The Pagoda Tree

Claire Scobie is an award-winning British journalist and author who has lived and worked in the UK, India and Australia. Her travel memoir, *Last Seen in Lhasa*, won the 2007 Dolman Best Travel Book Award. In 2017, a new memoir, *A Baboon in the Bedroom*, co-authored with her mother Patricia Scobie, is being released. She has written for numerous publications, including the *Daily Telegraph* and the *Observer*. Through her consultancy, Wordstruck, Claire advises companies and leaders on how to harness the power of storytelling as a strategic business tool. She runs writing courses in Australia, Asia and the UK and mentors writers one-on-one. In 2013, she completed a Doctorate of Creative Arts at Western Sydney University. *The Pagoda Tree* is her first novel.

clairescobie.com
wordstruck.com.au
@clairescobie

Praise for *Last Seen in Lhasa*

'Honest, deeply felt ... Ani is glorious'
David Davidar, author of *The Solitude of Emperors*

'*Last Seen in Lhasa* is enthralling [and] beautifully written'
Helen Garner, author of *The Spare Room*

'An intimate and moving account of a way of life that is fast disappearing'
Monica Ali, author of *Brick Lane*

'Utterly compelling'
Stephanie Dowrick, author of *Choosing Happiness*

'Claire Scobie's refreshing book shows how people can see their lives differently'
Xinran, author of *Sky Burial*

'Truly wonderful ... not only a deeply moving and inspiring account
but also an enthralling insight into a vanishing world'
Mick Brown, author of *The Spiritual Tourist*

'Rich, profound and deeply moving ... gripping'
Time Out

'A terrific book ... a story of courage'
The Age

'Absorbing and rewarding ... written in stylish, elegant prose'
Observer

'A wonderful book: warm and sincere about this extraordinary friendship,
alive and honest about the changes being wrought in Tibet ...
It stayed with me for weeks'
The Australian

'Required reading ... laced with gentle humour and great affection'
Sunday Telegraph

'A love letter to friendship'
Sydney Morning Herald

The Pagoda Tree

CLAIRE SCOBIE

Unbound

First published by Penguin Group (Australia), 2013

This edition published by Unbound, 2017

Unbound
6th Floor Mutual House 70 Conduit Street London W1S 2GF

Text design by Laura Thomas © Penguin Group (Australia)

Art direction by Mecob

ISBN 978-1-78352-370-2 (limited edition)
ISBN 978-1-78352-371-9 (trade hbk)
ISBN 978-1-78352-372-6 (ebook)

A CIP record for this book is available from the British Library

Printed in the UK by Clays Ltd. St Ives Plc

1 3 5 7 9 8 6 4 2

www.unbound.com

With special thanks to Tristram Kenton and Jane Scobie,
patrons of this book.

For Aden, with love

Dear Reader,

The book you are holding came about in a rather different way to most others. It was funded directly by readers through a new website: Unbound. Unbound is the creation of three writers. We started the company because we believed there had to be a better deal for both writers and readers. On the Unbound website, authors share the ideas for the books they want to write directly with readers. If enough of you support the book by pledging for it in advance, we produce a beautifully bound special subscribers' edition and distribute a regular edition and ebook wherever books are sold, in shops and online.

This new way of publishing is actually a very old idea (Samuel Johnson funded his dictionary this way). We're just using the internet to build each writer a network of patrons. At the back of this book, you'll find the names of all the people who made it happen.

Publishing in this way means readers are no longer just passive consumers of the books they buy, and authors are free to write the books they really want. They get a much fairer return too – half the profits their books generate, rather than a tiny percentage of the cover price.

If you're not yet a subscriber, we hope that you'll want to join our publishing revolution and have your name listed in one of our books in the future. To get you started, here is a £5 discount on your first pledge. Just visit unbound.com, make your pledge and type **pagoda5** in the promo code box when you check out.

Thank you for your support,

Dan, Justin and John
Founders, Unbound

AUTHOR'S NOTE

In the eighteenth century the word *pagoda* had a double meaning. It was both a southern Indian temple and a gold coin used in and around Madras. 'Shaking the *pagoda* tree' became a familiar expression among the English who went to India to make their fortune.

There is a legend among travellers about the fabled pagoda tree. Its roots are of silver, its branches of twisted gold. The leaves are fashioned from silks and satins, cotton and calico; the branches are encrusted with gems.

Merchants who voyage to India believe that when they shake the limbs, the ripe fruits will fall. What does not fall, they take. Some are lucky and fill their oak seachests with riches. Others perish scaling its heights.

For the goddess who guards the tree expects something in return. A drop of blood. A prayer. A show of gratitude. What she creates, she also destroys. Her emissaries are the lime-green parrots whose shrieks fill the skies at dusk. Those who ignore their messages do so at their peril.

INDIA
1765

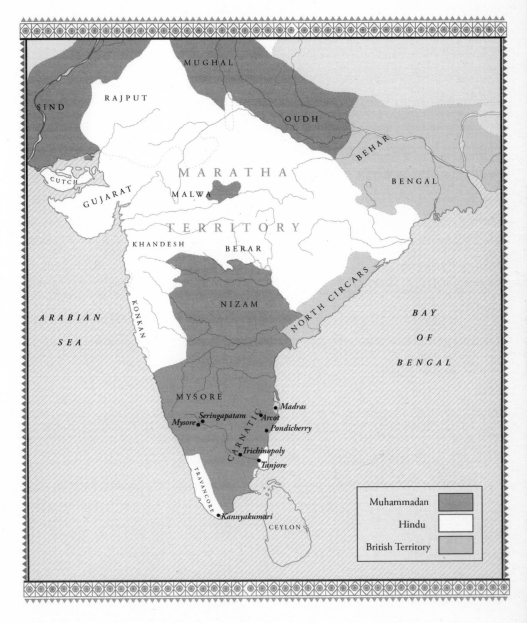

MUGHAL

SIND

RAJPUT

OUDH

BEHAR

CUTCH

BENGAL

GUJARAT

MALWA

MARATHA

KHANDESH

TERRITORY

BERAR

KONKAN

NIZAM

NORTH CIRCARS

ARABIAN
SEA

BAY

OF

BENGAL

MYSORE

Madras

Seringapatam

Arcot

Mysore

Pondicherry

CARNATIC

Trichinopoly

Tanjore

TRAVANCORE

Kannyakumari

CEYLON

Muhammadan	
Hindu	
British Territory	

Adapted from 'Historical Map (1769)', in *Imperial Gazetteer of India*,
v.26, Atlas 1909 edition

PART I
Tanjore, 1765

I

Maya stopped when she saw the splashes of blood around the well. They were fresh. Ants were already gathering around one drop, vivid red against the grey paving stones in the courtyard. Forgetting what she'd come for, she followed the trail through the kitchen and into the bedroom. In the shadows, her aunt Sita was crouching in a sari, knees pulled to her chest. When she saw Maya, she raised her hand.

'Leave me. Go and check on Leela.'

'Shall I get word to *Amma*?'

Sita shook her head, her eyes dull.

'Some water?'

She nodded.

Maya turned and ran. Reaching up on tiptoe, her fingers searched for the clay cup on the ledge. Carefully she filled it from the pitcher of water. Her aunt was sitting up when Maya returned with the cup. Sweat beaded her upper lip and Maya saw a dark stain on the front of the sari. A sweet metallic smell rose up, turning Maya's stomach.

'You're a good girl,' said her aunt. 'Now take your cousin outside.'

Maya hesitated. She wanted to ask what was wrong but feared the answer. Leela's shrill cry rang out from down the passageway. Maya turned to go to her before her wails woke the neighbours.

And then it was another day, and Maya was sitting in the corner of the courtyard, poking a stick between the cracks of the stones to see if she could unearth any beetles.

'She's nine years old. She's ready.' Her mother was sitting on a low stool with a grinding stone in front of her.

'We should wait until next year,' said Sita, sifting through a basket of snake beans.

'I can't wait that long,' Lakshmi said.

'Sister, *akka*. You know what was said at the child's birth.'

'You worry about your Leela and I'll make the decisions for Maya.'

'You talk as if I've never had a say in her upbringing.' Sita snapped a bean in half.

'Maya, you want to start dancing lessons, don't you?' Lakshmi called out.

Maya walked over to the two women. Sometimes she wondered if it wouldn't be better to have a mother and father. But her mother, her *amma,* always said husbands weren't worth bothering with. She stared down at her palms. 'I do want to dance.'

Lakshmi nodded approvingly.

'It's not the dancing that's the issue.' Sita patted the ground next to her and Maya sat down. 'It's everything that comes with it.'

Maya watched the muscles of her mother's jaw tighten. From the temple she heard the beating of drums, calling the women to prayer.

'Rao thinks she's ready. Uma too.'

Sita frowned. 'You've been to see him?'

'I told Rao I don't want to let the flesh wither on the branch before it has blossomed in the hand.'

Maya stretched out her skinny legs. Her knees were bony and one had a scab where she'd tripped over. She started to pick at the dry crusty edge.

'He agreed,' Lakshmi lied, throwing a handful of rice on the grinder. 'He said he'd check his *Panchangam* for an auspicious date for the initiation.'

Beneath the outer layer, the wound was pink and raw. Maya pressed it to see if it still stung. Not much. Not nearly as much as the fire-iron the priests would use during the ceremony. Some girls fainted before it touched their skin. A few soiled their clothes. Not Mother, though. She'd been strong during her initiation. *Just like I will be*, Maya thought, pressing the scab harder. *I won't cry.*

The sisters never let Maya out of their sight. The furthest she could go alone was to the banyan tree opposite their house on West Main Road. It was huge and shady with low branches and tangled roots hanging down like a curtain. Halfway up the main trunk was an old man's face in the burl and Maya felt safe there when she played. Their house was one of those owned by the Big Temple for the *devadasis*, the women married to the temple gods, whose duty it was to serve, care and dance for them. Inside were two living rooms that doubled as bedrooms, a small shrine room, and along the passageway from the *koodam* – the pillared hall – a simple kitchen. This led into a walled courtyard at the back. Maya liked the house when it was filled with the rustle of saris and tinkling anklets, the crackling of conversation and full-bellied laughter of women. When Sita and Leela were away, and it was just her *amma*, and her, the silence and dark walls pressed down.

In the season of *Karttikai*, in November, the weather was starting to cool. There were no festivals at the Big Temple so the women had only to perform their daily duties. Lakshmi was there at dawn to wash and dress the statue of Shiva, and offer the *kumbarti*, the sacred lamp.

After Maya finished her prayers, she was left to roam the enclosed temple grounds. It was there, parading up and down the shady corridors, practising the dance moves *Amma* had taught her, that her dreams took flight. She imagined she was leading a royal procession. The dancing girls carved in the walls were her attendants; the warrior kings were her suitors. The fantastical animals – half-men, half-beasts – were her private army, and she was queen of them all.

Most days Maya liked nothing better than to sit in the courtyard at home, staring up at the scaly branches of the frangipani tree and at the stripy palm squirrel as it edged along the wall. Her lime-green blouse and long cotton skirt hung limp in the afternoon heat. From inside she heard humming. Finding a shady spot, she waited.

Sita came out, Leela asleep against her chest. Carefully, she laid her in a cloth sling hanging from a branch. Maya stood up and stared down at Leela's small round face. They had the same square nose and wide brow. Sita began to rock her, cooing softly under her breath.

'Is that what you used to do when I was little?' Maya asked, peeling herself a small banana.

'Yes, and sing lullabies.'

'Did *Amma* sing too?'

'Yes.' She reached across and cupped Maya's face. 'Don't look so anxious.'

On the wall opposite, the squirrel sat on its haunches and gave a high-pitched trill.

'How much does it hurt?' Maya asked.

For a moment Sita looked confused. Then she said, 'The branding, you mean?'

Maya nodded, squishing the last bit of banana between her fingers.

'I won't lie to you. It is painful. Have you ever put your finger too close to a flame? It's worse than that.'

Maya's eyes flared.

'You have to see it as a great honour. You are offering your body to Shiva.' She lowered her voice, gesturing with her thumb to the neighbour's wall behind. 'Think of her. A common householder married for life to a husband like that.'

'Snake man, you mean?'

Sita rocked back on her heels, her mouth cracking open. 'Is that what you call him?'

'Yes.' Maya began to giggle. 'He looks like one, don't you think?'

Sita was covering her mouth now, as if embarrassed by the wideness of her luminous smile. 'Ssssh. She might hear.'

'She probably calls him that herself.'

'Or worse.' Her aunt looked thoughtful. 'I think your mother's right. By having the initiation now, you'll be able to start training.'

'Then why did you say I should wait?'

'It's a feeling I had, that's all. These rites of passage are so important.' Bending down, she picked up a fallen frangipani blossom. 'It's like this flower. The tree doesn't need to be told when its flowers are ready to fall, they just do. That's why we do everything according to the planets and cycles of the moon. Why we check the almanac to ensure the day is auspicious.' Sita twirled the flower between her thumb and forefinger. 'Everything has its time.'

'When I think about it, I feel scared.'

'Don't think about it then.' She squeezed Maya's hand. 'I've always believed in you.'

Maya felt herself expand inside. She wanted to be gathered up in Auntie's tight embrace – more fierce, more caring than her own mother's. Then the moment passed, and Sita rose to her feet, leaving Maya to play.

2

The night before the initiation Maya lay awake in the darkness. At dawn the throbbing of temple drums woke her. Her pulse quickened, her eyes squeezed shut. Before opening them, she waited until she heard her mother's footsteps cross the beaten-earth floor.

'Come, child. Slow to rise as usual. This day will not wait for you.'

Lakshmi's largeness filled the room as she bustled around her daughter. She pushed Maya towards the well in the courtyard. 'Bathe,' she said.

This first moment of washing was always Maya's private pleasure: when the chilled water startled her skin and she gasped from the cold. She wished she could be alone, but her mother stayed, scrutinising her.

'You'll turn out well,' said Lakshmi. 'You're strong in the legs; your arms can hold a pose. In time your backside will become shapely.'

She began to wash her daughter. She ground dried turmeric root and mixed it into a paste with gram flour, sandalwood, milk and honey. She smeared the mixture over Maya's back and neck, rubbing it hard under the ears and down across her narrow frame, her roughened hands scratching her most tender parts. By the end Maya glowed deep yellow.

Maya dressed in a cotton skirt and blouse. She moistened her lips and smoothed down the wayward strands of her hair, curling them behind her ears. She pinched her cheeks to make them fuller and teased at her eyelashes.

'I will go to the temple now to fetch the tray for the ceremony. Uma *akka* is there already, preparing everything,' her mother said.

'Why Uma *akka*?'

'As an elder she's helping the priest with the ceremony. Sita and Leela will be back later. You must fast until nightfall.'

Maya felt herself shrink inside. 'Yes, *Amma*.'

After her mother had locked the door behind her, Maya began her offerings at the household shrine. She felt very alone. As she lit the musk incense and oil lamp, the drums grew louder. She noticed then that her hands were trembling.

After shutting the door, Lakshmi bent down to rub her swollen knees. She grimaced. As she straightened, a flash of colour in the gutter caught her eye. It was the rose-coloured husk of a pomegranate, split open, its fleshy scarlet seeds scattered in the mud. She began to walk in the direction of the temple, trying to push away the nagging doubts. Perhaps Sita was right and she was being too hasty. It was still not too late to call off the ceremony. Her hand sought out the cloth pouch tucked on the right of her bosom. Through the folds of her sari she could feel the edge of one gold *pagoda*. If she delayed, she would have to pay the priests again. That settled it. The sooner Maya was initiated, the quicker she would attract the attention of a patron.

The flash of apprehension in her daughter's eyes made her remember the terror of when she was branded. She, too, had been nine years old when the priests had led her into the inner sanctum. She saw the flames licking around the iron trident of Shiva. She felt her eyes covered with a silk cloth perfumed with camphor. Once more she heard the hiss of burning iron as the head priest dipped the trident into water before searing it against her upper arm.

The rumbling of a bullock cart jolted Lakshmi from her memories. She was glad of it. She didn't like to remember that at her own initiation she had cried out. She always told Maya that crying was weak and weakness had no place in the house of a *devadasi*.

As dusk approached, Maya felt light-headed. She willed her mind to quieten. She had watched others make ready for the ceremony and knew what to expect. But she couldn't control her body. Despite the heat, she shivered. Sita and Leela were still not back and she kept fidgeting and looking towards the front door.

'Stand upright,' said her mother, as she fixed the sari around Maya's thin waist.

The stiff cotton felt scratchy on her skin as her mother gathered the material, tucking it around her waist.

'It's bunched up,' said Maya.

'That doesn't matter.'

'It feels uncomfortable.'

'Stop complaining.'

Sweat trickled down her thighs. The cotton was heavy. Silk would have been softer. She had wanted silk, but *Amma* couldn't afford it.

Her mother flung the tail of the sari over Maya's left shoulder, then stood back to admire her work, the tip of her tongue sticking out. She shook her head. 'The pleats aren't straight,' she said, unravelling Maya as if she were a ball of string.

Maya studied the vermilion cloth hemmed with silver and gold and a border of pyramids and stripes. It reminded her of the shrines and walls surrounding the temple. She liked that. The temple was her playground.

'Now you're ready. Turn around.'

Maya gazed open-mouthed at herself in the round mirror held up by her mother. She turned to the side to admire the way the sari sculpted her body. She'd never been allowed to wear one before. A shaft of late afternoon sunlight lit up her eyes, her earrings, the beads braided in her hair, and the sparkle of her nose ring. The filmy thread of the sari looked like the silken wings of a moth.

'Is that really me?'

For a moment, her mother's face softened.

'*Amma*, I won't let you down,' she said. 'I'll be strong like you.'

'I expect nothing less,' Lakshmi said, thrusting the tray of offerings into Maya's hands. 'Prepare this.'

Maya winced and turned away. She squatted down and in the centre of the tray she placed the *bottu,* the golden pendant the priests would tie around her neck to signify her marriage to Shiva, together with the posy of hibiscus flowers, half a coconut, cones of incense and betel leaves.

Sita's voice sang out and the front door slammed shut.

'At last. I thought we'd have to go without you,' Lakshmi said.

'Everything's ready at the temple. Uma *akka's* waiting with the priest,' Sita said, as she came in. 'My, you have done a good job, Maya looks—'

'Yes, yes. This is no time to chat. The musicians are waiting.'

Maya felt the weight of the occasion. Dressed in her red sari, as elegant as any Brahmin woman would wear on her wedding day, she rolled her shoulders back and held her neck high.

'Carry yourself straight as a pillar. Your eyes must betray nothing,' Lakshmi said.

Stepping over the threshold, Maya wavered for an instant, surprised at the crowd. Dancing girls and drummers, neighbours and children milled around, their faces illuminated by the last rose-gold rays of the setting sun. With Maya pressed in between her mother and her aunt, she felt herself carried along by the rapid rhythm of the *thavil* drums. Maya remembered her mother's words and gazed straight ahead. As they drew near the temple, she saw a man standing outside the gates. Dressed all in black, he wore an unusual triangular hat. He was a foreigner. His long hair was dishevelled, his pallid complexion ghostly. Her mother frowned: she, too, had noticed him. Only then did Maya falter. She'd seen foreigners before, but seeing him at this moment, as she was about to begin her life as a dancer of the temple, seemed a bad omen. He was staring at her, his pale-blue eyes wide, his mouth twisted. Even when she had stepped through the archway, still she felt his eyes on her.

3

Walter pulled back the curtain of the palanquin and stared out. Rice paddy fields stretched in a patchwork of lush greens criss-crossed by irrigation channels. The bristling shoots of the young rice reminded him of spring green buds back home. They were the same shade as the crabapple in the orchard, its trunk belichened, its leaves entwined with a spray of damask rose. That made him think of his daughter, Emily. He could see her now, her peat-brown hair falling around her, crossing the lawn in front of the rectory. He exhaled a long ragged sigh. The vice around his heart never released its grip. For so long he had privately cursed the God he preached to others.

His high-collared shirt clung to his neck. Although alone, it would be improper to loosen his necktie. In these parts, the loosening of one thing seemed too often to lead to another. He placed his black hat to one side, tugged at the curtains and lay back on the mattress, re-arranging the pillow under his head. At least he could stretch out in this bamboo litter, he thought, closing his eyes.

When he stirred, the sun was high. The palanquin juddered as the four bearers lifted it from their shoulders on to the ground.

'Lunch stop, *sahib* Sutt-sutt.'

Jiva opened the curtains to let Walter out.

'Come. We take rest at the *choultry*.' Resting his hand lightly on Walter's arm, he steered him towards the traveller's rest house, a simple wooden building among a grove of coconuts. 'By late afternoon we reach Tanjore.' He pointed across the alluvial plains devoid of any landmarks. 'See there? Tanjore's Big Temple.'

Even from this distance, the temple's giant tower reared up, a mythical structure, piercing the sky like a sword. It was the only building above the tree line.

'Jiva, it's Sutcliffe, not Sutt-sutt,' he said.

Jiva flinched at the irritation in Walter's voice.

'Sut-c-liffe.' He enunciated each syllable.

'Yes, *sahib*.' Jiva cleared his throat, his big hands out of proportion to his pole-like body. 'Not far to go now.'

Shortly before dusk, the litter passed through the east gate of Tanjore Fort, which was manned by whiskered watchmen holding short curved swords. After questioning Jiva and peering in at Walter, they waved them through. The streets of rammed earth were pockmarked and cratered; the low palm-leaf houses squashed together. There was a black hairy pig foraging among vegetable peelings and a bony figure asleep in the gutter. Walter craned his neck as the street widened. A refreshing breeze washed over him as they passed a large sunken tank of water. Above it was a grand white Palladian mansion with arched windows.

Ahead were the fortified walls surrounding the Big Temple. He rang the bell, signalling the bearers to stop, and alighted. A colossal stone gateway guarded the entrance. Cut into the wooden gates was a small door. It was open and in the centre, shaped like a pyramid, was the tower he'd seen from the plains. He stared up at the carved idols clustered around the pilasters, with their gaudy faces and garish gestures, and turned away in disgust.

Large black crows wheeled above, swooping across the sky in all directions. From up the street a screeching sound, like an off-key oboe, perforated the air. A procession was drawing near led by musicians and dancing girls. The crowd peeled apart and he saw two women with a child between them. The child was dressed in folds of red cloth, her hair braided with green and gold beads.

From a distance she looked more mannequin than girl. Then, as she approached, a torch illuminated her face. Her eyes, deep as mahogany, were warm and bright. Walter drew a sharp breath. She would have been about the same age as Emily. The child looked nothing like her but it was the intensity of her stare and the way the girl flicked her head that transfixed him. He took a step forward for a better look, but the crowd around her closed in and pushed the girl towards the small door in the temple gates. Walter stepped back, unsure of himself. As the group passed, he was assailed by a gust of rose. The heady perfume took him back down the cobbled laneways of Lewes to his daughter's china doll sitting on the bedroom dresser, gathering dust.

4

When Maya passed through the gateway, the memory of the man in black faded. She lifted her eyes. Ahead was the raised platform housing the central shrine. The carved figures of gods and goddesses vibrated honey-orange. Among the sculptures she saw a flash of green. And another. A pair of parrots was perched high up. Before she could point, her mother pulled her to the right.

'Look where you're going. Eyes straight ahead.'

They passed between the two Nandi bulls. The smaller one had a gleaming rump, from generations of worshippers who had touched it as they passed. She felt breathless and wondered if she would be able to stand the pain. As she looked up at her mother, Maya realised she had no idea how they would actually do it. *Amma's* face was drawn, her pupils wide. *She looks scared*, Maya thought.

The musicians were lining up at the entrance to the shrine, and as she passed between the square columns she blinked, her eyes adjusting to the semi-darkness. At the end of the lamplit corridor, Maya could see the head priest waiting for her, his bare chest marked with three stripes of ash. Behind him was the black, dome-shaped *lingam* of Shiva, decorated with garlands of marigolds and a white cloth. A charge passed through her. She'd never been so close to it; usually only the Brahmin priests were allowed here. Reluctantly, she cast her eyes down.

'It's hard not to look, isn't it?' the priest said.

She wasn't sure if it was a question or a statement and said nothing.

'It's right that you look. It's god's power you feel, it's Shiva.'

Her thoughts were racing. She remembered her mother's words. *Betray nothing.*

His face close to hers, he said, 'You have the mark of destiny upon you, child. Do not be afraid.'

Pressed into the narrow space were more dancers. She walked so close between the knot of bodies, she could feel the warmth of their breath. The floor was strewn with petals and oil squelched between her toes. She turned to look for her mother and aunt, but they had gone, and before she had time to hesitate, she was inside the inner sanctum.

'Follow me,' the priest said, ducking under a low archway into an adjoining room. Inside, in front of a large stone statue of Nataraj, the dancing Shiva, was a single wooden chair with armrests. Next to it stood Uma, her oiled black hair hanging to her waist, gold bracelets armouring her wrists. The older woman motioned Maya to sit.

Her feet didn't touch the floor, her calves swinging awkwardly. Sitting down, the sari scratched against her bare midriff. 'Where's *Amma*?'

'She's gone to get the tray with the offerings blessed.'

Uma busied herself rolling up the short sleeve of Maya's blouse on her left arm. With a piece of charcoal, she drew a cross, marking the spot. The priest entered carrying a fine silver instrument with the insignia of the trident. With care, he placed it on the burning coals in an iron pot. Maya bit down on her lower lip and gripped the armrests.

Outside the percussionists struck up and people were chanting. The cymbals were getting louder, the priest was shouting to his assistant. Maya twisted her head to look for her mother but she still wasn't there. How many times had she heard the story that *Amma* did not cry, that Shiva punished those who did.

'We have to do it now,' the priest said. 'The fire-iron can't get too hot.'

Maya thought it looked hot enough; the coals glowed liquid orange.

At that moment, Sita entered. 'Queues everywhere. Lakshmi *akka* is still waiting.'

'Hold the child's left hand, stretch it out,' Uma ordered.

'Can't we wait?' Maya said.

'It will be over before you know it.' Sita knelt down, placing her palm on top of Maya's hand to steady her arm.

When Uma went to tie the blindfold, Maya shook her head.

'It's easier that way,' she said.

'I want to see what's happening. Then I can prepare myself.'

Uma exchanged a look with the priest who was holding the silver seal. He plunged it into a pot of water and it crackled, the water spitting, steam billowing.

'You're sure?' Sita said.

Maya assented with her eyes. She was watching the trident, her body tense. She heard the murmuring of prayers and felt her aunt's grip tighten. The priest's hand was steady. She sensed the heat as the trident came closer, but when the seal touched her skin, it was like ice. Then a raging fire swept down her arm. Instinctively she shrank back, but Uma and Sita held her still.

For what seemed like minutes, yet was barely a few seconds, the priest chanted, 'O Shiva, take this girl to be your wife. See this *muttirai* as a mark of her devotion and your divine grace. She is your servant, your vessel.'

In front of her eyes danced a thousand bright lights. In her ears she heard the pounding of her own blood. A serpent-like wave of pain passed through her. When the priest pulled the seal away, her skin sucked back into itself, and a meaty charcoal smell pervaded her nostrils. Her insides curdled. She leaned forward, her mind blurry, suddenly afraid she would vomit. The heat in the room was suffocating. The pain in her arm lanced into every part of her body.

'Sit up, Maya. Sit up,' said Sita, placing a damp cloth over her forehead. 'Hold your arm out.'

She leaned back and closed her eyes, the tension leaking out of her. She felt her calves knock against the wood. Her buttocks were numb.

She flinched as her aunt placed a poultice of cooling herbs against the burn, wrapping it with strips of muslin to hold it tight.

'Water,' Maya said. 'Can I have some water?' Her lips were dry.

Uma helped her to drink. As Maya tipped her head back, she saw a painting of Shiva on the ceiling. His blue limbs shimmered. Around him was a circle of fire, and as she stared, feeling the water slip down her throat, she saw herself step over the flames towards him.

When she was steady enough to stand, she heard celebratory shouts and cheers from outside, and a crowd of faces at the door chanting Shiva's name. Behind them was *Amma*, holding the tray aloft. The priest asked Maya to bend her head, and taking the golden *bottu* on the yellow thread, he placed it around her neck. The disc sat flat against her damp skin.

'From today, your new life begins,' he said. 'You have started well.'

With that, he released her from his gaze. She looked up at her mother, but her eyes were unreadable. 'Where were you? They couldn't wait. But I did it, *Amma*. I did it.'

'She did well, didn't she?' Sita cast a sidelong glance at her sister as they watched Maya paddle in the shallows. She was naked, her long limbs glistening in the sunlight. 'The burn. It's almost healed.'

On Maya's arm, the insignia of the three-pronged trident was deepening to black. Only a few small blisters ringed the edge.

Lakshmi looked up. 'She did well enough.'

They were on the banks of the Kaveri, their washing spread out to dry on the flat grey boulders. Further up more women were bathing, their voices rising and falling. Dragonflies buzzed above the placid water.

'Is that all you can say?'

'You know what Mother always said. Show a child too much love and they go soft. Then the evil eye can strike. Ours is not a life where we can afford to be soft.'

Sita stood apart, arms akimbo. She was thinner than her older sister: a different father had given a different bone structure. Where

Lakshmi was solid and stubborn, with heavy-set features and a broad bosom, Sita was angular, wiry and restless. 'As changeable as the wind,' their mother always said. She could eat twice as much as Lakshmi and it never showed. All the fire inside her burned it up.

'Your problem is Mother always spoilt you,' Lakshmi continued, pummelling her sari.

Sita walked over to the nearby tree to check on Leela asleep in a sling. As she rocked her back and forth, she tried to imagine what Leela would look like seven years from now, when she was nine, and ready to begin her training. 'You don't recognise what you have. I'd go to the ends of the land for my daughter.'

'Where do you get such sentimental ideas?'

'Don't you remember what Adki said about Maya? It's not something to be taken lightly.'

'I don't. I just keep it in perspective. Otherwise we tempt fate. You, on the other hand, make a drama out of everything. You show Maya too much affection. Now help me finish the washing.'

Afterwards, Lakshmi roughly tied her sari around her waist and walked over to sit under the neem trees. Maya was half-lying on the sand, letting the water ebb back and forth over her legs. Already her frame was filling out. It was as if the initiation had hastened the body's natural process, as if a deeper current were at work.

When Lakshmi had entered the shrine room on that day, and looked down at Maya – her face illumined, her eyes proud – she'd seen a new strength in her daughter that, if she were honest with herself, she knew she'd never possess. Instead of sweeping her up in her arms and praising her, she had turned away. She told herself, *Maya must believe her own mother is strong; in that way she'll be strong too.*

She remembered her longing to have a baby, how it had consumed her. The times she'd gone down on bended knee at the fertility tree, praying for her belly to grow ripe. How she thought having a daughter would fill the emptiness inside. She'd put off having a child as long as she could. Her mother had warned her that once she did, the patrons would no longer call. Lakshmi hadn't believed her, but she'd been right.

On the day of Maya's birth, the sky had deepened to indigo, and a twisting spirit wind blew around their house and no other on the street. Afterwards, Lakshmi lay, spent, with Maya in her arms. While Sita was clearing up the bloodied mess, there was a knock at the door. When her sister answered, she gave a small cry. It was Adki with her coarse matted hair and thin wizened face. Adki, diviner of dreams and harbinger of omens.

She forced her way in. 'Where is she? Where is she?' When Adki saw Maya, she fell down in a state of grace. 'She is as I imagined.'

Too weak to resist, Lakshmi gave her newborn to the old woman. As if holding something that might shatter in her hands, she took Maya and examined her.

'She bears all the signs,' she said, handing her back to Lakshmi. 'Three moles – on her right cheek, at the centre of her chest and above the lips of her vulva. Signs of the goddess.' She stood up. 'To hold such power, she needs to be cared for well. The years between thirteen and sixteen must be calm. If not, madness can descend. The girl mustn't know before she bleeds. Once bleeding starts, you can tell her.'

After she'd left, Lakshmi had held Maya close to her chest, stroking the fine down of her black hair. 'How did Adki know where to come?'

'They say she has powers,' Sita said, squatting down. 'After all she's a *sadhvi* – a female renunciate – one of the few. She's travelled to all the places where the goddess herself has trod, her life an eternal pilgrimage.'

Lakshmi looked down at the sleeping baby. 'I should feel joy at her words but they leave me uneasy.' She glanced up at her sister. 'Are they a curse or a blessing? We all know the fickle nature of the goddess. There is always suffering for her devotees, rarely ecstasy.'

'Come now. Don't think like that. You have a healthy girl.' Sita leaned forward, her hands poised to take Maya. 'If she were my daughter, I would take Adki's words as a blessing. She is a wise woman.'

Lakshmi cradled Maya closer.

'And her name,' Sita said, her hands falling in her lap. 'Have you decided?'

'Mayambikai. Maya for short.'

'Will you pass word to the patron who fathered her?'

'No. Mother never told me of my father. Why burden the child? We temple women do better on our own.'

'You are still hurting that he left you.'

'Pah. Left me? It was me who showed him the door.'

In those early years, Lakshmi had entertained the thought that Maya needn't follow in her footsteps and that perhaps she could find one rich patron and settle down. Such things did happen. Now, as she watched Maya in the water, the sun's reflection transmuting her thin brown body to silver, she knew that would not be her daughter's fate.

That evening, when they went to the monthly meeting for the temple women, Sita stayed home, sick again. Lakshmi found a place at the back and told Maya to sit still. Since her initiation she wasn't allowed to stray from her mother at all. Not even to the banyan tree opposite the house.

It was as if eyes were watching her from every angle. Maya swivelled her head. Rao and Pillai were both looking at her. Straight away she averted her gaze, as she'd been taught.

The last women to arrive sat down on the ground. Everyone just managed to fit under the broad canopy of the pipal – the sacred fig – tree where the meeting was held every full moon in the town square. Only Arulsamy, the chief of the council, was seated. Either side, elders flanked him. Arulsamy was long and sucked-in, with a growth on the side of his head that his silver hair never quite covered. Softly Maya said, 'Lizard-face, up to no good, lizard-face.'

At the end of the meeting, the chief beckoned Lakshmi forward.

'The priest told me,' he said, pointing to Maya. 'No fear in the child's eyes.'

Her mother mumbled under her breath.

'You're keeping a close eye on her, Lakshmi?'

'Of course.'

'It's not only the priests who'll want her. The palace too. She might be lucky. The prince himself might notice her. The whole community benefits then.'

'Yes.' She gave a small bow.

Maya clamped her arms by her side.

'Don't be shy, girl. Look up.'

She hesitated. Her mother pinched her hard and her head jerked upwards. His bloodshot eyes narrowed. He bent closer and she caught the smell of arrack on his lips.

'The mole. It adds to her beauty,' Arulsamy said, tweaking her cheek. She forced herself to stay still, her eyes staring straight ahead. His fingers were moist and afterwards, as soon as she could, she wiped away the damp smear they'd left. Then, before her mother could stop her, she sprinted on ahead, ignoring the angry shouts from behind.

At home, Sita was sitting on a stool in the courtyard, staring up at the full moon. Pain skewered through her. She clenched her fists and ground her teeth down. *Oh mercy, Mother Goddess, take pity on me.*

It had started a year after Leela was born. The birth had been difficult and prolonged and the midwife had told her to prepare for the worst. That was enough for her to keep pushing. She couldn't lose another baby. One, already, had been taken.

She rubbed the bridge of her nose and, making her arms into a pillow, rested her head on them. At times like these her mind always slipped back to when she was fifteen.

Life was different then. You could still believe love was possible and a girl named Sita would be treated like her loyal and devoted namesake – Sita, the most steadfast and virtuous wife of Rama, hero of the *Ramayana*. Fifteen years old, when she'd seen the young Brahmin in the crowd at her debut dance performance as she was being presented to prospective patrons. His eyes brimmed with the adoration of youth, not the rheumy tiredness of old men. When she was dancing she kept looking at him, until she saw Lakshmi shaking her head, stony-faced. They always said Kama, the plump god of love, fires the heart with an arrow. For weeks she'd been aflame.

Nothing came of it, of course. He was penniless and Sita went to the highest bidder, a kind enough man, but three times her age and already married. She thought of Maya. Of her innocence. She wanted to protect it as long as she could.

Two weeks later, Lakshmi was scrubbing the pots from lunch when Sita arrived home, breathless and agitated.

'Where were you today? The priests were asking.'

'I went to look for some new cloth.'

'Is that all?'

She gave a small shrug.

'I saved you some *pongal*. Sit and eat. You look tired.' Lakshmi turned away and reached to hang up the griddle. 'I forgot to tell you, Rao and Pillai's eyes never left Maya at the last meeting. Arulsamy too.' She faced Sita, her stance wide. 'In no time at all the girl will be starting her dancing lessons. I'm taking her to see Pillai this week. He's the best in town.' She paused. 'Aren't you hungry?'

Sita didn't reply.

'You're not yourself.'

'Not myself? My life blood is pouring out of me and nothing I do can stop it.'

'Sister, I'm trying to take the load by looking after both the children. But you've got to—'

Sita held up her hand. 'Don't. I know what's coming. *I've got to be strong because weakness has no*—'

At that moment Maya came running through from the courtyard. When she saw her mother and aunt glaring at each other, she stopped.

'Is this what you tell Maya too?' Sita swivelled around, catching Maya's wrist.

'What?' Maya asked.

'That weakness has no place in our house.'

Maya didn't want to get involved. She looked at Sita, at her puffy eyes and lips pressed together. She missed Auntie's smile.

'Yes, sometimes,' Maya faltered.

'How does that make you feel?'

She looked from one to the other.

'Say something, Maya.'

'You're hurting me.'

Sita released her grip and Maya took a step backwards.

'I don't know. It makes me think I should be strong all the time. It means I don't cry.' She rubbed the sore part of her wrist. 'Not often, anyway.' She looked up at her mother. 'Not when I was branded.'

'Sita, calm down, you're scaring the child,' Lakshmi said.

'I just think—' Sita stepped towards Maya, her arm knocking a bowl from the ledge, which smashed, 'that it hardens us. It hardens us all. Our hearts. Our bodies. Sometimes there is strength in showing our weakness. In asking for help.'

'Here you go, putting ideas in the child's head. Confusing her. You're saying this because you're not well.'

'Maya, child.' Sita bent down so she was at eye level with her. 'What I'm trying to say is that there is another way to think, another way to be.'

'Sister, you're speaking gibberish.' Lakshmi turned on Maya. 'What did you come in here for anyway?'

'My stick.'

'Get it and go.'

Sita felt her sister's eyes needling her. She wasn't sure why she'd picked this fight and why she'd dragged Maya into it. She wondered whether she shouldn't just tell Lakshmi what she intended to do. But there was no point. Lakshmi would tell her she shouldn't go, she mustn't go. She was mad to even think about it, that going could ruin everything. She piled up the broken shards of the bowl and knew she just had to take the risk herself. It would only take fifteen minutes to get to the house of the Muslim doctor. She'd do it tomorrow when Lakshmi was at the temple and be back home by four o'clock. No one need ever know.

5

Walter's lodgings were built in the traditional Tamil style with narrow bricks of red earth, the same hue as the rich alluvial plain of the Kaveri delta for which the region was famous. In his bedroom, there was a cot with a straw-filled mattress, a washing bowl and jug. A single window looked on to the walled courtyard at the back of the house, and some fruit trees – mango, jackfruit, guava. He sat on the room's only chair and leafed through the empty pages of the notebook, a surprise farewell gift from his manservant, George. His eyes were drawn up to the crucifix carved from a piece of Macassar ebony. Christ's arms were pinned back, the stomach sunk to the backbone. It was the way the head hung down that disturbed him: in it, he saw no redemption.

He should have stayed with his original posting and gone to Cuddalore. At least it was on the coast. Here, there was no chance of dabbling in trade, no hope of shaking the *pagoda* tree. This place was as oppressive as his cell-like room.

Walter lifted open the top of the trunk, reaching inside for his wife's embroidered sewing bag. He held it in his hands, inhaling deeply. There was no trace of her perfume, only a lingering smell of wood smoke. He dropped it back inside and shut the lid. He looked again at the notebook in his lap. It was sturdy, an inch thick, with a hard brown cover patterned like an oil slick on water. Putting his private thoughts on paper always unnerved him. But a letter, that he could do. Smoothing out a piece of parchment, using the trunk as a desk, he began to write.

Tanjore, February 15th, 1766

Dear George,
I will not venture to excuse my delay in writing. Since I left Madras, I have been travelling and indisposed. I am now in Tanjore, 200 miles south-west.

At St Mary's in Fort St George I had the great fortune to meet Reverend Schwarz. He enlisted me to help minister to the English garrison in Tanjore. A few of my flock are awake to the love of Christ, but many soldiers who flood this land commit villainous crimes, usually because they are drunk.

It is truly a confounded place. Tanjore country is rife with idolatry. Schwarz urges me not to think of the Tamils as 'barbarous people', but I find their culture assaults my senses at every turn.

The pagoda practices repulse me the most. Recently, I saw a procession led by a young girl ready to be married to the temple god.

Under the guise of the Hindoo faith she dances for God but the priests debauch her for men. How I pitied that child. She would have been no more than eight or nine years old, the same as my dear Emily. I can only hope that through the word of our Lord, these poor souls may hear his blessings.

I promise to write again when I am in better spirits.
Yours affectionately etc.,
Walter.

6

Across the other side of town, in the palace, Palani lay face down. The table was hard and her hips hurt, digging into the wood. The maidservant began to sing as she rubbed Palani with warm sesame oil, coating her like an embrace. When the woman's fingers slid between her toes, she stifled a moan.

She pictured how King Pratap used to take her foot, as if it were his most precious jewel. She felt the touch of the feather as he caressed the sole. His tongue was next, licking the big toe, while stroking her other foot with the pads of his fingers. When she could bear it no more, he worked his way up the legs, his nose grazing her triangle of clipped hair. As he came closer to her swollen, plum-coloured lips, he demanded silence. It took all her will to draw in her desire and lie still, his moustache tickling the soft skin of her inner thighs, before he drank her in.

Only now can you make noise. Bring the town alive with your ecstasy.

She sighed deeply. Such exquisite pleasure.

'Madam, too much?'

She opened her eyes, startled. Her body must have given her away.

'Harder, harder on my feet,' she said, thinking, *Make it so hard it hurts.*

Back in her quarters, Palani sat on her wooden swing seat looking over the palace grounds towards the Big Temple. A movement caught her attention. It was a palm squirrel with black unblinking eyes.

A surprise will come, she thought, as she rang the bell. Her aged maid entered, bow-legged and bandy-armed. Her ear lobes were disfigured from pendulous jewellery, and her toe rings clipped as she crossed the marble floor.

'Bring me sweets. *Payasam, laddu, badaam halwa.*'

'Madam is hungry?'

'Madam is bored.'

'Massage no good?'

'Massage was fine. The new woman you found, I like her.'

Vimala jiggled her head.

'Don't look smug. I need entertainment. Bring it to me.'

'A man?'

'Sex? Not interested. That, you see, is my problem.' With a dismissive flick of her hand, Palani continued. 'The new prince is too busy. What I need is to feel young again.' She sighed, feeling the touch again of King Pratap on her breasts, over her belly, his hands squeezing her buttocks. How he had delighted in her body, how she'd surrendered to his touch. Aware that Vimala was standing, waiting, she said, 'Yes, maybe it is sex I need.'

'What is it you want, Ma'am?'

Palani frowned. Vimala was rarely so direct.

'A muse,' she said, at last. 'Someone to inspire me, since I no longer inspire myself.'

Vimala went to speak, but Palani shook her head.

'No. On this you stay silent. Your task is to find her. She can be young, she can be ugly.' She sat up. 'On second thoughts, she can't be ugly. But not too beautiful either. Find me someone who will teach me something I don't already know. Find me the best.'

Palani rose before dawn and took the back corridors to the tower. She gazed out across the south of the city, towards the Big Temple and the large *ghat* behind, filled with water the shade of pewter. She turned to the east, towards Manambu Chavadi, the last neighbourhood before the city walls. The newly built mansion of the foreigner was visible even from here: brash, white, haughty-looking, the arched windows like eyes staring at her.

At the heart of the palace were two spacious halls, one built by the previous Nayak dynasty, the other by the Marathas. Prince Tuljajee, the current Maratha monarch, sat in state in his Durbar Hall. The lingering scent of night jasmine mixed with the aroma of the first incense of the day. Below, a small army of servants began their daily chores, and outside the gates, a clanging bell announced the pariah pulling the night-soil cart.

She told herself she should feel grateful that she still had a place in court. The new prince could have sent her packing. She pressed her fingers in the middle of her chest, feeling for the point where her heart refused to heal. It had been years since King Pratap's death, and still, she thought of him every day.

To quell her mind, she retraced her steps through the maze of corridors, hearing muffled voices as she passed the wood-panelled *zenana*, and the queens' quarters, and retired into her own. After her body was pummelled and oiled, her hair washed and perfumed, her nails shaped and her eyebrows plucked, she began her day.

Her maid smoothed down the pistachio coverlet on the divan. Vimala knew well enough to keep out of Ma'am's way until she had smoked her first hookah. *Maybe today Ma'am would receive visitors. Company would do her good.*

'Bring me my parchment and tell the fan-bearer to wait outside. I'll call him in when I'm ready,' said Palani, her house gown hanging loose around her diminutive figure.

'Yes, Ma'am,' said Vimala.

'No interruptions.'

'No.'

'I mean that.'

'The pile is only getting bigger, Ma'am.'

'Yes, but is the prince among the invitations? Is he?' She felt the morning's equanimity slip away.

'No, the prince is not.'

'Then why should I waste my time with anyone else? He's all that matters.'

'If I could venture—' Vimala fixed her eyes on a point on the floor.

'Leave me.'

'Your hookah?'

'Get out. I'll tell you when I want it.'

A metallic grating made her look over at her parrot. Vikku had been a gift from King Pratap – to keep her company when he was busy with his wives – and she had taught him to speak. He was old now, the blue collar fading to grey. She stood up and opened the cage, coaxing him towards her. He tugged on the loose strands of her hair with his beak, but refused to step up on her hand.

Palani walked over to the polished corner cupboard, which housed her collection of inkwells from Rajasthan and the Mughal court in Delhi. She picked up one carved into the figure of Saraswati, goddess of learning and wisdom. Her breath became uneven and she laid the inkwell back down, not trusting herself. It was going to be another of those days. Another day when inspiration would not come, when the metre would fail to settle and the words would lie turgid on the page.

A wave of heat washed over her, then a surge of anger. The hot flushes were threatening her sanity itself. She should be rejoicing. Her time as a *rajadasi* – a royal courtesan – was coming to a natural end. To accept that with grace would give her the peace of mind she so lacked.

She stood up, suddenly defiant, and went back to the cupboard, pulling out the inkwells, knocking them over as she did. And then, she sat down to write.

Two hours later the quill was snapped in two and piles of crumpled and ripped parchment lay scattered around the divan. Outside the door Vimala hovered, but after hearing nothing, she crept away, hoping that Ma'am had fallen asleep.

Palani's eyes were closed but her mind was a bolting horse. Prior to these arid months, her muse had never deserted her. When King Pratap was on the throne, the words poured from her. Her gift lay in recasting the epics, not in the stiff language of the men of the court, but in the honeyed words of a woman whispering into the ear of her beloved.

As she lay on the divan, she remembered her moment of glory, reading her first one hundred verses to the packed court. King Pratap had sat motionless, his face inscrutable. At the end, he applauded wildly. 'Palani,' he cried, his hand outstretched towards her, 'you are incomparable.'

After that, she became mistress of the palace and the courtiers all answered to her. As she relived those moments, a lightness spiralled through her and she rose to her feet and took off her gown. She dipped her hand in a pot of perfumed oil and inhaled the fruity ambrosial scent. She ran her hands down her neck and over her breasts, letting her fingers trail over the curve of her belly, more rounded than when she was Pratap's favourite bedfellow, but alluring enough. Emboldened, she slipped one finger between her lips. The dryness took her by surprise. She pulled at the hairs, brittle and coarse. Silently, as a creek runs dry, her juice had leaked away. She looked down at herself, at the sagging breasts and loose folds around her waist, at the thighs threaded with blue veins, and suddenly, ashamed she would be seen, ran into the bedroom, pulling the door behind her.

The knock was too insistent to ignore.

'Madam is sick?' Vimala said, entering.

'Yes. What is it?'

'Rao *ayya*, Ma'am. He says he will cheer you up.'

Palani lifted her head. 'I can't see him like this.'

'No, you can't.' Vimala eyed the spittle on Palani's chin. 'Let me help dress you.'

Palani felt a squeeze of panic, as if she'd been found out. Then she wondered if in fact she had – and that all this time everyone else in the court knew that she was old and past her prime, but she was the only one not to notice.

When the retired court minister was ushered into her quarters, Palani waved a hand towards the chair opposite.

'You are looking as radiant as ever,' Rao said.

'Am I? Court life doesn't suit me these days. Even the ink on my quill has dried.'

'Your poetry is not flowing?'

She looked over his shoulder.

'I take that as a no.'

'The muse. She comes and she goes.'

Rao's hands lay folded in his lap. His fingers were his best feature, long, elegant, each nail manicured to reveal a half-moon. He was dressed in white, his turban slightly askew, his eyes limpid under bushy grey eyebrows. She'd always felt a tenderness for him. He'd helped her keep her place at court after the king's death. She permitted a cautious smile.

'That's exactly the reason I am here,' he said.

'You've been speaking to Vimala?'

'Not at all.' He gave a low raspy laugh. 'A woman like yourself needs a protégé, someone you can impart your knowledge to.' He rose to his feet and turned his back to her, facing the view.

'Are you implying I'm old?'

'Not at all. You are too well-versed in the arts of immortality to let the years reveal themselves.' He turned to face her. 'I can recommend one girl, only nine, and just initiated. I have checked your birth chart and hers, and you share several planetary conjunctions.' He took a step towards her. 'It is as if you are playing out each other's past and each other's future. You have been where she is going and she is going where you have been. A perfect combination for a guru and student. Her name is Mayambikai. Daughter of Lakshmi. Already known to Adki.'

Palani sat up. 'Since when?'

'Her birth.'

She pushed her lips forward in thought, wondering again if her maid had been talking to Rao. It seemed uncanny otherwise that he would bring news of this girl only the day after she had instructed Vimala to find her a muse. She looked at him. No, he'd come of his own volition. This made the girl more interesting, especially given Adki already knew of her. There was no arguing with Adki. 'I'll think about it. You're after favours, Rao *ayya*?'

Sitting down, he gave a short laugh. 'Not those sorts of favours. I gave up on that a while ago.'

'You're barely fifty.' As she said it, she felt her earlier despair. 'Time. She is a cruel mistress.'

His eyes were on her.

'So what do you want?'

'Some recompense for my work.' He shifted his weight in the chair. 'And I'd like to teach again in the court, starting with Maya.'

'The court is very crowded these days. Another band of musicians arrived from Poona this week.'

'Exactly why we need local talent.'

'Will the priests let her go?'

'I can take care of that.' He tugged at his moustache. 'Of course, once she has the eye of the prince, the priests will have no choice.'

'Pah. Who is in thrall to whom? The prince daren't leave the palace for fear of what the priests say.' She stopped abruptly, glancing towards the closed door. 'I'll leave the politics to you. Have the girl start her training and then let me see her.' She was tired now and wished him to leave. 'What else?'

'I wanted to invite you as the guest of honour to a concert. I've started playing the violin—'

'What's wrong with the *veena*?'

'Have you ever heard a *raga* played on a violin?' His eyes lifted towards the ceiling, lost in thought. 'It has a wrenching silken quality that the half-tones of the *veena* cannot emulate.'

'You seem quite taken with it.'

'I am. Also with English. The concert will be a mixture of local and European music. You, of course, can watch from behind a screen.'

'You're consorting with the devil.'

'If you're implying that my purity is in question. Or my caste—'

'I'm not implying it, Rao *ayya*. I'm telling you. Foreigners have no caste. Most have no religion.'

'I am not here to annoy you.' Rao straightened his legs, as if ready to stand. 'I only thought you might find it diverting.'

In a tone as civil as she could muster, she said, 'Where is this concert to be held?'

'In the house of Mr Strange in Manambu Chavadi.'

The white monstrosity she'd seen from the tower that morning.

'Thank you, but I am sure I can find other diverting ways to spend my time. Now, if you'll excuse me, I have matters to attend to.'

7

The day after Sita's outburst, Maya was left alone with Leela. *Amma* was at the temple and Auntie said she had to run an errand and would be back soon. Kneeling down, she opened the package Sita had given her. It was a folded lotus leaf loosely tied with twine and inside was a handful of yellow glass beads. She started to string the beads on a piece of cotton thread, imagining Leela's face when she saw the bracelet. Her keen eyes would light up; her tiny hands would grab it.

She heard the front door open and slam shut. Carefully putting the bracelet down, she stood up and began to rock Leela in the sling. 'Sleep now, ssshhh.'

'Maya, come quickly.'

Sita was standing in the hall, strands of hair plastered to her face, her narrow chest heaving. Her lips were moving but no sound was coming out. Maya could smell the sweat coming off her, and with it a pungent bitterness. She stood waiting for Auntie to say something. Minutes passed. Finally Sita crouched down. Her lips were dry and she kept licking them.

'I need you to do something for me.'

Maya nodded.

Taking Maya's shoulders, Sita leaned her forehead towards her. 'I know *Amma* doesn't like you leaving the house, but just this once, I want you to go over to the banyan tree. Just for a short while. I want

you to keep yourself hidden and if you see any of the elders coming
down the street, whistle loudly. You know our secret whistle? Will you
do that for me?'

Maya couldn't find any words to respond. Auntie's hands were heavy
and pressed down on her shoulders. The smell was worse close up. It was
as if every pore of Auntie's skin was sweating danger. She thought of her
amma. Now that she could go outside the house, she'd much rather stay
inside. She could see Auntie was trying to hold herself still. Her hands
were squeezing hard now, wringing the answer out of her.

'Can I take the bracelet I'm making for Leela?'

Sita's face broke into a brief smile. Her hands relaxed.

'Of course. Now go.'

Maya crossed the street and ran to the banyan tree. Bending down
under the branches, she sat cross-legged on the ground, pressing
her back against the trunk. She looked up through the glossy leaves,
searching for the old man's face halfway up and when she found it,
nodded to herself. Then she continued stringing the beads for Leela's
bracelet. Suddenly, her concentration was broken by the sound of
angry men's voices. She peered through the low-hanging branches.
A group of men were approaching the house. The voices grew louder,
gruffer. She didn't move. Then she heard a muffled scream and the
splitting of wood. A crowd was gathering: peddlers, neighbours, low-
caste cow herders in white *lungis* splashed with rust-coloured mud.

The head of the council, Arulsamy, was leading the group and
began banging on their front door. 'Lizard-face,' Maya said to herself.
A man pushed past him and started hammering with a club. Maya
clutched the beads. She heard Leela wail. Curling her top lip down,
she tried to whistle. Only a faint wheeze sounded. She tried again.

The men were shouting that Sita had to come out and explain.
They said an emergency meeting of the council was being called and if
she didn't turn up at six o'clock that night, they'd drag her by her hair
along the road.

The men started hitting the ground with their sticks and hecklers
chanted.

Dirty whore, show your face.

Have you no shame?

Maya felt as if she'd become another limb of the tree. She wanted to run out and stop them but she couldn't move. The men hit the door a few more times and then, led by Arulsamy, turned and walked back up the street.

She watched them go, wondering if they'd drag Leela, too. Maya ran her fingers through her own hair and tried to imagine what it would feel like: clumps would come out, leaving a trail of blood. She shut her eyes. When she opened them and peered up at the tree, the gnarly old man's face glared back. Her hands were shaking and she looked down to see the yellow beads scattering in the dust.

Maya had never been to Uma *akka's* house before. She hadn't seen her since the day of the initiation. A strong buttery smell filled the kitchen and Uma was bending down over a cooking pot. She stood up, wiping her hands on the front of her house smock.

'Leela's asleep,' said Lakshmi, handing the infant to Uma, 'and Maya will be no trouble.'

Maya looked up to see *Amma* and Uma talking with their eyes.

'Thanks for watching them this evening.' Lakshmi hesitated.

'I heard the commotion. Everyone did. Sita was lucky they didn't break the door down.'

'What are they going to do to Auntie?' Maya said, imagining Sita's long black hair stretching from the house to the town square. In her mind, it covered the road like a mat, mixing with cow dung and blood and vegetable peelings. Tears pooled in her eyes. She tried to stop them but they wouldn't be stopped and Maya watched, helpless, as they splashed on the floor.

'Be quiet now,' said Lakshmi. 'They won't do anything to her.'

She didn't sound convinced and Maya sobbed harder.

'Maya, snap out of this. Listen to me. Open your eyes.'

Maya took a deep breath and tried to focus. She moved away from her mother and Uma, keeping close enough to hear, but far enough so that they would think she couldn't.

'What do you think's going to happen to Sita?' Uma's voice was low.

'I don't think she stands a chance,' said Lakshmi. 'It was Padma who saw her come out of the doctor's house. You know she's always had a grudge.'

'Which doctor was it?'

'The Muslim one, from up north.' Lakshmi's face grew tight. 'I can't believe she did it. They'll make her leave.' She looked sidelong at Maya, mouthing, *I can't say any more.*

Uma nodded.

'I'm going now. See you later, Maya,' Lakshmi said. 'You're staying here with Uma *akka.*'

Maya felt desperate and ran to her mother's side, her body trembling. What if they were to drag *Amma* along the street too?

'Stop it, child.' She prised Maya's hands away. 'Be good now.'

Lakshmi took her time walking to the square. She kept dabbing her upper lip to stop the sweat dripping down. Around half the women were under the pipal tree, together with some of the priests, and the dance teacher, Pillai. When he saw Lakshmi, he shook his head and grimaced. She felt the full horror then. What it would mean, not only for her sister, but for her and Maya too. This would taint them all. There was no escaping it.

At the front sat the chief, Arulsamy; either side of him, elders stood with arms crossed. On the left, Sita was standing, her head bowed. On the right, next to Arulsamy, Padma was halfway through giving her testimony. *The bitch, she's enjoying it,* thought Lakshmi.

'It was just past three o'clock when I saw Sita, daughter of Javanthri, leave the house of the Muslim doctor. Her sari was in disarray.'

Sita was shaking her head.

'Did you speak to her?' Arulsamy asked.

'Yes, I called out and asked her what she was doing there. I didn't want to approach her for fear of being polluted myself.' Padma cast a snide look towards Sita.

'What did she say?'

'Nothing. She looked shocked. Caught out, like a thief. She began to run.'

The crowd murmured. The chief conferred with the elders and the head priest. Then he called Sita to stand forward.

'You've said already that nothing happened between you and the doctor. How can we prove that?'

'Ask him.'

'You know that isn't acceptable. As a temple woman who is well aware of the strict codes of purity, who has the privileged position of entering into the innermost shrines—' His voice had risen to a bellow. 'How could you even contemplate going to such a person's house? Your actions threaten to pollute the entire sacred complex.'

'I was desperate.' She looked up, imploring. 'Ask my sister, Lakshmi *akka*. She knows how ill I've been. I was told that this doctor can cure illnesses that others can't.'

Lakshmi shrank back, wishing the shadows would conceal her. She felt the eyes of the men on her and Padma's scornful stare.

'You can confirm what your sister said?'

'She has been unwell. That is true,' Lakshmi said.

'Did you know of her intention?'

'No.'

'Your Honour, I swear on our mother's life, nothing happened,' Sita interrupted. 'I covered my wrist with a piece of silk and the doctor read my pulse through a curtain. He did not see my face. He did not touch me. Then he passed me the medicine and I gave him the money. That is all.'

'Yet Padma says that your sari was in disarray when you left?'

'She's lying.'

'I saw her with my own eyes. Sita was sweating profusely. Her hair was unkempt. As she came out of the door, I could see clearly she was rearranging her clothes.'

Sita looked at Lakshmi and pleaded with her eyes. Lakshmi glanced at Pillai and thought of Maya. Any day now she should start her dance lessons with him. She felt a hardening inside. The men of the council were conferring among themselves. She knew they'd already made up their mind. There was little she could do to stop them. She knew Sita was telling the truth. But the law was the law, handed down by the sage Manu since the beginning of time. Lakshmi dropped her eyes, a bitterness rising in the back of her throat. She couldn't look at her sister's face when they handed down the verdict.

'We publicly denounce you, Sita, and find you guilty of breaking caste law. From this night forward you are forever outcaste from this community and banned from practising in the temple. Even in death you will not be recognised as a *nityasumangali* – an ever-auspicious woman.' A charge rippled among the crowd. 'You must be gone by first light.'

The next morning, before the silvery smoke from the cooking fires blackened the fresh dawn air, and while Maya was still curled asleep, Sita stole out of the house on West Main Road with Leela strapped to her back. Lakshmi gave her as much as she could spare and tried to make her take their mother's ring. Sita refused, insisting the family heirloom stay at the house. Lakshmi could not bring herself to say goodbye. She knew it would only make things worse. Only when she had pulled the door shut behind them did her knees give way, and with a half-strangled cry, she sank to the ground. She pressed her fingers against her eyes, trying to push back the tears. No sound came, only gulping, heaving sobs.

8

After the council declared Sita an outcaste, Lakshmi never heard the name of her sister spoken publicly again. The priests were brought to purify their small house, which she cleaned with dung of the holy cow. When they eventually permitted her back to the temple, they gave her the worst jobs – scrubbing floors, scouring the brass. Except for Uma, all the other women ignored her.

No one knew where Uma was from. As broad as she was tall, her mannish features matched her brusque manner. She rattled out orders and like water wearing down stone, usually got her way. She took on the position of the *taikkizhavi*, or *tai,* the female elder who organised the rites of passage for the girls and procured the most suitable patron when they came of age.

'You mustn't let the priests or council intimidate you,' Uma told her. 'Stand up for yourself.'

In time, Lakshmi listened. But she could not stop their house falling into disrepair. They had had to sell their milking cow and their possessions soon dwindled. Lakshmi would not part with her box of beauty wares. Nor her mother's ring. This she kept hidden, hoping secretly that one day Sita would return to reclaim it.

Each month, when the council met, Lakshmi forced herself to attend with Maya. Nobody spoke to them. Then one day, not long after Maya's tenth birthday, her mother noticed Pillai's eyes lingering on her daughter. It wasn't the first time.

Two days later, she woke Maya early, washed, dressed and adorned her, outlining her eyes with lampblack, and took her to the *Mangalavilas*, the school of the arts. Pillai retained a large room on the second floor.

When Maya looked up at the yellow-ochre facade of the three-storey brick building and saw the stone relief carvings of dancing girls, water bearers and musicians on the balconies and turrets, she imagined she was entering the palace of the prince himself.

Lakshmi turned to her daughter and said, 'If you perform the dance of flying the kite, he will not refuse you.'

'That one is too simple.'

'Do something simple and do it well.'

She followed her mother up polished marble steps that whispered under her feet. She could hear the footsteps of all the dancers who had gone before, and those yet to come. Upstairs, the classroom dwarfed her. The ceiling was decorated in midnight-blue and white tiles, like a night sky flickering with stars. Compared to their cramped home, here she could stretch herself and fly.

A class was underway and Pillai sat at the front, beating time. He was barrel-shaped with an owlish face and penetrating eyes. As Maya watched, she thought, *I can dance better than them*, noting the limp arms of one student, the rigidity of another.

Pillai made them wait all morning, then dismissed the class and nodded. With her hands in prayer, Maya raised her arms above her head and bowed low to Pillai *ayya*. She began with *alarippu*, showing off her footwork in an elaborate sequence of steps, punctuated by a series of single syllables *ta-tai-taiyum-tat-tam-kitataka*. The sound of her voice echoed in the lofty room as her soles struck the floor in the four-beat rhythm. A small jump and she opened her arms like a flower greeting the sun, sank to a half-sitting pose with her knees bent, heels together and feet pointing straight out. From there Maya gracefully moved into the dance itself, enacting the kite tugging on the string above her with precise hand gestures and expressive eyes.

Lakshmi watched as Pillai's surly features softened. At the end, he agreed to trial her once permission had been granted by the elders.

Back home, Lakshmi said, 'See, I told you, simple works best.'

Maya bit down on her lip and said nothing. She hung around, following her mother as she did the daily chores.

'*Amma,* why did Auntie have to leave?'

'Don't start again, child,' she said, her voice weary. 'They've gone, that's that.'

'Couldn't they have moved to another part of town so we could still see them, secretly?'

'You don't understand. Even to cross the threshold of your aunt's house would taint you too. At least this way she will have a life.' Lakshmi's back stiffened. 'I don't know what sort of life but she'll find a way.'

Maya hadn't meant to ask but now she couldn't let it go. 'Did you give her some money?'

'As much as I could. I wanted to give her your grandmother's ring, but she wouldn't take it. She said I should hold on to it for safekeeping. That, one day, maybe she'd come and get it. For our sake, I hope not any time soon.'

'Why?'

'Isn't anything obvious to you, girl?' She rolled her eyes. 'Pillai's only now agreed to accept you.'

Maya went quiet.

'What is it?'

'At my initiation the head priest said something about the mark of destiny on me. What did he mean?'

Lakshmi hesitated. *She's thinking what to say*, Maya thought, *like she does when something's important.* In her mother's eyes, she saw – what, exactly? Fear, that's what it was. So the mark of destiny was something bad, like the evil eye. She wondered where the mark was and touched the mole on the side of her cheek. Her mother was watching her.

'Is that the mark?'

'One of them,' said Lakshmi.

There's more than one.

'It means that great things will come to you.' Lakshmi felt the lightness of the morning drain away. She wanted to hold Maya's hands and look in her eyes and say, *You could become great, someone special. You have the sign of the goddess on you.* But to do that would only tempt fate.

'*Amma*, are you all right?'

Lakshmi felt the light touch of Maya's hand on her wrist. She bent down and pulled her daughter towards her, kissing her brow.

Maya softened inside as her mother held her close.

For once, Lakshmi let herself absorb Maya's warmth, and felt the child's heart beat against her own. 'Child, you did well today at Pillai's.'

When Maya began her dance classes, her life settled into a new routine. A head taller than the other girls, she liked the far-right corner of the classroom, by the open window. From that vantage point, she watched the birds. In the early morning, a flock of white cranes, wings dipped in silver, crossed the sky. Brown kestrels gathered at dusk on the eaves of the palace tower. Palani's tower, they called it.

She had grown up hearing stories about Palani. About her poetry, her power, her passion. Once a dancer of the temple, she was one of the few invited into the royal bedchamber. Sometimes, when Maya arrived early, as shafts of lemon sunlight slanted under the eaves, she saw a figure dressed in white on the top of the tower. Once, she saw her with a falcon. No one knew how old she was, or if she still danced.

Maya's gaze often travelled beyond the palace, towards the plains: flat, hazy smudges of green and sand, dun and rust. She yearned to know what lay beyond the city walls. She knew that Madras lay several weeks' travel to the north and to the east was the Coromandel coast. On sultry days, when the blue sky merged with the horizon, she imagined she was looking across the ocean – a world apart from her own. One day she wanted to feel the sea breeze on her cheeks and the sand between her toes.

'Spine straight, feet together, arms out,' barked Pillai, nodding to the drummer to begin. 'One, two, three, four. Right, left, right, left.'

As the girls rehearsed, he slapped his hand on his thigh to keep the beat. First he taught them how to recognise the *tala*, the rhythm, then the basic *jatis,* the steps. Next came the hand gestures. Every animal, bird, god and goddess had its individual symbol. And last, *abhinaya,* which Maya loved most of all, an entire language of facial expressions.

'Anger you show like this,' Pillai sucked in his nostrils, flattening his lips and doubling his eyes in size. 'But for cruelty, the brows must be knitted, the pupils fixed.'

Each week they learned a new glance. There were thirty-six in all, seven different movements of the eyebrows and thirteen of the head.

When Maya first joined the class, Pillai was struck by her unhurried gait and dreamy, fish-shaped eyes. He saw the other girls' jealous stares when Maya performed a new sequence effortlessly. She was fairer than her mother, her shoulders were square, her neck tall. She always wore a lime-green skirt and blouse to practice. The colour was beautiful on her. On the bottom of her right cheek there was a mole, and while some might see it as an imperfection, he often found his gaze drawn to it.

'Concentrate, Maya.' He clapped his hands. 'Eyes straight ahead. Posture like so.'

Although Maya drove him to distraction by drifting with the birds, he could see their flight in her dance. The swoop of a kestrel as her arm cut the air from left to right; the uncoiling of a swan's neck in the undulation of her torso; the strut of a maddened peacock when she stamped her feet on the earth.

One day he invited Rao to watch a class.

'You see Mayambikai now? How quick she is to learn?' Pillai leaned back, his belly spreading over his *lungi* like warm dough. 'It's not only her rhythm that is impeccable, it's how her movements mirror the exact structure of the music, and her face, though still young, expresses *rasa*. She does what the ancient texts on dance say every artist must do, she lifts the spectator from this mundane world and gives him a fleeting taste of bliss.' His rheumy eyes glazed over. 'I have only seen one other like her. And that is Palani. Yes, I know Maya's technique is not always correct. Her concentration wavers. Yet when she dances none of that matters. She surrenders to the dance. This is the mark of a true courtesan, this is what royalty looks for.' Pillai glanced in the direction of the palace. 'She will be our greatest asset.'

It didn't take long for Maya's reputation to spread beyond the *Mangalavilas*. Another Palani, that's what they called her. But all Maya wanted was to be accepted by the other girls. When the class crowded under the palm-leaf awning for their morning break, a silent circle surrounded her, which no one crossed. They would never let her forget that she was the niece of an outcaste.

9

Walter's life was overshadowed by the Big Temple. Every morning the somnolent drums woke him and on festival days the roar of firecrackers tore him from sleep. As the English troops were there to protect God and King, there were two garrisons, one near the palace and the other next to the temple. Almost daily, he walked or rode in his palanquin past the high granite walls. Through the wooden gates he caught glimpses of lawns and throngs of dark-skinned women in bright colours, hovering like flocks of gold and saffron sunbirds. Flitting among them were priests, flimsy white cloths around their waist.

On a sweltering day in January, he agreed to pay a visit. Standing next to his valet was a slim, raffish man with a slight stoop, and hoary eyebrows poking beneath a royal-blue turban.

'Mr Sutcliffe, I am Rao. A pleasure to meet you.' He gave a disarming smile and motioned Walter through the open gate. 'We leave our shoes with Jiva.'

'No shoes?'

'Not allowed.'

'Socks?'

'Better barefoot.'

Walter flinched at every step. Gravel, sharp stones, the squelch of rotting flowers. Rao walked ahead, turning every so often to wait. His voice was breezy, his English almost faultless.

'Europeans have putty feet. Look, mine are like leather.'

Walter looked down at his toes: white, foreign things, they rarely saw the light of day.

'I heard you like drawing. Did you bring your sketchbook?'

'No. I prefer to see places first before I draw them.'

Rao frowned. 'You intend to come back?'

'Yes, I was hoping.'

'For your visit I needed special permission. The palace. The priests. All have to agree.' He thought about it. 'But you are here because of Reverend Schwarz. I am sure something can be arranged.'

Walter had met Schwarz not long after arriving in Fort St George in Madras. As one of the few missionaries who spoke local languages, the German often acted as an interpreter on political missions for the English.

'This first court is no longer in use,' Rao was saying. 'The French turned it into an arsenal. Now it's considered impure.'

Walter looked across to the various shrines laid out in a formal design. 'An arsenal?'

'You seem surprised.'

'I had no idea,' he admitted. 'Such things aren't reported back home. You just hear of the victories – like Robert Clive beating the French at Plassey and Wandiwash.'

'Every time war breaks out between England and France, our ancient temples are desecrated. Our rice fields run with blood.' Rao stopped himself.

'Carry on.'

'You won't be offended?'

The sun's glare made black and red patterns swim before his eyes. *Listen with an open mind*, he told himself. 'No. I'd like to know more. It's hard keeping up with events here.'

'Let's pause a moment.' Rao pointed to a stone bench in the shade. Gratefully, Walter sat down.

'Since the Mughals in the north went into decline, everything is in flux in the south,' Rao continued. 'Rival princes and rulers fight among each other for land and supremacy. The English are quick to ally with whoever is stronger, while, of course, always trying to out-manoeuvre the French.'

'How does Tanjore fit into all of this?'

'The East India Company view Tanjore as the granary of the south – as do our two most powerful Muslim neighbours. To the north is the Nawab of Arcot, near Madras; to the west, Hyder Ali, ruler of Mysore. These days the English favour the nawab because he has more lands and revenue.' He gave a small shrug and stood up. 'But the Company have their eyes on Tanjore's wealth too.'

'I thought the English were here to defend the prince of Tanjore,' Walter said, rising to his feet. 'Haven't we been here for years doing just that? Now we're going to wreck the whole relationship by siding with the nawab?'

'No offence, but the English will take advantage of whoever is weaker and offer soldiers and arms to the highest bidder. These days it's the alliance with the nawab that's more important. He's dependent on the Company for military protection from his enemies and they are reliant on his income. It all comes down to politics in the end,' Rao said, as they continued to walk through the grounds.

'How do you know all this?'

'I was a minister in the palace for many years.'

When they stepped into the second court, Walter whistled through his teeth. He guessed the tower to be around two hundred feet. Raised on a square base, it was shaped like a pyramid with a dozen tiers, climaxing in a vast monolithic cupola. Classical in its execution and symmetrical design, the vast quadrangle brought to mind King's College in Cambridge. It had the same spacious proportions and sense of the dramatic. After the crowded town, he felt he had stepped into another world – of regal order, power and ceremony.

'You see this figure? This is Raja Raja, the Chola King, who built the temple,' Rao said.

Walter examined the brickwork. There was no trace of anything binding the stones together. He frowned.

'You see how clever it is? The stones fit perfectly.'

'How?'

'It's a secret. Only the families who built the temple know.'

That morning, Lakshmi had wanted to arrive early at the temple, but all the way, Maya dragged her feet. When they stepped through the entrance into the second court, Maya said, 'I'm tired of being left alone. I never have anyone to play with.'

'You shouldn't be playing here.'

Maya turned away, crossing her arms.

'Come, we're late.'

'I want to go somewhere else.' Maya could see the lines around her mother's eyes tighten.

The bells chimed. The women were being summoned.

'*Amma*, is it true that you could have stopped Sita leaving and you didn't?' The words came out, tumbling over each other. 'Is it true?'

The slap landed halfway across her back. The force of it propelled Maya forward, the ground hurtled towards her and she felt soft flesh on hard stone, her skin tearing, the taste of grit on her lips. It was the shock as much as the pain that caught her by surprise, and an awful windedness making it a struggle to breathe. When at last she could breathe, she opened her mouth and howled.

'Get up!' her mother yelled. 'Now.'

Maya shook her head, drawing her knees tighter in.

'Who told you that?' Lakshmi's shadow fell across her.

Maya tried to shut out her mother's voice.

'Get up or the next one will be harder.' She raised her hand.

And then a voice rang out across the temple forecourt. A hard clipped voice in another language.

What happened next remained a blur, as if Maya were watching the scene from above. Her mother turned, her hand still ready to strike, as a foreigner came briskly towards them. With his black hat and black coat, he looked more crow than man. The solid blackness of his clothes jarred against the space and light, the green lawn and her mother's turquoise sari. Her mother lowered her hand and turned back to Maya with such a scowl that she scrambled to her feet.

Maya found herself standing between the man and her mother. He took off his hat. His fine brown hair was flecked with grey and tied away from his face. Beads of sweat were forming on his forehead and upper lip. He took a white cloth and wiped them away. Almost immediately they came back.

He bent down and, muttering something, reached out his hand towards Maya. She backed away. She did not want to run to her mother but the man made her feel anxious. He looked familiar. She met his gaze and in it, she saw recognition.

As he stood up, Rao approached at a run, his chest palpitating. He pulled the foreigner to one side and spoke sharply to him.

Maya looked up at her mother and the pain rushed back. She snivelled as she touched the raw red scrapes on her knees.

The foreigner was staring at her and speaking to Rao, nodding vigorously.

'What is a white-faced *huna* doing here, Rao *ayya*?' Lakshmi asked, aghast.

Rao looked embarrassed. The foreigner's face remained impassive. 'He has permission, Lakshmi *akka*. He is impressed by our temple.'

'Tell him to go back to his own.' Maya felt her mother bristle. 'Tell him he has no business to interfere.'

Grabbing Maya's hand, Lakshmi strode towards the doorway of the central shrine and pushed her down the narrow passageway filled with oily fumes from hundreds of flickering lamps. 'See where your whining has got us? I'm late and a white-skin came close to touching you – defiling you – and all you could do was stare.'

Maya's eyes widened.

'Today, stay here, inside the corridor. Understand?' Lakshmi said. She nodded feebly.

'There.' Her mother pointed to the corner.

'Don't leave me.'

'Stop snivelling.'

'I'm scared. What if the man comes back?'

Lakshmi looked towards the open door, her face uncertain.

'He might come back,' Maya persisted. 'Can't I come with you?'

For a moment the tautness around her mother's mouth slackened. Then she shook her head. 'No. He won't come inside. Foreigners aren't allowed.' She pointed again to the corner. 'I will bring you a cloth to sit on.'

As Maya waited for her mother's return, she looked towards the open doorway filled by sunlight. She could hear birdsong and the sound of voices outside. It was hard to believe this was the same corridor she had walked through on the day of her initiation. Suddenly, it came back to her. The foreigner in black was the same man she'd seen on that day. Unsettled, she picked up one of the palm-sized clay lamps. At the far end of the corridor, she saw the figure of a dancer painted on the wall. Her arms were stretched above her, her breasts bare. Her hair was coiled on her head and her waistband was stitched with jewels. Next to the dancer's right ear hovered a green parrot. Maya lifted the lamp higher to reveal her full figure. She thought her magnificent.

As she stood motionless, she heard whispering. The whispers carried her name.

Maya, Maya. Let the divine flow through you. Let yourself be carried. I will always be here to show you the way home.

'Who are you?' she cried. The whispering continued, sweet like sugarcane juice on a ripe summer's day. A gust of warm air passed over her, carrying the scent of roses. Crimson rose petals were falling from above and she held out one hand to catch them. As they touched her skin, they dissolved. Then, she was sure the parrot took flight.

'Who are you? How do you know my name?'

Now the dancer glowed as if a thousand fireflies encircled her. The figure started to sway and began a slow courtly dance, her expression bathed with grace.

Maya felt herself become weightless and giddy. 'Take me home,' she said, flinging both arms up and dropping the lamp, which shattered around her. 'Take me home!' But the figure began to fade, Maya's vision blurred, and she felt herself falling, falling, falling.

That night, after putting Maya to bed, Lakshmi sat on a low stool in the back courtyard. The moon was a glowing lamp in the inky sky. She felt the heat breathing down on her and heard the rapid call of a gecko. Try as she might to let the sounds wash over her, she kept replaying the day's events. That foreigner, where had she seen him? She never forgot a face. A picture formed in her mind: the day of Maya's ceremonial marriage to Shiva, just over a year ago.

She went to fetch the wide basket sieve and bag of rice, and felt the dry grains run between her fingers. She threw handfuls into the tightly woven sieve, tossing it in the air to get rid of any chaff, and then picked through the grains. As she settled into a rhythm, her mind continued to run.

The town was used to the comings and goings of foreigners. The Portuguese had been first, followed by a few swarthy Armenian merchants. She'd been a young woman with a flock of suitors when the first English redcoats had arrived. First they built a barracks, then the encampment on the town's outskirts, now there was talk they would erect their own temple.

Lakshmi saw how many foreigners took local women. Whores were encouraged to settle down with them and were paid handsomely for their duties. One gold *pagoda* per child. She tried to imagine herself with a foreigner. The younger ones weren't so bad. But they were unclean, the lot of them. She shook the sieve harder. What was she thinking? After all that had happened to Sita.

She didn't deserve her fate, Lakshmi thought. *I could have done more. And I didn't. I let them abuse her, banish her.* Lakshmi's breath became shallow. She missed her sister. Even though their feuds lasted for months,

Sita was always a steady hand. She would know what to do about this devil man.

The sound of the slap rang again in her ears. That's what had started it today. Maya whining that she missed Leela. It must have hurt. But, surely, not enough to cause the girl to faint. She lay her hands down, the tension slowly dissipating.

She knew hard times lay ahead. She could feel it in the marrow of her bones. The world of her mother and grandmother was disappearing. The fate of her daughter was being affected by decisions made in a country far away, by strange men with triangular hats and pasty faces, who seemingly lived without honour or god.

Sighing, she packed away the sieve and the rice. Picking up the lamp, she took it over to the shrine of the Mother Goddess in the corner of the courtyard. Bending her forehead forward, she said, 'Sivakami, help me. Give me strength.'

Some weeks later, Lakshmi and Uma were out the back, counting out limes to make pickle.

'She's changed,' Lakshmi said, sitting down on the stool under the frangipani tree. 'Ever since that crow man cast the evil eye on her, she hasn't been the same.'

'What happened?'

'We were late arriving at the temple and Maya was complaining about being left alone. Then this foreigner dressed in black with a pale face – a face like death – came running towards us, waving a white cloth, this way and that.' The stool creaked as she shifted her weight. 'He was casting a spell, I'm sure of it. He reached out to touch her, to pollute her. So scared I was, I stood between him and Maya, yelling at him to stand back.'

'What did she do?'

'Nothing. She stared at him.'

'Was she scared?'

'No.'

'Just you were scared?'

'Yes, I think she was too shocked to be scared.'

'Then what?'

'Rao came running behind him apologising, saying that the for-eigner thought Maya was getting hurt—'

'Why?'

'Why what?'

'Why did he think she was hurt?'

Lakshmi didn't answer straight away, too focused on measuring out the correct amount of turmeric, coriander, cumin and asafoetida, and grinding them in the pestle and mortar. Uma began squeezing the limes. In the living room, Maya was waking up. The scent of lime wafted towards her and she was about to call out when she heard her mother's voice, hesitant at first, and then with more confidence, say, 'I walloped her. Just before the man came. I'm not proud of that—'

Maya could picture *Amma* shrugging it off.

'—but these things happen.'

'Why was Rao with him?'

'How should I know? He's everywhere these days. He's back in favour in the court, and now he's friends with white-faced *hunas*.'

Maya craned her neck.

'But as I was saying. After that I made her stay in the corridor while I did the *puja*. When I came out, imagine my horror, she was lying in a cold faint.'

Uma whistled. 'He took her soul away?'

Maya put her hand to her chest.

'You think he could do that?' Lakshmi's voice was shrill.

'I've heard it's possible.'

'What should I do?'

'Take her to see Adki.'

'But she lives outside of the city. I haven't time to go there.'

'If you're so worried, you'll make time.'

Maya sat on her haunches. She'd heard about the old sage Adki. When the late king had ordered her to cure his ailing son, she'd refused to come, except under cover of darkness. It was said she would evaporate if she were seen during the day. When the young prince recovered, Adki refused payment. She left the bag of *pagodas* the king insisted she take under the pipal tree in the marketplace, and only the needy, the sweepers and scavengers, could take the gold coins out of the bag. When the rich tried, the money turned to stone.

Her mother would resent going to Adki. The *sadhvi* lived in the forest, and the path was steep, narrow and prowled by tigers.

'It's too far,' Lakshmi said flatly.

Maya waited, holding her breath. If they found her listening, she'd get the switch. Still, she didn't move. She looked down at her hands, turning the pink palms towards her. How could he have taken her soul without her knowing? She pinched her forearm: solid and fleshy. The rhythmic pounding of the grinder began and then the menthol aroma of cardamom pods breaking. Her mother cleared her throat.

'The truth is, Uma *akka*, it's not just the crow man that worries me. Maya said she heard the voice of a dancing girl from long ago. That she danced for her in the shrine. I know, you think I'm joking.' Her voice became husky.

'Lakshmi, what is it?'

Her mother sniffed. 'Already I've lost my sister. Maya has lost her cousin and pines for her. I have no patron and little chance of finding another. I don't know if I can fulfil my duties for my daughter. My fears, they keep me awake at night.'

Uma stopped what she was doing. 'Pull yourself together, woman. Life is looking up for you and Maya. Take it as good fortune that she can hear the voice of a dancer. I saw how brave she was at her initiation and you said yourself she bears the mark of the goddess. How do you know that this isn't the way of the goddess to reveal herself?'

The next day, when they arrived at the temple, Lakshmi didn't leave Maya at the gateway and hurry straight in, she led her round the back of the tower.

'Have you ever wondered what these inscriptions are?' Lakshmi pointed to one wall covered entirely with writing.

'I've tried to read some of it. This says "Tiruvarur".'

'Yes.'

Maya's eyes brightened.

'Who built the temple?' Lakshmi quizzed her.

'I know, wait.' She scrunched her eyes, then burst out, 'Raja Raja the Great.'

'That's right. So these are all Raja Raja's records. All his staff, including the names of the four hundred dancing girls he brought to perform for him.'

'Show me.'

'Their names start here: Thangam, Selvi, Amuda . . .'

'I like Amuda,' interrupted Maya.

'It says she lived at 108 West Main Road.'

'We're almost neighbours.'

The temple bell sang out across the courtyard.

'What else does it say?' Maya tugged her mother's hand.

Lakshmi looked across the quadrangle. One of the priests was waiting.

'I've got to go.'

'Just tell me about one more.'

Lakshmi gave Maya's hand a light squeeze. 'Remember, don't go out of the gates. Meet me back here at midday.'

Maya watched until her mother had gone. Then she stared up at the rows and rows of writing and tried to imagine what the temple would have looked like when it was new, the carvings fresh, the paint of the frescoes still wet. The colours! Imagine. The clothes! An idea began to form in her mind as she started to walk. She broke into a skip, then ran to the furthest corner of the grounds.

There was a life-sized dancing girl carved into the pillar. Crouching down, Maya touched each toenail and the ridges of the ankle bells carved into the stone. She rubbed the head of the parrot that sat beside the girl's feet. Then she said out loud, 'Amuda, you're going to teach me how they danced back in Raja Raja's time.'

As she felt the girl's presence, Maya let her thoughts fly. Pillai had told her that if she were to dance the stories of the gods, she must imagine them. See them. Feel them. Only then could she become whatever and whomever she wanted – a swan gliding down the Kaveri, mischievous Krishna stealing the butter. Her feet found their own rhythm and she lunged and jumped from side to side of the arched passageway until her head spun. Laughing, she lay on the cool flagstones. Then, out of the corner of her eye, she saw a movement. She was being watched. A prickling ran down her spine. She scanned the grounds. The courtyard was empty. *Look straight across,* a voice told her. She waited.

Then, the crow man stepped out from behind a column. In his hand he held a dark-brown notebook. She stood up. She thought she would feel scared. Instead, she was curious. She knew he was straining to look at her. But he set off in the opposite direction in long looping strides. When he came to the corner, he stopped. Then he turned around and awkwardly raised a hand, as if in greeting, before disappearing from view.

I O

Palani was losing weight, her eyes were dull, her face jaundiced. Shivaratri, the festival to Shiva, was less than two weeks away and rumours about Palani's condition had reached the head priest. *Mistress never used to be like this*, her maid fretted. There used to be the occasional nip of opium after entertaining the king, not this wanton sucking on the agate-tipped pipe of her hookah.

Perhaps reminding her about the girl would help. After going quiet for a year Rao had arrived with the news that she was ready and a meeting should be arranged. 'The scandal attached to her has passed,' he'd said.

Vimala hesitated before she knocked on the door, then marched in.

'I didn't send for you,' Palani said.

'Rao *ayya* insisted I talk to you about that girl. In recent weeks she's been at the temple most days. Should I send for her?'

'I need to see for myself. Arrange the litter for tomorrow morning.'

Vimala tipped her head.

'Have you heard anything of Adki?' Palani asked, feigning indifference.

'Nothing. Why?'

'No reason. I never hear of her these days.'

'Do you want me to make enquiries?'

'No. First let's see how we go with the girl.'

Shivaratri marked the arrival of the hot winds. Maya was standing on the balcony of the *Mangalavilas*; her whole body ached. Pillai always made her hold poses longer than the other girls, so long that she had to suck in every muscle to keep still. If she strained to shut out the noise from the street, she thought she could hear her name being called across the rooftops. She saw a figure in the tower lean forward out of the arch with a bird on her wrist. It could only be Palani and the royal falcon. Maya's pulse quickened. She had an urge to wave, an urge to be seen. She watched as the falcon was released. It circled above the palace, and then, when Palani gave the signal, it returned to the tower.

Without needing to turn around, the gust of coconut oil that always preceded Pillai told her she was expected back in class.

For the next hour, Pillai singled out each girl to perform the sequence they would present at the festival. 'Maya, concentrate. What's wrong?'

Behind her, she heard a snigger. She tried again.

'That's enough.' Pillai banged the ground with his *thambu,* his wooden staff.

The morning of Shivaratri, Palani sensed her maid's presence outside her bedroom door before she opened her eyes. Her head throbbed and heat pulsed through her. She heard a cough.

'Curse you, woman. Why did you make me say yes?'

The maid opened the door. The sight of her mistress sitting up, the thin muslin gown hanging off her like a wilting blossom, constricted her throat. In front of her was a woman withering from the inside. 'It's time to rise. The sixteen adornments are ready and your bath is being prepared.'

'Get out.'

Vimala pushed on. 'Madam, if you don't act now, your quarters will be snatched up by Prince Tuljajee's next favourite.'

'Out.'

Palani's eyes were filled with splinters and Vimala breathed them in, letting the anger shatter around her. Then, next door, she heard

Vikku shrieking. All these weeks, the parrot had been silent, and now, in his cries, Vimala heard renewal. Quietly, she backed out of the chamber, and shut the door.

As Palani sank into the warm water, she gave a soft whimper. The blossoms of *roja, malli*, white lotus and holy basil grazed her limbs. She tried to keep her face hard, but when the maid turned her back, tears filled her eyes.

'Why are you crying? Your salty tears will sour the perfumes. Pray, stop.'

Palani lifted her head. Her maid turned and, bending down, she used the corner of her sari to wipe Palani's face and blow her nose. Their eyes met. For the first time in months Palani let herself see the sadness in the old woman's eyes and feel the loyal devotion in her touch.

As the water seeped into the emptiness inside, Palani said, 'Go on, tell me.'

'Madam needs to feel the dance again,' she ventured.

'You think that will be enough?'

Vimala nodded.

'Is this why you encouraged me to perform tonight?'

'The people love you. They will fill you.'

'What if I can't remember the dance?'

'It will remember you.'

Several hours later, after the saffron paste covering Palani had been washed off, the first queen's lady-in-waiting applied a solid line of lampblack to the inner rim of her eyes. Then she pressed *missi* paste over Palani's gums, giving them a mauve hue. As each of the adornments was completed, Palani felt her old vigour return. When her lips were hibiscus red, and gold bangles weighed down her arms, Palani drew herself up like a crane and demanded a beauty spot on the lower side of her right cheek – at the point of seduction. Then she was taken in her litter to the side entrance of the Big Temple and shielded as she slipped into the main shrine.

Ahead of her was the large granite *lingam*. She could feel a pulse deep in her belly, and unconsciously her fingers sought out the trident seared onto her upper arm. She walked through to the inner chamber and sat on the single wooden chair to wait. As she placed her arms on the armrests, it dawned on her that it was here that the girls were branded. She looked up. Above was a fresco of Shiva. As she stared, she heard voices whispering, women's voices. She smelt a hint of rose. The flames of the lamps gusted and outside the drumbeat built to a fury. She looked at the mirror ring on her thumb. The emerald eye of the snake in the centre of her headdress gleamed. She was ready.

By the time Maya, Lakshmi and Uma arrived at the Big Temple, the main courtyard was already crowded. The shadows were lengthening and the air hummed with expectation. For weeks Maya had been thinking about this moment. Every time she'd come to the temple with her mother, she prayed, 'Please let me meet Palani.' It was rumoured this would be the last time she would perform in public.

Maya and the women found a place at the back.

'*Amma,* have you ever met Palani?' Maya asked.

'No. But in front of his entire court, King Pratap said she was "incomparable among her kind".' She looked across to Uma, who was nodding. 'Our kind, temple women like us, Maya. But there aren't many like her any more.'

'I want to get closer to the stage.'

'No, we're staying here.'

'I can't see.'

The beat of the drums crescendoed as the bejewelled dancers took their places and people in front rose to their feet.

Shouting in her mother's ear, Maya said, 'Let me go to the front.'

Her mother shook her head.

Maya knew where Palani would be waiting before she went on

stage, that there was another entrance and she could squeeze through without being noticed.

'*Amma*—'

'Let the child go, Lakshmi,' Uma said. 'It would do her good to see Palani dance up close.'

Lakshmi looked from one to the other. Then, before she could change her mind, Maya ducked out of arm's reach and was swallowed up by the crowd.

By the time Maya reached the side door, she was panting. Somewhere nearby, she heard the sound of a chair scraping on the floor. Twisting her fingers together, she began to walk. The floor beneath was covered in a thin film of oil. When she reached the door at the end of the passageway, perspiration pooled in her lower back. Something caught her eye. Behind her was a finger-thin shaft of light to the left of the central *lingam*. It came from the inner chamber. Without stopping to think, Maya walked over and pushed open the door.

Sitting on a wooden chair was Palani, staring into the small oval mirror on her ring. She was wearing a headdress of rubies and emeralds; her eyes were lustrous, her lashes thick. She looked up and for the briefest moment, Maya saw her eyes widen with shock before her face regained its composure. Maya pushed the door shut and, in a single fluid movement, bent down at the older woman's feet in a deep *pranam*. Her feet were tiny, the skin papery and soft, smelling of citrus and flowers. As Maya touched them very lightly in a mark of respect, a current surged through her. Unsteadily, Maya stood up, taking a step back.

'How did you know where to find me?' Palani broke the silence, a hint of admiration in her deep, gravelly voice.

'I didn't, Palani *akka*. But I saw this door ajar.'

'The door to the inner chamber where girls are usually forbidden.' She arched an eyebrow. 'Yet you pushed it open.'

Outside the drumming grew louder. The room was stuffy and Maya found it hard to breathe.

'I have to go,' Palani said.

'You don't know who I am.'

'Don't I? You don't recognise me without the veil?' Palani said, her tone wry. 'I've been watching you dance, Mayambikai. You do it better alone than in a crowd.'

She stared at her feet, too overcome to speak.

'You must go. If they find you here, I'll be blamed.' Palani stood up. Her cloudlike sari was of woven silver and gold shot through with scarlet silk, and she'd pulled it up between her legs to form wide pantaloons. 'How do I look?'

Maya could only nod.

'Quickly, child. Run ahead.'

'Then?'

'Then?'

'That's it?' Maya said.

'Rao *ayya* will arrange everything else.' She placed her hand on Maya's arm. 'But keep quiet about this meeting between us. It is Shiva's doing.'

A few minutes later, Maya had found a place to sit at the front. Facing her was the *mandapa,* the stone pavilion opposite the central shrine. When Palani walked into the centre, the crowd cheered, and all the other dancers flocked to her like cygnets to a swan. As quickly as they'd come, they faded into the background.

As the singer started, Palani stood poised, a tiny, bird-like figure, whose presence still touched the furthest person in the audience. With crisp joyous movements, Palani began to woo Shiva and ask that on this, the dark night of the Lord, he be merciful to his wife and consort Parvati. A single warbling *nadaswaram* introduced her next round of devotional songs, accompanied by bell-like cymbals. Her body moved in sculptured poses, her hands fluttered in delicate gestures.

Maya watched as Palani orchestrated her performance like no other dancer she'd seen before; how she brought in musicians with the slightest nod of her head and told others to stop with the flick of an eye. She was both leading and following, improvising to a sudden flight of wild drumming with rapid foot movements and deep squats. Then she stopped the musicians and stepped forward to the edge of the stone platform, and with an imperious nod silenced the crowd. To a single drumbeat she began to perform a well-known *padam*, where Parvati soothes Shiva's fiery rages. As the cymbals crescendoed and Palani's feet moved faster, the flames of the torchbearers threw leaping silhouettes on the walls, magnifying her gestures of supplication and surrender.

Suddenly she transformed again – into a young woman, teasing her lover, playful and bawdy, thrusting her hips and pouting her dark-red lips. The crowd cheered, men and women vigorously shaking their heads. Through her facial gestures she expressed every emotion – fear, lust, anger, passion, innocence – as if she were not one person, but an entire cast. As if she were not only a woman, but the goddess herself.

Maya heard the crowd echoing the rattle of the drums, willing Palani, urging her, to bring the dance to its climax. She experienced a rush of pleasure and felt light-headed. As the dance drew to a close, Maya looked up, expecting rose petals to fall from above. At that instant, Palani stood in the centre of the pillared hall, her lips parted. As she spread her arms like frosted wings, devotion flooded the hall and the crowd gave a deafening roar.

Maya jumped up and a burst of light exploded behind her. She found herself calling out to Palani. She did not know why, but at that moment, she knew her life would follow a new course. She had done it. She had met the great Palani herself – alone and in the inner sanctum. And she had done so with Shiva's blessing. Walking back home behind her mother and Uma, the rhythm of the music pounding through her, Palani's words rang in her ears. For the first time since Sita had left, hope coursed through her. As she turned to go into the house, she looked upwards into the moonless night and mouthed a silent thank you.

I I

The following week, Lakshmi and Maya were ushered into the reception room where Palani took visitors. Without her headdress, Palani looked even smaller than Maya remembered. When she spoke she snapped her fingers, her eyes darting left to right as if performing, as if she never stopped.

Maya could barely bring herself to look around the panelled room, filled with divans and silk drapes, and in one corner, a desk with drawers. Ivory statues of Ganesha and Shiva stared down from alcoves. In the corner was a life-sized lamp in the form of King Pratap, the wick growing out of his cupped palms. Awnings in morning-bright colours stretched over the balcony. Everything was finely wrought – the sweeping arches, the swirling patterns of flowers on white marble columns. It was a place of dreams.

Her mother's face was tense. *She can't believe this is happening,* Maya thought.

'This is a great honour, Palani *akka,*' Lakshmi began, her words faltering.

Palani gave a small, kind smile. 'The honour is all mine.'

Lakshmi lowered her head.

'While I speak to Maya, you can discuss the girl's lessons with Rao *ayya.* He'll be teaching her languages. Marathi, Sanskrit, and improving her Telugu.'

'She knows the basics of Sanskrit. I taught her myself.'

'Excellent. You are welcome to sit in during her lessons. Rest assured the girl will be chaperoned at all times.'

Lakshmi nodded.

'I will be in charge of teaching her dance myself,' Palani said, reaching for the bell. Straight away her maid entered. 'Take Lakshmi *akka* next door.'

Her mother pushed herself up and followed the maid.

Once she had gone, Palani sat opposite Maya.

'Hungry?'

Maya shook her head.

Palani rang the bell again and ordered sweetmeats. She set the silver platter in front of the girl. Maya felt like she was being tested. Never had she seen such sweets: pink almond rosebuds, dark syrupy pistachio *halwa* and a mound of cashews. Saliva pooled in her mouth.

'Go on.'

Maya reached across and, picking one cashew, nibbled on it.

Like a squirrel, Palani thought.

'Thank you. I've had enough.'

The older woman smiled. She had the loveliest face Maya had ever seen. 'Try one of these.' She nudged the platter closer.

Maya felt her stomach contract.

'Go on.'

Hesitantly, she took the pink sweet between thumb and index finger. Just half. She popped it in her mouth. Palani's eyes were on her. The sweetness exploded. She let it coat her tongue and felt the perfumed syrup trickle down her gullet. Her cheeks flushed. To stop herself taking the other half, she slid her hands beneath her thighs.

Palani pushed the plate to one side. 'She's had enough, Vimala. Take it and leave us.' She watched Maya for a reaction. The faintest glimmer crossed the girl's face. Palani was impressed.

Maya was curled into silence. She studied the black-and-white chequered marble floor, imagining what moves she would perform between the squares. She sensed Palani's growing impatience, but her mind was blank. All she could think was, *Why me?*

At length, Maya said it. 'Why me?'

'I know Pillai *ayya*. Many years ago he taught me.'

Pillai taught Palani? The thought thrilled her.

'But that's not why I picked you,' Palani continued, thinking of the unexpected message she'd received from Adki. After months of silence, she'd appeared again, encouraging her to take Maya as her student. *You two have a special connection,* she'd said. *One that goes beyond this life.*

Picked me. I didn't know I had been chosen. Maya pressed her knuckles into the top of her thighs.

'As you know, I've been watching you dance in the temple.' Palani looked across at her. 'Which one is talking to you?'

Maya gave a barely audible gasp. 'Which one?'

Palani nodded and very softly she said, 'Which dancer?'

'You can hear her too?'

'Not any more. When I was your age, yes.'

Forgetting herself, Maya jumped up. 'There are two now.'

Palani arched an eyebrow.

'First it was the one in the corridor, the one with her hair piled on her head. She looks like she's trying to say something.'

'Does she?'

'Yes. She knows my name. I don't know how, but she does.'

Palani nodded.

Maya felt a lightness in her heart. At last. Someone she could – what? Confide in? Remembering who she was talking to made her nervous and the words dried on her lips.

'Go on.'

'The first time the dancer whispered my name and started to sway, I thought I was imagining it. But I wasn't. It was as if she lifted up from the wall and began this slow courtly dance, and the parrot at her feet flew around my head and rose petals fell from the ceiling and then,' she stared down at her hands, 'then I fainted.'

'What did your mother say?'

'She found me in the corridor and blamed it on the foreigner we'd seen that morning. I think it was seeing the dancer.'

'Does she believe you?'

'No. I don't think so.'

'You said there was a second?'

'She's a statue in the far corner of the temple—' Maya stopped mid-sentence.

'Yes?'

'I don't think I should tell you which one. She wouldn't like it.'

'Your secret will be safe with me.'

Maya shook her head. It wasn't that she didn't trust Palani. It was just a feeling that if she said too much, the dancer wouldn't talk to her any more. She blinked, uncertain.

As Palani stared at Maya, she heard the door creak. Drat that maid of hers. Palani put her finger to her lips and padded across to the door, pulling it open with a sharp tug. Vimala tumbled forward, her face startled as she rolled to the ground.

Palani and Maya looked at each other and burst out laughing. For a moment, Vimala lay stunned, before clambering to her feet.

'No wonder Maya didn't want to tell me. She must have known you were there. Get out. Leave us in peace.'

Palani beckoned Maya over to the balcony. The palace gardens stretched like an unfurling scroll. Tree creepers with scarlet and white blossoms wrapped themselves around the columns. Fountains studded the lawns and filled the air with the tinkling of water.

I want to know her secret, thought Maya. She started out as a servant of the temple. Now, she's as powerful as any queen.

As if divining her thoughts, Palani turned to her. 'You, too, can cultivate it. As you know, Maya, your name means illusion. All of this,' she gestured towards the gardens, 'is not real. What is real is in our hearts. But we have to know how to play the game. We must use what has been given to us. My mother and grandmother were eminent scholars and poets. And that is where we will begin. With poetry.'

—

Maya was sitting on the stool waiting for Palani. It was the first time she had been in her quarters alone; usually the maid asked that she wait outside. A squeaky metallic sound made her turn around. Vikku had shuffled to the end of his bar and was bobbing his head towards her. Some of the servants feared the old parrot, saying he had a sixth sense and knew when a maid stole food, crying out, 'Thief, thief.'

Over the next three years, Maya would spend hours sitting on that mauve-tasselled stool, its cushioned top embroidered with seashells. When she was alone, emboldened by familiarity and boredom, she would crouch near Vikku's cage and talk to the bird. In time he let her reach in through the bars to tickle his chin and scratch the top of his beak. If he wanted her attention he threw cracked seeds on the floor. She was sure he listened to what she said, but whether he understood, she never knew.

Rao was as punctual as Palani was erratic. Their lessons took place in a loft room. From the open window Maya could see the bright headscarves of the women working in the tiered paddy fields beyond the palace walls, their sickles rising and falling rhythmically as they harvested the rice.

If *Amma* wasn't with them during lessons – and now, thanks to Palani's influence, she was back performing her former duties at the temple – then an old maidservant sat in the corner as Maya's chaperone.

On the first day Rao gave Maya her own slate. A quick learner, after two months she could recite sections from the *Jamini Bharata* and understood the precepts of Puranic lore. While she sat cross-legged on a mat, he reclined in a rattan armchair. He wore a turban reluctantly and, halfway through the lesson, took great care unravelling it. His curling moustache was trimmed; his words lacquered.

Sometimes Rao brought his violin and Maya watched how his slim fingers cradled the instrument and turned the pegs. It took her a while to become familiar with the sound: lilting, flowery, wistful. It spoke a different language to the *veena*.

'Listen with your heart,' he told her. 'That's what you do with any music. You can't listen with your mind.'

When he was satisfied that the violin was in tune, Rao rose to his feet and started to play. Maya closed her eyes, letting the sound sink through her bones. Rao smiled as he coaxed the curved husk of wood to life.

Sometimes he would cancel the lesson and then she'd go to the temple with *Amma*.

'Where do you go?' she asked him one day.

'Don't pry.'

'I'm not.'

'Yes you are. I'm here now, aren't I?'

'You always bring something back, something foreign.' Once it was a coin engraved with the head of King George III of England. Another time, he was standing by the window, holding a long black tube to one eye, twisting it backwards and forwards.

'Unbelievable,' he was saying, 'just unbelievable.'

She waited.

'Don't you want to see for yourself?'

She nodded.

'Stand here. Look through this end. Now turn this.'

The distant view of the rice fields and the women flew towards her. She gasped.

'Amazing, isn't it?'

Slowly Maya turned the tube, and what was far became near. She could even see a white egret riding on the back of a buffalo.

'How does it work?'

He shrugged.

'Is it a trick?'

'No. This, Maya, is science.'

He held out his palm and she handed it back.

'It's not a toy, it's an invention.'

'What's that?'

'Something new, a discovery.'

A discovery. The thought pleased her. She watched as Rao eased the telescope back into its soft pouch. Then, he picked up his violin and began to play. Threads of music, curling and hypnotic, rose into the air.

I 2

'We will close the service with a prayer.' Walter waited as the soldiers knelt on the ground, their faces the same shade of pillarbox red as their woollen jackets. A dusty squall tore through the open courtyard. The sun was not yet high, but already it sucked the spittle from his lips. He was as eager to finish as they were.

'We pray for our fellow countrymen fighting against the Musulman Hyder Ali. We pray that the true God will reign victorious. We pray—'

'To leave this cesspit and go home.' The tight, cracked voice came from behind. Walter turned. A young private with a thatch of straw-coloured hair reeled forward, his jacket open, a bottle in hand.

'Sir. We are taking the Sunday service.'

'I don't see no church.'

'We have no need of a church to feel the presence of Our Lord.'

He raised his bottle. 'To the Lord, then.'

The man's head lolled to one side. His trousers were stained with piss and a dank, foetid odour rolled towards Walter. He could feel the eyes of the other soldiers on his back. This cur was making an ass of him. 'Either your name or leave now.'

The soldier sneered before stumbling away, swearing under his breath.

When Walter returned to the house, a letter from Reverend

Schwarz was waiting for him. He ignored it and, going straight to his room, tore off his wig and splashed tepid water over his face. When he turned to reach for the towel, a young, dark-skinned servant stood holding a cloth. Walter started; he had not heard him enter. After dismissing the boy, he began to undress.

Before taking off his breeches, he felt around inside the pocket, his fingers searching for the smooth rounded surface of the acorn. There was always a moment before he found it when he held his breath, and then, when he did, he relaxed. He placed the acorn with his silver pocket watch in a leather wallet and pushed it underneath the mattress.

'Jiva,' he shouted. 'Bring me tea.'

He sat down, pressing his fingers into his temples. He was so tired, so very tired. His mind glugged and lurched. He wished for coolness and rain. At home it would be midsummer and the days would be getting longer. But thinking of the rectory only made his shoulders sag. He chided himself for not writing to George. His manservant had helped him pack up the house. Now that Walter was here, he wished he had something of Emily, something other than the acorn. Her lace bonnet, her china doll. He had thought that leaving England and starting a new life would give him more than enough to think about. But he found the agony of forgetting worse than the pain of remembering.

He could feel the eyes of Christ on him. 'Father, I asked to do penance. Grant me forbearance.'

Taking a sip of tea, he replayed the morning's events. *I should have been harder.* His father would have damned the soldier to hell and then had him whipped for drinking on the Sabbath. *Weak-chinned you are, my son.* How many times had he heard that as he was growing up? He looked up at the crucifix. Some days he wanted to take the bloody thing down, but he couldn't. *If Schwarz found out*—Then he remembered the letter waiting for him. *Well, and what if Schwarz did find out?* The letter was brief, the handwriting exact.

Dear Reverend Sutcliffe,
I've heard troubling reports that attendance to your Sunday services
is declining. I know you conduct them extempore and the heat is
trying, but I urge you to increase your rounds of the garrison. Preach
wherever you go.

Once your congregation is loyal, you can start a school for the
half-caste children of the soldiers. The numbers only continue to
rise. These piteous wretches need urgent instruction.

It is well that I introduced you to Rao. Although a Brahmin,
he is quite agreeable. I think you will find him a diligent teacher
of the Tamil language. In time I pray that you will extend your
preaching among the heathens.

Your humble servant,
C. F. Schwarz.
June 23rd, 1767

In readiness for his first lesson with Rao, Walter laid out parchment, ink and quill. He couldn't imagine how he would master a language with a script so unfamiliar when he'd found Latin impossible.

Rao arrived holding a violin. 'Let's go outside. Under the mango tree will be cooler.'

He started repeating simple words by rote. After thirty minutes, Rao signalled for Walter to stop, and plucked the strings of his violin. 'Learning is better,' he said, 'with a calm mind.'

A few weeks later, he insisted that Walter accompany him to his barber, a short stocky man with wide flat feet.

'He has only shaved one *ferenghi* before, an English officer, and it didn't go well,' Rao said. 'He will shave you as long as you don't flinch at the length of the blade.'

Walter swallowed. 'I'm quite equipped to do it myself.'

'Every time I see you, you look worse. Now lean back.'

Rao sat beside him as the barber first washed and lathered Walter's shoulder-length hair. He *champued* the head, his fingers kneading the scalp, until Walter sank into the chair with a quiet, helpless moan.

Then the barber began to shave him.

When he brought a mirror, Walter was surprised at what he saw. His face was thinner and he looked peaky. He examined his yellowing teeth and when the barber was busy with Rao, stuck out his tongue. A thick white paste covered the back. *I should get a tongue scraper*, he thought. He held the mirror out from his face. He'd inherited his blue-grey eyes from his Scottish mother, his beaked nose from his father. He caught Rao's gaze and as he put the mirror down, heard Papa's stentorian voice. *Vanity is the most subtle and cunning of vices.*

Some months later, Walter was sitting in the courtyard waiting for Rao. The house was quiet but the mynah birds chattered in the branches like women haggling in the bazaar. He scanned the palm fronds to see if the monkey had returned but there was only a crow, jabbing its ugly beak towards him.

Rao sat down opposite him. 'We start with simple words. I say *Eppati irukkinga?* How are you? You say *Nalamaa irkken.* I am well.'

He repeated it. Ten minutes later, gone.

Rao said it again, slower this time.

Walter thought of how irritated he used to be with Jiva when he mispronounced his surname. And here he was, unable to count to ten after five lessons.

'You're getting better,' Rao said brightly.

'No need to be polite.'

'Languages aren't your strong point.'

He shook his head.

The Brahmin pushed a bunch of small bananas towards him. 'When we teach children, we give them something sweet. In that way they find the sweetness of learning. Eat this. I'll be back.'

Walter had tried the larger bananas in Fort St George. They tasted floury, with a woody texture. He broke off one from the bunch of six. It was the length of his middle finger and three times as thick.

He peeled back the thin skin and bit into the yellow-white flesh, the colour of shortcrust pastry brushed with egg yolk. It dissolved in his mouth, sweet and buttery. He took another. By the time Rao returned, all six were gone.

'I'll bring two bunches next time,' he quipped, looking at the mound of skins on the table, and putting down two clay cups of tea.

'Where did you learn English?' Walter asked.

'At the court. Before that, my father instructed me.'

'How do most boys learn?'

'Most don't.'

'The priests, though, they can read and write?'

'Yes. And often the Brahmins.'

'I thought priests were Brahmins.'

'They are, but not every Brahmin is a priest. Like me, for example.'

Walter thought about this. He'd been here close to two years now and yet he understood so little. He wondered if it would be the same if Rao came to England, or if life was more complex here. Or perhaps Schwarz was right when he'd said that Walter was a slow learner. The criticism still piqued. *Probably because it's true.* Dejection spread through him. 'I'm hopeless,' he said.

Rao looked up in surprise. 'Why do you say that, Mr Sutcliffe?'

'You never show impatience, yet I never improve.'

'It takes time, Sir. I was hopeless in English those first years. I couldn't make my mouth wrap around the words. I still have a problem with the letter "v" and your confounded "th".' He pushed his tongue to the back of his teeth. 'Through the thick thatch Tom thumped thistles.'

Walter laughed aloud. 'Who taught you that?'

'I made it up to learn how to make the "th" sound.' He tipped his head to one side. 'You know, I've never heard you laugh before.'

Walter caught himself, suddenly aware of how loud he'd sounded, how bold.

'Don't stop. It's good for you. We all need to laugh.'

As Walter took a sip of the spicy tea, he felt something inside him relax. He enjoyed Rao and his eccentric, bookish nature. If it hadn't been for Schwarz, he'd never have met him. He could thank the reverend for that.

When the hot months passed and the mid-year rains had come and gone, November brought cooler weather and Walter started to explore all quarters of the fortified town. He noticed how some Brahmins would only walk with a bearer ten paces ahead, hitting the ground with a stick to announce their arrival. He saw how dark-skinned pariahs jumped down from the road if they heard the higher castes coming, and if they were too slow, how brutally they were beaten. Although he told himself that the lower castes were no better than beasts of burden, their acceptance of life's lot unsettled him. The women were always bare-chested. Caste law prevented them from covering their upper bodies. The sight of the semi-naked women in the fields repulsed him, but one day, seeing a woman bent over, breasts hanging pendulous like ripe fruit, desire overwhelmed him. She stood up and, ashamed, Walter turned away – but not before she'd seen him.

Walter was granted permission to go to the Big Temple as long as his valet accompanied him. He'd pack his sketchpad, notebook, pencils, scale rule and pipe, and find a shady place to sit on the lawns in the second courtyard. From there he had a perfect perspective of the central shrine and tower above. He could also look across to the corridors and sometimes he saw the girl practise her dance steps, darting among the arches, hair streaming behind. Occasionally he'd see the girl's mother and give a polite bow, *Jack whore though she was.*

In the corners of his notebook, he started to sketch this flighty figure in green. In her wild abandon, Walter saw glimpses of Emily. Drawing her helped to anchor his mind and soothe the ache in his heart. But then his mind began to deceive him. Everywhere Walter went he saw Emily. Girls who looked nothing like her transformed before his eyes. Yet when he tried to picture his daughter, the contours of her face were slipping away. He could only just recall the timbre of her voice and her slight lisp. They said that time would heal. Four years on and he was still pining for her.

A crowd often gathered around him, pointing and murmuring at his drawings. The priests came and when they saw something he'd missed, they'd insist he take a closer look. That's when they showed him the carving on the north side of the tower.

'Like you.' The priest pointed at Walter.

He stared up at the figures. Usually he didn't look too closely, afraid of what he might see – sylphs in provocative poses with alluring gazes.

'See?'

Walter shook his head.

'Like you.'

Then he spotted him: a lone figure wearing a bowl-shaped hat that a European merchant might wear, a stout fellow, and undoubtedly a white man.

'Yes. I see,' Walter said, pointing to himself. 'Like me.'

The priest nodded, smiling. 'Foreigner. Up there. Carved into our temple walls.'

13

One day, when Rao was late to class, the maid brought Maya a bowl of *prasad* from the temple and she ate it slowly with her fingers, starting at the edge and working inwards, savouring the warm tapioca mixture. It tasted oily, sweet and comforting and made her think of Leela and how she would always suck her fingers clean. She tried to picture her cousin and shut her eyes hoping it would help. It didn't. She couldn't even remember how long it had been since Sita had left. The thought unsettled her.

'Come on, dreamer.'

Rao caught her off guard. She hadn't heard him enter.

They were halfway through the lesson when Rao announced, 'I think you should learn another language. You're doing so well with Marathi and Sanskrit.'

'Persian?'

'A foreign language will help you more. English.'

'Isn't the language of the Moghuls foreign enough?'

'The Moghuls are foreign to us, you're right.' He stared into the mid-distance. 'Still, I think English will be more useful.'

'Why?'

He turned to face her. 'You said you like the violin.'

'Yes.'

He smiled. 'That's foreign. Not everything foreign is bad.'

'Like that invention you showed me which made everything far away appear close.'

'The telescope.'

'Yes. So could you teach me?'

'The basics. One of my students is English.'

'That tall man who wears black? The one who became angry with *Amma* in the temple. Him?'

'Yes.' Rao frowned. 'That was when he first arrived. He's learned a lot since then.'

'What's he doing here?'

'He's an English priest who's helping another foreigner, Mr Schwarz. They give religious instruction to the English troops.'

'Why are the English here?'

'You're asking a lot of questions.'

'You're the only one who knows the answers.'

He laughed.

'In a short answer, money. And power. And politics.' He looked down at her empty slate. 'We should start the lessons.'

'What's his name?'

'*Sahib* Sutcliffe. Most people know him as *sahib* Sutt-sutt.'

'Is he nice?' She pulled at a lock of her hair. She could see he was thinking how to answer her.

'I don't always agree with him, but I like him more as I get to know him.'

At the end of class, as Maya turned to go, he said, 'Don't mention any of this to Palani *akka*. She's not keen on anything foreign. I've tried to explain the benefits but she won't listen.'

Maya nodded, glad to be part of a secret.

As the months passed, and the cooler weather once more turned to the torrid heat of April, Rao began to give Walter his lessons before sun-up. One morning, they took a stroll together along the riverbank. The water was sinking daily.

'The funeral *ghats* are over there,' said Rao, pointing to a paved area above steps on the opposite bank. There were four pyres of wood, each at a different stage of burning. People were gathered around and young boys with large sticks pushed the corpses deeper into the flames. From across the river, Walter could smell the sickening stench of burning flesh. He felt panicky inside and lifted his eyes beyond, to the bank of palmyra palms. In his mind's eye, he saw the charred frame of the rectory and the smoking roof. He tried to push the memory away, but he wasn't quick enough. Tightness spread across his chest. Aware of Rao's enquiring gaze, he searched for something to fill the silence.

'Some time ago we were discussing education. Do I take it that no women here can read and write?'

'A few only.'

Walter thought of Mama: her broad, swift handwriting that would fill a page in no time; her eleven o'clock daily ritual with a steaming cup of tea and the next chapter of Defoe or Swift.

'My mother could read and write. She said it gave her some space of her own. I always remember as a child it made me feel separate. Shut out, almost. She kept a journal locked and closeted away. I always wanted to know what she had written. But when she died, neither my brother nor I found it. She took her secrets with her to the grave.'

Rao was staring at him. 'Tell me more about your mother.'

'She was Scottish. She always missed the Highlands.'

Rao tilted his head questioningly.

'North of the border, the region is known for its high mountains and lakes,' Walter said.

'High like our Himalayas?'

'No. Small compared to them. High for us.'

'She was lucky to be able to read and write.'

'Lucky? Yes. Her mother schooled her. She thought it was important that a gentlewoman should know her letters.'

'Here it is only the temple women who know such things.'

Walter shook his head.

'The temple dancers? Why would they need to read and write?'

'To know the scriptures. The *Natya Shastra* is as old as your Bible. The women must know every dance posture and its meaning. In heaven it is only the *apsaras*, the celestial nymphs, who are taught to sing, dance, read and write. On earth it is the same. The temple women, we call them the *devadasis*, they have been given this gift and it is their right to use it. They are handmaidens to the gods. As the king is god's representative on earth, they entertain him also.'

Walter's forehead puckered. It didn't make sense.

'You asked me about that procession you saw. Remember? When you first arrived you saw a young girl being taken to the temple, dressed in red.'

He nodded.

'She is my pupil. Her name is Maya. On that day she was being dedicated to our god Shiva. Now she is being trained to the highest level. Some of the girls stay in the temples. You have women similar to this. Cloistered women.'

'Nuns?'

'Yes, some are like nuns. Others are too beautiful to stay inside. They become consorts to the king or the landowners. The men donate large sums to the temple and the women become their concubines.'

Walter thought of the girl, of Maya, on the first day he'd arrived in the town, her expectant face; her steady fearless eyes.

'Why do they offer them so young?'

'To begin their training.'

'And the priests?'

'Yes?'

'Is it true they have first rights over the girls?'

'Sometimes.'

Revulsion welled up inside him.

Rao raised his palms upwards. 'It is our custom.'

He thought of the girl and then of Emily. He shuddered.

'But not at that age,' Rao added. 'When they are older. When they are ready. Some have patrons and will stay with the same man all their life.'

'They sound like whores to me. Same as the dancing girls who flock the West End streets of London, touting their wares.' His voice swelled. 'How can dance ever be holy? How can it ever be in God's name?'

'Calm yourself, Sir. There are some things that are not easily understood. Once you have a better grasp of our language, it will open the door to our customs. They are not based in ignorance, although you might think so. They are divinely ordained.'

'Divine?' he spluttered. ''Tis nothing but heathen superstition.'

'Dance is divine. In our country, in the south at least, our god is Shiva and as he dances, the world turns and the universe spins; birth, life and death pass through their eternal cycles on the axis of creation. That is why he must dance and that is why the women dance to please him, so he never stops. You talk of your god, of Christ, who died and went to heaven and three days later was resurrected. What is that? I do not cast it as idle superstition. I see it for what it is, a story of rebirth, an allegory of the continuation of life. Even after we have breathed our last, our spirit, our soul – whatever you wish to call it – continues to live on. There are many ways, Mr Sutcliffe—'

'Please, call me Walter.'

'—to tell the same story.'

14

Palani was always more irritable after she'd been entertaining the prince. 'All he does is stay inside, getting visits from that Captain Berg.'

Maya sat quietly.

'He seems to have forgotten that foreigners are below untouchables. Why can't he be happy with his own courtiers?'

Maya bent further over her slate. The slate pencil refused to move and her letters came out crooked.

'The place is overrun with them.'

She wiped the slate clean and started again.

'Hurry up,' said Palani. 'What's taking so long?'

For months now she'd been feeling guilty that she was keeping a secret from her guru. She looked down, another mistake. *Concentrate, Maya.*

'I don't understand how they win people over,' Palani continued. 'Can't they see past their forked tongues to their blackened souls?'

Maya remembered the first time she'd seen *sahib* Sutt-sutt in the temple grounds. How black he was against the tower, at odds with everything around him. Now that she knew he was Rao's friend and she was learning English, when she saw him with his notebook she didn't mind. One time she'd waved at him.

On another occasion, when she, Rao and the old maid were walking outside the high granite walls, a clipped voice had rung out from behind. Approaching them was the *sahib*. The two men greeted each other like friends. Maya couldn't follow what they were saying and watched as a bullock cart rolled past. The boys on the back stood up, jeering insults at the foreigner. She saw Rao frown.

'Maya, this is *sahib* Sutt-sutt.'

She kept her eyes downcast.

'Look up. Say hello.'

She shook her head.

Haltingly at first, the *sahib* spoke to her, apologising for his poor accent. 'How pleased I am to meet you,' he said. Up close, the furrows on his forehead were like a ploughed paddy field. He had no moustache, and without it, his putty-coloured face looked bare. Watching him speak, as if each sentence was being wrung out, she warmed to him. When he stopped, she looked up. His blue-grey eyes were searching her own.

'You know, Rao, I often see her dancing in the temple grounds.'

'Do you dance there, Maya?' Rao asked.

It was hard to say anything when both men were looking at her. Not to reply, though, was silly. 'Yes, but not as often as I used to.' It had been months since she'd been there alone, months since she'd heard the whispering of the dancing girl.

'Nice to meet you,' she added, trying her first words of English on an Englishman. They flattened her tongue and changed the shape of her mouth.

Rao beamed.

'Very good,' the *sahib* said. 'Very good.'

She could see he wanted to say more. He hesitated, his eyes unsure, and then, doffing his hat, he said, 'Good day to you both.' His shoes clicked loudly on the paving stones as he walked away.

The sound of Palani rapping on the table brought her back. She looked up, startled.

'What's the matter with you, girl? You're in another world today.'

Maya took a deep breath. There should be no secrets between a disciple and her teacher. She would tell Palani plainly. As she gathered herself, she looked up at the fine tips of the palm fronds trembling in the wind. Then, seemingly from nowhere, a crow with glassy eyes plunged down and snapped up a beetle.

'Palani *akka*, I know you don't—' she began.

But Palani had turned away, and was staring at herself in the mirror, admiring her new string of lapis and pearls.

Whenever she was called, Maya went to the palace, and when Palani was in a good mood, she taught her poetry. 'You want to be a true courtesan. Learn from the greats,' she said, thrusting a rolled-up palm leaf towards her covered with spidery writing. 'First we start with Annamayya, master of devotion.'

Next came Ksetrayya.

'He teaches a woman passion. How to be ready to move on top.' She eyed Maya. 'Follow me,' she said, drawing aside a bottle-green curtain that revealed a low door leading into a dark passage. As she followed, Maya felt dust thick between her toes.

'Where are we going?'

'Be quiet. They can hear you.'

The corridor climbed upwards. Maya heard the sound of muffled voices coming from below. At the top of the stairs, the narrow passageway widened into a gallery and at the far end she saw daylight filtering through a latticework screen. In front of the screen was a bench where Palani indicated they should sit.

Maya pressed her eyes to the screen. Above were the high, vaulted ceilings of the great Durbar Hall. A drum roll made her look down. There, sitting on cushions on a large throne, surrounded by his ministers and lackeys, sat Prince Tuljajee. Female attendants stood either side fanning him with fly whisks, and musicians were tuning up. Dressed in an ivory-coloured *pyjama* with red dots and thick gold chains around his bullish neck, he reminded her of the plump partridges she sometimes saw near the river. His eyes were hooded, his face bloated.

Maya had only seen the prince once, when she and her *amma* waved to the royal procession as it travelled from the palace to the temple. She remembered how grand he seemed with his bushy black moustache and imperious wave, but now, close up, how unwell, how ugly he looked. The thought of being introduced to him, of dancing for him, made her stomach grizzle.

'Can they see us?'

Palani shook her head.

'Why do you come here?'

'To know who's in favour,' she whispered. 'You see the chief minister? The one with the giant turban bending down low. Last week he faced jail. Now, he's clawing his way back up. That one, he's the treasurer. He and the chief minister loathe each other.'

'Why?'

'One thinks we should side with the English, the other thinks the French.'

'What do you think?'

Palani's answer was lost as the drum roll sounded again. The crowd parted to make way for the new arrivals. Leading the group was a man dressed in black, his wavy silver hair drawn back from his face. In one hand he carried a triangular hat, in the other, a scroll. Behind him were four more foreigners, wearing stiff red jackets. As they approached, the chief minister stood to receive them. Prince Tuljajee's eyes slowly lifted.

'He's let them back,' Palani said.

'Who?'

'The *ferenghis*. For a while he wouldn't grant the foreigners an audience.'

'Why?'

'He blamed the English for allying with the Nawab of Arcot.'

'Did they?'

'What?'

'Ally with the nawab?'

'Of course.'

Maya looked at the foreigners. It was hard to tell them apart. The man in black reminded her of *sahib* Sutt-sutt, but he was older with a thin, angular nose.

'That tall, ginger-haired man is Captain Berg. He's the prince's friend.' Palani pointed. 'It's the one in black I don't trust.'

The prince was nodding, and with a wide sweep of his hand, the foreigner in black bowed low, cutting the air with his hat and handing the scroll to the chief minister. Maya watched as the three men conferred, their faces animated.

Shaking her head, Palani said, 'I've told the prince to watch him. They call him "the good Father". His name is Schwarz. He's trying to win the prince over with gifts. In return he wants his soul.'

Later that afternoon, after Maya had gone, Palani sat with her hookah on the swing seat. She sucked long and hard, streams of pungent smoke pouring from her nostrils. The maidservants lit the lamps along the balcony wall and those in the alcoves, bathing the room in soft orange light. She knew soon she would have to introduce Maya to the prince. *If he likes her as much as I think he will, that will keep me in favour.* A smile nudged her lips. She rang the bell, demanding her ivory inkpot and quill.

The words flowed, faster than she could get them down. It was a poem she'd started many years before about Radha, and how she instructs a young girl as she comes of age. *What would she tell Maya?* Palani thought. All that her mother never had.

She would say that when she is with the prince for the first time:

She should push him gently with her breasts.
If he gets tired while making love, quickly take over and get on top.
Love him skilfully, and make him love you.

She would tell her not to listen to the women in the bazaar who resent it when their husbands push their legs roughly apart. She would say that a woman must take control in the game of love. She put down the quill. *Maya is lucky that I think her good enough for the prince.* Yet unease crested through her. Remorse was there, guilt too. She found herself feeling sentimental for the girl. She enjoyed her company and would miss her.

She drew again on the hookah. The night sky was hypnotic, the stars incandescent. She felt the opium take effect. The life-sized lamp of King Pratap glowed. *Your son, the prince, is no match for you.* She could see the net was closing around Tanjore. It would not be long before the English and the Nawab of Arcot would be in charge.

As the opium took hold, her body became malleable and her thoughts fearless. She let herself soar. Of late, she always saw herself in the same place, where she wandered alone, feeling the earth through the soles of her feet, her toes splayed as they gripped rocky paths. She carried a staff and a bag and followed a narrow mountain stream among jagged snowy peaks. She wore a simple orange smock; her hair had become matted. She was stripped of all artifice, her mask had dissolved. No longer was she a seductress. No longer did she have to please her lord – for he walked beside her, white as jasmine.

As she picked up her quill, her hand trembling with effort as the opium pulled her towards the waking dream, Palani wrote:

> *Freed from rebirth and death I am,*
> *And all that has held me down*
> *Is hurled away.*

Beneath, scrawled across the page, she added, *So free am I, so gloriously free I will be!*

1770

15

One afternoon, Maya arrived at the palace and Palani was waiting for her. The table was laid out with dozens of her *paan* boxes, fashioned from wood and ivory, bone and silver. When mixed with other spices, *paan* was traditionally presented as a gesture of love and affection.

'Today's lesson is how you present *paan* to a patron. Then you will perform a dance,' Palani said, wrapping the glossy green betel leaves into perfect cones. 'With *paan* you offer the promise of what will come next. In that way, the man always returns for more.'

Tackat-tah tackat-tah tack-at-ter-tack. Tackat-tah tackat-tah tack-at-ter-tack. As the clipped hollow notes of the *thavil* drum rose to the rafters, Maya sensed a new spaciousness in her dance. She had no need of the dancing girls from long ago – now she heard their voices through Palani – and nothing gave Maya more satisfaction than seeing pride shine in her guru's eyes.

'Good,' Palani said, 'but lunge deeper with your squats and move faster with your turns.' She signalled Maya to stop. 'Come here now. Sit on the stool.'

Palani sat on the chair opposite and leaned forward, peering into Maya's face, as if reading it. 'How old are you now, girl?'

'Thirteen.'

'Only? Fourteen this year?'

She nodded.

'And you've been through your *sadanku* ceremony? You've started to bleed?'

Maya nodded.

'Then it's time to broaden your knowledge of the sexual arts.'

'How soon will it happen?'

'That's not up to me, that's up to your mother. When your training comes to an end here, you will be kept at home so no other man's eyes can behold you. Then, at the auspicious time, you will be presented to the prince.'

'Can't I stay here, inside the court, rather than go home?'

'I have to follow protocols. I'm already overstepping them by letting you visit as frequently as you do. You've no idea the competition from the other dance masters and their protégés.'

Maya said nothing.

'If you're wondering why I go to such lengths—'

She looked up.

'It's because in you I see my younger self.' Palani stretched out her legs. 'I don't have a daughter to pass my wisdom on to. Your mother doesn't value what she has.'

Giddiness passed through Maya.

'You might think I've forgotten how we started this conversation, but I haven't. A girl must be prepared for what happens next.'

Maya cringed inwardly. The first time she'd felt the warm seeping between her legs and the tight, hard cramps knitting her groin, she thought she was going to faint. She'd screamed at the sight of a splash of her blood on the paving stones in the courtyard.

Amma had come running. When she saw the blood, triumph crossed her face. 'At last, I thought it would never come.'

Once the days of bleeding had stopped, and she'd taken the cleansing bath, the week-long *sadanku* ceremony began, led by Uma. Maya's coming of age would normally have been when she also gave her first public dance performance in the temple, but her *amma* insisted that they keep it a private affair. Lakshmi wanted the formal presentation of her daughter to happen in the palace, with Prince Tuljajee as her

audience. She wanted Maya to receive her proper honour – and most
of all, her *inam* of seven *pagodas*.

Since then, every month, the sharp pains, the weakness. When
Maya had complained, her mother sat her down.

'See the blood as renewal. Let it touch the earth. You should not
leave the house; you cannot go to the temple. The priests tell us this
blood is impure, that we are unclean. We nod and say yes and follow
the strict codes of purity.'

Her mother had taken Maya's rag and rubbed the red viscous
liquid between her thumb and forefinger. She leaned forward, as if
letting Maya into a secret. 'But what do they know? This blood is life.
Each month the old runs away to be replaced by the new. Rejoice,
child. You are becoming a woman.'

Maya couldn't deny what was happening to her. The enlargement
of her nipples, ringed with small bumps across the dark aureoles. The
staleness of her sweat. The covetous looks from men. Even the bullock
drivers would turn their heads, their eyes shredding her sari. She was
glad, then, when the bleeding came. It was her time of seclusion, when
she stayed home and her mother prepared food for her.

She was becoming more curious about herself. One time, when
mother was sleeping, she had taken *Amma's* hand mirror and secretly
admired her small neat breasts. She no longer felt the crippling shy-
ness about her spreading hips and the curves of her waist. She ran her
palms over her narrow rib cage and down across her navel to the top of
her thighs. She dared herself to touch the dark mole nestled above her
moist slit and marvelled at the pinkness inside. Unfamiliar flutterings
in her belly made her want to laugh, then moan, when she touched
herself for the first time.

She heard a cough and was suddenly aware of Palani standing
there. 'The first rule, girl. Know thyself.'

After that, and in the following weeks, Maya learned everything about
the female form. She started with the sixteen adornments, which

comprised the various ways a woman could beautify herself, from her perfumed bath, to applying her make-up. Lampblack for the eyes, henna for the soles. She was taught which flowers in the hair evoked lust and which cooled desire. She mixed her own aromatic *javadhu* powder and blended her own perfumes. Sandalwood, rose, clove and musk. Palani blindfolded her and gave her scent after scent to feel the effect of each perfume on mind and body.

'Learn the arts well,' Palani said, 'perfect the moves. Write poetry and speak many tongues. Your body – you must exercise, nurture and adorn it. Of course, you have to do all that. But don't think that is why you do what you do. That is only the means. This is only your craft. What matters is this.'

Palani tapped her heart. 'What you radiate from within is what counts. Men think they want full-moon breasts and magnolia skin. Yet what they truly desire is a breath of the eternal. They want to feel the god within them met by the goddess within you.'

One stifling day, in the season of ripe heat, when the fragrance of the frangipani tree thickened the air to honey, Maya was given permission to stay late at the palace. *She wants me near her*, Maya thought, anxious that their time together was drawing to a close. Each week she expected to receive word of when she would be presented. But the prince, preoccupied with the threat of war hanging over the city, rarely left his chambers.

They were out on the balcony. Palani was lying on her swing seat, staring, like she often did these days, into the mid-distance. Alongside her, Maya was mixing perfumes with almond oil. She knew she should feel happy that she would soon be presented – *Amma* never stopped reminding her – but she didn't. *Palani's life is luxurious, yet she's never content*, Maya thought. *She's trapped, and if I'm chosen, I will be, too. My only window to the outside will be from the top of the tower.*

She put the bowl down, her hand suddenly unsteady. Without thinking, her fingers traced the three-pronged trident on her arm:

blackened, branded, enslaved. The words of her aunt came back to her. 'You are offering your body to Shiva. There's no greater honour than that.'

'Ready?' Palani said, lying back.

Maya nodded, attempting a smile, and began to rub the oil into the woman's coppery-brown feet. 'Is this the life you wanted for yourself?'

'There wasn't a choice.'

'Because your mother did it?'

'And her mother before that.'

'Did you ever want to get married?'

'I wondered where this was going.'

Maya pressed her knuckle into the soft pad under the toe; Palani flinched.

'It's normal to feel nervous,' she said. 'Just as you would before your wedding night.'

'I can't eat.'

'That's a good sign.'

'Isn't it easier just to have one husband?'

'And be chained to the hearth? A life full of drudgery. Ignorance. Can that be better than what you have?'

'No.'

'And you get to choose.'

'But do you?'

Their eyes met. 'You can choose in so far as any woman can. You will be educated. Any money you make is yours. Do housewives have that?'

'No. But they have—' she searched for the right word, '—security.'

'You prefer security over independence?'

'I suppose not.' She placed a towel over Palani's right foot, swaddling it.

'You must learn to wear a mask. It is your survival. Your *sadhana*, your sacred service, can only be achieved if you hold enough of yourself back. A man will want to take all.'

Maya thought about this. 'So it isn't just about the sex?' The word sounded coarse on her tongue.

'For some men, yes. They're little better than animals. Think of the maids. Their coupling is over in the fields in a few minutes. I imagine they rarely feel any pleasure. For you and me, Maya, we have the luxury of time, and knowledge. An ordinary householder won't be satisfied with a wife exhausted from the children and running the house. That is why those with money want a woman like us. To entertain and please them.' Palani yawned. 'But I soon realised that I needed something in return. I wanted recognition and fame.' She looked at Maya. 'What do you want?'

Maya fell silent. 'I want to be loved like you were when I saw you perform in the temple.'

Palani leaned forward and tapped her arm. 'It's nice you believe that I am loved. I'm not so sure these days. It is the folly of youth to believe that love is the answer.' Her tone was firm, but kind. 'It isn't. That's why we are married to god. Only god can give us true love.'

Maya looked across to the lamp of King Pratap. The halo from the flame cast a comforting shadow across the room.

A faint sigh escaped Palani's lips. 'You're right. I did love him. He was my lord.' She sank into thought. 'For all I have taught you, the heart can – and will – intervene. When we meet certain men, a spark of divinity is ignited that enlivens the senses and the passion – like *darshan*. We literally see the divine in the other and this aligns us to the Atman, the eternal soul.' She paused.

'This unity of man and woman re-enacts the sacred union of the gods. It is the eternal dance of creation. Shiva and Shakti. How could a man not want this? And this is our special power, this is what is unique to temple women like us.'

Maya stared into the velvety night sky, the stars blinking like heavenly fireflies. She was struck by the silence and serenity inside the palace walls. Here, the outside world was irrelevant. Perhaps, then, it was worth exchanging her longing for freedom for the contentment she would find here.

Palani lay back down. Her arm, crooked at the elbow, carelessly lying on the cushion, reminded Maya of a bird's broken wing.

'Maybe you too will find such love, but know that it will come at a cost. Everything does. Sometimes the only choice we have is to walk away.'

As she said the words, Palani's gaze slipped out of focus, leaving Maya uneasy. She tweaked Palani's big toe, but she did not respond. In her ears she heard a distant humming and Palani's foot fell heavy in her hand. It was as if her guru's body had become empty, her spirit threading its way through the air.

She's going to leave me. I know it.

'Palani *akka*,' she whispered.

Silence.

'What are you thinking?'

Palani did not respond.

That night, as Maya rose to leave, Palani gestured towards her corner cupboard. 'Find my *paan* box shaped like a parrot. Yes, that one.'

Maya held it in the centre of her flattened palm. The tail of the bird was also a whistle and the head was painted lime-green with a rose-pink beak.

'It's for you. Take it.'

For a while, Palani thought Maya would satisfy her sufficiently. The girl's presence had inspired her, and once more her days were filled writing poetry and composing *padams*. Yet she knew her status in the palace could not last. Her position was slipping and she no longer had the will to maintain it. Anyway, the visions kept coming. She was being called. And now she knew who was calling her. Adki. The old woman had brought her and Maya together only to tear them apart, for reasons that she would probably never reveal. Palani worried for the girl. She also worried for herself. She knew she had to follow her own heart's longing and feared where it would take her. She hoped that one day she would be able to explain everything to Maya and that she would understand.

As she counted down the days to when Maya would be presented to the prince, Palani felt herself becoming invisible. She thought she was immune to this. That she didn't care any more. Yet, as she tried to compose the last verses of her poem, all she wished was that Maya would be rejected and a message would come, imploring her to come back. She pinched the flesh of her arm.

Bitch. I'm a bitch. I've planned this all along, to prepare Maya, to use her. First as my entertainment and now his. 'Go on, just say it to yourself,' she said out loud. 'I used her.'

She reached for her quill, her fingers tense. She was determined to reach the end of the poem before the prince would bed Maya.

> *Just touch her lips with the tip of your tongue.*
> *Don't squeeze.*
> *Caress her nipples with your fingertips.*
> *Don't crush.*
> *Make love very very gently.*
> *Don't be wild.*

She lay back down, her head aching with effort. *It's so easy to give away money, to give away your family, to give your very life*, she thought. *But to give your man to another woman – what woman can do that?*

Forcing herself to sit up, Palani wrote down the final words.

> *Tortured by love, Radha couldn't close her eyes.*
> *Inside, she was burning.*
> *As for the prince, he was busy with the girl.*

The next day, Maya arrived at the palace as usual. Palani barely acknowledged her and went into her bedroom, slamming the door behind her. Some hours later, when she came out, she ordered Maya to recite the work of Akkamahadevi, the female saint who'd wandered naked, whose poems were dedicated to the lord, white as jasmine. The poems were dark, full of imagery Maya couldn't grasp – death, surrender, salvation. Each time she stumbled, she had to go back to the beginning and start again. She could see Palani was not listening, her fingers fiddling with a piece of ribbon, pulling it this way and that. To try and hide her mistakes, Maya spoke more and more softly. After a dozen attempts, Palani let her reach the end of a single poem. Maya's back was wet with sweat.

'You're a waste of time.' She spat out the words. 'You started out with promise. These days you make no effort.'

Maya's stomach felt hollow.

'Just going to stand there?' Palani threw the slate on the ground, the pieces skating across the marble floor.

Maya winced, helpless.

'I haven't got time for this, Maya. I haven't got time for you.'

Words still failed her.

'Get out.'

She didn't move.

'Get out.'

The words landed harder than any blow. Quivering, Maya backed out of the room, and as she walked then ran down the corridor, all she could think was, *I'll die if I can't see her again.*

16

Walter and Schwarz left early to go to the township of Vallam, four miles south-west of Tanjore. They were carried in palanquins and the climb up to the tableland made the journey slow. The air was fresher than in town and from some distance away, Walter could see the British Residency on the plateau. A row of coconut palms marked a natural avenue up to the low broad building with an arched portico at the front.

Together they walked up steps bordered by purple bougainvillea with blossoms growing thick as grapes. The paved area was lined with blue-glazed pots bursting with marigolds. A flock of liveried bearers presented them with a glass of slushy iced punch. Ice! Such luxury. They were shown through a doorway and in the centre of the domed reception room stood the Resident, Reginald Baldock, claret in hand.

'Ah, gentlemen, in good time,' Baldock said with a forced smile. He was short with sandy-coloured hair, the whites of his eyes a cloudy yellow. From inside, Walter heard the strains of a violin.

In the back courtyard a classical ensemble was playing Handel. In the centre stood a marble fountain of a Grecian water nymph and on either side, two stone bowls on pedestals were filled with petals – bougainvillea, frangipani and hibiscus – floating in water. Raised voices behind made Walter turn around. Baldock was flicking the back of his hand towards an Indian woman, her arms heavily adorned with fanciful bracelets, who had appeared through one of the beaded doorways off the corridor. After casting her eyes around, she retreated. Walter looked at Schwarz, whose thin lips were drawn tight.

'To your health,' Walter said, raising his glass. A little spilled over his hand.

'To Our Redeemer, may he deliver all from sin,' said Schwarz, who had declined a glass of punch. He looked across to Baldock. 'I see your work at the Residency keeps you absent from the Sabbath service. Mr Sutcliffe says he rarely has the pleasure—'

'Remind me. You're the junior chaplain at the garrison?'

'Yes.' Walter was colouring.

'Well, you should come and visit.' Baldock turned away. 'Much cooler here than on the plains.'

Aware that Schwarz was watching him, Walter said nothing. More guests were arriving. It was a long time since he'd been in such elevated company. Baldock was trying to get the attention of a tall, ginger-whiskered officer.

'Captain Berg, do join us.'

'Evening,' said Walter, who stretched out his hand, still sticky from the spilled punch. The captain's handshake was as fey as his porcelain features.

'Didn't think I was going to make it. Held up at the palace.'

'Prince Tuljajee didn't want you to leave?' Baldock asked.

'No. But I needed some air.'

'How is his mood?' Schwarz asked.

'Melancholy. No allies, few friends, huge debts. And too much of this.' Berg drained his drink.

Walter watched Baldock and Berg exchange glances. He wondered what they knew. Above, the sky was nudging to orange-red hibiscus, the colour of the petals in the bowls. He reached down, running his fingers through the perfumed water, and wondered if the Indian woman had picked the blooms, and where she was now. Baldock did have an English wife, he remembered, who was now back in England. The ensemble started up again and Walter and Schwarz turned to listen.

'So what's the latest?' Baldock murmured.

'The nawab and more English troops are on their way,' said Berg.

'Is that it? We've been hearing this for months. You're in a tight spot being so close to the prince.'

Berg shrugged. 'What is the council saying in Madras?'

'They're suspicious of the prince's loyalty. They think he sent a message to Hyder Ali asking for assistance for money and troops. That's enough to make them act.' He took a swig of wine. 'You know how the Company plays it.'

'So the amount the prince owes is irrelevant?'

'Yes.'

'Then an attack is inevitable?'

Baldock stared down at his glass.

'But will the Court of Directors in London agree?' Berg asked.

'The Court of Directors? Who listens to them? It takes a year for a letter to reach London and by then events have moved on. The council in Madras is a law unto itself. The prince doesn't stand a chance.' He stopped, as if he'd said too much. Baldock's voice dipped. 'Then, of course, the nawab knows how much he'll make if he and the English invade Tanjore. Both will reap the spoils when the city falls.'

'Turncoats, the lot of them.'

'Let's say, this might be the last party for a while.'

'That soon?'

Baldock nodded. 'General Smith is leading the charge.'

The punch was slipping down nicely. Walter's mind fizzed, his body tingled. After making his excuses he walked back through the reception to the front of the house. It was the first time he'd seen Tanjore from above and he noticed how the temple marked its centre, just like a church would in an English town, the tower rearing up above the horizon. It was hard to believe he'd been here nearly five years. He closed his eyes, laying his hand flat against his heart. These days the pain was less, but it was his mind he couldn't trust.

Inside, the musicians had stopped for a break and the waiters were refilling glasses.

'How's that junior chaplain of yours?' Baldock asked.

'He's good enough at his post,' Schwarz said. 'Although numbers have dropped off at the evening prayer meetings.'

'He doesn't have your touch, Reverend,' said Berg. 'There's something – how would you put it – lost about him.'

'A widower,' said Schwarz.

'I've seen him around with Rao.'

'Yes I encouraged him to take Tamil lessons, but he's a slow learner.'

'Better than me,' said Baldock. 'I can barely say hello.'

'Always has a notebook in hand. Heard that he particularly likes painting the young girls, the natives.'

Schwarz's eyes narrowed.

'One in particular, I was told. One of those dancing wenches,' Berg continued. 'Nothing to worry about, I'm sure.'

'Just as long as she's not too young. Doesn't set a good example for the troops,' added Baldock, dryly.

A gong rang out, hushing the crowd. 'Dinner is served!'

'I would like to discuss this further with you, Captain Berg,' Schwarz said, as they walked through the candlelit passageway.

The large panelled dining room was decorated with fine French mirrors and bland oil paintings of English landscapes; a forest of candles flickered in the central chandelier. Around the oval mahogany table stood a servant for each of the twelve guests. Walter took his place between Berg and a loud, bosomy lady. After a lengthy grace given by Schwarz, the guests began to eat. There were partridges stuffed with apricots and almonds, cubes of spiced mutton on a bed of *pilau*, boiled duck, and freshly caught carp roasted with herbs; exotic fruits and sugar candy, sweetmeats and milk puddings. After the sixth course, Walter feared his breeches would burst. His head grew heavy from the claret. The conversation was dominated by the spectre of war.

Days away.

Nonsense. Ignore the rumour-mongers.

It's the end for the prince. He's a pansy compared to his father.

Walter heard Schwarz's creaky voice rise above the chatter.

'Sir, the prince is greatly concerned about liaisons between the English soldiers and the native women.'

He watched Baldock as he swirled the claret around his crystal glass.

'What would you have me do? You know such relations are encouraged. It takes the troops' minds off the grog.'

Walter tussled with the tough duck's leg on his plate.

'I'm wondering what Mr Sutcliffe thinks about relations with native women.'

Walter found himself reddening. Baldock's eyes were hard. 'Immoral, Sir.'

'Immoral, are they, Reverend?'

Walter felt like he'd been caught out and wasn't sure why. He looked across to Schwarz; his eyes were blank but his upper lip puckered in disdain.

'You're staying awhile?' Baldock asked.

'As long as I'm needed to maintain religious standards among the troops.'

'Let's toast to that then, my dear chaps,' Baldock raised his glass, 'but let's not forget why we are here. We're not in the business of saving souls, only in strengthening trade.'

Every year Walter was warned about the build-up to the annual monsoon in June. Every year he thought he'd be able to cope better. But the summer months were unbearable. Sleepless nights, scorching days. To make matters worse, the heat brought a locust plague. For days the insects pelted down from the sky, covering the courtyard in a churning brown mass. Jiva muttered invocations. 'No good, no good. Bad sign, *sahib*.'

Walter took to his cot during the day but even with the servant boy waving the peacock fan, and the continual calls for cold water and lime, he was sucked as dry as a corn husk. Such weariness, such lassitude.

He had dismissed the warnings until the day he flogged his own horse until its rump bled and the switch snapped.

'*Sahib*, stop, I beg you. It is enough. *Sahib* Sutt-sutt, the horse has done no wrong.'

It wasn't until Jiva cried out that Walter recognised the sound of his own name. He turned then, his hand ready to strike, but on seeing his valet's expression, he slid off the horse, dropping the switch, and staggered towards the house.

The shame of inflicting cruelty on the beast hurt Walter more than the hostile stares from the servants. In a place where he should lead by example, he had failed. For the rest of the day he shut himself in his room, averting his eyes from the crucifix.

As Walter lay there, his mind turned to Rao, and how much he appreciated his friendship. He thought of the time when they'd met and Rao was with the girl Maya, and she'd spoken to Walter for the first time, saying, '*Nice to meet you.*' He'd been impressed. Yet it was the way she'd said it, scrunching up her eyes – just like Emily used to – that had stayed with him. *It is because she's the same age,* he told himself. *There are resemblances – that's all.* But the other voice in his head tormented him. *This is madness.*

Walter had never believed he was capable of feeling love like he did for his daughter. He thought he'd shut his heart when the woman he loved was betrothed to another, and he was left with the plain older sister. But at night, after his wife Margaret had put Emily to bed and he'd returned from making the rounds of his parishioners, he would sit at the foot of the child's cot and watch her sleeping. She didn't seem to belong to this world.

'You indulge that child,' Margaret said. 'She'll have no sense of what's real and what's not.'

He stared up at the wooden crucifix. At first, the grief was like walking alone in a dark tunnel. Then came a rage that left him breathless. But even that was better than this numbness, and the gnawing guilt.

He must have fallen asleep. When he woke, it was late afternoon. A mosquito whined by his ear. 'Damn you. Get away!' He scratched another bite on the side of his neck. It was enough to make a man cry.

Swinging his legs over the side of the cot, he peered through the window. Outside an unearthly amber hue was deepening to indigo, then charcoal, before a bolt of lightning fractured the sky. He jumped back. The crack of thunder that followed made the window frames shudder. It was like nothing he'd ever heard before.

Pushing open the door, Walter stared up at the gathering storm clouds. He could smell burning, acrid and foul. It made his eyes smart and his nose run. His stomach heaved. Quickly, he shut the door, falling back on the cot. The anguish began to rise in his chest. *I must be imagining it. I must be asleep and this is my dream.*

It was all still with him, as if it were yesterday. How many times had he replayed the events, going over each detail, each mistake, each decision he could have made differently; and now, in his cell-like room, in this godforsaken town so far from home, he let himself see it all.

It was Mrs Butterworth he had to go and see. She'd begged him to pay a visit. But Margaret was sick. As soon as his wife recovered from one illness, she went down with the next.

'Your parishioners are more family to you than your own,' she said as he reached for his hat and woollen overcoat. 'Fetch us some more wood for the fire. Emily's running a cold.'

Out in the wood-store, he grabbed the nearest logs: some seasoned, some green, moist and sticky with sap. As he filled the wood basket in the parlour he noticed again a strong odour of wood smoke. He'd smelled it that afternoon and looked up the chimney flue in case something was caught. Nothing. He boiled onion, garlic and honey and took the warming drink to Emily upstairs. Under the mound of blankets, she was shivering. He stroked her hair, smoothing it back from her brow, then bent down and kissed her forehead, leaving the drink next to her.

'It is there when you need it. I'll be back soon.'

Before striding out, he threw more logs on the fire, and taking his staff, pulled shut the door.

He'd only been gone two hours. As he approached the top of the hill, his pace quickened. Then, panic ripped through him. For a few seconds everything became very still. He could feel the brisk wind against his cheek and the solidness of the stick between the fingers of his right hand. He heard the distant scream of a barn owl.

He started to run. The soft chalky soil stuck to his boots like clay, making him slip and slide. By the time he reached the bottom of the hill, he was shaking. At first he could see nobody, only flames pouring out of the windows of the rectory, the roof ablaze. Then he saw George and a neighbour passing buckets to each other, and the housekeeper running back and forth to the well. Tearing off his coat, Walter ran towards the front door. The heat drove him back.

It was another hour before they could force their way into the house. The fire had started around the chimneybreast and spread through the first floor and into the thatch. The doctor was called. Using a chisel, they forced their way upstairs but the door to the landing, buckled and swollen from the heat, wouldn't open. George pushed Walter aside, telling him to fetch a hammer. In those moments, while he was in the shed, they brought the bodies down. Mother and daughter had been trapped, huddled on the other side of the door.

On the grass Walter's coat lay where he'd left it, the oil lamp to one side. The crunching of gravel announced the arrival of another neighbour and the crack of a horse's whip told him the doctor was approaching. They laid them on a blanket. Walter wiped the black soot off Emily's face and tapped her cheeks; he bent his head down on her chest. The doctor asked him to stand aside and held up the lamp. Only then did Walter see the colour of her skin: a deep, stained cherry red. Except for that curious colour, she looked like she was sleeping. The doctor opened Emily's mouth and her eyes. Both were a deeper shade of the same red.

'Inhalation of smoke causes the skin and blood to change to this colour. They wouldn't have felt anything. Be grateful for that, Reverend.'

Be grateful. Walter couldn't comprehend the words. His chest heaved.

He was given brandy and the doctor said he would take the bodies inside to be cleaned. Walter shook his head, his mind benumbed. He knew George and the neighbours were looking at him for direction, but no words came. The glass of brandy slipped out of his hand. When they went to pick up the bodies, he pushed them away and fell on top of Emily.

'Not her. Not yet. She doesn't want to go inside.'

He remembered hands prising him away as he reached for her small soft hand. Her palm was curled around an acorn. The acorn she'd found that morning. She must have gone to sleep holding it.

Then other hands were pulling him off and somebody was telling him to *show some control.*

Over the next months, Walter went from room to room. The smell of burnt wood pervaded everything. One side of the rectory had been spared. Except nothing inside was intact. He would remember something he needed – his father's quill, his own prayer book – and then would realise he couldn't get it. Then, he'd remember that he couldn't see her again. Sometimes between sleep and waking he'd forget what had happened and would hear her voice. *Papa, time to get up. Time to see what the day will bring.*

The only place he found solace was in the birch woods, with the puck-puck-puck of a startled pheasant as it shot out of the undergrowth. Every day he walked for hours.

They told him that he should leave the rectory. But that would mean forgetting. He moved into the servants' quarters, and after sawing off the charred beams, they boarded up the other half.

Sometimes he stared at his hands, at the fine lines, the deep grooves, studying them as if they were foreign to him. These hands, his hands, had chosen the wood. Were they to blame? Or was it his mind he needed to examine? If only he could rip that part out. He tried to believe that Margaret and Emily were in God's arms. But after one year, maybe two years, it didn't help. Nothing helped. People urged him to take another wife.

The shock of it kept reccurring, and so did the nightmares. He still could not revisit what had happened. It was as if the memory had been compressed into a tiny nut, an acorn, and he'd buried it, preferring to believe the lies he was told. That it wasn't his fault, that he'd done the right thing by going to see Mrs Butterworth, that fires happen, that it was God's will.

He stopped eating, stopped bathing, stopped sleeping. He became a ghostly figure, chatting to himself, chatting to them. It was George, his manservant, who took charge. He seemed to know the right thing to do. But George couldn't stop Walter blaming himself.

Now, as he lay on the bed, the fevered heat pressing down on him, the storm whipping through the palm trees, he realised that it wasn't himself he couldn't forgive, it was God. And if he couldn't forgive God, how could he stand there every Sunday and preach in His name?

Not long after, Schwarz paid another visit. Everywhere the German went, a crowd gathered. Walter trailed behind. He knew he should feel proud to be under the wing of the 'good Father', but he resented him. Schwarz had no qualms in proselytising to every person he met. Even the prince, Schwarz wished to convert.

The monsoon! At last. Walter woke to rain like he'd never heard before, hammering on the tiles with no pause or breath. Warm, refreshing, it carried with it relief from the months of infernal heat. As the night slipped away, the rain beckoned. He stripped off his nightshirt, wrapped a piece of cloth around his waist and slipped out of the door towards the centre of the courtyard. Tilting his head back, he opened his mouth, stuck out his tongue and let the drops fall in. He cupped his hand over his flaccid penis, rubbing the cloth against it as if trying to coax it to life. *This rain*, he thought, *could bring anything back to life*.

A door slamming brought him back. His stomach lurched at the thought of Schwarz finding him like this. He retraced his steps, slipped, and fell with a thud.

'Who goes there?'

Walter grabbed the wooden railing and propelled himself towards his room as loud footsteps approached along the inner corridor.

'Jiva. Come quickly, there's someone in the courtyard.'

He quietly opened the door to his room, his legs folding beneath him. He pushed his hands through his hair, and as he rested against the door, his shoulders began to twitch. Through a closed mouth he started to snigger, until, unable to hold it in any more, he opened his mouth. Silently, and triumphantly, he laughed.

The next day Schwarz left and the rain set in. Alone again, Walter began to experience a dislocation within himself, as if he were hearing his words echo back to him. It happened at the prayer meetings and in his private devotions before he went to sleep. He felt untethered, his nights oppressed by terrors.

His sermons were having no effect on the troops and incidents of drunkenness and brawling were reported almost daily. He saw the men in the garrison: bored and broke, their bodies crawling with lice, their digs filthy with vermin. Everywhere the familiar feeling of hopelessness dogged him. He cancelled his lessons with Rao and retreated to his room, feigning sickness. He lay listening to the bickering of the servants and the cockerel that crowed throughout the night. He wished to retreat from it all but could find no relief from his melancholy.

17

Lakshmi was in the courtyard enjoying a rare moment of idleness. The rain had stopped and the air was washed clean. As she was deadheading some flowers in the pots lining the courtyard, she heard a rapid knock at the door. Uma stood on the front step, her black eyes as brittle as coal. She did not wait to be invited inside.

Lakshmi started to walk towards the back of the house when Uma touched her arm. 'We should talk here,' she said, her voice so low it was almost inaudible.

She stopped, surprised. Uma was never one to talk quietly.

'I saw your sister. She's back.'

Lakshmi's jaw tightened, the freshness in her eyes fading. 'Where?'

'On the other side of town, near where the *ferenghi* soldiers have their encampment.' She waved her hand. 'I'll tell you why I was there in a minute. That's also why I came.'

She could see Uma was choosing her words carefully.

'Sita is with one of them.' Uma paused, for effect. 'And she has a son to him.'

'So Leela has a baby brother?'

Uma nodded.

'She saw you?'

'No. I made sure of that.'

'How do you know, then?'

Uma tapped the side of her nose with her finger. 'I know, Lakshmi, because I've started making enquiries among the foreign troops. Not the foot soldiers, they're mostly scum. The officers, and the other merchants and Company men who are moving to that part of town. You shake your head, but for those of us who aren't fortunate enough to be part of the great Palani's entourage, we have to make a living. I'm forming a dance troupe to perform *nautches* at the European houses. These days no party is complete without a *nautch*.' She crossed her arms. 'That's how I know.'

Lakshmi clasped her hands together in front of her chest as if to slow down her thudding heart.

'It's a shock, I know,' Uma continued. 'But I thought you'd want me to be the one to tell you first.'

'Oh Mother Goddess, why now? We are so close to Maya being presented to the prince. Any day we expect to have word.'

'You've been saying that for months.'

'I know. Palani *akka* always has some excuse for why the timing isn't right.'

Uma clicked her tongue, and motioned Lakshmi towards the courtyard. 'I've said what needed to be said. Now let's sit awhile.'

Lakshmi's whole body was quivering and she leaned on the older woman for support.

'You know what I've been saying all along about Palani. Yes, she's one of the greatest courtesans who ever graced our court, but her days are numbered. She doesn't have the prince's ear any more than you or I. If I were you, I'd start thinking of alternatives for your young Maya.'

'Alternatives?'

Another knock at the door made her look up. 'That will be her.'

Stiffly, Lakshmi walked back through the house, her mind racing with thoughts of how she could keep the news of Sita from her daughter.

'Come through, girl. I am with Uma *akka* out the back. No date, yet, from Palani?'

Maya shook her head.

'My, don't you look grown-up with your hair styled like that on top of your head,' Uma said, helping herself to the plate of *laddus* Lakshmi had put out for her daughter. She popped one of the round, sweet snacks into her mouth, and then another. 'And the silver girdle around your waist. Is that new too?'

'A gift from Palani *akka*. She wore it at my age,' Maya said, shyly.

Lakshmi gave Uma a pointed glance. 'Sit down over there, child.'

'I was just talking to your mother about the new dance troupe I'm setting up. Not for the palace, though. For the foreigners.' Uma's fingers jabbed the air. Her teeth were stained dirty red from the *paan* she habitually chewed.

'A troupe. The word makes me cringe,' Lakshmi said. 'How can the other women do it? What about the honour of working in the temple? What about their pride?'

'Your girl Maya has the right attitude. She's learning English, she knows what the future holds.'

Maya wasn't sure what the future held and started picking at a thread unravelling on the hem of her sari. She watched her mother, her clenching jaw. She wasn't sure what was going on or why Uma was being so insistent about the troupe. It was as if she were inviting her mother to join. She looked from *Amma* to Uma and back again.

Uma leaned across to Maya. 'I'm trying to show your mother that there are worlds beyond the palace and the court, and even the temple. My brother works in Madras now. Now that's a city with opportunities. There, the *dubashes* are like royalty. The foreigners dismiss them as middlemen.' She shrugged her plump arms. 'Yet these men are the city's most distinguished patrons. Their temple festivals are grander than those of the prince himself.' She pushed herself up, wheezing from the effort.

'You said it yourself, Lakshmi. Things are changing. We always have to be ready for what challenge the gods hurl at us next.' She patted Maya on the head. 'You finish the last *laddu*. I'll show myself out.'

Lakshmi woke with a start. Pushing herself up, she listened. Silence. She lay back down. Then she heard it again. *Cuu-kao, cuu-kao.*

It can't be, she thought. But there it was again. *Cuu-kao, cuu-kao.* The secret call that she and Sita used as children. She knew it had to come. She just hadn't known how, or when. She got up, and after checking on Maya, opened the door, hearing the faint click as the tongue loosened in the lock. The street was empty. Then, across the road she saw a silhouette, against the banyan tree, the face obscured. Dread flooded through her. To see her sister would be reckless. To shut the door on her would be unthinkable.

Ducking back inside, she took her shawl and was about to go back out when she remembered the ring. Lakshmi felt behind the statue of Durga, her fingers seeking out the silk pouch. There it was, the faceted emerald ring that had belonged to their mother. Quietly she closed the latch behind her. *Five minutes, that's all she can have*, she thought, crossing the road.

Dressed in a dun-brown sari, Sita was crouching low, her eyes sunken, her face gaunt.

'I wondered when I'd hear from you.' Lakshmi squatted down. 'Uma *akka* told me you were back.'

She said nothing.

'Come on, sister, I don't have long. You know what could happen if we're seen together—'

Sita let the veil slip. Greenish-yellow bruises covered her cheeks and jaw, a blackened shadow circled one eye, her top lip was split and swollen.

'Oh, Mother Goddess.' Lakshmi reached out her hand.

Sita flinched.

'What happened?' Despite herself, Lakshmi felt angry with her sister, that once again she might wreck everything. She looked at her, at her quivering lips, the fear in her eyes, a hunted look. This was not the sister she had known; this was a woman in fear of her life. 'You've got to leave him.'

Sita cast her eyes down.

'If our mother could see you now—'

'If Mother could see me.' Her voice was shrill. 'That's all you can say. You don't remember, do you, how the same happened to her. You'd already left by then. She always protected you from the worst.' She bit down on her lower lip. 'I'm not here to ask for your help, sister. I gave up on that a long time ago. If you'd wanted to help me, you could have done. But no, as always, you think only of yourself.'

Lakshmi felt the colour rising in her cheeks.

'I'm here for the ring.'

Stung by her comment, Lakshmi thought of refusing her. Then she reached inside her blouse. 'Here.'

Sita covered her face again with the veil. 'I know I can't stay long. I don't want to jeopardise Maya's chances.'

Lakshmi stared up through the gnarled branches of the banyan, like twisted arms knotted around each other, holding on for eternity. 'And little Leela. How is she? Maya still asks about her.'

Tears filled Sita's eyes. She tipped her face down.

Gently, Lakshmi reached out to touch her sister's arm. 'Sister, I can see how much you've suffered since you left. You say I didn't do anything to stop them banishing you. What could I have done? We aren't the ones who make the rules here. For the sake of Leela, leave him.'

'She has a brother now, you know? Babu.'

Lakshmi nodded.

'Does Maya know I am back?'

She shook her head.

'Can you find someone who will care for Leela? She's a good girl.'

Not now, not when Maya is so close to being accepted into the royal household. Lakshmi felt ashamed even thinking it. 'I'll do what I can,' she said.

'I'm scared for my children. I'm scared for myself.'

'How did it come to this?'

Sita's chest sagged. 'At first he was good to me. He took care of me. You should see his hair. So different...' She trailed off. 'Yellow, like the colour of straw. The English pay the women well who stay with the soldiers. It was either that—' she fell silent, '—or becoming a whore. Then he went off to fight. When he came back . . . I don't know what he'd seen – or done. But he started to drink heavily. It's much worse when he drinks.' She reached up to touch the swelling around her eye.

'You have to take the children and go.'

'They're going to attack, you know? The English soldiers are ready.' She looked at her sister. 'Any day, Tanjore will fall. You should be prepared. Maybe we can all leave – leave together?'

Lakshmi shuddered, looking up at the tree. 'I can't leave. Not when Maya is so close. Sister, send me a message when you've left him and I will try and place Leela.' She stood up. 'Please, for Maya's sake, don't come back to the house. There are eyes everywhere in this town.'

'I know. How is she? I've heard she's beautiful. Brilliant.' For a moment, her eyes lit up. 'Palani's favourite girl.'

Briefly their hands touched, before Lakshmi hurried back across the road.

After that, Lakshmi forbade Maya to leave the house. She sent a message to Palani telling her that she would continue her daughter's training herself and that Maya would stay home until she received the official summons from the prince. Nothing Maya did or said could dissuade her mother; she was as immovable as an ox.

As Maya sat in the courtyard under the frangipani tree, staring up at the squirrel, she thought about the lushness of Palani's quarters. Time swayed to a different tune when she was there. Lying next to her mother at night, nestling into the curve of her salty armpit, listening to the regularity of her snores, she no longer felt at home. When had home come to mean being with Palani? When had it all changed?

Lakshmi had hired a young maidservant, heavy-set with button eyes, to watch Maya. She didn't know how *Amma* could afford it, but there she was. Maya wasn't sure how long she could put up with the monotony. Every day, the same, only broken by the occasional visit of Uma, who prattled on about her latest *nautch* and the money she was raking in.

Then, one morning as the sun was rising, Maya heard a sound like rapid thunder, a rolling *tut-tut-tut*. Cries of alarm and screams rent the air and drifts of dark grey smoke appeared from the west.

Across town, Walter was sitting under the mango tree sketching when a monkey screeched. A flock of crows was taking it in turns to swoop down. The monkey turned and hissed, baring pointed teeth and pink gums. He picked up a stone and threw it towards the crows. As he did, the sound of distant cannon fire shattered the air. Grabbing his hat, Walter walked along the corridor and opened the door on to the street. The explosions were coming from Vallam on the escarpment.

That afternoon, he watched as a river of people coursed through the streets, seeking refuge in Tanjore's fort. Some drove cattle; others sat, heads bowed, on bullock carts, their faces covered against clouds of dust.

Later that week, Walter received a curt message from Schwarz. *The Nawab of Arcot wants Tanjore at whatever cost. The Company are backing him against the prince.*

When the English army sent reinforcements to the encampment on the western perimeter of town, Walter knew another attack was imminent. Eager to see how many troops had arrived, he went there as dawn was breaking. Small miserable huts with palm-leaf doors and straw roofs were clustered together. Outside, open-mouthed soldiers were sleeping. Next to many was a black woman. Some had a child between them. Further on were the natives' houses. Open drains made the air fetid.

Up ahead he heard screams, and out of one hut, one of the last in the encampment, ran a dark-skinned woman wearing brown garb, her hair falling over her face, one hand covering an eye. A yellow-haired man followed, shaking his fist. On seeing Walter the man wavered, his eyes glazed.

'Sir, restrain yourself,' Walter said.

'Damn you.'

'I am chaplain of the garrison. Talk to me like that and you'll be flogged.'

The man stumbled, his mouth twitching. He looked familiar; his hair was the colour of straw, his hands big enough to crush a skull. Walter looked around, sensing eyes upon him, but could see no one.

'Nobody for you to call on, Reverend.'

'There is always someone I can call on.'

The man stopped.

'As can you, Sir.' His voice was firm, his mouth dry. 'Christ will save even a sinner such as you. It's never too late to ask for forgiveness.'

For a moment, Walter thought he had him.

'Forgiveness?' The man's upper lip curled back to reveal a quarry of furred brown teeth. 'He could never forgive me, not after what I've done.' He looked over Walter's shoulder, his stare wide and vacant.

'God forgives every man.' As he spoke, Walter heard the words rise with conviction. For the first time in years he did not feel it was another who was talking. He saw the man opposite him for who he was: an ignorant commoner, brutalised by circumstance, no more in control of his life than he was of his own. 'Bow down and repent,' he said, his voice exultant.

The soldier stared at him, his face contorting into fiendish laughter. 'Go to hell, Reverend. Go to hell. That's where I'm going.' He pushed past, making Walter stagger back, and sprinted down the road. As Walter turned to watch him run after the dishevelled woman, the orange smudge of sunrise seeped to blood red.

18

The knock came after midnight. Palani was waiting for it, pacing up and down her chambers. As soon as she had dismissed the servant, Palani slit open the folded piece of cloth and read the palm-leaf note. *They are marching. Head north. We will meet at the crossing of the three rivers. Adki.* As she burned the leaf in the flame, calmness engulfed her. She went into the bedroom and dug out her mother's sandalwood prayer beads and the thick worsted cotton belt. She tried it on, pressing down on the seams to feel the faceted, metallic shapes. Despite its weight, the belt sat flat against her skin.

Then she sat at her desk and, piece by piece, took off the rest of her jewellery: the nose rings, anklets, bangles and armlets, the necklaces and rings. Unpicking one end of the belt she slipped in her two gold rings shaped like serpents. The necklaces she put in a pouch inside her sari. She rose to her feet. Without the jewellery, she felt naked. A metallic grating sound made her stop. It was Vikku. She opened the bedroom door and saw her parrot stabbing the air with his beak.

'Ssssh Vikku, calm yourself. Don't make it worse.'

She walked over and opened the cage, coaxing him towards her. As she whispered and stroked the velvety patch under his chin, his trembling lessened.

'You think I haven't thought about you? You'll be safe here with Vimala. She'll look after you.' The thought of leaving her maid, stealing away without telling her, caught in her throat.

Vikku swivelled his head away from her.

'My time has come. The visions are pulling me towards the waters of the Ganga. When I'm there, I will offer Mother Ganga this.' Reaching down into the cage, she picked up a cyan-and-crimson tail feather. A single tear splashed down. She ran the edge of the feather across her palm and saw the waves lapping against the *ghats* in the holy city of Benares. The pull was irresistible. 'I can't stay any longer. I'm losing myself.'

From the prince's quarters, she heard anguished groaning.

Inside his chamber, Prince Tuljajee sat alone, brooding. For days now, he had refused to see his queens or any of his concubines. His mood had darkened after the town was hit by the plague of locusts. They descended in ravenous swarms, obscuring the sun and raining on rooftops. Then came the storm that turned the sky amber. Lightning set fire to straw roofs and struck his sacred white bull. After a fearful bellowing it shuddered violently and then its knees buckled, acrid yellow-green smoke streamed out of its nostrils, its brown eyes bulged and wept blood. By the time the Brahmins permitted the prince to see it, the beast was a blackened carcass, its matt-white skin charred and smoking. The foul and unnatural smell of cooked meat pervaded the palace for days. No amount of incense and cleaning could remove the cloying sickly scent.

The prince declared that all temples, and especially the Big Temple, with its huge shrine to Nandi the bull, start a long ceremony to placate Shiva. But within a week, crows started falling from the skies, twisting and turning, their black wings useless; they hung suspended on the palm fronds, dropped on to roofs and littered the town's streets. They fell everywhere except in the Big Temple court-yard. People hastened to the temple, and in disbelief, saw that there was not a crow to be seen.

The gods are angry!

The prince is losing his power.

Stand by the prince! Tanjore is under attack.

Each crow was carefully taken and burned in a mass funeral pyre. When the flames licked around the mound of dead birds, there was a collective sigh of relief. The worst was over. But for days afterwards, the smell lingered and scorched black feathers fell from the skies.

Baba, the chief minister, was the only person to whom the prince granted an audience. Twice, he howled at him to leave. Baba refused. The prince sat with his head bowed.

'What should we do, Your Majesty? The nawab and the British forces are gathering. Already the people have fled Vallam.'

For minutes, silence. In a small querulous voice the prince said, 'How much more can we pay?'

'Fifty thousand *pagodas* if we raise the taxes again.'

'The people, what are they saying?'

'That the death of the bull foretells the demise of your throne.'

A tremor passed through the prince.

'They want reassurance, Sire. They need to see you to know all is well.' Baba bit his tongue. *What the people are really saying*, he thought, *is that the prince is a coward.*

'I should fight the nawab and the British, once and for all,' the prince said, his voice empty of conviction. 'But we do not have the army to resist.'

Baba did not meet his gaze. 'The nawab looks for any excuse. The British cannot be trusted. But in times like these, Your Majesty, when the foreign vultures gather round, when we no longer know foe from friend, when there are mysterious forces at work, a leader is required. You are that, Prince Tuljajee. Rise up and tell the people and their faith will be restored.'

When Walter heard that General Smith's regiment and the grenadiers were marching from Trichinopoly, he sent an urgent message to Rao. By the time he'd arrived, Walter had packed his trunk and was dismantling the house. He pulled up a couple of chairs at the table in the back courtyard. As he waited for Rao's breathing to settle, Walter was surprised by the affection he felt for the stooped Brahmin across from him.

'How close are they?' Rao asked.

'They'll be here by the end of the week.' He lowered his voice. 'This time their orders are to reduce the city.'

'Why are you telling me?'

Walter's head jerked back. 'To warn you.'

'So I can what – leave?' Rao gestured towards the servants packing up the boxes. 'This is my *ur*, my ancestral home.' He corrected himself. 'This was my home.'

'I thought you'd appreciate my letting you know,' said Walter. He hadn't thought it through. Too hasty, that was his problem.

'I'm sorry, I'm overwrought.' Rao pushed himself up from the table.

'I'm the one who should be sorry,' said Walter, standing. 'I wanted to give you this.' He handed Rao a flat bundle of papers.

Rao's eyebrows lifted. Inside were several sheets of music.

'We all need harmony in our lives, Rao, and you helped bring that back into mine when I thought I'd never find it again. I wanted to thank you—' Walter searched for the right word, 'for being a friend. I feel like I owe you an explanation.' He sat down again and motioned for Rao to do the same. 'These past months have been especially difficult. I told you I was ill. It was more than that.' He lifted his eyes upwards.

'Two years before I arrived in India, I lost my wife and daughter in a fire. It's a strange thing, grief. You think you have it under control and then, suddenly, it afflicts you again. It was the loss of my daughter, Emily, that affected me the most. I can't explain it. Not even to myself. There is an uncanny likeness between Emily and your student Maya. A likeness which probably only I can see. Over these past years I've done some drawings of her. Amateur sketches. When I saw her at the temple, or on the street with her mother. Foolish thought it might be, I wanted you to give her this notebook. You said she was learning English and perhaps it will be of value to her. Perhaps she will make better use of it than I.'

He handed the notebook to Rao, who stared at the swirling brown cover and carefully put it on top of the music.

Walter could see he was considering what to say. He let the silence deepen between them.

'I always knew there was something troubling you. Your eyes give it away. But there is a lightness there now.' He looked at the notebook. 'I will do my best to make sure it reaches her. She has asked about you, too.' He gave a small sigh and stood up. 'We can only ever know a tiny part of this infinity we call life. So you will be leaving Tanjore for good?'

'For now. They've advised me to move outside the city walls.' Walter stood, too, staring down at his bare feet. They were weathered and toasted by sun and no longer looked odd poking out beneath his breeches. 'The encampment of the troops grows by the hour. I went there yesterday to preach among the soldiers.' He frowned. 'Actually I saw Maya there.'

'In the encampment.'

'Yes. At dusk. She was with a woman. A native. I've seen the woman before, she lives there with one of the private soldiers. Maya was with her.' He stared at Rao, watching the colour drain from his face.

'You're sure it was Maya?'

'Definitely. I would know her anywhere.'

'You have seen her there before?'

'No.'

'*Sahib*, I must go. I will write to you care of Schwarz.'

When Walter reached out to touch his hand, the Brahmin seemed oblivious. Clutching the sheets of music and the notebook, he half-staggered, half-walked out the door.

It was the young maidservant who told her. The words slipped out. 'Sita's back.'

Maya thought she must have misheard. But the news landed like a blow just below her rib cage. She was learning to trust how her body responded. It seemed to know better than her mind.

When Maya questioned the maid, she denied ever saying it.

'You're making it up. Your problem is you live in a fantasy world. They made you soft at the palace.'

Maya knew the maid was lying by the way her hard shiny eyes slid sideways. There was nothing to do but wait. *Amma* was at the temple and Uma was coming later that afternoon. She sat in the courtyard and began to thread a necklace of yellow and blue beads, but her fingers were clammy, her mind distracted.

She remembered the bracelet she'd been making for Leela all those years ago. The one she never finished. Angry men's voices and Leela's wails came back to her. The emptiness when Auntie and Leela had left.

This time she thought, *I'll finish the necklace.* She held it up, watching the light refract through the glass beads. Maya counted on her fingers. Leela would be nearly eight now. *Ready to learn to dance, ready for me to teach her.*

It was frangipani season and the fruity blossoms were making the air heavy. She tried to imagine what Palani would be doing now. She kept hoping that she would demand that she return to the palace. She couldn't understand what she'd done wrong. And now, of all things, Auntie was back.

That evening, Maya complained of a headache. She insisted on staying outside in the courtyard with her mother and Uma. She closed her eyes, pretending to sleep.

'Have you seen Sita again?' Lakshmi whispered, glancing towards Maya.

'Yes. She's still living at the foreigners' army encampment.'

'I wish she'd leave. I told her to leave him.'

'And go where? You don't want her back.'

Maya couldn't believe that she hadn't worked it out before. *All these weeks, Amma kept me at home because she was worried I would see Auntie. It had nothing to do with Palani or the prince.* Yet this still didn't explain why Palani never called for her.

By the end of the week, when Maya had heard enough, she made her decision. She pleaded sickness and refused to eat. Then, when she knew her mother would be out and the maidservant asleep, she took the front-door key. Her hands shook so much, it took minutes before she could open the door. Then, for the first time in six weeks, she set foot outside.

The street was deserted. The heat pulsed through her arms, down to the tips of her fingers. She wrapped her shawl across her face so only her eyes were showing, kept her head down and walked westwards, cutting through the maze of lanes. Unaccustomed to walking through the city streets, Maya's feet ached; her heels were rubbed raw. Palani would be furious if she saw them.

It was another ten minutes before she reached the edge of the encampment. It was market day and piles of fruit and vegetables were spread out on the ground. Foreign soldiers milled around in their red jackets, buttons glinting in the harsh afternoon light. From one hut, she heard raised voices and a child screaming. Her pace slowed. To the left was the Kaveri, the brown water swollen from the rains. Large neem trees lined its bank. A memory rose up from when she was a child, and she, *Amma* and Auntie washed their clothes by the river. Up ahead, she could see the flat grey boulders.

Then she saw her. Sita was crouching down near one of the trees wearing a dull brown sari, her face partially covered. Maya had to stop herself from breaking into a run. She crossed the road and when she was close enough, slipped under the curtain of branches.

'Auntie.'

Sita looked up, eyes wide with shock, then scanned over Maya's shoulder.

'You came alone?'

'Yes.'

Sita pulled her close, pressing Maya against her. She could hear her aunt's heartbeat rattling and feel the rise and fall of her chest. She let herself be held. *Amma* never held her like this. She reached her arms around her aunt's back, and pressed her fingers into the sinew and bone, and wondered how she'd become so thin. Her breath was stale, her clothes unwashed. Sita clung to her and began to sob, only reluctantly letting her go.

'I can't believe you came.'

'Why didn't you come to see us?'

She looked down. 'I did. I saw your mother. I promised I wouldn't come back. I couldn't be the one to ruin your chances. Not again.'

They sat crouching together. She took a furtive look at her aunt. Her face was worn out, her lower lip quivering. There was bruising under one eye. *I should go*, Maya told herself. *Now. If I am seen with her*—She pushed herself up on her knees and peered through the branches. Except for one dog, the street was empty. 'How's Leela?'

'Nearly eight now.'

'I know. When can I see her?'

Her aunt shook her head.

'I want to see her. Is she tall like me?'

'I can't take you to where I live.' She stopped. 'Child, why did you come?'

Maya reached up to untie the necklace of yellow and blue beads around her neck. 'Will you give this to Leela? Tell her I made it for her.'

Nodding, Sita took it. 'I know you will soon be offered.'

'Everyone knows.'

'It's a small town. News travels fast. If you are seen—'

'I know I should go,' Maya said.

The sound of drunken voices and singing drifted towards them. A group of soldiers, shirts open, staggered past. She felt her aunt shrink back. 'Wait until they've gone.'

'Is it true you've got a son?'

'Who told you?'

'It's a small town. News travels fast.'

Her aunt didn't smile.

'Why did you go with a foreigner?'

Sita's face contorted. 'What did your mother say?'

'Nothing. She didn't tell me.'

'Does she ever refer to me?'

'Not for years now.'

Silence.

'Sorry,' Maya said.

'You don't need to be. I know how it works. You mustn't come back.'

'I won't.'

'Promise.'

She nodded, reaching out for her aunt's hand. It was cold and smooth and the nails were bitten to the quick. 'I missed you after you'd gone. I missed Leela. I missed your wide smile. I missed—'

'I know.' Sita swallowed, silencing her with her gaze. She squeezed her hands, wringing the fingers. 'You have to go now.'

She nodded.

'Maya, if you are seen, it will be finished for you. It's already finished for me.'

Maya looked down.

'You asked why a foreigner? Because no other would take me. I was desperate. In Trichinopoly they pay the women to settle there. When the encampment moved here, I moved also.' She looked down at her hands. 'But I have to leave him. He's a cruel man. The place where we live is bad.'

In her aunt's eyes Maya saw a haunting. A leaf dropped from above, quivering as it fell.

Sita looked up and down the street. 'The sun will go down soon. You must get back before dark. I will walk you to the edge of the encampment. There is a quick way to the house if you follow the city walls and then cut through. I'll show you.'

They started to walk, their feet falling into the same rhythm. A sticky dread pooled in Maya's mouth. Her knees felt weak. It was hard putting one foot in front of the other. She suddenly felt exhausted and had no idea how she would get home. She pressed against Sita, to feel her warmth. Her aunt's skin was greyish and flaking. Maya wished she could take her home. The thought of home made her slow down. She would have to face *Amma*.

'You must tell your mother to get ready to leave.' Sita waved a hand towards the dirt field on the left, filling with khaki tents and dozens of soldiers. The air crackled with shouting and the whinnying of horses. They stopped to stare. Maya had never seen so many foreigners. Her throat ached and she thought she might cry.

What will this mean for me? she thought. And Palani. She shook her head. She couldn't think of Palani at this moment. That world already felt distant, a dream from long ago.

'Any day now, the attack will start.' She reached out to hold Maya's hand again. 'I'm going to take the children north. When I know it's going to happen, I will leave. He won't be able to find me then. He won't be able to come after me. Tell your *amma*.' Her voice was hoarse, and she pressed her lips together, as if to seal them. Then, pulling Maya close, she kissed the top of her head. 'Warn her. There's no future for you here.'

By the time Maya arrived home, her feet were cut and bleeding. As soon as she opened the door, Lakshmi knew where she'd been. Maya expected shouting and the switch. She thought she'd shout back and blame her mother for not helping her sister. But she was too tired to speak.

Lakshmi dismissed the maidservant and without saying a word, went into the courtyard. Squatting down, she cut a thick fleshy leaf of an aloe vera plant, and started to pound it in the pestle and mortar with honey and some *ghee* she had cooked with sandalwood. Then she slapped the mixture on to a fresh banana leaf and went inside.

She sat Maya on the stool and bathed her feet. Then she smeared on the cooling mixture and wrapped each foot in rags. She gave her milk sweetened with honey and told her to lie down.

When Maya tried to speak, she put her finger to her lips.

'Enough.'

A few hours later, Lakshmi came into the room. Maya was lying on the thin mattress on the floor, her eyelashes fluttering. When she saw her mother, she rolled towards her.

'Feeling any better?'

'Yes,' Maya lied, clenching her fists.

Lakshmi peeled away the dressing on her feet. The cuts were weeping and the soles were bruised. It would be several days before Maya would be well enough to walk. She replaced the dressing.

Maya relaxed her hands. The cooling mixture felt good. Just as she was drifting off to sleep, she cried out.

Lakshmi came running.

'Auntie said I must warn you. They will attack soon. We have to leave.'

'Be quiet now. Sleep first. You have to get better.'

Lakshmi imagined that she'd be furious with Maya, yet she only felt despair. After ritually cleansing her daughter and herself, she swept the floors until the brush broke. She hoped if she could remove every shred of her sister, Maya would still stand a chance when the summons came from the palace. For the next two days, her hands were always busy with mending and sewing. Every few hours, she tended to Maya.

When Lakshmi saw her sitting up, her hands feverishly running over her skirt, back and forth, back and forth, the words of Adki came flooding back. *'Care for her well. The years between thirteen and sixteen are when madness can descend.'*

All these years Lakshmi had not allowed herself to think of the past: the secrets concealed, the opportunities lost, the sister she'd failed. And then, something inside her broke. She found it difficult to breathe. Her knees, they wouldn't hold her. But still she started packing what they would need to take. Just the basics, as much as they could carry.

'Come, child, tidy this up for *Amma*,' she said, giving Maya her special box of make-up, odd bits of jewellery and trinkets.

That evening, when Maya was asleep, Lakshmi lit a cone of incense and decked the bronze statue of Shiva with a garland of fresh marigolds. The bitter menthol scent of the flowers mixed with the pungent smoke. She said an invocation but her mind was elsewhere. She thought of her sister. *I can't help her*, she thought. *Even now I can't.*

She looked at the slim-hipped figure. The face of Shiva was impassive but she sensed his gaze penetrating her own muddy heart. She put her fingertips together in front of her chest and directed her attention towards him but a wave of self-loathing passed through her. Without looking up, she retreated.

Before dawn the following day, Lakshmi went to the temple when the maidservant arrived. She stood outside the vast ornate gates and looked up in awe. She stared longingly at the shrines and heard the beat of the drums. She couldn't go in. Not yet. She didn't feel pure enough. Nothing felt right.

Instead Lakshmi found herself walking along streets she never visited. Several times, she nearly turned back, but she made herself carry on. Uma had told her where she'd find the hut in the encampment: at the far side, near the river and opposite the well. There it stood, slightly apart from the others. As she approached, she saw the palm-leaf door ripped off. She began to run, her heart pounding. The unease that had plagued her rose up and she tasted bile at the back of her throat.

Inside, the mattress was slashed down the middle. A three-legged stool was split in half with one leg missing. It didn't take long to find it, tossed in the corner, smeared with dried blood. The walls were spattered with it, a pool of sticky darkness coagulating in another corner. In her mind's eye the image of the monster's face became clear. His straw-coloured hair, the gash for a mouth. Lakshmi felt her insides dissolve. *Sister, sister. What did he do?*

Her wails brought out the neighbours. Her wails woke the town. The sound travelled over the rooftops and swept through the empty streets, taking on a force of its own. It knocked on closed doors and rattled shutters, struck the bells on altars and lifted the bedsheets from sleeping bodies, it made the cows bellow and the roosters crow. Even the temple elephant turned its trunk skyward and trumpeted, frightening the *mahout* sleeping on the hay. The stray dogs took up the cry, and lifting their noses to the heavens, they started to howl.

Palani heard it in her dreams. She rolled over, burying her face in the pillow, but the sound would not go away. As if in a trance, she slipped from beneath the silk covers and padded across the marble floor. She walked into the adjoining room and in the semi-darkness saw Vikku trembling in his cage. She felt a prickling up her spine. Leaning over the balcony she listened. Nothing. *I must have dreamt it.*

Vikku rattled the cage.

'Tower, tower,' the bird cried.

'Not again, Vikku.'

Wearily, she placed a cushioned pad on her shoulder and clipped a ring around the parrot's right foot, hooking one end of a leash around the ring and the other around her wrist. Then she placed the bird on her shoulder and, carrying an oil lamp with the other hand, took the back passageway up to the tower.

She stood in front of the arch facing east. Dawn was coming. A cool wind ruffled the bird's feathers. She inhaled, filling her lungs. At this time, the air was fresh and filled with promise, not yet soiled by the day ahead, by the thoughts of common people. But a rank odour stung the back of her throat and nose. The smell was of decay, of dankness: the stench of death. The parrot quivered.

'Vikku, what is it?'

She waited, straining. She heard the distant croaking of a frog, the whistling of a brown kite circling above. She fixed her eyes on the horizon. She knew by now to trust Vikku. He was always the first to know of change. His head began to nod backwards and forwards, his long cyan-and-crimson tail feathers slapping her shoulder blade through the thin muslin *pyjama*.

As the first rays of light penetrated she heard the wailing, and the wave of sound that followed: the bellowing, crowing, caterwauling and howling, and on the horizon, she saw the cloud streaming towards the palace and the tower. The spectre of grief was coming.

By nightfall, Palani knew she would be on her way.

In the encampment in the west of town, the neighbours came through the door and clustered around Lakshmi. Some fanned out, looking for the bodies. Others told her they'd heard Sita's screams, but they'd heard them too many times before to bother. It was payday. Everyone knew what happened on payday. The bowls of toddy frothed over; the white-skinned soldiers filled the grog houses.

Inside the hut, the smell made Lakshmi retch. She went outside and vomited in the gutter, trying to expel every trace of the stench that clung inside her nostrils. Then, she followed the shouts that came from the well.

Sita hadn't fallen with the first blow. She'd got up; but then he'd hit her again, splitting her lip.

'Black whore, shut your gob,' the soldier shouted.

She covered her face with her hands.

'Get up, bitch!'

Sita's breath had become strained, the blood gurgling in her throat. His leather army boot flew towards her side, to the softness of her narrow waist. The toecap snapped a rib. Sita heard it crack; her lungs emptied of breath. He heard it too. The sound excited him. With one hand he grabbed her long black hair, pulling out clumps. With the other hand, he punched her face, pulverising her cheek. He felt the blood lust of the battlefield mixing with the arrack flowing through his veins.

Sick of her complaining he was, sick of her spending his wages, sick of the mites crying. They never stopped! Nothing more than pesky flies, like the ones buzzing around his head right now.

'Maggot!' the soldier screamed, taking aim again.

Leela rushed towards him. 'Stop, stop. *Amma! Amma!*' she cried, throwing herself on her mother's limp body.

He saw the stool and, lifting it above his head, he threw it towards her. Leela ducked, the stool hit the ground and a leg splintered. He grabbed the girl. She squirmed but was no match for him. He took the leg of the stool and swung it at her. The first time he missed. The second blow caught the back of her head and she fell forward.

Her mother, unable to see for blood, heard Leela's muffled cry. Silently, Sita prayed. *Mother Goddess, save her. Let him kill me, but save her.*

'Where's that useless son of mine?' the man cried, and seizing both children, he stumbled outside. Ahead he saw the stone well. Striding up to it, he leaned over, and holding the children by the scruff of their necks, he held them aloft, their legs pedalling the air furiously. He held them for a second before letting go. Their screams sucked downwards, swallowed by the depths and the water below.

He turned and went back inside. Sita lay inert. Taking hold of her ankles he started to drag her, then picked her up and slumped her over his shoulder. He retraced his steps and sat her on the grey wall around the well, and then, with one violent jab, he pushed her backwards.

The neighbours were gathering around the well and calling out to Lakshmi. She looked up. A man was holding a scrap of brown material, waving it like a flag. It was the same colour as Sita's sari, the one she'd worn on the night she came to collect the ring. Their mother's ring. She wondered where it was and if she could get it back.

After that, the details became sketchy. Lakshmi remembered walking towards the well and into a funnel of noise; everyone was shouting and arguing and she couldn't hear what anyone was saying. Blood was smeared on the inside wall of the well and when she went to look down, a woman pulled her back. She ignored her and leaned over. She saw Sita's brown sari and one spread hand sticking up, as if she had tried to pull herself up the algae-clad walls. Next to her was a yellow piece of cloth, and another limb. Lakshmi couldn't make it out. The limb was thin, like a leg, and she saw a knee. But it wasn't Sita's knee. The funnel of sound suddenly grew louder and colours swam before her eyes; she felt her body contract and expand. Her mind couldn't take it in. *He can't have done that, he can't have.* The woman was shouting in her face. She wrenched Lakshmi away from the well, tugging at her hand; she tried to resist but, defeated, she let herself be led away.

She must have passed out. When Lakshmi woke, flies were crawling over her face, sucking the moisture from her eyes and the corners of her mouth. She sat up and rubbed her head. She was lying on a mat in a small hut. Her clothes stuck to her skin. She looked down. Her fingers were curled round a scrap of brown cloth. It took several attempts to get up. When she did, she pushed open the door and looked across to the well.

Among the crowd, she saw a man dressed in black. She squinted. It was a foreigner. He was directing the people. In front of him was a body covered by cloth. Next to him, some men were holding a rope taut and a skinny man was being lowered down into the well. Lakshmi tried to run, but her legs didn't respond and she tripped, falling in the dirt. She wasn't sure if she'd be able to stand, but she tried, and she could; she began to walk. When she was close to the well, she called out. The woman whose hut she'd been in came over.

'The foreigner ordered the bodies to be taken out,' the woman said. 'Why?'

'He comes here sometimes to speak to the English soldiers.'

The woman gave Lakshmi's hand a squeeze.

'The soldier killed the two children as well.'

Lakshmi clasped the woman's hand. She became aware that the foreigner was talking to her. At first she thought he was speaking in his language, but then she realised it was her own. He was standing near her, his face clouded with worry.

'Your name?'

'Lakshmi.'

'Are you related to this woman?' He asked the question several times before she could find the words to reply.

Eventually, she nodded. 'Sister, she's my sister.'

'And the children that are in the well?'

'Her children.'

The foreigner's mouth twisted. He took a step closer to her. 'You are the mother of Maya?'

She stared blankly.

'These are Maya's cousins?' He tried again.

Lakshmi couldn't take that in. Maya. She began to panic. Where was Maya? She was plunged again into the funnel of sound. The man's face was familiar – *the crow man, that's who he is.* The memory of when she'd slapped Maya flashed through her mind, how he'd run towards them waving that white cloth, how she was convinced he'd cast the evil eye on her daughter. All these years later and here he was, standing next to her sister's dead body, and nothing made sense. She didn't know how he knew her daughter's name. She stared at him, into his tepid grey-blue eyes; his face rinsed of colour.

'I'm so sorry,' he was saying. 'I'm so sorry.'

She thought of Maya again. If any word of Sita's fate reached the court, Maya would never stand a chance. Her whole life, her future, all ruined.

'She mustn't know, *sahib*. Maya mustn't know. She mustn't know how Sita died, or that Leela died with her.'

Uncertainty crossed his face.

'How will you keep it from her?'

'We will burn the bodies today. Their souls are already disturbed.' She looked down at the three bodies. 'I can't tell Maya. It will ruin everything.'

PART 2
Madras, 1773

19

Mudaliar wasn't planning to go down to the beach that day, but a ship arriving in Madras Roads always triggered such a frenzy that staying inside became impossible. With no port to anchor at, the ships were forced to wait until high tide; only then would the fishermen risk ferrying passengers to shore. All day they had waited for the signal, and now a storm was fast approaching. If they didn't get the foreigners to the Fort soon, they'd be spending another night on board.

The reedy ululation of the *paan* seller and the smell of roasting peanuts rose from the street below. He hadn't eaten since breakfast: enough reason to have a break. But he had a few more things to finish first, and rang the bell for his assistant.

'Take this to the chief judge,' Mudaliar said, handing Ramesh a pouch bulging with coins. 'He must get it before the court opens.'

'Any message?'

'No. He knows what I want.'

In front of him on the long teak table were the month's accounts and piles of money: gold *pagodas*, *fanams*, copper *annas*, Company rupees and grubby *paise*. He wrote a brief note to Mr Scattergood, the Secretary of the East India Company, congratulating him on his recent promotion. 'Take this letter to the Fort. Ensure it reaches Scattergood directly. That too.' He pointed to a square box, levered the top open and plunged his hand inside, letting the fragrant coarse tea leaves fall through his fingers. 'It's fresh in from Canton. An exceptional brew. He'll know I mean business.'

The sound of gunfire carried from across the water. The guns of Fort St George answered with puffs of smoke and tiny reports like the *pop-pop* of a musket. Mudaliar crossed to the open window. There were two ships now, a Dutch Indiaman, the *Fazant,* had cast anchor alongside the *Gloria*. The sea was too shallow for such large vessels to moor any closer. The surf thundered up the beach and some of the fishermen flew like sticks as they thrust their *masula* boats into the waves. The bright sun made him wince and he dug his thumb into the side of his forehead. Nothing seemed to relieve the pain.

'Sir wants to go down to the beach?' Ramesh asked.

Mudaliar sighed. He wanted nothing more than to go to his village and walk through his gardens with his son's small fingers coiled around his own. It had been months since he'd seen him.

'Why not? Afterwards we go to the temple in Mylapore. Bring all the guards.'

Behind the red, white and blue ensign of the *Fazant,* the sky was darkening to charcoal. *Someone won't survive the crossing today*, he thought. The omens were all there. He shrugged, turning away. That's what comes of being impatient. Every white-faced *huna* wants to be the first to arrive, all greedy for the best pickings.

Thomas half-jumped, half-fell into the centre of the small boat thrashing in the waves. It was just a few broad planks lashed together with twisted coconut fibre, six feet across. There were ten men on board, with a navigator at the stern, wrestling to control the vessel. His feet sank into something green and soggy. It scratched the skin through his thin stockings. He looked down to see a gorse-like plant. A thick layer of the stuff covered the base of the boat, but it wasn't enough to stop the seawater seeping through. One man's job was to continually bale out water. He kicked against the plants coiling around his ankles and was gripped by a swift wave of nausea.

Now he was here, he wished he'd opted to stay on board ship rather than hazard the crossing. He looked up, hoping to see Sam still on deck. Only the lady passengers were left on board, sheltering under a thicket of parasols. For all their chatter about making an elegant entry into Madras, they looked like tired tulips, their ringlets limp, bonnets sagging. Flora Sickles, the captain's fubsy daughter, waved. He ignored her and, leaning forward, braced himself.

It was only five hundred yards to shore but landings on Marina Beach were fraught, drownings common. Catamarans were close at hand in case of accidents. Thomas could see the British flag frisking in the wind and the gunmetal-grey ramparts of Fort St George; close by was the chalky white spire of St Mary's church. To the north was an indistinguishable mass of buildings that made up Black Town. Along the length of the beach were rows of brightly coloured wooden fishing boats and hundreds of onlookers.

The man behind prodded him to bend lower and he tucked his head down as the natives began yelling, 'Yalee! Yalee!' The navigator struggled to hold the boat straight as the oarsmen stuck in their long oars. Then, like a bucking ass, they shot through the waves. For a moment they teetered on the crest, then the bow came crashing down, soaking him through. They'd survived the first bank of surf, but there were two more ahead. The boat was filling up and the navigator seemed unable to hold it straight. He pushed down the rising panic and hunched lower. Ahead was a foaming avalanche of whiteness. His guts flew upwards, the sea roaring in his ears, and then with a thud they hit the sand.

Two of the men hoisted him like a marionette into the shallows. After months at sea, he could barely put one foot in front of the other. He felt weightless, his body no longer his own. All around him coolies, black and bare save for a white loincloth around their waists, were carrying wooden boxes. Children with curious stupid eyes tugged at his blue jacket. On the road, a battalion of the king's army marched past to the jaunty beat of a drum.

Palanquins were lined up to ferry the new arrivals to the Fort, but Thomas waved them away. He'd come so far, it had taken so long, he wanted to walk the short distance himself. Halfway up the beach, a short Indian man wearing a white *lungi* grabbed his arm. He was quickly surrounded by others dressed the same.

'You need a *dubash*? Need money?'

It took a few moments to register that the man was speaking English in a coarse guttural voice. Thomas yanked himself free.

The man rubbed his thumb and index finger together. 'Currency. *Pagodas*. You want some?'

Within seconds a crowd surrounded him, all with black curling moustaches and coiled white turbans, jostling and shouting in his face. He'd been warned about these gangs of *dubashes,* the middlemen and agents to the Company men. No fellow worth his salt could do without a *dubash*. But how could you tell who was decent? Their faces blurred together. He tried to squeeze through them, but they wouldn't let him pass.

Further up the beach, Mudaliar was standing under the shade of a tas-selled yellow umbrella held by his roundel boy. No one caught his eye. As he turned to go, he scanned the stragglers. Even from this vantage, he could see the terror in one lad's eyes as the boat vaulted the final bank of waves. He couldn't have been more than eighteen, his face flushed pink. A writer, no doubt, coming to try his luck. The man shook himself like a dog, momentarily floundering in the deep sand, before walking on.

Mudaliar started down the beach, watching as the young man approached. He could read them easily now. He himself had started as a writer – a glorified clerk – when he was thirteen, working in the Sea Customs office. For years he'd scrutinised arriving foreigners and their booty. It wasn't the big fellows you went for, they sickened too quickly; it was the leaner ones, those with a hungry look. Ahead, a crowd of *dubashes* swarmed around the man, but Mudaliar didn't quicken his pace. He could bide his time. He knew when to strike and what to say.

'Lodgings. Good price,' one man said.

'Thirsty? Arrack?' said another.

Thomas looked from one to the other. 'Later, later.'

'I'll help you.'

'Don't listen to him.'

The sunlight was searing, the sand blistering through his soft leather shoes.

'Seachest. You have one?'

Oh God, his seachest. Thomas turned around, gazing across the beach. There it was, the only one painted rust-red. *What an ass to leave it there.*

'I'll get it for you.'

The man's voice demanded attention – his English was more fluent than the others. A yeasty smell, overlaid with spices and musk, rolled off his skin. Gold chains hung around his thick neck and his fingers were heavy with rings.

'How much?'

'No charge.'

The other men were still arguing. He just wanted to get inside, away from them all.

'I'll bring it to you,' the man persisted.

'Where will you find me?'

'The Fort's not a big place. Your name?'

'Thomas Pearce. You?'

'Papanasam Subbaraya Mudaliar. I am a *dubash*, and at your service, Sir.'

Thomas shook his head. The name made no sense.

'Don't worry. You'll get it in time.'

Thomas pointed. 'It's that red chest. You'll bring it straight away?'

'Yes, yes.'

Thomas pushed on. There wasn't far to go now. Not fifty yards away was the small, compact Sea Gate of Fort St George. As he climbed the steps towards it, he noticed with wry amusement that Reverend Sutcliffe was being carried on the back of a wet fisherman, clinging on with grim determination. He waved at him before walking under the archway, flanked by a line of liveried musketeers. Punching the air with his fist, he said out loud, 'India! At last, I've arrived.'

Several miles south of the Fort, Lakshmi was walking along the main street of Mylapore. She quickened her pace. The doctor only saw patients for a couple of hours a day and it was already late afternoon. She couldn't put it off any longer; she'd been shitting blood for weeks now. Hammering filled the air. They were rebuilding the temple and workers were passing baskets of sand from one to the other. A squat foreman paced up and down, singling out those who were slow and jabbing them with a bamboo prod. Armed guards holding standards with red, white and black flags embossed with the bull stood nearby.

The doctor took Lakshmi's pulse and checked her tongue. He felt her stomach and shook his head. Most likely a tumour. He gave her bitter medicine to drink three times a day and said, if she was lucky, the growth would shrink.

'If not?'

He shrugged. 'Then it's a matter of time.'

She flinched.

'Next.'

She couldn't face going home. Nothing felt like home here. She mourned their little house on West Main Road and found no place for herself in this sprawling city with wide rushing streets. The hollow church bells from San Thome chimed in a language she did not understand. Without the rituals at the temple, her days had no order, no meaning. There were no cries of the palace peacock to bring her back to port. At night, the sound of the ocean pulsed through her veins, disorienting her dreams and stoking her nightmares.

She decided to take a slow walk to Uma's house. She'd been avoiding her for several weeks. *If I tell her I'm sick, maybe she'll give me some extra time*, she thought. She couldn't repeat what the doctor had said, not to anyone. If she didn't repeat it, maybe it wouldn't be true.

When she arrived, Uma was reclining on cushions. A gleaming brass statue of Shiva looked down from the newly carved teak altar in the shrine room. All Uma could talk about was the success of her dance troupe.

'Maya still hasn't come to see me,' she said.

'Tomorrow morning she'll come.'

'Lakshmi, when I first met you, your daughter obeyed you. Since you left Tanjore, something in you has given up. The girl can sense that.'

'Perhaps you can have a word with her?'

'Gladly.'

'She'll be back soon, I should go.' Lakshmi hauled herself up.

'Haven't you forgotten something?'

Uma's brother appeared in the corridor. He'd been listening. Lakshmi hesitated, then searched inside her blouse for her purse. The *pagodas* were moist and she wiped them on her sari before handing them over. When she gave him two, he stood waiting.

'I think you know by now that two isn't enough.'

She swallowed. 'If I give you three I won't have any more.'

'If Maya worked with me you wouldn't need to pay such high interest,' said Uma. 'I'd accept it in kind. Think about it.'

Later that afternoon Lakshmi was trying to get comfortable on the rush matting when she felt the breeze freshen. She pulled a cloth over her eyes. The hairs on her arms pricked. A crisp cold sensation jolted her upright. The room was empty, yet the spirits were all around. Not just Sita this time. Others, too – all women – all parading before her. They would come for her next.

She shuddered, thinking of those last days in Tanjore. If it hadn't been for the English *sahib* ordering the untouchables to fetch the bodies out of the well, and Uma paying for the funerals, they would have been thrown in the river. All she had left of her sister was her ring. By a small miracle she'd found it in the hut, clotted with blood. Shame flooded through her. *My only sister, and I failed her.*

When the city fell, she and Maya had joined Uma in the exodus. More than once she'd feared the girl was losing her mind and slapped her to stop the keening. Maya was devastated when she couldn't say goodbye to Palani, heartbroken, when Lakshmi told her that Sita had taken the children and gone north.

It was Uma who had advised Lakshmi to wait before she told Maya the truth. *Wait until the girl is more stable, until she's settled.* That moment had never come.

I must tell her, Lakshmi thought. *Maya must know.*

A sharp pain gripped her. She whimpered, covering her face with her hands. Slowly Lakshmi let her hands drop in her lap. The room was silent. She was alone again. The women had left her this time. She looked around at their few scattered possessions – they fitted in a wooden box no bigger than a brick. That was all she had to leave Maya. Worse, though, were the debts. They would cripple the girl. When they had left they only took what they could carry and in the intervening years, they'd relied on Uma. The old woman had already paid for the funerals of Sita and her children. *Next, she'll be paying for mine.* She thought of Uma and her nuggety black eyes and knew Maya would have to go and do the woman's bidding. It would be years before Maya could repay in full.

20

Thomas lay awhile listening to Sam's rhythmic snores. Down below, carts were arriving with provisions and a noisy chorus of crows announced sun-up. He stepped out of bed and poured a jug of brown water into the washbowl, splashing his face and neck.

'Time to rise.' He prodded Sam.

'It can't be morning already.'

Their fusty room encased him like a shell. They had just enough space for two cots, two seachests, a small table and a dresser. Muslin mosquito curtains rigged between the beds added to the general clutter.

Thomas dressed, smoothing down his velvet jacket. He'd bought it from a Bristol milliner who said the colour would remind him of home: *'The exact same shade as the common blue butterfly.'* Styled in the latest fashion, it gathered at the waist and was cut away below the hip. Out here, though, it was suffocating. He rested the hand mirror on the dresser and fixed his sandy-coloured wig, powdering the front with care. He sniffed. A foul smell drifted towards him.

'For God's sake, Sam, go and live in a pen.'

'Uhh?'

'Get yourself to the privy.'

'Go to hell.'

'Get up. You'll be fined if you're late again.'

Thomas untied and re-tied the bow at the base of his wig.

Sam pushed himself up on his elbow. 'Something fancy on today? Another meeting with that *dubash* of yours?'

'Trollop. It's Scattergood I'm trying to win over.'

'Aye. He's as shrewd as they come.'

Thomas nodded gloomily. He cupped his hands on either side of his long, chiselled face, looking at his blunt nose and the deep indentations either side of his mouth. His beauty had always been a source of aggravation. Women loved him; men mistrusted him. 'This place ages you.'

'It's the monotony.'

'The heat, too. Hard to believe it's already April. How long have we been here?'

'January 18th we landed. We should get ourselves down to the whorehouse near the Navy Tavern.'

'That's for the troops. We can do better than that.' Thomas fastened his breeches, sliding his hand over the bulge of his sex. 'You're right though. I'm in need of some cunny.'

'Keep it to yourself.'

He laughed. 'We survived ten months in the same cabin on the *Gloria*. You've nothing to worry about. Why would I be attracted to a hairy red nut like you? You've the arse of a monkey and the belly of a sow.'

Sam leapt up with a yell. 'You'll wish you never said that, you tousle-haired, green-eyed macaroni.' He wrapped his arms around Thomas's head, pushing his face towards his armpit. 'Breathe it in.'Tis the scent of a man.'

'Curse you.' Thomas pushed him off, wiping his face. 'You've wrecked my wig.'

Sam fell back with a hoot.

'You stink, Sam. Here the pariahs are cleaner than you. They wash more times in a day than you do in a month.' He rummaged around in a bag. 'Try this. The natives call it soap nut. It will clean even the slime that grows between your toes.'

'You're more vain than a duchess. Next you'll be telling me you've got yourself some rosewater.'

Thomas fell silent.

'You have, too. You're as bad as Purley, who trots around in silks and smokes a hookah.'

'Christ almighty, Sam, who doesn't want the life of a *nabob*? Isn't that why we're crammed into this godforsaken Fort, isolated from the rest of the civilised world and dying like flies? So we can become something we could never be back home. Think of your father. He did it.' With a toss of his head, he left the room, his footsteps echoing down the long wooden corridor.

From there it was a short walk to the Company offices. Thomas strode upstairs and on to the balcony. The streets were clean, the new buildings handsome, their shiny white polished exteriors redolent of Italianate marble. The Fort itself, built with rugged ironstone, covered around a hundred square yards with four bastions at each corner, the governor's house in the centre, and four gates, with the Sea Gate facing east. From the balcony Thomas could see the new arsenal, customs house, refectory and mint. In between the lodgings, where Company servants lived cheek by jowl with soldiers and officers, were storerooms for the goods, and the new houses of agency, which were multiplying as trade routes opened up, and free merchants and Company men clubbed together to reduce the risk of loss.

He went back inside to wait. Eventually the door opened and a brown bony finger beckoned him in. It was Scattergood's long-serving assistant, a rake of a man with hawkish eyes. The secretary was bent over a desk, peering at sheets of accounts through a gold-rimmed magnifying glass. At length he looked up.

'Pearce.'

'Sir.'

'You come recommended by Pinney. You know the family well?'

'I do, Sir.'

'A loathsome man. I knew his father.'

Thomas felt the heat rising up his neck. 'When I say "know" – I've made his acquaintance.'

'Know, or not know? What is it, Pearce?'

'A family acquaintance. If he's not to your liking, look to my other patron, Lavenham.' He pointed to a letter on the desk, his godfather's ornate writing instantly recognisable.

'No need to point.' He glanced down. 'A writer of responsible worth. Excellent at sums. Family good merchant stock from Bristol. Father traded in tobacco in the West Indies.' He looked up. 'Is that you, Pearce? Have you got what it takes to last or will I be burying you before the next season?'

Thomas blinked.

'We're losing a dozen a day. Fever. Flux. The pox. Your predecessor lasted six months. He was found dead in the gutter. He'd only lain there a few hours before the crows picked out his eyes and the blacks stripped him bare.'

Behind him, Thomas heard a snigger, disguised as a cough.

'You've picked up some Portuguese, I hope?'

He nodded.

'Good. You've learnt your currency tables?'

Thomas looked blank.

Scattergood waved a hand and his assistant handed him a scroll. The secretary unfurled it on his desk and beckoned Thomas around.

'There are over a dozen currencies in use here. In the Madras Presidency we tot up our accounts in *pagodas*, *fanams* and *paise*. Here you have the current rates of exchange between *pagodas* and other currencies like the Company rupee.' He reached for his magnifying glass and peered at the figures. 'The rates differ depending on where they're exchanged. Currently the Company exchanges forty-two *fanams* to one *pagoda*. And two-and-a-half *pagodas* equals one pound.'

He put down his magnifying glass. 'It's a devil of a system. The golden rule of thumb: ensure that your receive change in the same currency in which you paid, especially when dealing with merchants and your *dubash*. I hear it's Mudaliar. He clearly saw something if he picked a fresh-faced griffin like you.'

'Griffin, Sir?' A blush spread up his neck.

'A new arrival.'

He nodded, pointing. 'Where do I get a copy?'

'This one's yours.'

Thomas went back around the front of the desk.

'Your trading contract is in calico.'

'My mother's favourite.'

'Well, you can be a dutiful son and send her some.' Scattergood scrutinised him. 'You know the rules? No private trade. Your job is to run and manage the Company's trading contract. That's what every writer does. Don't get ambitious, Pearce. Don't think you can be like your father. I know all about him, too.'

He felt himself shrink under the secretary's paternalistic gaze.

'I'll be watching. Understand?'

'Sir.'

The writers weren't required to start until eight o'clock, but Thomas was down at the Sea Gate at daybreak. The chaotic atmosphere in the exchange and around the warehouses crescendoed each time a ship was ready to weigh anchor, followed by weeks of lethargy when the bay emptied and the trade winds failed. Then, the days dragged as he copied letters in triplicate, in case they miscarried on the long voyage back to Leadenhall Street.

Trade was the only topic of conversation. Rumours of who had made the best sale and whose ship had gone down swirled around the Fort like the north-westerly squalls. Periodically jealousies broke out into public spats or dawn duels on Marina Beach.

Company rules kept most of the natives outside the Fort walls. Inside the exchange, Thomas mingled with officers, free merchants and Madras old-timers, the Wynches and Boddams. There were pearls from Tuticorin, sandalwood from Mysore, tea from south China and bolts of blue and red patterned calico, muslin and chiffon, ivory, spices and vermilion, taffeties and tobacco. And to pay for it all, chests of silver bullion from Manila. The quantities made his head spin.

At the back of the building, Thomas noticed the chaplain of St Mary's trying his hand.

'Found anything, Reverend Sutcliffe?'

'Oh, you know, I'm just observing.' Walter looked down at his shoes, his face sheepish.

'No need to be shy.' Thomas gave a slow, easy smile. The man was always so uptight, as if he had a broom shaft up his backside. There was some scandal attached to him. Something about a girl. A native girl.

'You seem to think you know more than me, Pearce. You seem to think that about everyone.' Walter's eyes narrowed. 'Remember who the griffin is around here.'

'I forgot,' Thomas said drily, 'that you've spent time here before. Tanjore, wasn't it?'

'That's right. In service to the eminent Reverend Schwarz.'

'Miss it?'

He hesitated. 'Yes. Actually, I do. Loathed it at first but it grew on me. This place gets under your skin. Mark my words, Pearce.'

'I'll be sure to, Reverend.'

'I haven't seen you at St Mary's since you arrived. Now you're on dry land you don't have any excuse.'

'No.'

Walter waited. Ever since their argument on the *Gloria* about the rights and wrongs of missionary work, the lad had irritated him. Beneath his boyish charm there was an arrogance. 'So, I can expect you at the Sunday service?'

'Without a doubt.' Thomas didn't try to hide the sarcasm. 'Good day to you, Sir.'

As Thomas weaved his way back through the throng, the word 'griffin' stuck in his throat. He felt his newness and despised it.

Empty-handed, Walter returned to his lodgings at the back of the church. The walls were of exposed brick and the small window afforded no view. He thought he'd get more as the Company's chaplain of St Mary's, but he had less than when he was a junior chaplain in Tanjore. Yet here, his duties were more onerous.

Aside from the festivals, funerals and marriages, he took charge of the offspring of English soldiers and native women, and was expanding the Fort's military orphanage. The children came to him malnourished and illiterate. After a few weeks, they could recite the first line of the Lord's Prayer, and on Sundays, ate plum pudding out of a bowl. This they did with their hands. In time, Walter hoped they would learn to use a spoon.

If only I could make a bit extra, he thought, flinging his black jacket on the back of the chair. Some two-storey apartments on James Street had become available. Now that would be the place to live. He'd be able to hold court there. Perhaps even Schwarz would grace him with his presence.

As soon as Walter had arrived back in Madras, after the long tiresome voyage from England on the *Gloria,* he'd written to Schwarz. Three months later and there was no word. *The man was always so busy*, Walter thought, loosening his white necktie. He couldn't risk putting on his pantaloons at this hour. The warden would call soon and then lessons would begin.

He missed that about Tanjore: the freedom to dress as he pleased behind closed doors; that, and Rao's regular visits. He hadn't heard from him, either. Rao always made him think about that girl Maya. He wondered how she'd fared; where she and her mother had gone after the city fell to the nawab. He sat down. He'd been a fool to give her his notebook. *Getting ahead of myself, interfering in matters that I had no right to.*

He breathed out. *What's past is past.* Outside, the second gun salute of the day made the earthen cup tremble on the table. Nine o'clock. Time for breakfast.

2 1

Maya stood by the wall, watching her mother grind the spices and toss them into the pan of spitting *ghee*. 'What did the doctor say?'

'Pass me those chillies, will you?' Lakshmi slit open a bloated red chilli, stripping the innards, cutting out the rotten parts and putting half the seeds to one side. 'I shouldn't have so much hot spice, that's all.'

Clouds of yeasty-smelling steam billowed as her mother placed the round fermented rice-and-dhal cakes on to cook. When they were ready, she crouched down and served the steaming *idli* and coconut coriander chutney on two plantain leaves. They ate in silence.

The next morning, Maya woke to find the room empty and her mother sitting on the step into the courtyard, asleep, a line of spittle running down her chin and gathering between her breasts. When she coaxed her back inside, her mother could barely walk.

'*Amma*, what did the doctor really say?'

'I need to rest.'

'Did he give you anything?'

'It's over there.'

With difficulty Lakshmi sat down on the mat and Maya squatted in front. Her chest was straining. 'Why can't you talk to me? Telling me what's wrong isn't a sign of weakness. All it does is build a wall around your heart. A wall between us. You always hide things from me. You think it's to protect me, but it's to protect yourself.'

'I'm too tired for this.'

Maya rested her hands on her mother's knees. 'You're not well. I need you to be honest with me.' She stared at her mother, trying to read her face, but her eyes were expressionless – a doorway to an empty house. Maya knew if she stayed any longer she'd get angry. 'I'm going for a walk along the beach,' she said, standing up.

'Get back here now. We're going to Uma's this morning.'

'You're not well enough to go anywhere.' Maya was already walking out the door.

Their lodgings were three streets back from the beach in Mylapore. The palm trees arched in the stiffening wind, the fronds clacking together like blocks of wood. Ahead, the shingle was exposed as the waves sucked in and out. Maya licked the salty air from her lips and looked across the bay to the horizon, to that line of infinity where sea and sky met. It was at that point – suspended between worlds – that she wanted to be. That was why she loved to dance. It took her to the same timeless place. She ground her feet down, squeezing the warm sand between her toes. Not that she was dancing much these days.

At least here, though, she was no longer watched. No priests, no Rao, no palace spies. After the enclosed fortress walls and dusty narrow streets of Tanjore, Madras was a revelation. More than anything, it was the expanse of the ocean. She'd always known it. Somehow the ocean had always called her. The immensity of what lay beyond made the tightness in her chest lessen. It helped her gain her bearings.

But nearly three years on, and some things still made no sense. No sense at all. The mysterious flight of Palani. The sudden disappearance of Sita. Maya tried calling out to her aunt in her mind. *Auntie, I know you wouldn't just leave me like that. Tell me where you are. Tell me where I can find you.*

She waited, hoping to catch a glimpse of something. But her mind was too full of fleeting images and passing thoughts. She shook herself. She should get back now and see *Amma*. Yet, she continued to walk north towards the Fort. Taking long supple strides, she swung her arms by her side. She forgot her mother's suffering, and her own, and dreamed of flight.

Later that week, Lakshmi and Maya were walking together towards the fish markets along the seafront. To give her mother time to catch her breath, Maya kept pausing.

'See that tall woman up ahead, that's Kuttamma. Her family is from Tanjore, too. She sells the best fish,' Maya said.

Lakshmi shrugged.

'*Amma,* you could learn to like it here if you wanted.'

'We should never have left Tanjore.'

'We couldn't stay.'

'Others did.'

'You said you couldn't abide living under the nawab.'

'He's gone now. Prince Tuljajee is back on the throne.'

'We can return then.' She looked at her mother. Dark rings encircled her eyes, her skin was sallow and washed out. Maya's voice softened. 'When you're better, we'll go on pilgrimage. We can stay at the pilgrims' rest houses along the way, stopping at shrines. You've said yourself pilgrimage is the best way to heal body and soul. We'll go to Kannyakumari, to where the three oceans meet.'

'All you ever talk about is the sea. What good does it do you?'

'It lifts my heart.' Maya stretched her arms up, her bracelets jangling against each other. Her hair blew across her face.

'It doesn't bring in any money.'

'I've said I'll go and see Uma *akka.* I'll join her dance troupe if I have to.'

'We should never have left.'

'We had no choice.'

'It's the English that are to blame. They took everything.'

'Don't start again. What's done is done.'

Lakshmi said nothing.

'*Amma*, let's go and sit in the shade.' She steered her mother away, her voice rising and falling, pointing out the stallholders she'd befriended and those who would cheat them, and like a child, her mother let herself be led.

Uma took it upon herself to instruct Maya how to please a man. She said that if Maya was going to lead the dance troupe, she needed more training. Maya wished she would leave her alone.

'A patron needs to be arranged. You're sixteen.'

She went quiet, feeling knotty inside.

'Pay attention. I'm only going to explain this once.'

Uma showed Maya which herbs to mix to help an ailing erection and the point to press for quick ejaculation; the bitter herbs to prevent pregnancy; the love elixir to bewitch a suitor and the sour tonic to end it; the two twigs to perform an abortion and the poultice from the preserved petals of the *asogam* tree to cease the bleeding. She taught her the days when she could have sex and those when it was forbidden. Then she taught her the art of classifying men: their caste, their wealth, whether they were prone to liquor, and how to keep a man in the house.

As they walked along the street, the old woman tested her.

'This one. What caste?'

'Chettiyar.'

'Wealthy?'

'Yes.'

'Wrong. Look at his slippers,' Uma said.

As he walked past, Maya saw the soles were worn through.

'Next one. Virile?'

Maya tittered.

'What's so funny?'

'I can't tell.'

'Course you can. That man would damage a girl like you.'

'How do you know?'

'How does a man know a good horse? He trains his eyes.'

She cast a sidelong glance, feeling queasy.

'Now see that one there, coming out of the temple—'

Across the road, in front of the newly painted sea-green doors of the temple, stood a tall, broad-shouldered man dressed in white muslin with a gold border on the edge of his *lungi*. He was deep in conversation with a squat man with the flattened nose of a boxer. On either side stood bearers carrying ensigns in black, red and white, painted with the symbol of a bull.

'He'd be good for you. He's from a rich farming family. Yes, you might pull a face, young girl, you might think that his caste is below yours, but they're the ones with money in this city. His name is Mudaliar and he's chief *dubash* to the English. There's nothing he doesn't trade in – cloth, diamonds, it all passes through his stubby fingers. See how he affects such airs.' She squeezed Maya's arm. 'That sort is easy to manage. You play to their weaknesses and flatter their strengths. His heart's never left the village, even if he struts around here as the new *dharmakarta* of the temple.'

'He's head of the temple?' Maya was incredulous.

'Yes. He's bought off everyone – including the priests. He's rebuilt that temple to honour his father, who the British accused wrongly. The poor fellow died penniless in prison. Mudaliar's been trying to claw his way back up ever since.'

Maya watched the *dubash* barking orders and the hunched figure of the priest scurrying through the open doorway.

Back at Uma's house, the *tai* taught her to sing bawdy *padams*.

'Show us more passion. You must bewitch the patron.'

'What if I don't like him?'

'I decide who you like and who you lie with. You are there to please a man.'

'What about my pleasure?'

'Pah, Palani *akka* has gone. The palace has gone. You don't have the luxury of choice. If you're going to be part of my troupe, then you do as I say.'

'What if I don't want to be part of your troupe?'

Uma's lips puckered. 'You have no choice.'

'You don't own me.' Maya stood, defiant.

'I do.'

She stared at Uma, trying to hold the older woman's unflinching gaze, but she could not.

'Ask your mother.'

'*Amma* wouldn't just sell me off.' Her voice faltered.

'You better start facing reality, girl. You've lived a life far removed from the ordinary. Get used to the mundane.'

22

Thomas was waiting outside the Sea Gate for Mudaliar. A scudding wind made the palm trees wave like sails. A storm was on its way. Every few minutes he stopped and scanned the bay with his telescope. It was a futile exercise. There was only the *Fazant* lying at anchor; no sign of the *Gloria* with its secret cargo of tea.

He looked through the telescope towards the Dutch ship rocking in the swell. It was the same vessel that had anchored alongside the *Gloria* on the day he'd arrived in Madras. One man was sitting on deck, as you might in a park on a Sunday afternoon. His clothes were a mixture of European and native, with a loose crimson coat and open-necked shirt. His face was ruddy, his nose beaked. Thomas felt as if he were spying on him, yet he continued to watch until the first drops of rain fell and trickled under his own starched shirt collar. Only when the rain became heavy did the man go beneath deck.

The whistles and shouts announced the arrival of his *dubash*. Standard-bearing guards preceded the litter, and running alongside was Ramesh. When Mudaliar alighted, another servant was quick to put up the fringed roundel, another to pass him a cloth to wipe his beetle-browed face.

'I need a horse,' said Thomas.

'You brought me out in the rain to ask me that?'

'It's been nearly a year – most writers don't last six months. My health is robust enough to live out my term.'

'You still haven't paid me for the gingham shirts and the advance to buy cloth. Pay me back with 12 per cent interest and I'll consider a loan for a horse.'

Mudaliar turned to go, the red and white flag with the black bull billowing behind him. Thomas kicked his shoe in the dirt, cussing under his breath.

That evening, Thomas was working late. He sat back on his chair and stretched his arms above him. It was the currency that drove him to distraction. He picked up the gold star *pagoda*, pancake-flat and embossed with a five-pointed star in the centre. It looked flimsy, inconsequential, yet here it was the equivalent of two weeks' wages. He groaned, cross-checking the figures again. Everything tallied. Why, then, this persistent sense that Mudaliar was cheating him?

Thomas made it his business to examine all the cloth he purchased. He demanded that his *dubash* take him to the filthy quarters where the Company kept the weavers, dyers and fullers, their hands stained blue from indigo, resentment etched in their faces. He stood up, spreading his fingers on the edge of the desk. Papa's words came back to him: *'Don't be fooled by the figures, go to the source.'*

Thomas must have been twelve. It was a bright morning with hoarfrost on the Downs when he and Papa walked briskly down to the warehouse on Broad Quay. His father opened the side door, signalling Thomas to be quiet. At the front of the warehouse were ten hogsheads of tobacco. Around the back, under the foreman's desk, another bag of offcuts. The foreman had kept the right amount, but syphoned off enough baccy to sell on the side and make a few guineas. His father fired him that same day.

Thomas shuffled the palm-leaf accounts back into order.

'My *dubash* is a bloody liar,' he told Sam later.

Outside, Thomas could hear drunken voices. Inside their room, the air was worn out.

'What do you expect? Everyone knows they are two-faced. They undercut the native merchants and us,' Sam said. 'Forget about him. Any day now the *Gloria* will arrive and we'll make a profit.'

He sighed audibly.

'Tommy, you have to take risks to get the returns.' Sam reached across to snuff out the candle, then rolled over to sleep.

As Thomas lay in the darkness, he knew Sam was right. He'd never make it back home if he didn't earn more than his paltry £10 a year. He wondered what time it was there. Sunday afternoon. Elsie would be sitting on the high-backed sofa, needlework on her lap, hot buttered teacakes on the table next to Mama's prized china teapot, the only one she'd managed to hide from the debt collectors. In the morning, he would finish writing that letter. Even with no money to send home, he would write.

Last thing before bed, Mudaliar sat on his raised dais and read two or three lines from his holy texts. His head ached and the twinge in his left knee was worsening. *Maybe I need to go on a pilgrimage*, he thought. *To appease the gods.* He'd been promising his wife they'd go. He rarely thought of her these days. The city air didn't suit her. He would tell Pearce plainly that he needed time away. Just to be in those sacred places was enough to revive a man.

He wrapped the palm-leaf manuscripts in the cloth and looked across to the single straw mattress on the floor. What he needed was a woman: someone to entertain him, someone to rival Vedacala's mistress. Now she really was a beauty. He'd see that old hag Uma again. He'd talk to her about this girl she had for him.

Mudaliar swung his legs down to the floor and stood up. He spat on the ground and examined his teeth in the small mirror. The *paan* was eating away at his gums.

As he lay down to sleep, he consoled himself with the thought that, at heart, he was a good man, a generous man. *When I am head of the temple, my rivals will see that. They'll see I'm a man who can be trusted. They'll reward me, as they should …*

Above, the rats continued to gnaw the thatch and the rest of the house slipped into slumber.

Lakshmi was dozing when she heard the knock. It took several minutes for her to gather herself and open the door.

Uma was standing with her arms crossed. She took a step forward as if to march inside, and then stopped, her nose wrinkling. 'Lakshmi, you haven't replied to my messages. I had no choice but to come myself.'

Lakshmi looked across to the other side of the street. Uma's brother was there, watching them. She pulled down her blouse. A sour smell erupted from her armpits.

'It's more than your knees that are troubling you,' Uma said.

'The doctor said it's nothing to worry about.'

'If that's the case then I'll wait.'

The open-air tank at the end of the street was as far as Lakshmi could manage to walk. After they had both bathed, they sat under the neem trees and dried their hair in the stippled sunlight. Not since Tanjore had she done this with Uma, who insisted on combing her hair.

'Be honest, now,' Uma's voice was soft. 'I know what the doctor said. He said you were dying.'

She swung her head away and grabbed Uma's wrist. The force of it took the older woman by surprise. 'The doctor had no right to say that. How much did you pay him?'

For a few seconds they eyed each other. Then Lakshmi let go. 'It always comes down to money with you, doesn't it?'

'Always.'

'So what have you decided?'

'Mudaliar is the most likely. He'll pay the highest.' She started to comb her own hair. 'Your daughter is my daughter too. I'm looking out for her best welfare.'

'When will it happen?'

'Once the rebuilding of the temple is finished. He says he's too busy until then.' She leaned forward. 'Think of it, Lakshmi. She'll be on the arm of one of Madras's most eligible *dubashes*. You must be proud.'

'How can a middleman who works for a foreigner be as good as Prince Tuljajee?'

'Your problem is you live in the past. Maya's place at the court in Tanjore is gone forever. These days Madras is where women like us can shine. We can be more than dancers, we can be courtesans to the wealthy and famous. As mistress to Mudaliar, she'll still be able to perform at the temple—'

'Impossible.'

'Why not? He's head of his own temple. He dictates who performs there. Why do you think he's spent thousands rebuilding the temple in his father's honour?'

As Lakshmi listened, she thought of the first time the palace gates had opened and she and Maya had sat before Palani in her elegant quarters. It seemed like a memory from a former life.

'They have all the power here,' Uma was saying.

'Who?'

She rolled her eyes. 'The *dubashes*. They might not have the knowledge of the Brahmins, that I grant you. Some are uncouth. Mudaliar,' she paused, letting her streaked grey hair fall to her knees, 'he is a bit of an oaf, but Maya can cope. I've told her what to do. I'll be there to help her.'

'You'll be there?'

Uma put the comb down. 'I'm sorry, Lakshmi. I know I'm a hard woman. I don't know how I'd be feeling if I were you. We all think we know how we'll be when we face it. The truth is, we don't.'

Lakshmi bowed her head, covering her face with her hands. Maybe she'd release Maya from the debt. Maybe she'd take pity on her. Slowly, she looked up. Uma's face was rigid.

'I can't do that,' Uma said. 'There will be your funeral costs on top of the ones I already paid for.'

'How much is still owing?'

'One hundred and eighty *pagodas,* including interest.'

'So much?'

'You've lived off me for three years now.'

'How much will Mudaliar pay?'

'Eighty is the best I can hope for. You still have Sita's ring. Give me that and Maya's payments will be reduced by a quarter.'

Lakshmi fell silent.

'Have you told her yet what happened?'

She shook her head.

'You must. You can't carry it with you. The girl still lives in hope of seeing her aunt again, of her coming back.' Uma stopped. 'That's even more reason to give me the ring. How will you explain to Maya when you told her that you gave the ring back to Sita before she left?'

Uma was right. She could have it. That ring was cursed. 'You have the ring.'

Uma looked suspicious.

'If it helps Maya, better you have it.' She pushed herself up. 'I ask only one thing. When she's settled, tell her about her aunt. You know what Adki said all those years ago. The years between thirteen and sixteen are when she's at her most vulnerable. She's through the worst of it now.' Her eyes lingered on a single pink lotus flower poking through the murky green water of the pool. 'And very soon she'll blossom. I'm only sorry I won't be there to see it.' She was struggling to hold herself upright, and, covering her head with the tail of her sari, Lakshmi walked away.

Mudaliar arranged the meeting inside his temple. At every opportunity he went there. Not only for his *puja*, but also to sit in the cool courtyard as worshippers performed their ablutions; to watch the temple women as they sang and danced for the gods and encircled the shrines with the trays of flaming *aarthi*; to stand before the statue of his father.

As he made a simple *pranam* at the statue, he said, 'By building this, Father, I've rebuilt your reputation. I've immortalised your name. Future generations will know that you were an honourable man...'

A figure in the doorway made him turn around.

'Lord.' Uma bowed low, touching the top of his feet with a flourish. 'Each time you look more magnificent, your eyes more wise, your—'

'Enough. You came alone?'

Resting her hand lightly on his arm, Uma steered him towards two seats in a quiet corner. 'Her mother is gravely ill. It's not timely for me to show her.'

'Always an excuse.'

'I'm here to finalise details.'

'I need to see the girl properly. It's not enough that she walks past me, head down, veiled.'

'This is why I am here. Mayambikai loves to dance. She becomes the dance. It is why she was a breath away from becoming the *rajadasi* of Prince Tuljajee himself. Her dance can steal a man's soul. Trust me.' As she sat down, she widened her legs, locking him with her stare. 'I will send you a message when I know she is coming to the temple. She likes to practise after lunch, when the priests are asleep. I promise you, you will not be disappointed.'

'When?'

'My lord,' she gave him a reproachful look, 'the girl's mother is dying.'

'How much will she cost?'

'First you see her. Then we make our final price.'

'How can I believe that she is still a virgin?'

'I swear on my life, my mother's life. She was Palani's protégé, trained for the prince himself. No one was allowed near her.' She shook her head. 'Then the war came to Tanjore, our lives were thrown into chaos. All this time she has been under my care. I've waited patiently to find her the right patron. A little ripe, yes. But who never liked the sweetest mango from the tree,' she gave him a coy look, 'the sweetest flesh you could ever imagine.'

23

For days Lakshmi had been lying in the corner. The doctor returned, carrying a jar of thin black leeches, their heads lifting, circling for food. He left with the leeches fat, their bodies sated, and *Amma's* arms spotted with blood, her eyes rolling back in her head. After the bloodletting, a fever set in and she muttered jumbled words in her sleep – for her mother and for Sita. Her body betrayed her, her bowels loosening over Maya's hands as she tried to undress her. Then she fell into a stupor.

The doctor came back and gave her a spicy powder to inhale, waking her with a start. He told Maya to call the priest to administer last rites, then stayed a while, repeating prayers. The smell was unbearable, Lakshmi's face, legs and arms were swelling. When the doctor left, she heard the splatter of vomit in the gutter outside.

Maya sat down next to her mother. It would be a matter of hours now. She heard rattling, as if there were stones bouncing inside her rib cage, as if she were trying to capture every last breath. A deep gurgling pushed out the final whistle of air, and with it, a gust of decay. At that instant Maya felt her mother's soul float up from the centre of her chest. She thrust out her hands to snatch it, but was too slow. Taking a cloth, Maya wiped away the sticky black mixture gathering in the corners of her mother's mouth. She closed *Amma's* eyelids and ran her hand down the centre of her chest, checking there was no heartbeat.

Then, Maya lay down next to her. She was too numb to cry. As she lay there she became aware of a subtle shift in the room: a thickness, a stirring of ether, her own heart expanding as her mother's light faded.

Then she went to Uma's and together they told the priests to arrange for the cremation the next day. The following morning, in recognition of her mother's status, Uma ensured that she was accorded the special honour of receiving the fire from the temple kitchen to light the pyre. Lakshmi's body was taken around Shiva's idol for a final time. As a woman married to god, she would leave this world as a *nityasumangali* – an ever-auspicious one – married for eternity to her lord.

Maya watched from a respectful distance as the flames took hold. She knew she mustn't cry. This would only keep her mother's soul attached. She imagined her *amma* like a boat, the moorings cut, drifting on the vast ocean.

When only her skull was still glowing and one charred foot visible, Maya left. Uma tried to make her stay with her for the night but Maya insisted on returning to the house. She wanted to be alone with *Amma*. She sat in the corner where she could still feel the warmth of her presence. The room was bathed in peace.

Uma did not wait long. Two days later she was banging at the door, demanding Maya repay the rest of the debt. When Maya refused, she said she'd be back and take everything she owned.

'I know you're in there, you lazy good-for-nothing.'

Maya didn't move from the corner.

'If you don't pay me, I'll beat the door down.'

Maya covered her head with her mother's sari.

When Uma called again, Maya didn't open the door. 'I can't pay you.'

'You can.'

'Leave me alone.'

'Not until you repay me.'

'I don't have anything.'

'We know that's not true, Maya.'

Two weeks later, when the funeral rites had been completed, Maya went to the temple in the afternoon. It was lunchtime and the place was deserted. Quietly she laid to one side her anklets threaded with silver bells, together with her bracelets, nose-ring and hair ornaments. She took her time flexing her fingers and cracking her knuckles, spread her arms and stretched her shoulders. As she let her body lead into the dance, she heard the internal beat, passed down from generation to generation of women.

This one is for you, Amma. She imagined her mother squatting in between the pillars, slapping out the rhythm with her hand on her thigh. So vivid was the image, Maya felt she could reach out and touch her. When she did a double twirl, she was sure she saw a glimpse of her mother's turquoise sari, but when she looked again, it was gone.

Maya lunged, her body lengthening, and like the luminosity of a flame, let her devotion fill the temple until she saw herself as a blaze of light. When she could hold it no more she pulled herself back in, leaving enough as an offering to the divine, but not emptying herself completely – otherwise, how could she do it all again? As she folded her hands in the centre of her chest and closed her eyes, she felt body and spirit realign.

At that moment, she felt a lurching inside. An intruder. Slowly, she opened her eyes. She saw the white turban first, the face obscured by shadow. She stifled a gasp. Mudaliar.

'Why, you are spying on me?'

Her boldness caught him by surprise.

'Spying? I wouldn't call it that.'

'When the temple is closed it is common knowledge that we perform our duties for Shiva's eyes alone.'

'What can be seen by the lord can also be seen by me.'

'Now you are head of the temple, you are also Lord Shiva?'

'Impudent woman.'

'Sir, you do me a great dishonour. I will not talk to you when I am unclad.'

'I will wait for you.'

'I am busy.'

'I could have you thrown out on the street for this.'

'You wouldn't, though, would you?'

'No, I wouldn't.' He took a step towards her.

She folded her arms across her chest.

'Uma was right about you after all.'

She looked up abruptly. He was staring at her, taking all of her in. His teeth were stained red from betel nut and tobacco, his cheeks wide and fleshy.

'Uma *akka*?'

'That you dance like royalty. I want you to perform for me.'

He took a step closer.

'You will perform at a special party for the secretary and Company men.'

She was silent.

Irritation crossed his face. 'Have you lost your voice, Mayambikai?' He said her name slowly, as if tracing his finger down her cheek and neck. 'It has all been arranged. You will be relieved of your duties here.'

'What will you offer me?'

'That's not for you to question. I've arranged everything with Uma.'

'You want me because of my training under the great Palani.' She ran her fingers through her hair. 'Yet you treat me like a common whore who can be bought and sold. Who performs at *nautches* for foreigners like some travelling bard. That's not how I will be treated. What more can you offer me?'

He scratched the back of his head. In his eyes she could see he was calculating her worth. He said nothing.

'It seems you've lost your tongue now.' She paused. 'I'll tell you how it will work. The money you arrange with Uma *akka*. The jewels, with me. As for the lodgings, I want my own quarters and an allowance. I'm not going to bed down in some vermin-infested attic. Nor anywhere close to your wife.' She pulled herself up tall and remembered how Palani would always end her conversations with a dismissive turn of her head. 'Understood?'

She was aware of his gaze on her. He no longer bristled with anger. His eyes were glassy. He gave a curt nod and walked out.

Foolish man, she thought. *The prouder they are, the more stupid.*

When she heard the door swing behind him, Maya went slowly to the pile of her belongings and slipped on the bracelets and anklets. She wrapped the scarf around her head and neck, wiping the perspiration from between her breasts. She did everything with absolute deliberation, as if nothing else in the world mattered. In that way she did not have to think about what had just happened, or what would happen when she went to Mudaliar's. Right now, she wanted to stay with the beauty of her dance. As she cast her eyes around the courtyard, she hoped for a sign that *Amma* was close by, but there was only emptiness. Outside she heard the clanking of the chain as the priest opened the gates. If she hurried to the fish markets, Kuttamma would have saved her the best catch.

Mudaliar set Maya up in his Mylapore property, a two-storey brick building in a walled courtyard. At the age of seventeen, she became a mistress and a housekeeper. Her quarters were not as lavish as those of Palani, but she could come and go as she pleased. The rooms were on the second floor, above the room where Mudaliar met with merchants and Company men, and with a view across the bay.

On the ground floor were a series of small, low-arched storerooms for all the bales of cloth, vats of arrack, chests of tea and other merchandise the *dubash* bought and sold. When trade was going well, he gave her presents: a pair of yellow songbirds in a gilded cage; later, a silk Persian carpet from Delhi, and bolts of burnt-orange silk from Benares.

According to tradition, Uma decided the first night he would come to Maya's quarters. It was not a public affair, but not private either. The whole household knew for days beforehand. She hated that. And she hated that it was Uma who oiled and plaited her hair, and not *Amma* or Auntie. 'Stop jutting out your lower lip. You're making yourself look ugly. No man wants that.'

'Stop fussing around me.'

'Girl, he paid decent money. He expects the goods.'

'I'm not chattel,' she hissed.

'No, that you're not, but you're not Palani *akka* either.'

Maya shook her head, the plait unravelling.

'Now, remember what I said. You want it to last long enough that he's satisfied, but not too long that he does any damage. Lift your hips when you hear his breath quicken—'

But Maya wasn't listening. She felt a quivering run through her and pressed her thighs together.

'I'm going to call for Pari to come. She can plait your hair,' Uma said, crossing her arms. 'Anything to lighten your mood.'

An hour later, Pari was combing Maya's hair. The stiff teeth of the coconut shell had a calming effect, as did her friend's presence.

'It's worse beforehand,' Pari said.

'What if I can't get it hard?'

'That won't be your problem. It will be that you can't get him to stop.'

'How is it with your patron, Dorasami?'

'Good enough.'

'Too old?'

Pari shook her head, breathing through her nostrils. 'Too quick.'

'Quick?'

'It's done and he's asleep.'

She'd only met Dorasami twice, a thin, blustery man, always rushing, always on to the next thing. He'd been *dubash* to three governors already. 'Your patron, he's never satisfied, is he? He's worse than Mudaliar.'

'That's why they're so competitive.'

'They're all competitive. Everyone in the circle is trying to outdo each other.'

Pari squeezed Maya's shoulder. 'That's why it's nice that we aren't rivals. That we have each other.'

They had met through Uma's dance troupe. Pari was the

better singer, rounded and vivacious, her rosebud mouth set in plump cheeks. Maya reached up to Pari's hand and squeezed it.

'You're ready for this, Maya. I can see that.'

She looked up. 'You weren't, were you?'

Pari tipped her chin down. 'No, at thirteen I wasn't. But enough of that. This is your day.'

Pari had been right, Maya thought later, as she squatted over the bucket, douching herself with lemon juice. It's better now it's done. She ran her finger along the lips of her vulva, still tender to touch, and slightly bruised. He'd been careful, though. More than she thought. He'd rubbed oil there first, and on himself. His penis was almost black, as if all the colour of his body was concentrated there. The head was domed, like a helmet, and when she touched it, the effect was instant.

In time she grew to enjoy it. He was diligent in his affection and always in a better mood afterwards. As with everything, he lacked a certain finesse. He was thorough, though, she could give him that.

Once a month he asked her to organise a *sada* and the house thronged with poets, singers, patrons and their courtesans. These events lasted until dawn, earning Maya a reputation as the best hostess in town, and Mudaliar as the *dubash* with formidable largesse.

Maya was standing in the centre of the rooftop terrace, ordering the servants in the final preparations. The *paan* seller was making up coned *ghouris* in one corner, hookah *birdars* were filling the pipes in another. Kovalan and Javard were adding the final touches to the poems they would present that night. Down below Maya could hear the muffled click of dice and the lonely call of a hawker touting his wares. Beyond, constant and comforting, the distant roar of the surf.

'Arrange the cushions on that side, under the awning. Hurry.'

For the third time the bearers rearranged the low divans, draping the brocaded and mirrored cloth across them. She watched the violinist tune up, cradling the instrument like Rao, but never with the same reverence. Pari beckoned her over and she sat down on the wicker stool as her friend finished braiding her hair. She felt Kovalan's besotted gaze follow her own and gave a small smile. Pari tugged at one of the braids.

'*Aiyoo!*'

'I saw that.'

'What?'

'You're lucky your patron's not around.'

'An innocent smile, that's all.'

'It won't get you anywhere.'

'Does it always have to?'

'You of all people should know.'

'Anyway, Mudaliar wouldn't notice. He's too preoccupied these days.'

'With another?'

'No. Not in this town. That, I wouldn't allow.'

'Is he coming tonight?'

'Once he's finished at the Fort. That red-faced secretary always has another errand for him.'

'But business is good?'

'Couldn't be better.' Maya smacked her lips together. 'So busy, I rarely see him.'

Once Pari had finished her hair, Maya allowed herself a moment of quietness before the guests arrived. She watched Kovalan as he uncoiled and recoiled his silk turban. He'd found a rose to match and twirled it absent-mindedly. She knew he was penniless but it never stopped him being elegant. His robes were ivory with a border of flowers at the cuffs and hem. He was of slender build with an oval face and his lips were wide and sensual. Everything a poet should be. Everything Mudaliar was not. *Mudaliar pretends to enjoy the intellectual jousting that poets thrive on*, Maya thought. *In truth, all he cares about is his reputation.*

She sighed. Sometimes she longed to be free of him – free of it all.

Kovalan approached her.

'This poem is for you.'

She said she'd read it later. He waited. When Maya didn't invite him to sit, he pulled up a low stool.

'Is it true that you were taught by the great Palani?'

'How did you know?'

'Mudaliar mentioned it in passing.' He gave a bow. '"Palani, incomparable among her kind." Isn't that what King Pratap said?'

She laughed.

'He could have said the same about you.'

She felt herself redden and looked up to see Pari shaking her head. Maya's eyes dipped and she turned away, careful not to encourage him further. It had crossed her mind more than once to take Kovalan as a lover. But it wasn't worth the risk. First, she needed to become established. Guests started to arrive from five o'clock as the sky folded itself in a soft pinky embrace, bathing the rooftop terrace in golden hues. She and Pari stood at the stone balustrade, watching as the sun sank rapidly into the ocean. As dusk fell and night came, the blackness unfurled like a curtain from above.

By nine o'clock, the women were up dancing. Mudaliar and the other *dubashes* reclined on cushions, pushed back in a wide circle. The men were clapping, waving their hands. All eyes were on the dancer in the centre. *Paan* was offered again, fresh pipes smoked. Maya heard shouts and knocking from below. More guests were arriving. Among them was a *ferenghi* who sat next to Mudaliar.

On the opposite side to the men, she sank into cushions. Her feet ached and she beckoned her maid over. Vedacala's mistress took centre stage: her hips thrusting, her hands spiralling. She was sleek and sinuous, her sari the same green as the tree creepers with white star blossoms that grew up the colonnades. Vedacala sat, open-mouthed.

'He's fallen at her feet,' said Pari, sitting down beside Maya.

'She robs him of every last coin.'

'But how she moves.'

'Like a street girl.'

.'Cruel!'

'She has no class,' said Maya shortly. 'She leaves nothing to the imagination.'

They watched as the woman lowered herself, coiling and grinding downwards as the drumbeat slowed, until she was on her knees, at eye level with her patron. The beat rose again, goading her on, and like a cobra rising out of the basket, she wound her way back up, never pausing for breath. By now, all the men were entranced, their eyes fixed. Vedacala was oblivious to all but the girl.

Mudaliar beckoned Maya across. Reluctantly she extracted her foot from the maid's hands and went to him.

'I want you to meet Jacob Haafner from Holland. I've known him many years.' Mudaliar's eyes were bloodshot, his words starting to slur. 'He is a great admirer of our poetry and once this slut has worn herself out, you and Pari are to perform together.'

Slowly the frenzied beat returned to a moderate tempo.

Maya peered at the foreigner. Accoutred in a burgundy-silk *banian*, his hair flowed loose down his back.

'What would you like to hear?' she asked.

'The most beautiful you know. I want to be reminded of life's wonder.'

'Mr Haafner, such a romantic.' Mudaliar patted the man's arm. 'If only there were more like you, there'd be less war in this sorry world of ours.'

Maya smiled. She wandered over towards Pari and, clasping her hand, pulled her up from the low divan. As the pair took to the floor, the dancers sat down for a rest and the bantering of the poets fell silent. Mudaliar stretched out his legs and Jacob called for another hookah. A hush descended. Maya looked at Pari and nodded. Her rich tones soared, blossoms falling on a hot summer's day, and Maya began to recite the love poems of Ksetrayya, as if all the court of Tanjore were watching.

24

One afternoon in late March, Walter was finishing up in the classroom when the warden beckoned. Schwarz had just returned from a meeting with the governor and was waiting for him in the square opposite.

'At last,' Walter said. 'I have written several times. Have you not received my letters?'

'I'm very busy these days.'

Walter stood, uncertain. 'Have I offended you, Sir?'

'You have offended yourself.'

His mind clouded.

'Let us walk,' said Schwarz, looking around him. The Fort was quiet. It was close to sundown, when the Company men took their daily walk on the Esplanade. Even the birds were silent. 'In Tanjore, it was told to me by people I trust that you had a fascination with the native girls. One in particular. A dancing girl young enough to be your own daughter. That you were intending to solicit her.'

Walter heard the words plainly. The shock of them made him stop. Then a memory reared up from that night at the house of the British Resident. Baldock's pointed questions about relations between the soldiers and local women. The awkward silence around the table when he'd fumbled for the words. And silence from Schwarz ever since.

'Reverend Sutcliffe, I gave you a position of trust, of responsibility. You betrayed that.'

'No, Sir. No. Those are falsehoods. There was a girl who I liked to draw—' He stopped. How could he explain? 'She was a pupil of Rao. I once saw her with her aunt in the encampment of the English soldiers. Her aunt lived with one. There was nothing beyond that. Where did you hear such lies? From whom?'

Schwarz scrutinised him. 'How can I take your word?'

'Ask Rao. You trust him?'

'Rao is no longer in Tanjore. He left not long after the nawab arrived.'

'Jiva. He will speak for me.'

Schwarz said nothing.

'Or is he the one who told you?'

He looked away.

Walter licked his lips. Dry, dusty. 'You're right only about one thing, though. The fact that she would have been about the same age as my daughter.'

Schwarz waited.

'If I have committed a crime, that is the only one. The native girl is called Maya. She was the same age as my daughter Emily would have been, had she lived. She and her mother were killed in a fire. Looking back, I realise that I was not always in a sound state of mind. I thought coming to India would help me forget. I thought it was a way to do penance.' Now the words were coming, he didn't want to stop. 'This is not the best place to confess. But for many years I blamed myself for their deaths. There was a likeness between Emily and this girl Maya. So I started to sketch her. One time I spoke to her when she was with Rao. Any other rumours are false. If I am guilty of anything, it is of letting my grief get in the way of my duties.'

For the first time since he'd met the German, Walter let himself truly look at him. The grey eyes, a wintry sea; the tight lips, a closed heart. He realised that he didn't need the reverend's understanding, any more than he needed his pity.

They stood still for several moments. Then Schwarz looked down.

'I fear I have wrongly accused you.'

Walter waited for an apology. None was forthcoming.

Schwarz continued to walk. 'After you had returned to England, I didn't expect you to come back to Madras.'

'Nor I.' He raised his palms skywards. 'But as soon as I was home, I sold the rectory and took the first ship back. It's here that my destiny lies.'

Each time Schwarz paid a visit, he commented on the progress of the military orphanage and on Walter's 'natural ability to improve the heathen half-castes'. Once he said that he thought Walter had found his calling in life.

Walter began to believe so, too. 'They have helped make the fire within me blaze again,' he told Schwarz. 'I want to let all the dross burn away until I am naked in the eyes of the Lord.'

25

Jacob pressed his knuckles on to the frame of the open window. The wind was warm and within minutes of taking his bath, he was dry. He started to lay out his clothes. English gatherings, how he loathed them. Yet there was no way out of this one. The secretary's party was the best place to find this Captain Sickles and piece together what had happened to his share of tea stolen from the warehouse.

He struggled into the slim-fitting breeches, starched shirt and leather shoes. After months dressed in Dacca muslin *pyjama* and open sandals, he felt an impostor. As he powdered his face, flattening out the tawny shine, he wondered if others would see through him. Only the colour of his hands, as dark as any mulatto's, he couldn't change.

By the time he reached the residence of the secretary, guests were spilling on to the lawn. Waiters in white zigzagged from one side to the other bearing trays above their heads laden with glasses; inside, tables groaned under platters of sweetmeats. With a glass of punch in hand, Jacob scanned the crowds, searching for a familiar face. He caught the eye of a young man, mousy-haired and foppish, wearing a pompadour waistcoat. A pale, chubby fellow was talking to him, but the young man was staring across at Jacob. He looked behind, thinking the gaze must be directed at somebody else. There was no one there.

'Mr Haafner, we meet again.' The Tamil voice rolled low and fast.

'You're looking well,' he said, turning to see Mudaliar, the gold brooch gleaming at the centre of his turban.

The *dubash* surveyed the room. Satisfied, he gestured Jacob towards the garden. 'Business couldn't be better.' He flicked his eyes in the direction of a man well salted by the Orient.

'Who's that?'

'Our host, Mr Scattergood. I'm his chief *dubash*.'

Surprised, Jacob feigned indifference. 'You've come a long way since the first time we met.' He gave a cough. 'After your father's demise.'

'Yes, it's not something I like to dwell on.'

'I'm sure.'

'Those days are behind me. I never think of them.'

'Truly?'

'You know how the Company is. So many die. Those who survive have short memories.'

What does he want? wondered Jacob.

'My past is not well known,' said Mudaliar finally.

'Scattergood doesn't know?'

'He knows a little. But he has his own secrets.'

'You can trust me with yours,' said Jacob.

'You must come to the inauguration of the new temple in Mylapore constructed in my father's memory.'

'That would be an honour.'

'I know how much you appreciate our culture.'

Jacob shot him a look, but Mudaliar was serious. 'You are one of the few.'

As they wandered back across the lawn, Scattergood strode towards them tossing the dregs of his claret on a bush of peach roses. Bacon-faced, his red sagging jowl and small black eyes exuded an arrogance peculiar to the British.

'Mudaliar, a fine display you've laid on.'

'Glad to be of service.' He indicated Jacob. 'This is Mr Jacob Haafner, our esteemed Secretary Bookkeeper of the Dutch East Indies.'

Jacob clicked his heels together, smiling through gritted teeth.

'How's that young Pearce coming along? I see he still dresses like a dandy.' Scattergood tipped his head towards the man wearing a waistcoat like a floral display. 'Making any good deals yet?'

'He's hungry,' said the *dubash*. 'He'll go far.'

Thomas had chosen the pompadour cloth at the market, claiming it was for his sister. The silk seduced him like the body of a woman. Back at the Fort he had found a tailor and ordered a waistcoat with a gold brocade trim and matching buttons. The print was bold, the colours garish – bottle-green, crimson and mauve. He thought it splendid. Sam refused to walk with him when they entered, but the new arrivals – 'the fishing fleet' – with their crinolines still creased from the long journey, flocked to him. Thomas quickly tired of the women's prattle and made his excuses.

On the other side of the reception hall, Maya was helping Pari with her outfit. They were both wearing nine-yard silk saris, pleated and stitched to create loose-fitting pantaloons, and held in place with a low-slung belt. Their necks were draped with gold jewellery and their long plaits entwined with flowers.

'Quickly, what's wrong with you?'

Maya's fingers kept slipping. She pressed hard on the clasp of Pari's choker.

'*Aiyoo*. You hurt me.'

Maya made herself slow down. 'All done.'

'How do I look?' Pari pushed out her chest, her lips stained red.

'As ravenous as Radha on her wedding night.'

She squealed. 'My hair?'

'Just the back needs arranging.'

'Come on, girls, enough fussing.' Uma was bustling among them, fixing a belt here, tidying a strand of hair there. 'I'm coming to you yet, Maya.'

Her stomach was tight. This was the first time she'd performed publicly with the troupe. The first time in front of foreigners. Palani wouldn't approve.

A gong boomed and the dancers assembled. The crisp white house was all angles and sharp corners, the rooms and corridors marching away, out of reach. A silent throng of servants filed in and out of the kitchen. Pari was leading the first dance, then Maya would follow. Mudaliar insisted she perform alone.

They were performing at the far end of a high-ceilinged reception room and Maya waited behind a latticework screen. Most of the guests had hardly noticed Pari give the first recital, one woman clapping her hands over her ears when the musicians struck up. Her eyes combed the room. Her patron was nowhere to be seen.

Two young *ferenghis* hovered near the table of delicacies. One was plump with reddish hair. He piled his plate with sweets, pushing them into his mouth as he talked. His friend, slight and leggy with chiselled features, wrung his hands like a washerwoman squeezing out a wet rag. His gaze flitted around the room, as if he were trying to find a place for himself. Only his short-sleeved jacket was bold: a riot of bougainvillea, palm fronds and purple oleander. Even from this distance, she could see he had an eye for cloth.

Peering through the gaps in the screen, she was back with Palani watching the Tanjore court, and listening to her husky laugh as she pointed at the men below, to see who was climbing the ladder and who was on the way out. These two foreigners barely had their feet on the first rung. Still, Maya continued to watch. Beneath the swagger of the slim one wearing the colourful jacket, there was a certain bafflement and awkwardness she found quite charming.

The two young men turned and walked out towards the garden. Maya pulled her face away from the screen and smoothed out her sari. In the end she'd chosen the gold seamed with scarlet, the same colours Palani had worn at the Big Temple festival. All those years ago, yet she could still see her now in those final ecstatic moments and hear the roar of the adoring crowd. She wondered where she was; if she were still alive. The hurt at her leaving without saying goodbye had faded, replaced by a yearning to see her once more.

But now Maya had to forge a new path for herself. Mudaliar had thrown her a challenge: dance for men like you dance for the gods. She couldn't do that. That would only invite their displeasure and sully the sacredness of her art. Yet she would make the guests notice her. She'd chosen a section from Jayadeva's *Gita Govinda* to perform, and would play the part of Radha, yearning for the return of her beloved Krishna. This would be a dance they would remember. When the signal came, the invocations crossed her lips. As she stepped into the hall, she heard *Amma's* words. *Betray nothing.*

As Jacob and the others walked back into the hall, the drums began to roll.

'Mudaliar, I'm looking for Captain Sickles. Do you know him?' Haafner said, his voice becoming lost in the music

'Sickles? He's just arrived back in port. He's right there.'

Jacob turned to see a whiskered man surrounded by women with large bustles and bonnets.

Scattergood pulled a face. 'Not another damn *nautch*. Haven't we seen enough?'

Jacob looked to see if Mudaliar had heard. The man's eyes were fixed on the lead dancer, the same girl who'd danced on the rooftop terrace. He wondered why she was veiled when her troupe were not. He took another step towards Sickles, reluctant to let the opportunity pass. As he did so, the rapid beat of the *thavil* drums and cymbals grew louder.

To the right of Jacob, Scattergood had half an eye on the *nautch*, and his head tilted towards Sickles. 'I can only keep the tea in the warehouse a week,' he was saying. 'Then you've got to get rid of it.'

'If the winds are on our side, we'll sail down. Otherwise I'll send it overland,' said Sickles.

'Are you sure only the Frenchman was involved?'

The captain hesitated. 'Yes, no one else. I can assure you.'

Before Scattergood could say more, the music drowned out any further conversation.

Thomas was standing at the back when the performance started. After the usual staccato beats that jarred his nerves, the music softened and a violin began accompanying the singer. Then, a single dancer bowed low to the audience. Her hands and feet were stained red and her arms were muscular. Her sari, shot through with gold thread, reflected the light of the flickering torches. Only her mahogany-dark eyes were visible above the veil. The fact he couldn't see the rest of her face drew him closer.

Leaving Sam, he walked up the side to the front. There was something captivating about her. He understood enough to know that she was performing a story of a woman waiting for her lover. She was brushing her hair, holding a mirror and putting on make-up. There was a knock at the door and, through her gestures alone, he could see the man enter. The dancer's eyes flared and her glance beckoned him in. As Thomas stared, his insides became hollow and all other thoughts fled his mind.

Her dance began at the tips of her fingers and moved flame-like through her fingers, wrists, arms, until her entire body undulated. Yet each movement and each expression was done with such precision it was as if she were talking to him. He took a step forward. She was down on one knee now, her face anguished, both arms thrust out with the palms upward, pleading to her lover.

All around, the chatter was falling silent as people turned to watch and her presence filled the hall. He forgot himself, as others did. Her hands caressed the air and her feet moved like quicksilver. The slow tempo quickened and, with a turn, she transformed Phoenix-like from the devoted wife to the scorned woman. He wanted to get closer still, to smell the scent of the perfume that she was surely wearing. He wished she'd look in his direction but her gaze never once met his. Her eyes seemed to be everywhere and nowhere at the same time.

As the performance drew to a close and the music sweetened to a lullaby, a rousing applause filled the hall. He spun round to see the secretary guffawing and raising his glass towards the *dubash* Mudaliar. When Thomas turned back, the dancer had gone.

'First class, Mudaliar,' said Scattergood. 'Haven't seen one for a while that's held my attention. Is this troupe down from Calcutta?'

'No Sir, hand-picked from our own Madras artists.'

'We must get them again. Especially the lead girl. She really has something.' Scattergood snapped his fingers for a refill. 'Perhaps you could introduce her?'

Jacob watched as confusion crossed Mudaliar's face, before he regained his poise. 'That won't be possible, Secretary. She is a *devadasi* and resides at the temple.'

'I thought they were all women of easy virtue. Temple or not.'

'The lower caste may have that reputation. The upper caste have strict rules.'

'None, surely, that can't be bent for the right price?'

'Enquiries can be made, Your Honour,' Mudaliar stammered.

'This, Sir, is why you're the best at the Fort. Arrack from Goa when everyone else has run dry; loosen the nawab's purse strings when cash is needed. Nothing is too hard.' He slapped the *dubash* on the back, winked at Sickles and, chortling quietly under his breath, ambled away.

'If you'll excuse me,' said the captain.

'I was just going myself,' said Jacob. 'Perhaps we could leave together.'

As they approached the door, the young man in the brightly coloured jacket came barging towards them, rubbing his hands together. 'Captain. There you are. I've been trying to get your attention all evening. Don't we have to talk about that tea—'

'Another time, Pearce.' Sickles gave him a withering stare before sweeping out of the door, his tails flapping behind.

Thomas stared after him. 'Such an amenable chap usually.'

'I'm sure,' said Jacob, eager to depart himself.

'I didn't introduce myself. Thomas Pearce. Are you the chap I saw on the *Fazant*?'

'Yes,' he hesitated.

'I thought so. Very impressed I was by your—' he struggled to find the words, '—composure during that squall. Forgive me. I was watching you with my telescope from the Sea Gate. I remember when I first arrived here myself. After that many months at sea, I was desperate to get off the ship. You seemed quite at home, even when the rain came down.'

A smile crept across Jacob's face. The young man wore his naivety like a medal. 'When you've sailed this coast as often as I, and you've spent that many years at sea, another day on the ship makes little difference. For a newcomer arriving, it can feel like the longest day of your life. Now, if you'll excuse me, I must run.'

26

With the arrival of the *Gloria* back in port, Thomas and Sam tripled their earnings overnight. Dressed in his brightly coloured waistcoat, his head shaded by a parasol bearer, Thomas crossed the square in front of the Sea Gate, ignoring the cold stares from the other writers who walked without a parasol. His pace quickened, the bearer struggling to keep up. Only twenty minutes before the bales would be sealed and the next shipment finalised. He had timed it perfectly. Thomas repaid Mudaliar with interest, and a week later, his *dubash* delivered a grey mare to the Fort.

Thomas called the horse Piper. She was a skittish creature with a white dart down the centre of her forehead. After hearing no word from Mudaliar for a month, Thomas decided to pay him a visit at his Mylapore house. He guessed his absence was in reaction to the latest Company decree, which forbade even *dubashes* privileged with a palanquin to wait outside the Fort gates.

After all this time, Thomas still couldn't read the man. A servant showed him upstairs. Mudaliar was standing next to the window. He nodded when Thomas entered. Between them was a wide polished teak table, which doubled as a desk. On one side Mudaliar had his feet parked firmly on the floor. On the other, paced Thomas.

'We need twice as much calico,' Thomas began. 'And better quality.'

'You don't know good cloth from bad,' Mudaliar snorted. 'Last month you went behind my back and paid three times as much for two lousy bales.'

Thomas scowled.

'Did you think I wouldn't find out, Mr Pearce? The Fort is a small place.'

'I wanted to test you.'

'You think I'm cheating you. If you want to succeed, first know your cloth.'

Over the next weeks, Thomas combed the streets of Black Town, haggling with the local merchants. He began to understand the weave, the texture, the weight. As soon as he could, he took off for a few days, scouring the weaver villages in the arable Arcot districts, west of Madras. The artisans there were famed as the most skilled of all. Finally, at the last stall of the monthly market, he found what he was looking for: bolts of eggshell-blue cotton, with a weave so tight that when laid out, it shimmered like a Gainsborough. Thomas bought the lot.

On his return, he didn't go in person to Mudaliar's. He sent a single swatch on a black velvet cushion. When he received a message to come to the house at once, he knew the rules had changed. This time Mudaliar sent a palanquin with scalloped silk curtains and a cohort of peons ran ahead clearing the street. In Mudaliar's lofty room, Thomas was invited to stand on the same side of the table. He accepted the offer of a Spanish cigar and took the same wide stance, his hands loosely held behind his back. Facing the open windows and the ocean, the pair stood in silence, wreaths of blue smoke curling above them.

A week later, Thomas called again. He was shown upstairs, and as he sat there, his gaze was drawn to the right-hand corner of the room, to an area of latticework. Last time, he fancied he'd seen something glinting and a flash of colour. Then, he heard the creak of an upstairs floorboard. Whoever it was trod lightly. The step of a woman. Shoeless, certainly. Stockinged, perhaps. The thought sent a pleasurable chill down his spine. He saw the eyes of the dancer again and her hands caressing the air.

Tired of waiting for Mudaliar, Thomas rose to his feet, leaving the latest swatches of cloth on the table. As he turned, a glint of silver caught his eye. Bending down, he saw a short silver chain with small bells attached to it and slipped it into his pocket. With nothing to rush back for, Thomas decided to take the horse for a ride south, past San Thome. He dug his heels into Piper, who fell into a brisk trot.

After the dusty streets, Thomas followed a rutted track towards the Adyar River. He passed some of the garden mansions owned by the governor and Company directors. Their weekend retreats were glorious – stuccoed Palladian palaces set in gardens with clipped topiaries. A white-throated kingfisher darted among the foliage, its red beak vivid against the deep shades of green. Piper slowed down, struck by the afternoon torpor. Thomas urged her on, ducking under fleshy-leafed creepers and trailing vines.

Further on, they came upon a patch of cleared land. Ahead were wrought-iron gates and a long driveway. He let Piper's reins fall slack. A mauve dragonfly floated past on wings of iridescent filigree. In gold embossed writing, there was a sign on one of the gateposts. Cheyney's Castle. A lick of excitement ran through him. He'd met William Cheyney on the *Gloria*. In fact, he'd saved the man from going overboard after one too many bottles of claret. Thomas gazed up to the newly built classical house with two white turrets. The gardens were laid out in the latest fashion, low hedges interspersed with blocks of colour from circular rose beds. He stood up in the stirrups for a better view, wondering what it would take to own such a mansion.

From behind, he heard the crack of a whip. He turned to see a black polished hackery approaching with two peons running along-side. Suddenly aware that he might be seen as loitering, he jumped off his horse, pulling Piper to one side. The carriage came to a halt.

Through the open window Thomas could see Cheyney asleep, his dove-grey wig askew. Thomas watched, uncertain, then he took a step forward. 'Ahoy there, good Sir.'

The man started.

'Forgive me. I had no idea you lived here. I was out for a leisurely afternoon ride and decided to let the horse lead the way.' Thomas slapped the side of Piper's neck. 'We followed this track and found ourselves on the edge of your estate.' Thomas bowed. 'Mr Pearce at your service once again, Sir.'

The man's nose twitched and he clapped his hands. Straight away a peon opened the carriage door. Out stepped a stout, blowsy-faced man in breeches. His cheeks were puffy, his eyelids heavy.

'Mr Pearce?'

'From the *Gloria*, Sir.'

'The *Gloria*?' His words were thick and rusty, as if buried under the weight of his tongue. He tottered and the peon jumped to take his arm. 'I remember. You're damned lucky I do, young man. Or else I'd have had you shot for trespassing.' He held up his right hand, his two fingers sticking out, his thumb cocked. 'Hah, hah. Only joking.'

Two more servants appeared. Cheyney turned, as if swatting a fly.

'Get along. I don't need three of you to help me.' He turned and climbed back into the carriage.

Thomas hesitated, unsure, and tugged on Piper's reins.

'Where the devil do you think you're going?' Cheyney shouted. 'I haven't forgotten that time off the coast of the Isle of France. Wouldn't be here today if it wasn't for you. I don't think I ever repaid your kindness. The least I can do is offer you a glass. Get in and let Klipper take your horse to the stables; she looks like she could do with a drink too.' He waved his hand towards a gilt-frocked man. 'He's my head bearer.'

They pulled up at the steps to the front porch. Gripping a wooden cane with a fluted silver handle, Cheyney took each step one at a time and Thomas followed behind. At the top was a hexagonal entrance hall. In the centre was a French *jardinière* cascading with white lilies. Following Cheyney's lead, Thomas took off his shoes.

His stockings had been darned a dozen times and reeked of meat hung too long on the skewer. Cheyney gave him a sidelong glance but said nothing. A statue of the portly elephant god Ganesha stood on one side of the door, and above there was a simple wooden crucifix. At Thomas's expression, Cheyney quipped, 'Got to keep the gods happy. All of 'em.'

They entered a high-ceilinged drawing room, hung with muted oils of English country life and crossed the parquet floor to French glass doors, which opened onto a wide verandah running around both sides and the back of the house. Terracotta pots lined the walkway, brimming with salmon-pink geraniums. Straight away Thomas could feel the coolness from the Adyar River.

'You've seen the rose garden?' Cheyney was saying, as he pulled out a weed. 'I have the best in town. But here, on the verandah, is where I enjoy myself. Anything grows in this country. Succulents mixed with forget-me-nots, Cape strawberries and orchids.' He looked over his shoulder. 'Come along, Mr Pearce, I can see you're not a gardener.'

He shook his head. 'Thomas, please.'

'Right you are. I may as well give you the grand tour. I don't get many visitors these days.'

Thomas followed, making appropriate noises about the plants. The warm tiles underneath were sunbaked and comforting. In stockings, he felt he could glide. If he'd been alone he would have done just that: glided as if he were ice-skating on the Avon. The verandah at the back of the house looked over the river. Thomas walked across to the stone balustrade, jumping back with a small yelp. In the sun, the tiles were scalding.

Cheyney laughed. 'You're not the first. One just wants to rush up to get closer to the view. To dive into it.'

In front of Thomas was a palette of sky and space and a smooth, wide expanse of water. The flatness of each layer merged with the next, creating a mirage of reflections. It was only the dense bank of green on the opposite side of the river that gave the view perspective. To the left, the Adyar widened to its mouth and Thomas could just see the silhouette of a ship on the horizon. They continued round to the other side of the house.

'Our bedroom is over there,' Cheyney pointed. 'The kitchen, scullery and what have you, down there. I have a cold room underneath and sometimes we're lucky enough to have ice.'

There were steps down to a shady paved courtyard with a fountain. In the centre was a carved statue of a woman. Her nose was pierced with a ring and jewels adorned her ears. Her breasts were pert, her waist narrow. One foot was planted, the other pointed; one arm was stretched out in front, the other rested naturally on her hip.

When Thomas came closer, he saw she was an Indian dancer with anklets and a slew of bracelets up both arms. He remembered the silver chain he'd found and pulled it out of his pocket. It had the same small bells as those carved around the dancer's ankle on the statue. He thought again of the footstep he'd heard that morning. Desire shot through him.

'Where did you get her from?' Thomas asked.

'Tanjore.'

'She looks like she could do a pirouette right there.'

'That's why I chose her. Bloody heavy to cart back, though. She weighs half a ton.'

The lawn led down to the river, where two rowing boats were tied up.

'Go boating much?' Thomas asked.

'Not now. More when the children were younger.'

'Children?'

Cheyney continued, rushing his words. 'The river looks as placid as a millpond, but there are strong currents. You have to pick your day.'

On the opposite bank there were some young boys swimming. Their whoops and cries reminded Thomas of that hot summer's day back home when his father had thrown him into the river to teach him to swim. He couldn't have been more than ten years old. The smack of icy water and the fear as the weed wrapped around his ankles, pulling him down. Those long terrifying minutes underneath, before his uncle had dived in. As he stared out, his mood darkened.

'Where's home?' asked Cheyney.

'I was just thinking of it,' said Thomas.

'I could tell. It's a particular look.'

'Bristol,' he said, trying to snuff out the unwanted memory.

A servant appeared. 'I'll show you the roof later,' Cheyney said. 'Right now, it's time for a house special. Crushed ice, lime and arrack punch.'

Later that afternoon, when they went inside, Thomas noticed how the front of the house was furnished with European rosewood card tables and chintz curtains, and how at the back, it became oriental. Rattan chairs and a chaise replaced upright settles; a swing seat rocked on the back verandah. *Truly the lifestyle of an English nabob*, he thought. *And what a life it is, too.*

Flocks of servants milled around: plump women in saris, bewhiskered men in an odd medley of *lungis* and feathered hats. A dozen gardeners speckled the lawns, sweeping leaves and pruning the orchard of guava, mango, banana, jackfruit and papaya. One young lad's sole job was to keep the crows at bay with his slingshot. Thomas guessed there were over seventy staff, kept in line by Klipper, the head bearer.

'It's another job, managing them all,' said Cheyney, when they reached the top of the circular staircase to the flat roof, his breath coming in short bursts. 'They're always squabbling and fighting.'

'Why have them all then?' Thomas asked, as he watched a young girl tearing across the grass chased by the cook.

'They each have their own job. It's not like back home where the mopsqueezer will muck in for the kitchen maid. Here, you give a task to one and he won't do it because it's below his caste. You give it to the next and they pass it down the line.' He shook his head, leaning on his walking stick. 'It takes some getting used to.'

In the corner of the garden was a small building with a monkey sitting on the roof. A woman came out dressed in a fine sari, her black hair coiled on her head. When she saw Cheyney, she shook her fist in the air. He stared down at her, his eyes thoughtful. He seemed to be about to say something and then changed his mind, turning towards the back of the house and the view over the river.

'I never get tired of this view,' he said.

'Is that why you decided to build here, rather than on Choultry Plain?'

He nodded. 'I came out here not long after arriving. About your age, I guess, and it was all jungle then. Well, much of it still is. You can see a few other white roofs at the mouth of the river.'

As they started to walk back across the roof, a woman's singing broke the silence. It was reedy and piercing, and wavered as if trying to find its way along a dark passage. Then the notes gathered strength and carried high over the treetops, raining down on them. It was the woman standing in the garden, her arms akimbo. Cheyney stopped, his shoulders hunching tight. Under his breath, he murmured, 'I knew she'd come round eventually. They always do.'

Over the ensuing years, Thomas would become a regular visitor at Cheyney's. His Sundays were taken up with long lunches, boating trips, picnics and afternoons spent around the card table. Sometimes Cheyney had other guests, and Thomas met current and former councillors, and shiny-booted officers and their dull, tittering wives. On one occasion William Hickey visited from Calcutta, regaling the party with his scurrilous tales of Reverend Tally-ho. On another, Governor-General Warren Hastings sermonised for hours on the sublime quality of the Hindoo sacred texts. But Thomas preferred it when he and Cheyney were alone, playing backgammon or whist, and sinking into a companionable silence with the placid Adyar River flowing by.

'Don't you ever get lonely?' Thomas asked one day, when they were sitting on the verandah.

Cheyney jerked his head towards the garden. 'I have my *bibi*, Prema. She keeps wonderful company.'

'*Bibi*?'

'My mistress.'

'You've never introduced me.'

'I'm not like William Hickey. He parades his *bibi* like she's a circus act.'

Thomas gave him a blank stare.

'You probably don't know Hickey well enough, but he's got a reputation for boring his friends with his tales of his beloved mistress, Jemdanee. He's always writing about her, getting her portrait painted and what have you.' He swallowed the last of his drink and rang the bell for another. 'I prefer to keep Prema to myself. It doesn't go down well in certain circles. Anyway, she doesn't approve of the drinking and smoking and gaming. She has her life and I have mine.' He paused, sucking noisily on a slice of lime. 'And most of the time we're happy.'

Thomas wanted to know more about Prema and wondered if she was the mother of Cheyney's children. He'd never forgotten hearing her sing, the first time he came to the house when he and Cheyney were standing on the roof. He thought again of the dancer. He wondered if she was Mudaliar's mistress and if the natives shared their women around. Not the wives, although he'd heard the Moors did that. But the concubines.

Here, it seemed anything could be bought and sold. Only the other day, a woman had offered him two rupees for her child in the bazaar. He couldn't tell if it was a boy or a girl, its body was so skeletal. Worse than anything he'd ever seen. The gin drunks on Bristol quayside were brimming with life compared to these poor wretches.

Thomas looked across at Cheyney and was about to ask. But the last arrack had been one too many and the old man's eyes were sinking, his cheeks pickled. Suddenly, his head jerked up. 'Got to get my affairs in order. Best to be prepared,' Cheyney said. 'You never know.'

Not long after, Thomas arrived at Cheyney's unannounced. While waiting for him, Thomas took a slow stroll around the garden. His thoughts flitted like swallows at dusk over the river. He stopped and lifted his head. In front of him, by a tree, stood Prema, motionless.

He jumped back. 'I'm sorry, I didn't see you there.'

'You must be Thomas.' Her words were precise, her vowels curling on the tip of her tongue. 'He's away on business.'

'Oh?'

'Back at the weekend.'

He stood, unsure.

'Shall we take a walk?' she said, bending down every so often to snap off a fading blossom from the rose bushes. The white jasmine tressed in her hair was fresh and the perfume washed over him.

'He's very fond of you.' She stooped to pick up a frangipani flower. 'I can see why.'

Thomas waited.

'How old are you?'

'Twenty.'

'The same age as Benjamin would have been.' Her vowels elided to a whisper.

'Benjamin?'

She paused. 'Our firstborn.'

He stopped. 'How many do you have?'

'I still say three. Only two remain.'

'I'm sorry. I didn't know.'

'He never talks about them?'

Thomas was quiet. 'Once.'

'I find it hard to believe.' She shook her head.

'Where are the other two?'

'England. Where else?' Her mouth puckered and she stared down at the flower in her hand, her distress plain to see. 'I'll let him know you called,' she said.

As he watched her walk away, Thomas could see she was a proud woman, and yet he felt pity for her. Cheyney's words came back to him. *They all come round in the end.* Thomas wasn't sure he believed that and, as he turned to go, he couldn't shake the feeling of unease.

27

For over a year, Maya put up with the servants Mudaliar provided – the grumbling watchman who mistreated his wife; the gossiping house girl from his village who filched her bangles. Worst, though, was Ramesh, with his bent nose and guttural voice. He'd taken an instant dislike to her. Anyone who came between him and his master was a threat.

It wasn't enough to have Pari there during the evening *sadas*, she needed an ally in the house itself, her own maid. She'd never forgotten the fierce loyalty Vimala had for Palani. She was brushing her hair when she heard Mudaliar enter. She watched him, unwinding his turban. Already the signs of excess were showing: his stomach, hard and round like a watermelon, the pallor of his skin.

He bent towards her and let his moustache graze the side of her neck. She had to stop herself from flinching.

'Maya, my beautiful princess. Every time I get close to you, you get further away.'

She feigned a dry laugh. *Business must be good*, she thought, holding the mirror close and turning her face from side to side. Red veins were threading through her eyes.

'Rub my feet, will you. They need your special touch.'

He lay down on the straw-filled mattress, and she sat at the other end on a low stool. The heels were abrasive, with the texture of unpolished granite.

'Talk to me. You never say much these days.'

'You're not here, that's why,' she said.

'I'm here now.'

There was the subject of pin money. She'd been wanting to raise it for a while. Then, the issue of the maid. She had a girl called Nila from Cheranaadu picked out. She moved one hand around to the top of the foot where it was softer and then with the other, dug her nails in, carving a valley up the centre of the sole. He jerked back ever so slightly. She alternated between her nails and a light touch with the tips of her fingers, between hard and soft strokes. Then she slowed down to let his breathing settle.

'Where did you learn how to do this?'

'Tanjore court.'

'On the prince?' Alarm sounded in his voice.

'No. Palani *akka* taught me. I've been taught by the best.'

'I can see.'

'Then I should be treated as such. Every mistress must have her own maid.'

'You have a maid.'

'That house girl? She's casting spells on me. She's giving me sleepless nights.'

'Be quiet. She's a simple woman from the village.'

'Send her back then, to the cowshed where she belongs.'

'I have too many expenses as it is. Three houses to upkeep. My family. You. The inauguration of the temple.'

'So, what's the cost of one more maid?'

'Why do you have to keep asking?'

'You wanted me because of my beauty. Now, I must maintain it. Palani *akka* had a dozen maids. I'm asking for one.'

'Palani, this. Palani, that. You're not at the palace now, girl. You have a tailor at your beck and call. You host the *sadas*. None of that is enough?'

She continued to rub his foot, her irritation brewing.

'Of course, my lord.'

'Then?'

'You said I would receive some money.'

'Why do you need money? You have everything you want.'

'To make donations to the temple.'

'I do that.'

'You do it for yourself.' She looked at him as she continued to trail her fingers across the bridge of his foot. His eyes narrowed a fraction.

'I'm not about to bargain with you.' He pulled his foot away from her grasp.

'I want my due, Sir.'

'To spend on what?'

'As I like.'

'On who?'

'On no one.'

'I've seen the way Kovalan looks at you. I've seen how his eyes linger.'

'Sir, please.'

'I know he has a big debt and what will happen if he doesn't pay it by the end of the month.' He leaned forward, his face close to hers. 'He's asked you, hasn't he? Asked you to help out in return for small favours.'

'Nothing of the sort.'

'Well, why the urgency? Why now?'

She jutted out her bottom lip, attempting a sob. 'To make an offering for my mother's passing at the temple.' She felt humiliated telling him the real reason – to clear her debts with Uma for good. She was tired of the old woman's surreptitious messages, more urgent as each month passed.

He was watching her. 'You're a good actress, Maya. But those aren't real tears.'

'My lord, you think I want the money to help some poor poet out of a fix?' She threw back her head, her laughter crackling like mustard seeds in hot *ghee*. 'Then you do not know me. Why would I waste my money on that? Or my talent?'

She leaned forward, pushing him back down on the bed, letting her hair fall around her face. 'Why would I do that when I have you?' She ran her finger over his lips, tugging on his ear lobe. 'It's not as if you can't afford it.'

'At the end of the month. You'll get it then.'

A week later, her maid Nila arrived. She had arched eyebrows and a narrow nose, and was lighter skinned than the other servants, who resented her preferential treatment. Every day when she *champued* Maya, she chanted, her hands moving in long flowing strokes. Maya was left vibrating, her mind empty. The maid washed her down with a coarse herbal powder mixed with water, the colour of cow dung, the texture of silk. Then she took a muslin cloth and rubbed her dry. Straight away, Maya was back in the courtyard on West Main Road and *Amma* was drying her after her morning bath. Except when Nila did it, there were no harsh words, no jabs in the ribs to turn around – only a caring touch.

On a quiet day at the end of December, as the year 1775 drew to a close, Thomas was in the exchange when a message came to join Mudaliar at the silk bazaar in Mylapore. He was shown down a dimly lit passageway and wondered if he'd come to the right place. Then, it widened into a huge warehouse filled with long trestle tables and piles and piles of cloth. Natives in long *lungis* walked up and down the aisles. Sunlight penetrated the narrow windows, illuminating the billows of dust that tickled his throat, and setting the silks ablaze.

Oh, my, why hadn't he come here before? What use was cotton, when you could buy silk with gilded dragonfly wings embroidered into the cloth? Take that stall there, not one choice of purple for Elsie, but a dozen: lilac and mauve, lavender and mulberry, Windsor violet, aubergine and amethyst.

'I'd like to buy a couple of yards for my sister,' he said, putting out a hand to steady himself.

'You are unwell?' Mudaliar clicked his fingers. 'Tea!'

A young lad holding a tray above his head weaved through the crowd towards them. Mudaliar gave him a small earthenware cup, the size of an eggcup. The tea was sweet and creamy, and he gulped it down.

'It's the choice,' Thomas said simply. 'I thought I was beginning to know the cloth market. Then you see this. I need some air. Shall we take a walk?'

It was cooler outside. While the palanquin was sent on ahead, two peons stayed close by. He was surprised what a stir Mudaliar's presence caused – like a squire back home walking through his estate. Shopkeepers made deep bows, one man almost bent double. Thomas noticed that nobody else approached him directly. Even the maimed and the lame kept their distance.

'You've always lived here?'

'For the past ten years.'

'You are well known.'

'I'm a third-generation *dubash*. My father held a position of great honour here. I built that *pagoda* in his memory.' He pointed to a granite temple on the side of the road. Cut into the main door was a smaller sea-green door studded with carved flowers. Mudaliar paused, rummaging around under the folds of his pleated *lungi* and pulled out a large key.

'Have you been inside one of our *pagodas*?'

Thomas shook his head.

'You're not allowed into the inner sanctum, but I can show you the courtyard.'

He handed the key to a peon, who slid it into the lock and hoisted open the padlock. Thomas took off his hat and stepped inside. The smell rushed at him – greasy, overpowering.

The *dubash* was standing in front of a pillar, his palms pressed together at his chest, eyes closed. As Thomas approached, he saw that carved into the pillar was the figure of a man with an uncanny likeness to Mudaliar. He was dressed in identical flowing robes, except the chest was bare. He shared the same powerful jawline and wide forehead, and the same hardness in the eyes.

'My father,' said Mudaliar, with some difficulty. He touched his right index finger to his lips, forehead and heart, and then, bending forward, placed both hands over the carved feet and whispered under his breath. The gesture was elegant and emanated from the depths of the man's soul. Thomas looked away, trying to imagine such filial loyalty to his own father. He couldn't picture it. *These Hindoos may be soft*, he thought, *yet they have a reverence we lack.*

He walked over to a table of flickering lamps. A movement in the shadows caught his eye. It was a woman crossing the courtyard dressed in diaphanous silk. Her arms were bedecked with gold bangles, her hair plaited. As she entered the shrine opposite, he saw she was wearing a hooped nose-ring, and on her right cheek was a prominent beauty spot. As he strained to see more, he sensed Mudaliar's gaze and turned to find him staring at him. The familiar hardness had settled around his jawline. He searched Mudaliar's face but it was impassive.

'We should go. They will open the temple soon.'

'Thank you for showing me,' he hesitated. 'You must be, um—' He searched for the right word. 'Greatly proud of your father.'

Mudaliar stayed silent. As they reached the doorway, he said, 'He did great work and achieved much in his lifetime. But he was wronged by the Company and suffered a lonely death.' His voice was ragged, the tone accusatory. 'I, the eldest son, could not light the funeral pyre of my own father. There is no greater dishonour.'

Thomas was taken aback. 'I had no idea.'

'This temple serves to resurrect his name. Perhaps you could join us, Mr Pearce, for its inauguration.'

'Gladly,' he said, thinking only of the girl. Aside from her nose ring, she was an image of loveliness.

The date for the inauguration of the temple was the week after Pongal, in January 1776. Two days beforehand, Maya began the sixteen adornments. When the tailor arrived, laying out the saris on the divan, she gasped. Mudaliar had excelled himself and this time she could forgive his bad mood. Before her were the most expensive silks on offer. As she squatted, Maya half-closed her eyes and saw the colours merging into a shimmering patchwork. Then, she saw the one she wanted. She snapped her fingers and pointed. It was deep purple, with dragonfly wings and mother-of-pearl beads sewn into the border.

On the morning of the celebrations, she took her bath before dawn. Then she was massaged with perfumed oil. She'd made the mix herself, spending hours in the Mughal Perfumery until she'd found the right combination: four drops of attar of rose, three of sandalwood, one of frankincense, two of frangipani, three of clove.

As she was being dressed, Pari came to braid her hair.

'You won, then.' She glanced towards the maid, who was opening the shutters.

'Eventually. It came at a cost, though. These days Mudaliar is hard work. He loses his temper at the slightest trigger.'

'The stress of inviting half the Fort to the celebrations. The priests are unhappy and say *ferenghis* shouldn't be allowed,' Pari said.

'It's all too much.'

'No good complaining. Sit still, let me get your parting straight.'

Maya held the mirror away from her face. 'Perfect.'

'You'll have to train the maid.'

'No. Let me keep one job for you, otherwise when will we be able to gossip?'

Pari laughed and tugged her hair. 'You look magnificent. Now go.'

At midday, Maya ascended the steps of the *howda* and parted the curtains. When she gave the nod, the *mahout* prodded the elephant with a sharp metal spike. As the animal got laboriously to its feet, its trunk curling upwards, she swung wildly, left to right. With its giant ears flapping, the beast began to walk through the narrow streets. Ahead was Mudaliar, and either side, guardsmen on horses were holding his flag in red, white and black.

The elephant slowed down as the road narrowed and the crowds gathered. When it halted, Maya leaned forward to rub its tough scaly skin, the coarse hairs like fine wire. She looked down. That was a mistake. The ground seemed so far away and her stomach dropped. She heard her name and saw Uma waving, giving an exaggerated bow. Maya ignored her and kept looking ahead. As the curtains flapped in the wind, she saw she was level with roofs and could see inside people's attics. *I'm here*, she thought. *I'm royalty. I've made it.*

'This way, mister.' The peon showed Thomas to his seat. He walked past the crowds to the front, where he sat under an awning on one of the dozen chairs reserved for foreigners. The heat sapped his enthusiasm and the smell of incense and body odours invaded his mind. He let the din roll over him – the beating of drums and shrieking of that awful oboe-like instrument. He felt a tap on his arm and was surprised to see the Dutchman take the seat next to him. He hadn't seen him since the party.

'Just made it in time,' Jacob said.

A procession of elephants was approaching. Each had intricate painted designs on its forehead and ears. The first and last beasts had elegant litters on their backs. At the front, Mudaliar sat cross-legged on the bull elephant, dressed in fine cream muslin, waving to the crowd. Some people leapt devilishly, catcalling and clapping.

'I had no idea he was held in such respect,' said Thomas.

'He's the *dharmakarta*, the head of the temple. That's the highest honour, bar royalty, that can be bestowed on a man here.'

'Bestowed or bought?' Thomas asked.

'In his case, probably the latter.'

'You've known him a long time?'

'I knew Mudaliar when he was a young apprentice.' He paused. 'How times change.'

Behind the elephant was a buffalo with painted horns and a large bell clanking around its neck. Then a dozen dancing girls, sheathed in red silk, gold sashes cinching their waists. They moved in a V-formation and each carried a gilded plate with an oil lamp in the centre. Thomas looked at the lead dancer but she had none of the royal presence of the woman he'd seen at the party. He craned his neck, looking at the others. None had her eyes. After the pantomime of the dancers, came priests. Then a wooden litter, carried on the shoulders of eight men, with a bronze deity bedecked with orange cloth and ribbons. They walked like pallbearers, their faces solemn. Following the main male deity were two more idols: a female figure and a child.

When the idols passed, the crowds surged forward. One girl was flopping and leaping, her head falling from side to side like a rag doll's, her mouth open and eyes lost to the world. As she convulsed – was it with ecstasy, or horror? Thomas wasn't sure. Four peons stepped forward to hold her back. They could not restrain her; she was possessed. The crowd thundered. He wished he hadn't come – the heat, the flies – and he needed to piss. Ahead were more elephants. Thomas looked up and in the last of the lumbering beasts, sitting on a litter surrounded by blush-coloured curtains, Thomas could make out a single figure. A woman. The curtains around her parted in a gust of wind. It was the dancer, the woman who had pierced his days and haunted his nights.

As the procession approached the temple, Maya saw the *ferenghis* sitting under an awning, being fanned with peacock feathers. Mudaliar was waving to the crowd surging towards him, then backing away as the elephant chose that moment to dump a pile of steaming manure. The foreigners turned their faces in disgust. Maya smiled to herself.

As she drew closer, she saw the young leggy foreigner who came to visit Mudaliar, next to Jacob. She'd spied on the Englishman through the latticework. He was staring at her. In spite of herself, in spite of all she'd learned about the danger of meeting a stranger's eyes – and revealing the truth in her heart – she stared back. For a few seconds she met his gaze. Then she lurched forward as the elephant bent one front leg, then the other. With as much decorum as she could muster, she stretched out her hand to a waiting attendant, and descended to the ground, following the procession into the temple.

Two hours later, when the ceremonies had finished, the dancers walked back out of the inner shrine.

'The deity stays there now,' Jacob was saying, 'and the performances begin.'

At the back of the temple complex, in a pillared hall next to an open-air tank, a large black, red and white tent had been erected. Cushions were laid out and musicians were tuning up. Bending under the arches, Thomas followed Jacob's lead and sat on the far left. He was glad that he'd decided to wear his pompadour silk waistcoat. The Dutchman had taken it a step further. His trousers were in the Calcutta style, wide in the leg and narrow at the ankle. 'They're loose and airy, unlike the dreadful things I wore in Amsterdam.'

'Is that where you're from?'

Jacob nodded.

In front of them was Scattergood. Wearing long black woollen socks, a checked gingham shirt, jacket and wig, his reddened face was a picture of endurance.

As Mudaliar crossed the courtyard towards them, he seemed to have grown in stature. Thomas looked across at Scattergood, whose eyes were smouldering. *He'll bring the dubash down a peg*, Thomas thought. *Scattergood loathes an upstart.* He watched Mudaliar greet the other *dubashes,* who bowed and scraped before him. All of a sudden, the secretary rose to his feet, and waving his hands, gestured towards the door. For a moment Thomas could see Mudaliar was trying to stop him, but then he dipped his head, escorting the secretary out.

Musicians came and went; trays of dainty sweetmeats, made from milk and sugar, were brought. A singer strutted into the hall and began to perform to a flute. Jacob was nodding his head and mouthing the words.

'How do you know them?' Thomas asked.

'I've seen this one before.'

Jacob passed him the coiled pipe of a silver hookah.

'Just inhale, do you?'

'First time?'

He nodded.

'Yes, watch for the sting at the back of the throat.'

Thomas sucked hard, too hard, triggering a coughing fit. He leaned forward and Jacob clapped him on the back. He washed his mouth out and tried again, this time more gently. He hadn't liked to ask what was in the mixture, but straight away he started to sink, his mind orbiting around the hall. He sucked again. His body sank deeper into the cushions, his feet into the floor. His bones liquefied, his thoughts loosened. He found himself smiling and nodding at Jacob, but wasn't sure why, or if Jacob had said anything to him. The room began to turn, or was it the dancers? Time passed more slowly.

The hookah-bearer refilled the bowl with another bud of opium mixed with rosewater, sugar and tobacco.

Thomas inhaled again, and then closed his eyes. That was a mistake. He was on a spinning top, like the one he had as a child that skedaddled over the shiny parlour floor. He twitched, violently enough to jolt his head up. He looked across at Jacob but was relieved to see the Dutchman looking the other way. His mouth was tense, his teeth jittery. He wasn't sure if he was hot or cold. He stared at Mudaliar. He'd never seen him smile before; the man looked puffed up, a right royal peacock.

'Jacob . . .' Thomas heard himself say, and then his voice petered out. He thought he might vomit. His mouth and lips were dry, a bitter taste at the back of his palate. Yet his body felt delicious, like it did after that warm bath and *champu* in Surat, when they'd laid him on the marble slab and rubbed him with oil.

Jacob leaned forward. 'These songs are beautiful love poems. They could rival your Milton.'

'Truly?' He tried to sound intelligent.

'The Tamils are renowned poets.'

Thomas glanced up in surprise. 'You can read Tamil?'

'Yes. It's a coded language, a doorway to an ancient past. Drink?' He lifted his glass. Thomas lifted his.

'I've come to love this country more than my own,' Jacob continued, his eyes wistful.

Thomas had never heard a European talk with such admiration about the place. He looked across at Jacob. He was a man of wit, you could see that, a man of the world. The creases on his forehead were like the folded parchment of a yellowing atlas. He wanted him to keep talking; it soothed him. 'How long have you been here?'

'Madras?'

'India.'

'I first came when I was fourteen. I stayed some years and then went back to Holland. I couldn't bear the cold winters or my mother's nagging. I wanted a life at sea and I've been here ever since, sailed dozens of times up the Coromandel coast.' He leaned forward. 'But I've never seen a dancer bedazzle like her. She has the wildness of the Orissi women from Jagannath and the poise of a royal courtesan.' He indicated towards the door where a woman was entering. On the border of her sari were the fine golden wings of dragonflies. They seemed to whir in the deepening light.

It was her. Dropping the tail of her sari, which she'd used to cover her face, she stepped into the centre. Thomas inhaled on the hookah again. Bonhomie diffused like bubbles through him. His legs felt light; his senses alert. Everyone's eyes were fixed on the dancer. Her skin was cinnamon, her eyes deep mahogany. As she came closer he caught a whiff of her perfume. Rose was there, lemon too, and underneath, something spicy, like gingerbread or mulled wine – he couldn't place it. He inhaled again, closing his eyes.

Maya pressed her hands in prayer, lifting them to the heavens, to the brass statue on the shrine beside her, and to Mudaliar. Then, to mother earth. Poised, she stood in perfect balance, waiting for the signal from the percussionist. The bell-like cymbal began at a medium tempo, matching her crisp movements. The paving stones were warm from the day's sun and the atmosphere charged from the priests' rituals. She could feel the deity next to her, the power of Shiva. For weeks she'd been preparing herself, fasting, praying, practising her dance. Her body glowed. She sensed her inner fire, her *tapas*, coursing through her limbs as she settled into the repetitive beat. The temple itself, freshly dedicated, seemed to respond, the columns wrapping themselves around her. As her feet moved faster and faster, the percussionist was twitching and jerking, nodding his head and crying out. She heard the thump and slap of her soles and felt the swish of silk between her thighs. Her mind suddenly emptied as the drumbeat slowed and Pari began to sing.

This was Maya's cue to begin the central piece of the recital, where the heroine yearns for her beloved. Now, she became Parvati, consort to Shiva. With one hand against her heart, she let her fingers trail down the side of her face, feeling his touch. With the rippling of her hips, she let ecstasy surge through her. She could see Shiva clearly, and as she embodied his essence, and felt his pleasure, the audience felt it too. There was a thickening around her, a sinking into bliss, gasps from the crowd, whistles and catcalls. Without altering the steady gaze of her eyes, she saw Mudaliar reduced to tears. And the foreigner, he was licking his lips, his body taut with desire.

Thomas felt himself harden. He leaned forward, wanting to absorb everything about her. The shining dark mole on her right cheek and tilt of her modest chin. Her curved hairline and forehead dashed with vermilion. There were birds in her dance and he saw their flight as she slipped from one sequence to the next. Her body created geometrical shapes, but her face did something else entirely. It described the entire world and everything in it. Her limbs expressed love with such longing he could barely watch. She arched her neck, pushed up her breasts and with her arms wide, seemed to encircle the temple, and everyone in it.

He sucked again on the hookah and blew the smoke in her direction. It was oafish but he felt reckless and did it again. All this time she'd never looked at him but she was close now and the smoke made her nose wrinkle. He ignored the murmurings behind and Mudaliar's incessant clapping to the side. The music became deafening. They were reaching the end now, surely. It had been going on for hours. He wanted to strip off, lie down on the cushions and demand that she come to him. He would have her tonight. As he thought that, he looked up and she levelled him with her eyes.

Thomas turned to see Mudaliar swaying, tears coursing down his cheeks. He'd never seen the man betray a shred of emotion, and here he was, a jibbering wreck. Within moments, the dancer bent down and offered the *dubash* a silver tray with parcels of *paan* leaves; his fingers lingered on hers, his shoulders shaking. Thomas was jolted back into his skin.

The offering of the *paan* signalled that the festivities were over. He pushed himself up and, nodding thanks to Mudaliar, made his way over the sea of cushions to find his shoes, blinking in the late afternoon sunlight. He noticed a sparrow pecking at crumbs around a pedestal and followed the column upwards. At the top, phantasmagorical figures with bulging eyes stared down. He'd forgotten he was in a temple. His mouth was dry.

'Thomas, travelling back to the Fort?'

He'd forgotten about Jacob, too. 'I think I'll take a walk,' he said, and left.

Out on the street, Thomas headed towards the sea. His fogginess lifted, leaving him with a pleasant sense of ease. For the first time, it seemed, he began to observe his surroundings. His eyes met those of the passers-by and he noticed piles of crimson and green scaly fruits spread out on the pavement. A cameleer was coaxing his beast through the market stalls. There was a small shrine of the red demon goddess next to a stall selling copper cooking pots.

Out of the corner of his eye, he noticed the entrance to a tiny shop, Mughal Perfumery. He opened the heavy door, the bell clanging above.

A woody citrus scent rushed up Thomas's nostrils, strong enough to taste. Inside were shelves lined with rows of small cut-glass bottles filled with floral attars. In front stood an old man, who introduced himself as Mahomet from the Moghul's court. His fingers were stained brown, green and red, the nails long and yellowing.

'This is the queen of them all.' He reached up to the top shelf and brought down a small square bottle, pulled out the glass stopper and pushed it under Thomas's nose. 'Used by Emperor Akbar himself.'

At three *pagodas* a bottle, it was exorbitant. But it was the closest Thomas could get to the perfume of the dancer. He'd always had an unusually acute sense of smell. Both a blessing and a bane, he'd lost friends and business because of it.

After dabbing a spot on his wrists and the centre of his chest, he opened the door on to the street. His whole body vibrated like a tuning fork. His vision was clearer, his senses more alert.

He kept walking. It dawned on him that nothing could prepare you for the intensity of the light in India, or the suffocation of the heat. It was hard to remember what cold was like, or the perpetual darkness of home. How free he was here. Back in Bristol, he was always one of many. In Madras, he was one of the few. He no longer wanted to play by the rules. Here, he could make the rules. He thought of the dancer again. He wanted to follow the scent of that woman until he could smother himself with her. From the way she'd looked at him, even for that instant, she wanted it too.

When Thomas arrived at the beach, he stared out across the foam-flecked waves, at the blueness, bright and sharp. What was it Cheyney had said? *'It makes you just want to dive in.'* That's what he wanted right now. To dive into it all.

28

By eight o'clock in the morning, Walter's high-collared shirt clung to his neck. Usually a draught through the open sides of the shed relieved the worst of the heat, but today, everything was still. The ocean becalmed, the children silent. Of the fifty boys sitting there, dressed in long trousers and blue calico shirts, a dozen were asleep. When lessons ended at midday, he instructed the warden to grant them an extra hour of rest. Then he ordered his bearers to take him in his palanquin to George Town. A councillor had succumbed the previous week to smallpox and his personal effects would be auctioned at lunchtime.

Inside the parlour, Walter began flicking through a pile of books. He felt someone's gaze on him and turned to see Thomas Pearce standing nearby. Since he'd last seen him, he'd lost some of the boyish sheen.

'Anything I should be reading, Reverend?'

'*Pilgrim's Progress.*'

'I could do with something lighter. How about this?' He picked up *Travels in the Mughal Empire*. 'Have you read it?'

'As a boy.'

The room was filling up.

'We should take a seat,' Thomas said. 'Close to the front.'

Several members of the council came over to shake Walter's hand. He made a point of personally thanking one officer who'd made a recent generous donation.

'You've moved, I hear,' Thomas said.

'On James Street now. You should drop by for tea.'

Bidding began. Scattergood took the carved rosewood bed. Thomas put in a bid for the silk jackets but was too slow. By the time they came to the sundry items, most people had wandered off to the polo match on the other side of the square. The auctioneer mopped his brow as he held up a drawer of mixed pieces.

'A *pagoda* for the lot.'

'I'll take it,' said Thomas.

'I'll give you two,' said Walter.

'Three.'

'Five.'

Thomas raised his palms. 'I had no idea a reverend could be so aggressive. You must have learned a thing or two since I first saw you at the exchange.'

'I'm getting a taste for it now.'

As Thomas made to stand up, Walter put his hand on the man's arm. 'Pearce, we've had our disagreements in the past. But, I'm wondering if you could—'

'Show you the ropes?'

'Yes.'

'All for a good cause.'

'Exactly.'

'I'm sure we can come to some arrangement.'

When Walter was back in his lodgings, he tipped the contents of the drawer on to the card table. There was cutlery, a leather snuff pouch and a knife with an ivory handle. But it was the sketchbook and tin of watercolours that had caught his eye. He crossed over to his easel in the corner, facing the bay window. He placed the sketchbook next to the half-finished drawing of the girl in lime-green running among the temple arches. It was her eyes that still eluded him.

Shortly afterwards, a note arrived. The writing was unfamiliar and he hoped it wasn't an urgent message to conduct last rites.

It's been too long. I heard from Reverend Schwarz you were stationed at the Fort. I will be staying in Black Town until further notice. Ask for me at the paan seller next to the flower bazaar. Yours, Rao.

By mid-afternoon, he and Rao were travelling in a chaise and pair along the Esplanade. Walter thought it worth the extravagance. Rao's stoop had worsened and the hardness of the intervening years was etched in the spidery lines on his face.

'I thought I'd never see you again,' Walter said.

'I wasn't sure I'd return. I've been all over on pilgrimage. You read about these holy places in the *Ramayana*. But to experience them – to bathe in the waters of the River Ganga herself.' He sighed. 'I can die content now.'

'You've been here a while?'

He nodded.

'Without letting me know.'

'I wasn't sure, Reverend, how you'd receive me.'

'I'm delighted you're back.' He leaned forward and motioned the driver to return to the Fort. 'I'd like to show you my work here.'

They alighted in front of the military orphanage.

'This shed is for the boys. The girls are housed over there.' He pointed to some flimsy huts. 'Once we have more donations, I'll provide shelter for them, too.'

'What do you teach them? To read and write?'

'No, they learn only what is needed for their station in life. The boys learn basic crafts; the girls are taught needlework. But I drill them for work. I instil Christian values into them.' He looked at Rao. 'Their native mothers teach them nothing; their English fathers are intoxicated. After several years with me, they become an asset to society.'

In front of them was a line of young girls dressed in chequered cotton dresses, waiting for their clothes to be inspected. The church-warden paced up and down, slapping his palm with a stick. One girl, her hair pulled tight into pigtails, looked up at Walter. The fear in her eyes was unmistakeable.

'An asset to your society, not ours,' Rao said, with a small shrug.

'Yes, I grant you that. But here they are given a chance. Their numbers will only rise as more and more English arrive, yet the Company isn't willing to take responsibility for them. If things carry on as they are, there will be entire communities of these half-castes, forever stranded. Denied a place by their own and by us.'

Rao was quiet on the way back to Black Town.

'You did as much as you could, those last days in Tanjore,' he said at last.

'What do you mean?'

'I found out after you'd left that you helped get the bodies of Sita and her two children out of the well.'

Walter didn't reply.

'I can see it affected you deeply,' Rao continued.

Walter frowned at the unwelcome image. These days he rarely thought about it. Most affecting had been the small hands of the girl, the nails broken and the skin ripped where she'd scraped at the wall of the well. Then, the face of the straw-haired soldier; his gash of a mouth, eyes and veins bulging, the scorn in his eyes. Walter found himself chewing his bottom lip. He stared at the street scenes passing by.

'You did the best you could,' Rao said again.

'The soldier got away scot-free. He could do it again. These children you saw today. They won't suffer the same fate.' His voice was louder than he intended.

They both fell silent.

'Did you hear any word from the girl?'

'Maya? Nothing. They went north. That's all I know.'

Two weeks later, Thomas saw Walter at the exchange. Merchants surrounding the reverend were all talking at once. When his eyes came to rest on Thomas, a wan smile lit up Walter's face and he beckoned him over.

'You're just the person I was hoping to see. Anything I should know about?'

Leaving the natives to argue among themselves, Thomas led him to the best bales of Andhra calico and showed him the piece goods that would earn him a profit. An hour later, having made his purchases, and given Thomas a slice of the commission, Walter said, 'Between you and me, we should do this again.'

At the Fort there was a time for buying, a time for selling, and a long wait in between. After months of inertia when the monsoon and the trade winds drove the ships off course, the bay was full once again. Merchants and *dubashes* jostled for space and the frenzy around the Sea Gate was building to a fever pitch. All morning Thomas and Sam went through the details of the latest deal.

'Thomas, this is a sound ship. The captain's sober; his crew are old hands.'

'I think we should stick with the *Gloria*. She did well for us last time.'

'We can't wait.'

'Give her till the end of October.'

'You can. I am going with Captain Tiler.'

'It's too much of a gamble,' Thomas said, pressing the telescope to his eye as he scanned the bay. Tiler's ship, the *Elizabeth*, was listing in the calm sea.

'What? You're happy to just lose it at the gaming table?'

'Sam, you're a man of fortune. If I put in a thousand *pagodas* and the *Elizabeth* goes down, these past three years will have been for nothing.'

'You can get a thousand now?'

'Mudaliar finally agreed to lend me eight hundred and fifty *pagodas*. I can stump up the rest if I don't send anything home this year.'

'She'll make it. I have a good feeling about her.'

He wished he didn't trust Sam's judgement more than his own. He thought of Mama's letter by his bed. She was still paying off the cost of his thirty-pound passage out to India. If this gamble worked, he'd be able to settle his debts.

'So?' Sam said.

'I'll put in the lot.'

'Good man.'

Mudaliar was sitting at the table, his eyes vacant. It was past mid-night and the accounts lay unfinished. However much he bought and sold, it was never enough. Each month, there were more bills to pay. The flickering oil lamp made the figures dance across the page. His thoughts skittered just as fast. The rot had set in after the inauguration of the temple. The cost had drained his coffers and he'd fallen out of favour with Scattergood, losing the Company account. *That man, like Saturn, plagues me so.*

He thought of his father, how he'd lost everything. All those years, a loyal *dubash*. All those years in service to Murray. Then the son-of-a-bitch had cashed in twelve thousand *pagodas* of forged bonds and escaped to England with the money. *And Father, you paid the price*, Mudaliar said softly into the night, the familiar anger rising through him. *You served the sentence and died a broken man.*

He couldn't let the same happen to him. If business didn't improve soon, he'd be forced to sell the Mylapore property and auction its contents to pay his debts.

Each morning, he should start by reading the holy texts; he'd be better for it. Take yesterday, he might have restrained himself from hitting Maya. Or not so hard. She'd taken minutes to get up. It wasn't the image he wanted to cultivate.

Under his breath, he began chanting the mantra given by the astrologer to weaken his enemies. They were stabbing him from all directions. The merchants were swindling him and Pearce was hiding something. Mudaliar stared down at the accounts. The numbers in front of him – they held the answers to all man's problems. But he kept flitting back to Pearce, to when he'd seen him outside the Mughal Perfumery, his face flushed, his eyes shining.

1777

29

Maya was upstairs on the verandah when she heard Pari's voice from below. She leaned over the balustrade and beckoned her up.

'Is he here?' she said when she arrived.

Maya shook her head.

'Not back yet?'

'Back and gone again.'

'So, come out to the temple. Kovalan and Javard will be there.'

'He might return at any moment.' The fear made her weak inside.

'And?'

Uncertainty crossed Maya's face; she should confide in her friend. Turning aside, she busied herself with the darning in her hand. Her palms were clammy and it was hard to hold – twice it nearly slid away.

'What's wrong? You haven't been yourself of late,' Pari said.

'Just tired.'

'How can you be tired when your patron is away?'

Maya hesitated. She felt ashamed of what was happening to her – by what she was allowing to happen. This horrible whiny voice told her that she should accept the fact that sometimes Mudaliar flew into a rage and hit her, that he was the richest *dubash* in Mylapore and she should make the best of it.

'Maya, you're not—' Pari was staring.

'Pregnant? No. Nothing like that.'

Ten minutes later, they were sitting by the *ghat* in the temple. Gnats buzzed above the waterlilies in the still water. Kovalan sat closer than he would usually dare and Maya didn't stop him. Her mind was vacant, her spirit listless.

'I heard some news about Palani *akka* when I was journeying south.'

She roused herself. 'From whom?'

'A courtier from the palace.'

If it wasn't for the longing to see Palani again, she sometimes wondered if she hadn't imagined it all.

'She left Tanjore on the night the English marched through the defences. They slaughtered the guards and passed through the breach. Somehow she found a way through. After she'd gone, her parrot went berserk and escaped from his cage, flying around the corridors of the palace shrieking. Furious, the prince ordered the bird's head to be cut off. Not long after, the palace fell.'

'Vikku!' she cried.

Kovalan stopped.

'Go on.'

'The rumours are that Palani *akka* is still alive. She's been seen dressed in orange, her hair matted, carrying a staff. She's taken a vow of silence and speaks to no one.'

She looked at him, trying to take it in. Then very softly, she said, 'Thank you. Your news gives me hope.'

Later that evening, as she and Pari walked back together, her friend linked her arm through Maya's. 'Tell me the truth. He's not treating you well, is he?'

'How do you know?'

'The way you press yourself into corners.'

Maya slowed her pace.

'When did it start?'

'After the inauguration of the temple he lost much of his business. That secretary is punishing Mudaliar for doing so well. And he started to take it out on me.'

'There are no excuses, Maya. You can do better.'

'He'll leave again. I'll have some peace then.'

Pari shook her head. 'Go on pilgrimage.'

'Why are you saying that?'

'Isn't it you who told me that the body never lies? I can read your body, not your mind. Your fire is almost out.' She turned Maya towards her, holding both her hands, then kissed the side of her cheek. 'Just go.'

'I couldn't do it alone. Can't you come?'

'You're never alone on pilgrimage.'

She thought of what Kovalan had told her about Palani. She tried to picture herself, on the road. Alone. Fear widened her eyes. 'He'd come and find me.'

'Just go.'

The following week, Mudaliar arrived back from Benares. Another failed deal, another furious outburst. That night as she lay beneath him and heard him panting, she knew she could have been any of them: his wife in the village, the woman he saw in Vellore. She turned her head to one side and focused on the golden hoops swinging in his ear lobes. She thought of the Englishman again, the intensity of his gaze. She should never have returned it. He was creeping under her skin and invading her mind. She had to stop thinking of him; stop before she did something she'd regret. The panting was louder now, the breath coming in short bursts. Mudaliar was nearly there; his eyes were glazed. It would be over soon.

Some hours later, Maya lay on the wooden swing on the flat roof. The sea breezes breathed over her and she felt her stomach expand and relax. She kicked her foot against the balustrade and began to rock. The house was still. Dogs howled in the distance and a single cock crowed. Maya nestled deeper into the cushions, but there was no warmth there except her own.

To distract herself she began counting the fishing boats, their lanterns twinkling in the bay. Below she heard the scraping of the bolt and the sound of the heavy door opening. She stepped off the swing and padded downstairs. Snores punctured the air. Mudaliar lay on his back, mouth open. She slipped past the bed, picking up a shawl, and crept out of the room. On shutting the door she put her ear to the wood. The volley of snores continued.

Once out of the house, she covered her head and face with a chequered indigo-and-red shawl, the sort a weaver woman might wear and began to walk. In the distance, fishing boats were coming to shore with their catch and up ahead, women were selling fish. They were rough, their faces shiny from the salt and sea. Maya knew she shouldn't go alone here and she could send the maid, but she liked the sense of space the beach gave her. Mudaliar would be angry if he found out. Her skin crawled at the thought of him. Her pace quickened.

As she passed the baskets filled with fish, one of the women, shrieking an obscenity, launched herself at her neighbour. A man waded in and pulled one of them out, whacking her smartly across the face. Maya cringed.

When she saw Kuttamma, Maya waved. She enjoyed talking to the tall woman from Tanjore, who always knew the neighbourhood gossip. A foreigner was bargaining with her. He crossed his arms, pointing to one of the other women beckoning him. Kuttamma shrugged. She knew she had the better fish.

Maya slowed down. *It was him.* The Englishman who called at the house. Up closer, she saw his eyes were green not brown, and he was taller than she'd remembered, his face pinker. She wondered if he would recognise her dressed like this. She wished he would.

She watched to see if the fisherwoman would back down. With one hand on her hip, Kuttamma dangled a mackerel in the other. When the Englishman handed over the coins, she jerked her thumb out to sea.

'Ship?' Kuttamma said.

'You speak English?' he said.

'A little.'

'No, the Fort.' He turned towards Maya and she looked away.

'You speak English too?'

Maya pulled the shawl tighter.

'Shame.' He took a step closer.

Panicking, she cast her eyes downwards.

'You. What's your name?'

She shook her head.

'*Sahib*, take your fish and go.' Kuttamma waved dismissively.

He hesitated. Maya felt his eyes on her. For a moment she imagined looking up and smiling, letting her body naturally follow the tilt of her heart. It would change everything. She knew that. But she couldn't. Not here. Not in public. The consequences would be – she thought of Mudaliar – *hell*.

'I'll be back.' He turned, waving at Kuttamma.

Maya never lifted her eyes from the ground.

'You know him?' the fisherwoman asked.

'Mudaliar deals with him.'

'The foreigner is doing well for himself. Every time I see him, new clothes. Always the nails are clipped, clean and polished. He's not bad.' Kuttamma jutted her pelvis forward with a playful smile.

'Don't they all smell?'

'I've seen worse.'

'What would your husband say if he could hear you?'

Kuttamma wiped her hands on her apron, leaving a trail of fish scales and slime. 'He does his work, he drinks his toddy, he sleeps. Sometimes he beats me. Tell me, *akka,* what have I got to lose by noticing another? I've heard they are better to their women.'

Maya snorted. 'Men are men. The colour of their skin makes little difference. When they drink they are all beasts.' She bought her fish. 'Does he come every day?'

'No. Once a month at best. Why?'

She shrugged and started to walk back. The mackerel was awkward to carry and Maya held it upside down by its tail, wondering if the *ferenghi* was doing the same. She couldn't tell how old he was, early twenties probably. Her stomach tightened. By the time she reached the house gate, she was breathless.

After leaving the fish with the maid, Maya slipped out of her shabby clothes into an aqua sari with coral beading. An angry voice carried from below and she heard the crack of Mudaliar's hand against the table. She forced herself to walk downstairs, her feet dragging towards the last step.

He was standing in front of the table, tobacco smoke rising above his head.

'Forgive me my lord. I couldn't sleep so I went to buy fish.'

The knot in the centre of his forehead grew, filling his face with darkness.

'What woman are you to leave me and go alone to the fish markets? You have servants for this.' He covered the space between them in one stride, pressing her against the wall, sniffing her like a dog. His breath was sour. 'What are you hiding?'

'Smell my hands.' She pushed her fingers towards him. 'I've nothing to hide.'

He pinned one hand around her neck, smashing her head against the wall. 'If you go there again, I'll throw you out.' With the other hand, he grabbed her wrist, twisting it behind her back.

She refused to be cowed.

'If I find out you've seen Kovalan, I'll beat you again.'

She stood her ground.

'Will you lower your eyes or not, woman?'

She felt the blows as if they were happening to another. She stood them for as long as she could before he flung her to the side. 'Get out, you worthless whore.'

Maya had ignored all the others, but Uma's latest message sounded desperate. All the debts were cleared; she owed the *tai* nothing. Yet still the old woman persisted. She said she was going to Tanjore and she had to see Maya before she left. As Maya looked through her saris, she deliberately chose the dark plum-coloured one. It hid the bruises better. She held it against her. It had been a gift from Mudaliar in the early days. She tried to remember how it was back then; when he still called her 'my beautiful princess'. Why had no one ever warned her that a relationship could sour as quickly as buttermilk in the noonday sun?

As she fixed the gold necklace around her neck, an image formed in her mind. She saw herself standing under the banyan tree on West Main Road with yellow glass beads in her hands. Approaching her was a mob of angry men waving sticks and hammering on the door of the house. It caught her by surprise, as if floating up from a long-forgotten well.

Uma was sitting on a wall near the tank, her hair grey, her body run to fat.

'You are alone?'

Maya nodded, sitting several paces away from her.

'Smell, do I?' She tried to smile. 'If you think it's money I want, you're wrong.'

'An apology would be nice.'

'Apology for what, girl? You've done well for yourself.' She cast her eyes over Maya's sari and necklace. 'Your mother would be proud.'

Maya's eyes were hard.

'None of them are perfect.' Uma shrugged. 'You can always leave him. He doesn't lock you at night with a chain.'

Tiny droplets of sweat were gathering at the corner of Uma's nostrils and she wiped them away with the back of her arm.

'What do you want?'

Uma put her hand inside her bodice and pulled out a cloth purse. She handed it to Maya. Inside was a gold ring with a faceted emerald in the centre. She frowned, turning it over. 'Where did you get this?'

'Your mother.'

'I don't understand. This is Sita's ring. Mother always said that Auntie took it with her when she fled Tanjore.'

'There's never a good time to say these things. Your mother should have told you years ago.'

When Uma had finished telling her everything, Maya looked down to see her hands gripping the ledge of the wall. She thought that if she were to let go, she would fall. Uma's face blurred. Her lips were moving but Maya could not follow the words.

'He killed them all,' she was saying. 'Your mother arrived too late. That crow man, the *ferenghi*, he was there too. He helped arrange the funerals. It was me who paid for them.'

'Why didn't *Amma* tell me herself?' She thought of her mother's last days, crying out her sister's name. And then that brief, precious moment when the delirium had lifted and she'd turned to face her daughter, reaching out her hand. 'Accept all that comes, it is the will of the goddess. Bend to her, and your life will be easier.'

'She blamed herself, Maya. She never got over it.'

'What happened to the English soldier?'

She gave a half-shrug. 'Nobody knows.'

They sat for several minutes. A small lizard darted across the stones in front of them.

'I think I always knew. Somewhere deep inside, I knew Auntie was never coming back.' Maya stared across to the pink lotus flowers in the water. 'Poor *Amma*. Seeing it all. Carrying it all those years to protect me.' She rested her hands in her lap.

Uma rubbed the bridge of her nose, her face ashen. *She's not long for this world*, Maya thought, with a twinge of – pity? Sadness? She reached out to touch the old woman's arm. 'Thank you for keeping the ring. You didn't have to.'

She jerked her head up. 'I made sure you paid for it.'

'Of course you did. It always comes down to money in the end.'

'Always.'

A few days later, Thomas called at the Mylapore house. He was surprised when he was shown into the empty room. When a deal was close at hand, Mudaliar was usually there. He sat down to wait.

In the bedroom above, Maya was stirring. When she opened her eyes, pain jabbed into the back of her skull. The egg-sized swelling had subsided, but the side of her head throbbed. She pulled out her mirror and examined her face. The bruising was more vivid today, a blackish-blue and purple stain ringed her left eye. She should never have asked Mudaliar for money.

From below she heard the squeak of a chair along the wooden floor. She frowned. At this time of day the servants would be sleeping off their lunch. No one else was home. She wrapped her shawl around her head and went downstairs, creeping along the verandah. Inside the room opposite, the young foreigner was sitting, gazing towards the open window.

Alarmed, she retreated, her heart racing. Then, she edged forward towards the open door. He turned, startled and stood up.

'I'm waiting for my *dubash*.' His Tamil was stilted.

She looked around, checking no one was about, and then went inside.

They stood awkwardly, the table between them.

'Do you speak English?' he asked, at last.

'A little.'

'I'm Thomas.' He stretched out his hand, only to bring it sharply down. *Fool*, he thought. 'What's your name?'

She hesitated. 'Mayambikai. Or Maya.'

'Where is Mudaliar?'

'Gone to his village.'

She found herself looking at Thomas's hands to see if the nails were clean and clipped. Kuttamma was right: the nails were polished. She felt naked standing there in her blouse and cotton skirt, the shawl barely hiding her bruises. She could not bring herself to meet his gaze. From the prickling sensation she felt between her breasts, she knew well enough that his eyes were sweeping over her body, lingering. Her hand travelled to the ring – Sita's ring – that she'd hung on her neck-lace. She took a deep breath. The servants would wake soon.

'My lord is sorry to have missed you. He asked that you leave three *pagodas* for the cloth.'

Surprise crossed his face. That would barely buy a few yards. 'Is that enough?'

'Five would be better.'

Thomas noticed how the mole on her right cheek was in line with her mouth, and how, in a way he couldn't explain, it held the essence of her face. Women back home would be envious of such a beauty spot. Sliding his hand into his pocket, he imagined how it would feel to trace his finger over it, and her lips, and kiss the nape of her neck. He inhaled. Beneath her floral perfume was musk, more bitter than he'd expected, and beneath that – he stopped. It was unmistakeable. The smell of fear.

She could see a dozen thoughts running through his mind. Yet lightness burst through her. A flicker of joy and a racing heart.

After all this time, here was the dancer standing before him and Thomas could think of nothing to say. He didn't believe for one moment that Mudaliar had asked for the money but he didn't care. He pulled out five coins and laid them on the table, darting her a sly look. 'Be sure they reach him.'

'Of course.'

'When is he expected back?'

'I don't know.' As she shook her head, her scarf slipped. She pushed it back, hurriedly, but not before Thomas had seen the bruising and congealed blood around her left temple. He was jolted. The pile of gold coins gleamed on the teak table.

To be seen talking to her would make matters worse. The servants could be listening. Mudaliar might return at any moment. *Mudaliar, the brute.* Thomas couldn't stop himself. 'I've been thinking about you. Ever since I first saw you. Your perfume—' He was being reckless. 'Why don't you come with me?'

She gave a small bow. 'You must go.'

'Leave him.'

'I can't.'

'Think about it.'

A voice in her head told her to be careful, that foreigners couldn't be trusted. *Look what happened to Auntie. Get him out, now.* Before he could say another word she turned, crossing to the door and calling out, her voice brittle. 'Maid, escort the gentleman out. Right away.'

When the front gate slammed shut behind him, Maya slipped back into the room and scooped up the coins, remembering how the Englishman had slid his hand into his tight breeches; how he had not taken his eyes off her when he slapped them on the table. She had thought they would make a noise, but at the last minute he laid them down gently. He had seen everything about her in that moment. She had laid herself bare.

She began to walk around the table now, trailing her right hand along the edge, feeling the slip and grip of the varnish. In her left hand, she held the *pagodas*. She saw the large bare room for what it was. There was nothing special here; nothing worth staying for.

She opened up her left palm. The gold coins were as thin as a *dosa*. She looked closer. Each one bore an imprint of a five-pointed star. She squeezed them tight. As she walked back upstairs, relief spread through her. With the evening still ahead, she could prepare everything and be gone by first light.

30

That night Maya dreamed of flying. She was carrying a bag that contained a sari, a *paan* box and a parrot with red-and-blue tail feathers like those of Vikku. As she flew, she met people from her past and they called out to her to stop. She told them she couldn't because someone was waiting.

When she woke she still carried that curious weightlessness of flight. Rays of golden light suffused the room. Outside, she heard the cracking of whips on bullocks' leathery backsides. The sweepers were sweeping and the pedlars were hawking. The watchman was clearing his throat and the cook was stoking the kitchen fire. Soon the maid would knock on her door. She knelt down and began to pray. 'Please, Mother Goddess, guide me. Show me the way.'

She wondered if the Englishman had given her the money out of pity, or lust, or both. If he were also the sort of man who would hit his woman.

She wanted to get up, but couldn't move. A scared voice inside told her that staying with Mudaliar was safer than striking out alone. He'd hunt her down and denounce her. Her stomach churned and cramped.

Then, she smelt a gust of fresh lime. She saw herself in the front room of the house on West Main Road while *Amma* and Uma made pickle. Fragments of the conversation came back. The crow man.

Sahib Sutt-sutt. It was years since she'd thought of him. She had no idea why she should think of him now.

She managed to stand; her legs were soft and woolly. So as not to raise suspicion, she had packed only what she could carry in her blue cloth bag, including some of the gold jewellery that she'd hidden from Mudaliar. Then she remembered her mother's box. The wheedling voice told her if she'd forgotten about *Amma's* precious things, then she was unfit to travel, and should stay. Opening the cupboard, she dug around for the box.

Inside was her mother's copy of the *Panchangam* and the brown notebook given to her by the *sahib*. A musty perfume of camphor escaped: the smell of her mother. She shut the box to try and keep the smell inside. All she wanted was to be held, her forehead stroked.

She had to leave, now. Now, before she changed her mind again. She left some money hidden for her maid, packed her mother's box into her bag and crept downstairs and out the back door, and into the morning crowds thronging the bazaar.

It was the beginning of the hot season, when mangoes were at their sweetest; when everyone slept outside, anything to find a whisper of a sea breeze. The time when saffron-robed sadhus appeared like apparitions, and people closed their shops and walked away from their mundane lives to renew their faith and go on pilgrimage.

As Maya ducked between the stalls, the crushing feeling inside began to lift. She came to rest in a strip of shade on the opposite side of the road to the temple.

A group of women were standing in front of the sea-green door. Most were her age, dressed in inexpensive patterned cotton saris, bangles jangling. Their palms were stained red-brown, their eyes kohl-darkened: a travelling troupe of *devadasis*. With them was an older, stout woman, who rapped a bamboo staff on the ground to keep order.

One stood apart from the others. Her skin was fair, her braided hair wound around her head, her clothes dusky pink. As if sensing Maya's gaze, the girl looked across and smiled at her. With one hand, she beckoned. With the other, she made the gesture of a bird in flight.

Maya looked at the woman in charge, doubtless the *tai*. She thought of Uma and shook her head.

A bullock cart half-filled with pilgrims was approaching. The girl beckoned again. Everywhere noise: the *tai* shouting at the driver, pilgrims clapping, a flute playing, and then chiming through it all, this high enchanting voice.

Maya heard the words quite clearly – as if the girl were standing next to her.

The tai is not so bad. She listens to me. She will not hurt you. Come, join us.

No, mouthed Maya, baffled that she could hear the girl above all the other noise.

As the group climbed aboard, the girl was still beckoning. Again Maya heard the voice.

There is still time. Act now.

But Maya only watched as the cart rumbled away in a cloud of dust. Then she stood there, her forehead drawn. She wondered why the girl's face was so familiar. She thought of her prayer that morning and wondered if the goddess was telling her to join the troupe, even though they were low-caste *sudras*.

Maya suddenly realised how thirsty she was. Crossing the road, she was about to go inside the temple when she saw Mudaliar's assistant, Ramesh, arguing with the priest. She shrank behind the door and went back on to the street.

Another bullock cart of pilgrims was coming and this time she yelled at the driver to stop. When he shouted that he was full, she ignored him. Grasping at the forest of hands that reached down for hers, she found a place between two older women. As the cart juddered from left to right heading out of the city, she covered her face with her shawl and soon fell into a dreamless sleep.

Two days later, the bullock cart ground to a halt. The two older women next to her stirred.

'Everyone out,' said the driver.

'Where are we?'

'At the *choultry* on the crossroads. South towards Pondicherry; west, Arcot.'

'We can't stay here,' said one woman. 'This is bandit country.'

'The beasts are lame,' the driver said.

Grumbling, the women started to walk to the travellers' rest house among a grove of coconuts.

'I'm going to stretch my legs,' Maya said. 'Would you keep me a place inside?'

'Yes, girl, but don't be long.'

Outside the *choultry* was a pump and Maya washed the grime from her face. It was still an hour before dusk and the breeze rustling through the tamarind trees felt delicious on her wet cheeks. She walked towards the sacred grove outside the village. In the centre of the clearing was a stone shrine housing a statue of the Mother Goddess. With no defined features or limbs, she was a symbol of the void roughly cast into form. Maya looked for something to lay on the statue. No flowers or lamp. What could she offer? *Only myself.*

The mournful call of a koel sounded in the treetops. As Maya stood opposite the statue, her hands in prayer, she felt the rhythm of the dance through her bare soles. She sensed the shapeless statue take form, rising up to become Durga, the warrior goddess, sword held high. As she breathed in Durga's strength, she felt the *darshan* – the exchange between the goddess in stone and her own breath of life.

Then the sound of men's voices cut through her in mid-flight. Thugs. Bandits. Kicking the leaves over where she'd been dancing, she squeezed herself behind the statue. The voices grew louder. Two men, maybe more.

'Are you sure she went this way? This place looks disused.' Ramesh's voice was distinct, guttural and as hard-boned as the man.

'I don't know. This was the general direction.'

'Maybe into the village?'

'What did the old women say?'

She pressed her nails into the palms of her hands to stop them shaking.

'That she'd be back soon.'

'We should wait for her at the *choultry* then.'

Maya heard a leaf falling and scraping on the roof. The dust was making her want to sneeze. She had a sudden urge to pee. Something scuttled nearby and she drew her knees closer. Cobras liked dark shrines, so did rats. Her mind flitted to the Englishman. Maybe he'd been the one who told Ramesh. She was stupid to have asked him for money. Outside, laughter. One of the men cleared his throat and spat.

'You go to the village. Offer a *pagoda* to anyone who's seen her.'

'She won't get far. If the thugs don't find her, the wolves will. These paw prints are fresh.'

'Fool. Mudaliar won't give us anything if we bring back a corpse.'

'I know. He wants to decide her punishment himself.'

After the men left, Maya stayed behind the shrine. The sounds of the forest settled down. As night fell, she heard rustling leaves and breaking twigs, then a cry from a single koel. In the distance jackals were barking, but closer, much closer, there was a larger animal sniffing around. More than one. In her mind's eye, she saw the yellow eyes and bared teeth; she smelt the foul carnivorous breath. She could never outrun them. They'd tear her to death, limb by limb. Then, would the villager who found her still get a *pagoda*? Her jewellery, they'd strip; her body, leave for the maggots.

She forced her mind to slow down. She had to take control. Better the wolves than return to Mudaliar. Better the wilderness than enslavement.

Better to choose, Maya thought, *who I will be enslaved to*.

Her mind was turning in on itself. The inside of her mouth was dry, her body numb. Akkaamahadevi's words came back to her. The saint who'd wandered naked, who'd tamed the animals and birds and fought off men with wandering hands. She remembered those last frantic weeks with Palani. When she had to stand and recite Akkamahadevi's poems to the 'Lord white as jasmine'. She'd never understood why. It was the only time her guru had lost her temper with her. Now she understood. It was Palani's way of telling her that she was leaving. That she had to follow her own path.

Maya thought again about choice. Hadn't the choice already been made for her: by her birth, her mother, by the *muttirai* on her upper arm? If so, at least she could claim it as her own. The goddess may be the one who would lift her up. It was Shiva, seared on her body, who would carry her to the other side.

She shuffled out from behind the statue. All around, the eyes of wolves pierced the darkness. Through the trees was the leader of the pack, with silvery fur and nose low to the ground. She began to walk. It was moonlit and the path through the forest opened up. The koel left her at the edge of the grove, and an owl took its place, swooping from branch to branch. She wasn't sure if the wolves were following her, or she was following them. As the night slipped away, so did they. By dawn, Maya had reached the edge of the forest and was greeted by a flaming red sun. Ahead lay the road south.

3 1

It was busy at the Sea Gate. A fleet had arrived bringing tea from Canton and spices from Batavia. Thomas was hoping the *Elizabeth*, now several months overdue, was among them. He was the first to see her captain in the crowds, his face thinner than when they'd waved him off, his clothes dishevelled.

'Sir.' Thomas waved.

The captain stared from Thomas to Sam.

'Captain Tiler.'

'I couldn't save her.'

Thomas felt a void open up inside. 'You lost everything?'

'All the cargo?' Sam said.

'Everything lost. Everything shivered.' He turned, his mouth twitching. 'For flaming Christ, look to more than your purses. All my crew went down. All this—' he gestured to the cloth, '—you can replace.'

Thomas wasn't to be pushed aside. 'We need to know the facts, Sir. I'm sorry for your losses, but it was our money that was under contract.'

The captain pulled out a snuff bag. Rubbing several strands of baccy between his thumb and forefinger, he lodged the ball up his left nostril. Thomas looked at Sam, who cautioned him with his eyes to wait. Then came a gurgly, rackety sound, and the man's eyes watered.

'The ship was insured?' Sam said, feebly.

'No.'

Vertigo overtook Thomas. He glanced at Sam, a faint redness on his cheeks the only sign of his anguish.

'I'm sorry, gentlemen. A full report will be made and submitted to the secretary. Good day to you both.'

'Fuck, Sam, you told me the boat was insured.'

'Tiler said it was.'

Thomas needed to keep hold of himself. Thinking about spilled milk was like coming home to a house empty of furniture, his mother mute on her armchair, his father locked up in the Marshalsea.

'We'll find a way of getting it back,' Sam said.

Thomas felt the old loathing come up. That Sam could afford to lose a thousand *pagodas*; that for Sam, this was all a game, passing time until his inheritance came through. He tried to shut the voice down.

'We might still be able to sue.'

'Sue a man who's lost everything?'

Sam looked up. 'I'm not thinking straight.'

'Scattergood has demands on me, as do my family. Already six months have passed since I promised to send back their yearly allowance. I must have the money, Sam. Without it—' Thomas stared at the floor, 'I face ruin. You promised me that this was a good ship, a sound ship, that I'd make 100 per cent.'

'Thomas, be a man about it. You invested money. You lost it. That's what happens.'

'Yes, but it's all I have.'

'Deal with it.'

'I can't run back to Papa.'

'Damn you. I'm tired of hearing the same story. I could have discarded you years ago, like all your other friends did when your father lost his mind. I stuck by you. If it wasn't for me, you'd still be knocking around the Bristol docks.'

'He didn't lose his mind. He was swindled.'

'Face the facts.'

'Are you calling my father a madman?'

Sam went quiet.

'Say it.'

The redness was spreading, an angry blotch travelling down the side of Sam's neck.

'Or are you calling him a cheat?'

'That's what everyone else called him.'

Thomas looked up at the austere grey wall of the Fort. The cries of the merchants sounded distant compared to the blood clamouring through his veins. He wanted to knock Sam flat. Men died for saying such things.

Sam was watching him, his eyes narrowed. He was waiting for Thomas to do something, to challenge him to a duel. When he didn't, Sam shook his head and, with a scornful look, walked away.

32

After several weeks of travelling, Maya arrived at the southernmost tip of India: Kannyakumari, where the three oceans meet. It had always been her dream to travel there with *Amma*, to the ancient temple honouring the goddess in her virgin form. The promontory was jagged, the beach stony. Ahead, an endless horizon. Behind, the land. A surge of *bhakti* – of devotion – swept through her and she fell on to her knees and kissed the earth. It was as if she had been waiting all her life to let the land take her as one of its own.

Fully clothed, she made her ritual bath. She prayed for it all to be dissolved by the sea: the shroud of grief since her mother's death, the violence suffered at the hands of Mudaliar, the pain of losing Sita. The current was strong and the sand pulled from under her feet, her sari becoming tangled in the surf. Water filled her nostrils and as she tried to stand, another wave caught her from behind. When she finally broke through to the surface, gasping, none of the other pilgrims had noticed. She shivered. The hand of the goddess was fickle.

The next day, she took a fishing boat across the narrow stretch of water to the tiny island where the goddess Parvati had stood on one foot, praying to Shiva. Inside the small temple was the clear indentation of a footprint in the rock. *Where she has stepped, I will step*, thought Maya.

The keeper of the shrine was an old woman and when she went to take lunch, Maya slipped through the gap in the door and placed her left foot over the footprint. A powerful charge passed through her. She evoked Parvati in her incarnation as the moon-faced maiden, and understood that when she had first stepped on to the earth, she had carved the land from herself.

When Maya stepped outside, the goddess was there also. Her brass statue was being carried on a litter and a group of temple women were dancing, chanting her praises in ecstasy.

Maya held the doorframe for support, her mind giddy with bliss.

When the old woman came back and saw Maya sitting there, she offered her a bowl of *prasad*.

'You should go to Maruda Malai, child. You don't look well.'

Maya sucked the warm tapioca pudding sweetened with jaggery from her fingers.

'You'll find other pilgrims who'll be going. Head north, it's the only hill rising up from the plains.'

The pudding was comforting and Maya wondered if the old woman would give her more. But she turned away, reaching inside the shrine, and dabbed her thumb in a pot of red *kungumam* powder. Then, she pressed it firmly between Maya's eyes in the centre of her forehead. Maya stumbled back. 'Go straight away and when you get there, ask for Mother. She will help you.'

Two days later, at Maruda Malai, the mountain covered with healing plants, Maya saw her. She was sitting at the entrance of a cave. Her body was emaciated, her skin buckled. All her curves were gone, ravaged by the rigours of the road, her once elegant face cracked as a dry riverbed. Her frail body was close to the end but her spirit was soaring. Maya fell at her feet, kissing the blackened skin.

'After all these years I've found you. I had given up looking.'

'That is the only way,' Palani replied. 'When you give up the search.'

Their time together began with a dance. Palani kept the beat as

Maya performed on the natural stage of granite rock in front of the cave. She started with her arms crossed over her chest, her hands clenched. Then, with a confidence she had never had at the palace, Maya transformed anger into the agony of separation. The suffering of her guru's sudden departure was enacted through the subtle inflections of Maya's eyes and the jerkiness of her flicking fingers. The years of waiting were shown in the deep bows and mournful glances; their reunion in a simple gesture of two palms touching in front of her heart. At the end, Palani stood up, her eyes fierce with pride.

'This time, do not kneel. This time, stand and meet my gaze.'

The effect was swift, the current strong. Just as Maya had felt at the shrine of Parvati, she sensed the same communion when she stared into her guru's eyes. No longer was she simply receiving a blessing – somehow Maya had learned to give it back. Without another word, Palani gestured towards her cave, inviting Maya to stay.

The days began with a teaching and ended at dusk with a story of Palani's wanderings. Maya made a strong brew of tea. Palani sat on a tiger skin by the fire; Maya on a flat stone. It was hard to believe she was the same woman. In only seven years Palani had transformed from the great courtesan that she had been to a gap-toothed *sadhvi*.

'Those first months, I was terrified that the nawab's soldiers would find me and rape me.'

'Why did you leave?'

'To be inside the palace for all those years was stifling. I thought the prince's favours would help. Then that you would be enough to re-inspire me.' Palani bent forward stoking the flames, the ridges of her spine clearly visible. 'First I wanted you as an offering to the prince and then I wanted you for myself. Then I realised I didn't want either. You were a threat to me.'

Maya became very quiet inside.

'I used you,' she said, eventually turning to face Maya. 'I used you and I'm sorry.'

Like wind passing across water, Maya felt the words ripple through her. Part of her wanted to tell Palani that she understood. A deeper voice told her to feel the depth of her hurt and sit still. 'I only wish you'd told me you were going. That pained me the most.'

'I couldn't. I just had to go. The fall of the city gave me a chance of freedom. And then—' she stared into the embers, '—I knew Adki was leaving. That gave me courage.'

'You knew Adki?'

'Of course. That's why I chose you.'

'I always thought she didn't exist. Nobody I knew had actually met her.'

'Your mother did. And your aunt.'

Maya frowned.

'Your mother really told you nothing, did she? Adki came to her on the day you were born. She'd seen the omens. She told your mother you bore the signs of the goddess and she should take special care of you. I'm sure she tried. But she was incapable and life intervened. Many years later, Adki encouraged me to take you as my student. She said we had a special connection. One that went beyond this life.'

Palani broke some kindling and threw twigs into the fire. 'They say that the power of the goddess came to her at a young age. But her parents were from a poor seaside village in Andhra and had no use for a daughter who could not scale and gut fish. One day her mother found her on the beach, passed out cold. They took her to the temple but the priests turned them away as unclean. As they were carrying her home, they saw a sadhu. All night the holy man sat with Adki, and then he left.'

'So what happened?' Maya asked, edging closer to the fire.

'Adki kept falling into a trance. When she awoke, she could foretell people's futures. There were spontaneous healings – even the sores of lepers were cured by her touch. Word spread and the sadhu returned, and she became his disciple. They spent their life on pilgrimage, giving teachings wherever they went. When he died, she settled near Tanjore.'

'How did you meet her?'

'I too come from Andhra. I heard of her when I was growing up,'

Palani said vaguely, rising to her feet. 'She sought me out after I had arrived at the palace: there was no refusing Adki.'

Maya waited.

'She told me that I would have to give up everything one day. Then, much later, she told me about you.' She squatted back down, her hands resting on Maya's knees. 'Life has been hard on you. We each have our fate: that is written in the planets. Yet more and more I believe that within our destiny, we have choice.'

'I thought we only had duty.'

'That is what women are brought up to believe. But there are always those who have gone before us. You say that you thought Adki didn't really exist. It's true, in some ways she didn't. I've never known a person to be so closely merged with the divine. She was more spirit than matter.'

'Was?'

'She died four years ago. Alone. As she wanted it.' Palani stared into her hands. 'I spent two years with her. More precious than all my life put together.'

The next night, Palani continued. 'Adki and I journeyed north. Sometimes separate, sometimes together. We took a vow of silence.' She paused, her mind elsewhere. 'I shaved my head and renounced all my worldly desires. I gave away my jewellery—'

'Your jewellery?'

'Hard to believe, I know.' She gave a wry smile, cradling her clay cup of tea.

Minutes passed. They sat staring into the flames.

'By the time we reached the foothills of the Himalayas we had entered a luminous state of communication where words were no longer needed. The following spring, when the mountains were covered with wildflowers, our feet barely touched the ground.' She stopped again. 'We followed the trail up and up, the river narrowing to a mountain stream, until we reached Gomukh, the source of the Ganga. Thick snow and blue ice covered the river. In the cave where the spring pours forth, Adki left me, saying I had to continue my practices alone.'

'Were you frightened to be alone?'

'At first. But I always felt her nearby. Eight months later, Adki died. I felt her go.' She swallowed. 'It left a gaping hole in my heart.'

Maya hugged her knees to her chest. She wanted to reach out to the old woman but feared her hand would pass straight through her. She wondered if Adki was here with them. All around she felt the unseen pressing closer, wanting to share in the story and warmth of their bodies.

'You and I were chosen from birth to be handmaidens to Shiva. For many years I saw that as serving my king. It is easy to become lost in the ritual. You remember I taught you those ecstatic poems of Akkamahadevi who sang to the "Lord of white jasmine" – to Shiva himself?' She did not wait for an answer. 'I realised they held the truth that I was looking for. I could not find this truth outside of myself, only within.'

'I don't understand, Palani *akka*. Are we forever slaves to men, when we were consecrated to god?' Maya's voice was reproachful. 'You haven't heard what happened to me. How my mother died and Uma sold me to a rich *dubash* in Madras. How he beat me. Where is the sacredness in that?' Her face contorted.

'You have not had the protection that I did. I know that. I heard that the Prince of Tanjore is a slave to the English now. We are all slaves to someone.'

Maya felt the stillness thicken. The ancestors were everywhere now. The circle was complete. 'Do you feel them around us?'

'They are here, yes. You must know that you are never alone, whatever happens. The goddess never abandons her children.'

As Maya plummeted inside, the dark night descended. She was poised between worlds: the unfathomable within and vastness without. 'How will I learn to trust in her voice?'

Palani stared straight ahead. 'When your heart is ready to listen.'

During the day, a trickle of pilgrims came to ask Palani for advice and healings. She was known as the Mother of the Medicine Mountain. Sadhus carrying tridents, their faces coated in yellow turmeric, naked *babas* smeared with ash, eyes crystalline, they all came to pay their respects. Palani tired of the holy men quickly. Then she tired of talking altogether.

As Maya's mind drained of the usual listless thoughts, old memories rose to the surface and then sank again. Her senses became more acute. She began to feel a vibrating illumined field all around her. In her mind – or was it outside, she couldn't be sure – she saw the gods and goddesses parade before her and experienced the unique essence of each one. With each day, the *muttirai* on her arm burned stronger and her body began to tremble. When she closed her eyes, suns exploded; when she opened them, the world around her danced.

She wanted answers yet knew words were inadequate. Once again, she sensed Palani slipping away and could do nothing to stop it. When an eagle flew above her as she lay on the ground, she found she, too, was soaring high. A loud clapping brought her back. Palani's face was a hand's breadth away.

'Enough. You are not ready. Nor your body.'

It was the first time she'd said anything in weeks.

That night she gave Maya warm buffalo milk and fussed over her. Maya preferred the silence.

The next day, Palani told her that it was time for her to leave. 'I was waiting for you, my child. I was singing you. Now I must return to my solitude.'

'I haven't learned everything there is to know.'

'You've learned all you can.'

'I know nothing.'

'Show some respect.'

Palani took a step towards her. Maya drew herself upright. Once again the current ran between them. Maya felt the tingling through her body and lightness filling her mind. She saw Palani felt it too.

'When I see you now, it is I who feel I have much to learn. But that is our fate. Rao always said we are each other's past and each other's future.'

'Will I see you again?' Maya asked, knowing the answer.

Palani shook her head. 'But we have met before and we will meet again.'

All afternoon Maya brooded, her distress clawing to be heard. When a filthy, long-haired man arrived and Palani went to him straight away and did not return till noon the following day, she sat paralysed, her eyes fixed on the empty horizon.

'You cannot abandon me again,' Maya said, when Palani finally returned.

Palani lifted one eyebrow. 'Again?'

She took Maya's left hand, turning it over thoughtfully, tracing her dirt-encrusted nail over the faint lines crisscrossing the palm, sucking in her cheeks as she did so. 'Your destiny is not easy. The woman who carries the mark of the goddess also bears the shadow.' Palani closed her eyes and blew across Maya's palm.

A shudder passed through her and she tried to pull her hand away but Palani's grip was firm. The old woman's forehead dipped into deep crags, and then, as Maya watched, there was a slow peeling back as if a curtain was lifting inside Palani's mind. Maya gulped for air. Palani continued to blow over her palm, until Maya slumped down.

'I always thought it was with your mother that you had the pact. I see it was with your aunt.'

Maya sat up.

'What happened to her?' Palani asked.

The urge came again to pull her hand away.

'She was murdered in Tanjore. Along with Leela and her brother. Killed by an English soldier too drunk to remember his own name.'

Palani made a whistling sound through her teeth.

Maya's hand fell limp, her palm burning. 'My mother didn't tell me. Uma *akka* did.'

Palani let her hand go.

'What do you mean, pact?' she said.

'A debt that we carry, handed down from one of our ancestors. Usually it is from mother to daughter; in my case it was from my grandmother. In yours, from Sita.'

Maya shook her head. It didn't make sense.

'When Sita was outcaste, you took that upon yourself. Out of love. Part of you, too, was cast out. Your mother could see what was happening and tried to stop it.'

'You knew that Sita was outcaste?'

She nodded. 'I had to wait over a year before it was safe enough for me to invite you to the palace. Still, not until now did I realise how much you carried. Nor how much Sita suffered. She was a kind woman. Too soft for the role she was born into. Too loyal. Like her namesake.' She looked at Maya.

'Whatever path you choose, never forget the meaning of your name in the *Vedas*. Maya means "glory of the goddess". Yet also realise this—' she picked up Maya's hand again. 'As a goddess, Mayambikai understands this world is illusory. That is very hard for humans to understand. But you can grasp this. It is your gift.' Palani patted her knee. 'Lay your head in my lap, child.'

As Palani sang a lullaby and stroked Maya's hair, she felt herself slipping into sleep. She tried to fight it, wishing the night would never end.

When she awoke, Palani had gone. The fire was out, the ash scattered snake-like around the pit, and on the pile of Maya's clothes lay two parrot feathers, cyan and crimson.

Once Maya was certain that her guru had gone, she uttered a single anguished cry, leaned forward and retched. When the pain grew too large to be contained inside, she sobbed until there was nothing left to spill. Then she picked up the two feathers. They were from Vikku.

Palani had kept them all this time and now she'd left them to her. Maya lifted up her arms, a feather in each hand, and brought them down sharply. The feathers cut the air with a hiss. Her mind was racing now. The dream she'd had of flying on the day she left Madras. The same day, seeing that girl outside the temple and hearing the girl's voice in her head. Since then, it was as if she'd been on another current, parallel to the world she'd known yet no longer part of it. The owl, the wolves, had she dreamt them too? Wolves didn't live this far south. She'd asked people and they'd told her she was mistaken. Palani had simply nodded.

She was not dreaming. Yet her mind was malleable. She rocked backwards and forwards blowing over the feathers, like Palani had done across her palm, and her heart began to soften. Palani could have turned her away after one night. She felt the tenderness of the old woman's touch and the ferocity of her gaze. Standing up, she stretched out her arms wide, a feather in each hand. She looked up to the sky, and very softly, she said, 'I know that the goddess resides within me. Now it is up to me to make the most of what I have learned.'

Thomas could not forget her face. Nor her perfume. When he'd finished the bottle from the perfumery he sent his valet to buy another. He came back empty-handed. 'The shop, it's gone.'

He went searching himself. He passed the small shrine of the red demon goddess with her tongue sticking out, a man's corpse beneath her splayed feet, and the stall selling copper cooking pots. There was no sign of the Mughal Perfumery. The stallholders only pulled faces of incomprehension. When a child tugged at his sleeve for an *anna* he knocked him to the ground, cursing the idiocy of them all. Cursing himself.

That night he did not return home, nor for several nights afterwards.

His skin started flaking, first behind the backs of his knees, then on the crease of his elbows, down to his wrists. His hands, too, they swelled and cracked, the fingers weeping, red and puffy. Holding a quill became agony, then impossible. He wore brown silk gloves to hide them, but in the sticky air, infection set in.

Thomas tried his mother's spirit of lavender. It brought back the scent of childhood and easy homecomings; it did nothing to help his hands. He fell into a listless fever.

As he lay on his cot, he saw a movement at the top of the blinds above the window. Then, a spiralling, twisting shape. He sat up. A slate-grey snake with fine white markings was hanging down, the forked tongue darting in and out. He froze. The snake curled back on itself and began to hiss, low and menacing, its body tensed, the hood and the neck quivering. His thoughts seemed to be slowing down as his heart speeded up. His sword was too far to reach. He saw himself dying there, having achieved – what?

In one swift movement he rolled away from the wall, landing on the floor. In another bound he leapt across the room and gave a loud, rather ludicrous, scream. He pulled his sword from its sheath and slashed the air. The snake reared up. Thomas jabbed again and sliced through the string holding up the blinds. His hollers brought the servants running.

'*Sahib*, what is it?'

'Snake.'

'Where?'

'On the blinds.'

'Big head? Wide?'

'Yes.'

'Put the sword away. Holy snake.'

'For crying out loud the snake is above my bed. Kill it.'

'Where, Sir?'

Thomas looked. The blinds were empty, swinging from side to side. The wall was bare. He blinked, suddenly aware of the tension in his arm holding the sword, and the ache where his hand gripped the handle.

'There was a snake,' he said. 'I saw it. A big snake.'

'*Sahib* has fever.' The servant held out his hand for the sword, tutting at the sight of the chapped hands. 'I'll get you something for this.' Nudging Thomas's arm, he motioned towards the cot.

'No. I can't sleep there.'

'*Sahib* rest now. No snake.'

Thomas moved out of the Fort to a house in Black Town. He spent his afternoons visiting friends and his nights at the gaming table. There was no word from Sam.

'Another, Sir?'

He clutched the bar and tried to respond. The tavern owner's face separated in two.

'What time is it?'

'Eleven o'clock.'

'You're closing soon.'

'We've just opened.'

His right leg buckled. The man's face divided again. He held a bottle of Madeira towards Thomas. When he uncorked it, the sickly smell made Thomas heave.

'Later.' He stumbled out of the door. The sun was already high, his mouth was furry and his breath foul. He looked down at his oatmeal breeches stained with vomit. He had no idea what day it was or how long he'd been there. He started to head towards Black Town, keeping to the shade. After a few minutes he stopped, disoriented. *I have to go home. I have to leave this place.*

When Thomas woke, it was night-time. He was strapped down, his arms pinned by his side. A surgeon walked past shouting orders, his apron blood-soaked. Thomas tried to lift his head; his throat felt desiccated. He called out but no sound came.

They kept him in hospital for several days. They bled him and cupped him with blistering poultices to draw out the evil humours. The surgeon said he'd been frothing at the mouth and running a fever that should have killed him. They'd tied him down for his own good. He'd been delirious, lashing out, crying like an infant. He was lucky that Reverend Sutcliffe had found him when he had.

For the next few weeks, Thomas lay on his cot in his room staring up at the patch of mildew in the corner, at the spreading stain. He couldn't face seeing the reverend in person and sent a letter thanking him for his charitable actions. A day later, when Sutcliffe called, he pretended to be asleep. The humiliation of taking leave of his senses only added to the slippage he felt inside. A message came from the Fort. He had a choice: go home on furlough or take two months' leave. Thomas decided to take the leave.

Some weeks after Palani had left, Maya arrived at the *choultry* from where she'd fled. Outside the rest house a man was standing by a richly decorated palanquin. His face was darkened from sun; in his hand he carried a silk fan.

'Every time I see you, you look more like one of us,' the *choultry* owner called out.

The *ferenghi* laughed, looking most pleased with himself. She recognised him immediately: he was the Dutch friend of Mudaliar.

From behind the building, she heard shrieks of laughter. A short man with no neck appeared, shaking water from his hair. 'You'll be sorry, girl,' he shouted.

Maya went around the back. Sitting on a bench, wearing the dusky-pink sari, was the girl she'd seen on the day she'd left Madras. The girl tilted her head forward.

'You,' she said.

Maya looked down at her hands.

'I'm Mamia. What's your name?'

'Don't you already know?' Maya laughed, rueful.

'Only your face. You're travelling alone?'

She nodded.

'Which way?'

'I'm not sure. Madras, perhaps. You?'

'Wherever the *tai* thinks we can find an audience and enough to feed ourselves. We go where we please.' She pulled out a small cloth bag from inside her blouse to reveal gold earrings and a necklace. 'We are paid generously for our work.'

The cry of the *tai* shattered the peace. The girl sighed, rising to her feet, her manner languid. 'When I come back you must tell me who trained you.'

'What do you mean?'

'Only a *dasi* walks like the whole world is watching.'

After the troupe had performed, Maya went to their encampment behind the rest house. Mamia was sitting outside her tent while the *tai* combed her hair. She dismissed the old woman and brought out a cushion.

'You dance well,' Maya said, sitting down. 'Where did you learn?'

'In Surat, where I'm from.'

'The foreigner certainly enjoyed it.' Maya said.

'He's biased. We've been lovers for some time.'

'Really?'

'You seem surprised,' Mamia said, winding her long hair into a bun and fixing it with a wooden clip. 'I offered him the lover's *paan* some months ago. At first he rejected me – fool that he was. It didn't take long for him to change his mind.' A smile hovered on her lips.

'You don't care that he's a *ferenghi*?'

'He's almost one of us. See how he speaks? How he sings along to the songs?'

Maya laughed. She thought of the Englishman. How he'd looked at her. The lust in his eyes.

From the other tents Maya heard the rumbling laugh of the *tai*. She had the same physique as Uma: short, with a square face and a wide mannish forehead. She looked across to Mamia. The girl was young, sixteen maybe. Still innocent despite all she'd lived through. Maya wanted to ask how she could hear the girl's words so clearly in her head.

'It's a gift,' Mamia said. 'And sometimes a curse.'

'How can you know what I'm thinking?'

'My father was the village healer. He always taught me that I could hear everything if I listened carefully enough. For many years I tried. Then it happened one day. It scared me. I meet people first in my dreams and then in life. Like you. Sometimes I know too much. About myself. About others.' Her voice sank to a whisper. 'I know I will die young.'

Maya found herself shying away.

'Don't be scared. I don't mean any harm.'

She thought of Palani. How they, too, had communicated in the silence.

'Where will you go, Maya?'

'I'm still not sure.'

'Join us. I know you're worried that you'll lose your caste, but they look after you as if you were family. Even the *tai*, she is like a mother to me.' Mamia yawned.

'I'm keeping you up,' she said. 'Your patron won't be happy.'

'I'm having a night off.' Mamia winked.

Maya couldn't sleep. She knew that the *tai* would be happy enough if she joined the troupe, and she felt an inexplicable kinship with the girl. She thought of Palani staring into the flames and telling her, *Read the signs that life presents*. As she lay on the rough matting, it dawned on her that she could decide which way to go: that had been Palani's lasting gift. Neither *Amma* nor Sita had had such choice. But she was free to choose.

The next morning, outside the *choultry*, Maya asked Jacob if he'd heard news of Mudaliar. He told her the *dubash* had lost all his business after the Company closed his account and the secretary had returned unexpectedly to England.

From the road Maya heard a loud whistle announcing the arrival of a bullock cart. It was coming from the west and as it pulled up, her spirits lifted. She'd learned enough to know she could find her own way in Madras.

At that moment, Mamia came running from behind the rest house. 'Have you decided where to go?'

'Madras.'

'There is someone for you there?'

Maya half-smiled.

'If he's not there, come back and find us.'

'Or you come to the city and find me. I'll be in Mylapore, near the beach.'

As the bullocks strained and the wheels began to spin, Maya turned to wave. All the troupe had come out to see her off and Mamia, a crown of pink flowers around her brow, stood next to Jacob, both of them waving.

PART 3
Madras, 1778

33

Maya took cheap rooms in Mylapore close to the beach. To pay for them she sold the last piece of jewellery Mudaliar had given her. By asking around, Maya heard that not long after she'd left Madras, the *dubash* had faced bankruptcy and sold two of his properties. A trip to Benares to salvage the losses had failed and on the way back, Mudaliar had succumbed to cholera. Since then, an indigo merchant had taken over his residence. Now, she stood outside the gates, looking up to the rooftop terrace, and recalled those glittering nights as hostess of the *sadas*. Despite the luxury of it all, she felt only relief that that chapter of her life was over. Pari had been right – going on pilgrimage had not only released the heaviness in her soul, it had stoked her fire for life.

She wondered where her friend was, and if she'd be able to find her. The city was changing so fast. Villagers were streaming in from the north as rumours spread that Hyder Ali's forces would return. Already reports of *looties* were coming in from outlying districts. Soldiers and stragglers from Hyder Ali's army came at night, stripping what they could, seizing women and possessions and burning the rest.

Now that she was back, she regretted not staying longer with Mamia and the troupe. After spending that time with Palani, she imagined that she'd be different, that she'd be less attached to the world and the temptations around her. But her teacher had been right – Maya was not ready to give up her earthly pleasures.

The Englishman was crowding her mind. He was there when she woke and went to bathe in the temple *ghat*, pitcher in hand, breasts bared. Twice she thought she saw him on the beach near the fish market. But Kuttamma said she hadn't seen him for months.

It made life complicated. His smell – that was one problem. Unclean. Unwashed. His foreignness – that was another.

Still she thought of him. His neat clipped nails. The square shape of his jaw. His lips, full and pink. She repeated his name to herself. *Thomas*. And again, *Tho-mas*. It was awkward to say. More awkward was finding him again.

She knew the English walked the Esplanade in the hour before sunset, so one afternoon, she prepared herself.

Once washed and dried, she oiled her hair with coconut, and lit the *aarthi* and several cones of incense. Then, still naked, she offered the flaming lamp to the statue of the goddess, repeating the words Palani had taught her. Warmth travelled up from the base of her spine, around her groin and belly, and she felt her own hungry desire. She placed the clay dish of burning incense on the floor and squatted down, close enough to feel the heat. With one hand she waved the smoke towards her vulva, running her fingers through her coarse black hairs – to scent them; to invite him in.

Two hours later, dressed in a purple sari, she was out on the Esplanade. Along the avenue of palm trees groups of foreigners walked and chatted. A horse and buggy passed and both men turned to stare, laughter erupting. *Let them talk. Let them laugh.* She rolled back her shoulders. *Walk as if you have all the time in the world.*

Maya saw the white women avert their eyes and the men's mouths grow slack. Up ahead, she recognised one man with reddish hair. He was the man who'd been with Thomas at the party. As he came closer, she told herself, *I have nothing to fear. The worst they can do is tell me to leave.*

Next to him was a woman. Their arms were linked and there was a playfulness in the way she stroked his arm. Maya had always thought foreign women ugly in their starched dresses, their faces bone white with a dab of pink in the centre of each cheek. Yet this woman, with her wheatish hair styled into curls, was quite beautiful. Maya marvelled at their public display of affection, at the tenderness of his gaze. A sharp sting of regret, then despair, gripped her, and she quickened her pace. *Why would the Englishman want me*, she thought, *when he could have this?*

At that moment, the redheaded man looked up. His eyes narrowed. When they were almost level, and when Maya knew they expected her to drop her gaze, she slowed down again, and said it.

'Hello. Good evening.' She gave a slight bow.

The man blushed. She saw him hesitate and the woman frown, then they passed by. Moments later she heard raised voices from behind her. Maya continued to walk, her heart thumping.

By the time she'd reached the end of the Esplanade, sweat was trickling between her shoulder blades. She wanted to sit and cool down. She hadn't intended to come all this way. In fact, she hadn't any idea what she would do once she finished her walk. He wasn't here. Or perhaps he was, and she'd just missed him. He could be anywhere – with anyone. *If he wants me, then he should be the one finding me.* She wished, then, to be rid of him.

Later that week, Thomas decided to pay a visit to Cheyney. There was still no word from his friend since his departure for England. Thomas lay back in the palanquin, bracing himself when he heard the synchronised grunt of the bearers as they stood, levering the bamboo poles on to their shoulders. When he arrived, the gates were padlocked and the windows of the house boarded up. The grass was knee-high; the topiaries overgrown. He double-checked the side gate and called out. After ten minutes, Klipper appeared.

'Mister Thomas, too long, too long.'

'Where's your Master?'

'Gone. Wait here.'

Cheyney's head servant ducked back through the gate before re-appearing some minutes later holding a letter.

'He said you must have.'

Thomas reached into his pocket to give the man a coin but Klipper shook his head. 'Only doing my duty.'

Once back in the palanquin, he broke open the seal.

My dear Thomas,

I write in haste before leaving. I gather you are out of station as my messages have gone unanswered.

I've never had the courage to say this to you directly. Believe me, I have thought it in my private moments. You are the closest I have to my first born, who we lost. In my absence I am making you Executor of my affairs subject to your agreement. You know the house well enough by now …

The words were hard to take in. What about Prema? He should have thought to ask. He folded his arms tight across his chest and looked once more through the gates. In his heart, he knew that Cheyney wouldn't be returning. Beneath the palanquin rocked. He rapped the side ordering the bearers to follow the coast road. He needed time to think.

The letter amounted to an open invitation. If Cheyney's bibi had left, and the house was vacant . . . It was foolish to think that he could . . . But surely, Cheyney would want me to have the house.

Somehow, he had to find the money. The only option was to borrow from the Nawab of Arcot – the Company's banker of the south, as he was known. The interest would be high, but it would be worth it. Life was too short. The last few months had shown him that.

Outside, the Mylapore streets were unusually quiet. Ahead, on the left, were the large wooden doors of the temple. For old time's sake, he called his bearers to stop and, leaving his shoes in the litter, pushed open the sea-green door. He walked past the statue of Mudaliar's father and towards the back pillared courtyard. The place seemed empty and, emboldened, he continued, his tread softening in the still air.

At the edge of the inner courtyard he hesitated, more fearful of finding nothing than of the priest chasing him away. He realised he was holding his breath. He edged forward and saw a pile of clothing and beaded bracelets. He waited. First came a drenching of coconut – she must have coated herself with it – then an aromatic spice he couldn't identify. He heard humming and a papery sound of bare feet rubbing against stone.

She was alone and unveiled. The sunlight was streaming behind her and one by one she unclipped her anklets and hair adornments, teasing her long black hair loose, then when she stepped from the light into the shadow, her figure became clear. Thomas slowly exhaled through his nose. His legs were trembling and he pressed his hands on his thighs to stop them. Then she unwound the shawl and, arms akimbo, began to dance.

34

That evening when Thomas arrived at Maya's lodgings in Mylapore, he wasn't sure what to expect: other women perhaps, small cubicles divided by shabby patterned curtains. An ugly madam ready to filch his money. Instead a servant showed him into a simply furnished house. Seagulls were squawking through the open window. He sat down on the low settle.

Upstairs, Maya was panicking. Holding her mirror, she examined her kohl-rimmed eyes and pulled at the tendrils of hair falling from her temples. She rubbed her wrists behind her ears to even out the *javadhu* powder. She should go to him. At length, she entered.

She had changed from earlier and was wearing pale-blue silk seamed with green leaves. Her hair was intricately woven with beads, a gold hoop dangled from one nostril and her mother's single chain hung around her neck. The whole effect made her shimmer. In her hand was an earthenware plate piled with shiny green packets of *paan*.

Thomas stood up, bowing awkwardly. He was a head taller than her, his body slight. She wondered why he had stood up when she entered, and motioned for him to sit. Now he was here, she wished he'd never come.

'A drink?' she said, and went to fetch a glass of dark-red liquid. 'Pomegranate juice.'

He sniffed it, warily. *She could have given me something stronger*, he thought. 'Delicious. Thank you,' he said, the Tamil words sticking together in his mouth. He sat down again.

She watched him drink. His neck and cheeks were pink and bare. *I should try and speak English.* She passed him the plate of *paan. I can smell his breath from here. Rotten.*

'I made them specially.' She attempted to smile.

He hoped she hadn't seen him grimace. 'I need to freshen my breath with *paan?*' he said jokingly.

She nodded, her gaze serious.

He ran his tongue over the back of his front teeth. His mouth did feel grubby, his breath was stale. He could smell his sweat, too. He wished she'd stop looking at him. He put one parcel of *paan* in his mouth and began to chew. A bitter astringent flavour exploded on his tongue, followed by perfumed sweetness. The taste was overwhelming and made him cough. His eyes filled with water. She reached for the spittoon. He spat out most of it, still unchewed.

No man had ever rejected her *paan.* She was mortified.

'You don't like it?'

'Yes.' His eyes were streaming. 'But too strong.'

'Try another?'

He shook his head.

He can't like me, she thought.

Thomas rose to his feet.

That's good, he's leaving. Foreigners don't understand anything about manners. She went to the door.

I need a stiff drink, he thought, putting the empty glass on the table.

'Another?' she said.

'Do you have anything else?'

'Tea?'

'Arrack?'

They all drink. All the ferenghis. 'I'll order you some straight away.'

While Maya was outside sending the servant off, Thomas began to pace. The *paan* made his mouth and his nostrils burn; a mild euphoria swept down his legs. He wondered if his breath was that bad. He was sure he'd seen her recoil when she'd first approached. *I can't sit here all evening. After the first drink, I'll go to the club.*

She sat in silence as he downed the first arrack, and the second. His hands were less jittery after the third. She noticed they were chapped and red. His nails looked less polished, his face thinner. Then he stretched out his legs, and desire licked through her. She'd never wanted a man like she wanted him. *I can't. He must bathe. And then, could I?*

Thomas turned the glass in his hand, watching the candlelight flicker through it. Gusts of her perfume breezed towards him but it was the smell underneath, her bodily scent, that lacerated him.

'Shall we—' he started.

'You need to bathe.'

'I had one earlier this week,' he said.

She rolled her eyes. 'You *ferenghis* are so dirty.'

He looked at the curve of her waist between the folds of cloth. He tried to imagine undressing her and where he would begin. 'Where can I?'

'At home. Come back tomorrow night when you are clean.'

He thought he must have misheard. 'But we haven't even begun.'

'Come back tomorrow, but come earlier.'

She stood and called to the servant who entered immediately. Thomas wanted to say no. To insist that he couldn't go – not now, not when she was so close. When he came back, she might have disappeared, like the perfumery. He'd lose her again. He stood up, his stomach hollow.

She was standing by the open door looking at him, her face impossible to read. In truth, he had no idea who she was. Her name was Maya. That was it. He'd never find her again.

'Tomorrow, then?' he said. 'You're sure?'

'Come before sunset.'

'The bath house before that.' He tried to make light of it.

She tilted her head. 'Until then.'

The next day he arrived at five o'clock. Maya had given the servant the night off. She showed him upstairs onto the rooftop where there was a chair and a swing seat. He was dressed in a clean pressed white shirt and pantaloons. She noticed the tightness around his eyes and the way his chapped hands turned over uneasily in his lap. She offered him a drink and sat cross-legged on her seat and began to sing.

When she finished, he asked who had taught her.

'My mother. I started when I was four.'

'You learned to dance then, too?'

'Yes. It's all part of our training.'

She stood up and walked to the walled edge. He came to stand beside her. She could feel his warmth and her heart pounding in her chest.

'When I saw you yesterday in the temple, I saw birds in your dance.'

She looked down, smiling.

'How do you dance without music?'

'I can hear the music all the time. It never stops. The beat—' She thought about it. 'It's been there ever since I was born. From my mother, and her mother too.'

She pressed her hands against her belly. Her heat was rising, but not enough. Simmering only. She let them drop by her side. Then, he drew a finger down the soft centre of her forearm, and into her palm. He pulled her close, his chin tilted downwards. She could hear the sound of water splashing from the street below. The moon was already sinking into the ocean. She pulled away. Yet still she sensed where his finger had touched her arm.

'Not here, we can be seen,' she said. 'That is not our custom. Such moments should be private.'

She led him downstairs into the bedroom. It was sparsely decorated with only a thin narrow mattress and a stool. In one corner was a wooden box and a cushion. He saw, then, what she'd given up by leaving Mudaliar. She'd lost everything. He hesitated and leaned forward to kiss the side of her neck, pushing away her hair, and nuzzling his nose and mouth into the hollow where her neck met her collarbone. He felt her breasts pressing against his chest.

Her arms encircled his narrow muscular frame and her fingers pressed down on the ridges of his spine. Part of her still wanted him to leave but she knew she wouldn't be able to let him go. Not now. She felt the heat between them and was helpless to stop it. He bent down and through her blouse started to suck her nipple, nibbling one, while caressing the other. When she looked into his eyes it was hard to hold his gaze. She realised, then, what Palani had meant when she'd talked about the *darshan* of love – how through the eyes two souls can merge. Swift – and terrifying.

With her eyes never leaving him, Maya undid the knot of her sari, took a step and turned, step, another turn, unravelling the single piece of cloth as she did so. In English, she said, 'Nine yards. All nine yards.'

Thomas stood open-mouthed, staring at her. She stood in a sea of pale blue silk. The blackness of her mole and the symmetry of her eyes gave her face a rapturous quality. Her shoulders were straight and her face was proud, and he saw that she was shivering.

After he'd gone, she went upstairs and lay back on the swing. He'd washed properly, using a floral scent that she didn't know. She wondered what colour the flower was and what it looked like. She would ask him. He would be back the following night.

She hadn't kissed him. Too unclean, too soon for that. A few quick grunts and it was over. *Ferenghis*, they weren't taught any better. He'd been more uncertain, more boyish than she'd imagined.

The third time they lay together, he pushed himself up on one arm and leaned over her. He looked down, taking her all in.

'You must leave now,' she said.

'Why do you always send me away? I've been waiting for you for so long.'

She half-sat, her hair quilting the pillow. This time had been better; he'd held it for longer. Still, he had much to learn. She jerked her head towards the door, her eyes firm.

'I've lost my head over you,' he pleaded.

When he'd gone, she lay back down. He'd told her the scent was lavender, his mother's spirit of lavender. A lilac-coloured plant, with small grainy flowers that grew in his garden back in England. Next time he said he'd bring her a dried flower. Maybe she could grow a new one from seed – grow it for when he left. As she knew he must, as they all did.

She rose, unable to sleep, and went up to the roof. The moon was nearly full. A frail white disc hanging in the night sky. If he was losing his head, she was losing her heart.

Thomas never knew what to expect when he paid her a visit. Yet the fear that she would not be there never left him. As he turned the corner of the narrow street, he always felt the same nervous excitement. Sometimes other musicians were there and Maya would dance for the small gathering on the rooftop. He kept asking her to move to his lodgings in Black Town. He was sure she took other lovers and the thought of it made him sullen. Yet when he was with her, his resentments evaporated. *It's like I've always been running and now I can stop.*

Maya began to let him stay the night. She bathed his feet in blossom-filled water and *champued* warm oil over his body. One night, she let him kiss her. His tongue prised open her lips and slipped inside, and she didn't pull away in disgust. Tentatively she let the tip of their tongues touch. When he pressed more firmly against her, pulling her towards him, he felt her nipples harden. Her tongue responded and loosened in his mouth until, breathless, they pulled away. Then she angled her head towards him and started kissing him again.

He savoured the moments after they had lain together, and when she got up to bathe. She didn't glide exactly, but her poise, bearing and suppleness combined into a single fluid line. There was ease in her movements, naturalness; she was utterly comfortable in her own skin. Her hair, a curtain of coconut-scented blackness, nearly reached her waist. He knew that she knew he was watching her and could see she liked it. She was used to men admiring her. Seeing her like that made him hard and he wanted her all over again.

With women he'd always felt brutish and clumsy. Women's cunts were dark unknown slits – places he'd barged into, often drunk, in the dark. Fumbled affairs between layers of clothing with whores or maids. He'd only touched one gentlewoman, and she would do nothing except let him kiss her hand.

With Maya, it was skin on skin, by candlelight. She washed him before they lay down, and afterwards, they often bathed together. He took his time rubbing the soap nuts over her back, and over her firm apple buttocks. Occasionally a vague twinge of guilt rose up – that he was enjoying himself this much, and with a native, and a dancer – but he pushed the thought aside and saw how the cold water made her nipples become ridged and erect.

It didn't take him long to realise that she was more educated than he was. Two months after they'd met, she spoke to him in lilting English.

'Where did you learn?'

'In the palace in Tanjore. My tutor thought I should know English over Persian. Maybe he knew things that I didn't,' she said, a wry smile flitting across her face, as she rolled towards him.

'You speak more languages than I do.'

She counted on her fingers. 'Five. You?'

'Three, four if you count my broken Tamil.' His eyes narrowed. 'The palace. Are you royalty?'

'No, but my mother hoped I would be presented to the prince. My teacher was the city's most famous courtesan, a great poet, too.'

'Why did you leave?'

'The English invaded.'

'Oh. I'm sorry.' He grimaced.

'In one way it freed me. In another—' She turned away.

'What?'

'Nothing.' She sat up, pulling the coverlet around her, and pushing away the fleeting thought of her aunt. 'Where are you from?'

'Bristol in south-west England, by the sea.'

'So you grew up always knowing the sea?'

'Yes. As a child I often spent time with this old man called George who lived on the docks. He was blind in one eye and spent his days repairing the ropes. A real old sea-dog—'

'A man who was a dog?'

He smiled. 'No, it's just an expression. He'd spent his life at sea and his hut was decorated with objects from all the places he'd visited. Like India. He showed me a silver *pagoda* and told me stories about life here. The palaces, the jungles.'

'Is that why you wanted to come?'

'I suppose. But nothing can prepare you for what it's really like here.'

She lay back down and nestled her head against his chest. 'I can't imagine being anywhere else. This is all I've ever known.'

Thomas always left at dawn. Then he ran through the narrow streets to the beach, swept clean by the tide. He loved this time of day: the bright orange disc of the sun rising fast in a blue sky feathered with cloud, the streets stretching into life. He could smell Maya on his skin and would feel her for hours afterwards. He pressed his palms over his nostrils, breathing her in. One night she'd shown him how to touch her, guiding his fingers as she whispered words he didn't understand. Then she fell silent, her breath coming in short fast gasps.

Those first few months together, life was glorious. His lust for her was insatiable. He wished each day to be over, just so he could be with her again. Sometimes when he arrived, platters of food were laid out. Crispy savoury *vadais* served with white coconut chutney; chunky vegetable and dhal pancakes smeared with butter and dark-brown sugar, and to wash it down, small bowls of tangy *rasam*, spiced with chilli. Friends of hers would drop by with their musical instruments, wary of him at first, but gradually more accepting.

When Maya was lost to their rhythm, envy scorched him. But with a nod of her head, the beat would change and she would stop singing and begin to dance. He saw, then, how quickly the male musicians were subdued by her easy grace. It pleased him knowing that they would leave when the night was over and he would be the only one to stay.

After months of asking, Maya agreed to live with him. It went against the grain and her mind told her she would regret it.

'What will I be, if I move in?'

'My mistress. My *bibi*. That's what you were to Mudaliar.'

She thought about this. 'With him, I had standing in the community and in the temple. I'm giving that up for you. I know how the foreigners treat their Indian *bibis*. I don't expect to be put in an outhouse, if that's what you're thinking. I expect my own quarters.'

He looked at her. Her defiance only made him want her more.

'Why don't you find another *dubash,* then?' His voice was flint-edged.

He was testing her and she played along with it.

'Nobody would have me. I've been touched by a white man.'

'Is that such a sin?'

'You know the answer. Even the untouchables are better than you.'

He stood up and walked behind her. Leaning down, he blew on the nape of her neck, and up to her ear. He slipped a hand around her waist. Her breath quickened but she stayed firm.

'Do you regret it?' he murmured, his tongue tasting the salt on her skin. When she tried to turn away, he held her tighter. Momentarily her resolve weakened, then she slipped out of his grasp. 'You would pay me?'

'No. I would keep you. You would have pin money, the household to run.'

'I would have no status.'

'And you have status now? Living here, entertaining a few poets who come by?' He was irritated. 'If you're asking me whether you'll ride atop elephants and dance at temples, no, you won't. For that you should have stayed with the likes of Mudaliar. As you say, you don't want that and you are now sullied, then you'll have to make the best of things with me.'

The discussion was running away from her. She felt it again – the nagging fear that this would end in disaster. Yet she couldn't bear to leave him. There was a force she couldn't stop, that wouldn't be stopped, that was bigger than both of them. But there was too much sacrifice involved. *All my sacrifice*, she thought. *He gives up nothing.*

'Where would we live?' she said, at last. 'There isn't room in your Black Town house.'

'No. I will keep that for business.' He turned away, thinking of the bonds he'd signed that week to the nawab's moneylenders. 'I cannot tell you yet, but I can assure you it will be most agreeable.'

Three months later, in the season of ripe heat, she and Thomas were travelling in a chaise and pair southwards, past the mount of San Thome. His hands were turning over in his lap. As the buildings thinned out and the foliage grew thicker, he leaned out of the carriage. When they came to some large gates he ordered the driver to stop. He alighted and offered her his hand. Maya stepped out, the sharp gravel pricking the soles of her bare feet and crunching beneath his shoes.

Together they walked down a driveway. Ahead was a huge white house with two turrets, set in large gardens. There were rose beds and frangipani trees and clipped hedges in the shape of peacocks and swans. For a moment, she was back at the palace. She felt a sense of wonder and joy swelling through her. He began to strut, his eyes shining, his angular face flushed with laughter. She let his excitement encircle her, and when he began sprinting towards the front door, she followed.

'All of it, all of this, is mine.' He spread his arms wide and then, turning to her, he gripped both of her hands. 'And you are the only person I want to share it with.'

3 5

After finishing up at the Fort, Thomas often spent his evenings paying social visits and, to keep up appearances, met with other covenanted Servants. Now that he and Sam had patched up their differences, and his friend was back in Madras newly married to the daughter of Colonel Paunceford, Thomas visited their new house on the Choultry Plain. He would watch Sam and Lily together, their faces turned towards each other, sharing a private joke. He could never get that close to Maya.

One day, as the late afternoon breeze swept away the foul odour of the River Cooum, and they walked along the Esplanade, Sam turned to him. 'Now, Tommy, when are you going to settle down?'

He had an answer all prepared. A wife was too expensive. First he had to provide for his mother and two sisters, still at home and without enough income to enter polite society.

'You're not getting any younger,' Sam added.

'Twenty-three is hardly old.'

They nodded to the Marion sisters as they walked by, each holding a frilly peach-coloured parasol. Thomas noticed that the younger girl's ringlets bobbed up and down and wondered what it would be like to pull one and watch it recoil. He must have been staring, because she tipped her face down.

'See. She'd be a good match. Her father's just been promoted in the royal army. He's got three daughters to get off his hands.'

Thomas looked out across the water. 'It's not the right time.'

'You're not taken by that dark hussy, are you?'

He felt a prickling in his chest. 'She comes and goes.'

'I saw her once, you know, walking along the Esplanade alone. She had the gall to say "Good evening" to Lily and me.'

Thomas felt a fleeting moment of pride. *That's my Maya. She won't be cowed.* 'She speaks good English,' he said.

'And stays with you now, I hear?'

'From whom?'

'Don't be an ass, Thomas. Nothing's a secret in this town.'

'I don't live in this town.'

'What, you think news can't travel a few miles from Cheyney's to the Fort?'

'What are people saying?'

Sam waved to Reverend Sutcliffe on the opposite side of the road. 'That you're wasting your time and could do better. She's not a Christian after all, she's a temple whore.'

For a moment Thomas thought he might punch him and bloody his short smug nose. He clenched and unclenched his hand.

Sam must have sensed Thomas's irritation because his tone softened. 'I'm saying it for your own good. Isn't it better I tell you than you hear the gossip? You have to think about your prospects. Things are changing here. It's not like the old days, when every Company servant had a *bibi* or two in the outhouse. Madras is becoming more like Calcutta, sophisticated, with taste.'

'Sophisticated!' Thomas exploded. 'It's a dreary pedestrian backwater. We're years behind Calcutta. Aeons behind the London fashions, though your Lily pretends otherwise and tries to keep up with the latest in Emperor-yellow wallpaper and china teapots. Just because you're under the thumb of your approbate wife, don't lecture me.'

Sam reached out to steady his arm, but Thomas shrugged him off. 'No need to drag my Lily into this.' He tightened his grip and pulled Thomas back, turning to face him. 'If you're seriously carving a place for yourself here then you need to play by the rules. Have her on the side if that's what you want, but get a proper wife. A pretty heiress to run your household, to give you some social standing. God knows you need it.'

'What do you mean?'

'How you manage your accounts is your business. But you've come running poor often enough for me to know that you need a stable income. Since England is losing its grip in the Americas, trade can't be relied on, and God knows what will happen now that we're at war with France. Cheyney's would have cost a mint and until you can pay it back, you're a sitting duck, waiting for the next downturn.'

'Cheyney bequeathed it to me.' He looked over Sam's shoulder without meeting his eye.

'He did what?'

Thomas stared across the water.

'What about his children?'

'Both dead, I presume. They were sent to England years ago and no one's heard of them since.'

'No wife?'

Thomas gave a sharp intake of breath. Sam didn't know about Cheyney's *bibi,* then. 'No.' He said, firmly. 'No wife.'

'You're on shaky ground, Thomas. Claims could be made against you. Surely Cheyney would have other family in England.'

He gave a small shrug.

'And you didn't have to pay a guinea?'

Thomas twisted his hands. 'Well, there were some costs. Cheyney had outstanding debts, which were passed on to me. The house required work. It's not cheap running a household like that.' He paused, wondering if he should say more.

'But where did you get the money for that?'

'A loan from the nawab.'

Sam shook his head. 'You're a fool. Look how many Company men have ended up in the gutter doing that. The nawab loans the money, then demands it back at preposterous interest, and when you can't pay, his debt collectors will come knocking. It can't last, either, Tommy. The web of corruption between the nawab and the Company stretches all the way from here to parliament. They're calling us crooks.'

'Crooks?'

'You talk as if it's a revelation. Edmund Burke and other Whigs in parliament are saying that we English *nabobs* are making our money from ill-gotten gains. Mixing trade with politics.'

'It's envy, isn't it? Envy that middling men can come out here and make a new life for themselves.'

'It's more than that. Robert Clive may have won the Battle of Plassey, but it didn't stop him being questioned for three days in parliament over how he returned to England with such a fortune. The politicians have a right to know. I thought you were above all of this. After all that happened to your father.' He stopped himself and sighed. 'I can see you're not listening.'

'Sam, you're proabably right. But I love it at Cheyney's. I've never felt happier. I've wanted that place ever since I first saw it. Living there—' he stared again at his palms, '—makes me feel like I've finally achieved something in my life. I've found my station.'

They started to walk again. The wind was picking up.

'Anyhow, I've told the governor to consider me as a deputy collector.'

Sam frowned. 'Are you sure you've got the mettle for it? It can be a grim job.'

'It gets results.' Thomas stared at the buckles on his shoes, coated with a film of dust.

'Yes, at what cost?'

'C'mon Sam, you can't tell me you've kept your hands clean all this time. Anyway, better that than getting a wife. She'd only cost me more.'

It was a Tuesday morning and Thomas was at home when he heard the jangly rattling of the runner's tambourine. Immediately, it triggered a chorus of cries as each servant called out and the message was relayed

from one to the other. The runner had a letter from the Fort and
Thomas told him to wait for the reply. Holding the envelope bearing
the Company seal, he took the front steps two at a time. He started
to cross the drawing room towards the back verandah. Raised voices
made him turn back. Maya and his valet, Flam, were sparring again.
Tall and willowy, with a fringe pinned down with a lacquer of coconut
oil, Flam kept the servants in line. Thomas had no wish to intervene
in their domestic dispute. Maya always seemed to be in an ill temper
these days.

He retraced his steps towards the front of the house and climbed
up the circular staircase to the roof. From there, the view across the
river still gave him as much pleasure as it had on that first day with
Cheyney. More so, now that it was his own.

He felt the folded parchment between his fingers. Too thick for
an invitation. Too thin for a bill. As he slid his knife to open it, he ran
through a list of debts outstanding. There was nothing that would
warrant such luxurious watermarked paper. Scanning the contents,
his pulse quickened.

Thomas read the words out loud. '*We have pleasure in offering you
the position of Deputy Collector, effective immediately.*'

He offered his thanks skyward. All the revenues of the farming
and cloth-producing districts north of the Palar River would now go
through him. He could feel the weight of the gold *pagodas* already.
This was going to be his tree and he'd shake it for all its worth. His
predecessor had stayed barely four years in the post before retiring to
England, and with the profits he'd bought a manor, a title and a seat
in parliament.

Later that afternoon, he took a slow stroll up the river. The shadows were lengthening and swallows sculpted the air above. He heard
the laughter of children and saw them, naked and shining, as they
ran along the opposite bank, where lazy water buffaloes stood in the
shallows among creamy waterlilies. *India*, he thought, *how sublime*.

What had Cheyney said, as he'd drowned in his cups the night
before he left for England? '*The more you try, the less she'll give. She's as*

fickle as the sea and as changeable as the moon, but when you're ready, she'll shower you with gifts.'

Thomas wasn't sure if his friend had been talking about a woman or a siren or the place itself, but as a shaft of golden afternoon sunlight illumined the scene before him, he thought that everything in his past had brought him to this moment. This single moment with its promise of liberty and the chance to make a man of himself; to release the Pearce family from debt; to erase the shame of his father's demise in the Marshalsea. He wanted to bottle it, savour it. Then he noticed the dome of a single cupola on the other side of the river poking through dense vegetation, half-hidden, forgotten, a memory of another era now reclaimed by the jungle.

As he stared at it, the flame inside him fizzled out. He suddenly felt the freight of history behind him, the layers of peoples and cultures that had come before – and his own insignificance in it all. He thought again of Cheyney and his final words of caution. *'Whatever you do, remember you're the guest here. Don't outstay your welcome.'*

By the following Monday, Thomas had accepted the position and was packing to go north.

As Maya watched him leave, she was reminded of Mudaliar. Next to Thomas's palanquin, peons ran, bullying people out of the way with wooden staffs. Flam jogged alongside, nodding as Thomas shouted his final orders. Behind were bullock carts with supplies, coolies carrying luggage, and a pair of guardsmen at the rear. Anyone watching would have thought Thomas was a general leading a campaign. Only Maya noticed the nervous folding and unfolding of his hands. Despite everything she did, his eczema was worsening.

After he'd gone, the weeks stretched out ahead. She put her tiredness down to the weather, the sickness to stale food. Listless, she wandered from room to room.

She missed the sounds of the temple and the screech of parrots as they flew among the statues. She thought of the rituals her mother performed. Dawn, mid-morning and dusk. They gave her life order. Now that Thomas was going to be away regularly, she sent a message to Pari, along with another message to Nila, asking her to return as her maid. And another to Mamia. She wondered what had happened to her and the Dutchman. She was in need of the company of other women.

Two months later, on the morning of Thomas's return, she completed the sixteen adornments with her maid. The call of the watchman announced his arrival. She waited at the top of the steps and ordered the servants to line up on either side. In her hand, she held a platter of freshly rolled *ghouris* of *paan*. As Thomas stepped down from the chaise and pair, he looked momentarily taken aback by the liveried staff. He tugged his jacket down and pushed the hair back from his face, weathered from the sun. He took his time, greeting each of the servants, and for that, she liked him.

At the top, his eyes swept over her, widening slightly. She felt a subtle current run between them and wondered if he'd felt it too.

'Welcome home,' she said, offering him the platter. He couldn't refuse. All eyes of the household were upon him. He hesitated, taking the smallest. She'd made that the strongest. His eyes blinked rapidly as he began to chew, then, with a faint smile, he carried on inside.

All that day he was in his study. Peons came and went. Sam made a visit and they arranged to go to the governor's ball together that weekend. The day was a firecracker and by mid-afternoon, the ink dried on the quill before he could get the words down on paper. He went out on the verandah. Maya was sitting on the small swing seat, with her back to him. Where her blouse ended and her sari began was a strip of exposed flesh, a thumb's width. His breath caught in his throat. He'd missed her. Such long trips were no place for a woman, but they would be more enjoyable if she were there.

'You are finished for the day?' she asked.

She senses me before she sees me, he thought.

'I will call for a house special.'

'No rush.'

He stood next to the swing.

'That pink is radiant on you,' he said.

She stared straight ahead and he couldn't see her reaction. Her back lengthened slightly. 'Your time away was everything you hoped for?'

'Good enough. Travelling here is never easy. Some of the villagers,' he shook his head, 'they've never seen a foreigner before. I was mobbed in one place. Treated like royalty in another. Collecting taxes is not for the faint-hearted.'

She pressed her lips together.

'People are nervous. They all ask what the Company are doing to keep Hyder Ali – the tiger of Mysore – at bay.'

'You know what they say about the tiger? There can only be one king in the jungle,' she said quietly. 'Everyone knows he's angry since the English seized more of his lands.'

'Let's not talk about it, just sit awhile. I missed you.'

They sat together on the divan. He stretched out and she perched beside him. She pushed down a squeeze of nausea – his feet smelled unbearably of wet leather. She could see the journey had strained him. The skin around his lips was taut and he was thinner. She preferred it when he dealt with cloth, rather than stealing villagers' livelihoods.

Everything about her is fresh, he thought. He felt grimy. Not only from the dust and heat. He hadn't reckoned on it being so ugly. He'd seen the gangs of thugs; he'd heard the screams. He knew the chiefs who collected money on his behalf went to every length to make the peasants pay.

'Come closer,' he said. 'Or do I smell that bad?'

She edged towards him. Then she took his hand, turning it over. The skin was cracking; the knuckles were inflamed. She brought the palm against the side of her face. Then slid it down over her body to lay it flat against the mound of her belly. She wished he could guess, that somehow he could know. 'Thomas, I am with child.'

His eyes flared. For a moment, his arm flinched, but his hand stayed where it was.

'How long?'

'Four months.'

She could see his mind calculating.

'January?'

'Yes.'

The memory of that night came back to her. She felt it now, in her body; in the way their legs touched, falling against each other. They had been walking across the wooden-floored drawing room together. The servants were asleep and it was past midnight. He had uncurled her fingers one by one and taken her hand in his. As she faced him, he pressed his other hand into the small of her back. Then he began to count.

'One, two, three; one, two, three. You have to imagine hearing the music. The violins would start first,' he whispered, his lips grazing the side of her ear.

As he counted the beats, she began to hear the rhythm of the waltz. It took two attempts for her to master the steps. Once she trod on his toe.

'In England we call it two left feet,' he teased, steadying her.

All these years she had danced alone and this was the first time she had danced in a pair. As they spun around, laughter bloomed through her. She let herself be led, revelling in their symmetry. Her head spun, her shoulders rose and fell. Faster and faster they danced, weaving figures of eight around the room; closer and closer pressed their hearts, until they came to stop and stood trembling in each other's arms.

Then they took a mattress on to the roof. After the giddiness of the dance, it was his stillness that surprised her. He held her close, his fingers tracing the outline of her shoulders and her waist. Her thighs become moist. She scrunched up her toes, her body taut. He pulled her hair, cupped her cheeks, his palms and fingers moving across her brow, the arch of her nose, the fullness of her lips.

They started to undress and she bent down to suck his nipple, pulling at the faint hairs surrounding it. When she looked up, his pupils were dilated. He went down on his knees, pulling her towards him and burying his face between her legs. His hands clenched her arse.

'What do you want? Ask me anything,' he said.

She looked down at him over the dip and rise of her body. His hair was ruffled, his eyes adoring. Then she pushed him down on the mattress and laid him flat. She lowered herself on to him as her fingers plunged deep into his mouth. Her hips arched and her head flung back. In the distance she heard the sound of the sea sucking over the rocks and the surf rushing in. Her groans were unstoppable.

The sound of his voice brought her back to the moment. 'January, you say. Are you sure?'

'Sure? Yes.' Uttering the words out loud made them real, and her face broke into a wide smile. She could believe it for herself now.

The smile caught him unawares. The joy of it streamed through him, too, dousing any fears. He burrowed his hand deeper, his palm cradling her belly. He wished to lay his face there and that night, in the darkness, he would do that.

'And I'm the—' He stopped, uncertain.

'Absolutely.'

36

Over the next few months, as her belly swelled and the baby grew, Maya felt the loss of her mother and aunt keenly. Following tradition, she left Cheyney's at the beginning of her seventh month. From then, until the baby was twelve weeks old, she had no contact with Thomas – or any man. She spent the last months of her lying-in with her maid and Pari in a separate house in Mylapore. Between them, and a local midwife, Maya gave birth comfortably to a tiny girl, and named her Suranita.

Three months later, after the spring festival of Pongal, Maya returned to Cheyney's in a palanquin. When the bearers stopped outside of the tall wrought-iron gates, she handed Suranita to the maid and checked herself once more in her ring mirror.

At the front porch, she took her time getting out of the palanquin. When she put her first foot down on the brushed earth, she felt a sweet sense of homecoming. Relief swept through her. She looked up to see Thomas on the stairs rubbing his hands together. There were shadows under his eyes. *He has not slept well.* The thought that he had lain awake thinking of her sent a shiver down her spine.

'Welcome. I trust your journey was comfortable.' His voice was husky.

Their eyes met. She tried to still the quivering of her mouth.

He hoped he didn't look as tired as he felt. The few drinks with Sam had turned into a long night.

She pushed away a fleeting anxiety.

'Come along. No need to dawdle.' His voice was sharper than he intended. She looked frail, standing there on the bottom step, straightening the folds of her sari on her shoulder.

From inside the palanquin came a mewing cry. He stopped. His eyes widened, first with alarm, then a slow dawning of recognition. Maya reached inside and the maid passed her Suranita. Thomas bounded down the stairs.

'I didn't think—' he said, peering down. 'I wasn't sure.'

She pulled back the muslin cloth from the baby's tiny round face. Her forehead puckered and the bright light made her blink. Tentatively her eyes stayed open. They were the colour of liquid amber: dark brown with darts of light chestnut around the pupil. He gasped, bending his head closer.

'Her eyes?' He looked up at Maya. 'Never have I seen such eyes.' He reached down and with his index finger stroked her hand. She unfurled tiny fingers and gripped his own.

Maya laughed. 'You're caught now. She's strong.'

As she followed him up the steps, holding Suranita against her chest, she tipped the child's forehead towards the carved stone Ganesha in the entrance hall, reaching to touch the red *kungumam* on the forehead of the pot-bellied elephant god, and dab some between Suranita's eyebrows.

Thomas waited for her. Her lustrous black hair was pulled back from her face accentuating her high cheekbones and long neck. *The woman undoes me, damn her.* He wondered if she could smell the cheap perfume of the brothel on his shirt. *Or is it in my hair?* he thought, running his fingers through it.

'I have made some changes while you were away,' he said, his tone brisk. 'We now have the corner room at the back of the house. The maid can sleep next door. I've had the living room redecorated, too.'

'Thomas, I am tired. I am thirsty.'

'Yes, of course.'

He showed her into the living room, the walls now clad in a sickly yellow. Maya sank into a cushioned armchair, suddenly weary. Heavy wooden furniture was arranged in a circle around a low table. On one wall was an oval mirror, on another, a painting of an English family with dogs at their feet. The faces of the women were marble white; the men all shared the same red cheeks. The father dominated. She wondered if Thomas was the young boy at the front, kneeling, his hands folded in his lap, his eyes staring anxiously back at her. She found herself calculating how much it would have cost to import the European furniture. Business must have gone well in the months she'd been away.

Thomas was trying to keep his composure. The tiredness from the previous night, and all the other nights, was catching up on him. He looked at Maya and the bundle in her arms. Now he had a child to think of, too. He rose to his feet, clapping his hands, and called for Flam in the haughty tone Cheyney liked to use. 'Sweet lime. Bring it now.'

On 25th July 1780, an emergency meeting of the council was called. Afterwards, Thomas declined the offer of luncheon and went in search of the reverend, who always knew more than anyone else. As the ear of Schwarz, he seemed to know Hyder Ali's next move even before the ruler of Mysore himself. As Thomas started in the direction of the school, he saw the distinctive figure in black approach. Under one arm was the Bible, under the other, a sketchbook.

'The council has just finished, yes? Come along, we'll talk about it over a cup of tea.'

Thomas almost had to run to keep up. All the while, Walter talked. Each time they met, the reverend was becoming more forthright. In a place where many Company men only knew Sunday by the flag at half-mast, Walter's fiery castigations, infused with the new evangelicalism out of London, were costing him his parishioners. In his eyes, Thomas saw the zeal of a crusader, a man who had finally found his mission.

Once in the parlour, Walter busied himself stacking the Company dispatches into a pile. Thomas stood at the window, looking down on to James Street. It seemed a lifetime since he and Sam had shared that small airless room together in the Fort. He was glad they'd reconciled.

He looked across to Walter. He was grateful the reverend had never mentioned finding him on the street, frothing and insensible, after he'd – he could barely admit it to himself. *After I lost my mind.* Walter had been true to his word and kept quiet. They'd had an exchange of letters and that was that. Thomas scratched the back of his head. In such a small place, the merit of a man could be judged by a single indiscretion.

'The school is going well?' Thomas asked.

'We need to build another wing. All these troops coming from England.' He pulled out a chair, motioning Thomas to sit, and rang the bell. Then Walter fixed him with his stare. 'More and more I believe it's the Indian mothers that are to blame. The state of concubinage in which so many live corrupts all decency. But it is their innocent children who suffer. Ill-gotten bastards who've never heard the name of Our Lord cross their lips.'

Thomas shifted his weight, wondering if the reverend's sermon was because he'd heard about the birth of Suranita. Outside, the three o'clock gun salute split the air.

A woman entered. Her hair was looped around the back of her head and fixed with pink blossoms. Her shoulders were muscular, her carriage erect. She was gripping the wooden tray so tightly Thomas thought it might break. As she placed it down, some tea slopped out of the spout. She dabbed it dry with a corner of her sari and retreated from the room.

'Your house warrants a housekeeper now?' he said, raising his eyebrows.

'Oh, her? My man had to go back to the village. He begged me to give his sister some work. Phoebe's a recent convert, and most devout.' Walter stirred two sugars into his tea. 'Now to the matter at hand. What was the outcome of the meeting?'

'The council is going to send another mission to Mysore and build up the defences around the city.'

'They still don't take Hyder Ali seriously?' He shook his head. 'He has an alliance with the French and over eighty thousand troops. Yet, when he declares war on the English, the council adjourns for lunch. It beggars belief.'

'The governor said, "It wouldn't hurt the tiger of Mysore to get his knuckles rapped,"' Thomas said.

'When will they get it?' He swept his hand towards Thomas, spilling the jug of milk, and barely pausing to mop it up. 'If we lose this war, we stand to lose everything.'

The following week, Thomas was riding through Mylapore. By late afternoon the streets were usually coming back to life after the soporific malaise of the day's heat. But with the declaration of war and news that Hyder Ali's forces were on the move, fear had already paralysed the city.

As the road widened, he dug his heels into the flanks of the grey mare. The reverend's words thrummed in his ears. 'Children at the mercy of their Hindoo mothers should be taken from them at the earliest opportunity.' The horse flattened her ears and snorted, breaking into a canter. He drove her harder, as if he could drive away Sutcliffe's words, as if by fleeing the Fort, he could escape its grip.

Ahead the track narrowed to a path, and bamboo created a natural archway, blocking out the sunlight. 'Good girl, easy there, girl.' Thomas pulled up the reins and Piper slackened to a walk. Home was close yet he wasn't ready to go back. He couldn't keep his daughter a secret from the world. He couldn't keep ignoring Sam's requests to visit.

But Maya would never convert to Christianity. She'd never marry him. She couldn't marry him, she said. She'd rolled her sleeve up and pointed to the three-pronged black trident on her arm. The branding. *In my culture I am already married. I know you don't understand. But I am wed to Shiva.'*

Thomas thought of Cheyney. He'd managed by keeping Prema, his *bibi,* in a separate bungalow, calling it *a zenana for one.* He didn't want Maya anywhere but in the main house with him. These days, with the threat of *looties* – raids from Hyder Ali's soldiers – it was too unsafe.

The horse began to pick her way down the path. As it opened out to the clearing and Thomas saw the white turret of Cheyney's, he wondered where they'd found Prema. He wondered from which tree they'd cut her down, and if grief had driven her to it, or defeat. Or a mother's despair at having her children taken away.

The woman's voice still haunted him. He'd never forgotten that first time when he and Cheyney were standing on the roof, and she'd started to sing, her deep-pitched voice laced with longing and rinsed with regret. He thought of Maya, at how she looked at her daughter with such tenderness. He couldn't send Suranita away. He'd have to find another solution. He leaned forward, draping his arms over the mare's neck, smelling her oaty sweat, and groaned quietly.

Two weeks later, Thomas was shuffling through his papers. He would be gone again before the month's end and his Company accounts were overdue. Maya was at the temple and the house was quiet. He walked out of his study on to the verandah. The maid was sleeping on the ground. In her hand was the end of a piece of rope. The other end was tied to the wooden cradle above in case Suranita stirred. He hesitated, not wanting to disturb them.

Then, quietly, he approached. Beneath the gauzy muslin, the child was sleeping, her face turned to one side. Her thick eyebrows were sharply drawn. Against the white sheet, her skin was the colour of burnt caramel. He took a step closer. He could see his sister's likeness in the child's face. Her blunt nose was identical to Elsie's. He looked for something of himself, too. He saw it in the angular lines and the chiselled chin. He bent down and blew her a kiss. Her skin emanated a milky scent. He wanted to imprint the image of her in his mind: her promise, her innocence, her sweetness. He wanted to leave for the districts with that image seared in his heart.

That afternoon Thomas shut himself away in his study, his food untouched. Maya ate her fish curry and rice quickly and alone, and then went back to the verandah to wait. The cook had laced the fish with too much tamarind, leaving a bitter aftertaste. She wished Thomas didn't have to go. She wished she had family close by. Her friends were scattered now. Mamia had gone north but said she would return soon. There was no word from Pari.

Maya rocked the cradle. Suranita was twitching in her sleep, making sucking noises with her lips. Her heart swelled. This love was unbearable at times. She wondered if *Amma* had ever felt the same way for her, even if she hadn't been able to show it. She could understand, now, how love was something to be feared. That to show too much love – too much *anpu* – was tempting fate. Auntie had never feared it, though. *And nor do I.*

She heard his footfall in the corridor. He stood behind her, looking at the child. Tentatively, he placed his hand on her shoulder. She stiffened and he stepped away. She heard the sound of footsteps and turned to see Flam with a tray, a glass and a carafe. Thomas pulled up a chair on the other side of the cradle.

'These past days you've been very quiet,' he said.

'Do you have to go?'

'I'll only be gone three weeks.' He sipped his drink. The arrack smelt offensive.

'I want to go back to Tanjore,' she said. 'I want to go home.'

His face emptied of colour. 'You can't. It's not safe. Hyder Ali's troops are already in the south.' He put down the glass, knocking loudly against the wood. Suranita stirred. Maya glared at him and nudged the cradle with her foot.

'Clumsy me.' He attempted a smile. 'Isn't this enough for you?'

She could see he was trying. More than Mudaliar ever did. She wished she could speak the truth, that despite everything, she never felt safe. There was always a threat. His eyes were on her, willing her to speak.

'You will never understand me,' she said at length. 'I will always be less than you.'

'And you were an equal with Mudaliar?'

She turned her head to one side. 'Thomas, I know you've had other women. But that's not why I don't trust you.'

She stood up and walked to the far corner of the verandah. He came towards her.

'I don't trust any Englishman.'

Her hands sought out the ring hanging on the chain around her neck. Sita's ring. She pressed hard on the faceted emerald.

'Maya, I don't always understand you. That's true. I don't always understand myself. But I love you.' He reached out for her hand. 'I know that you miss your family. As do I.'

She pulled her hand away. 'You have no idea about my family.'

'You never talk about them.'

'You never ask.'

'I don't like to pry.'

'You don't care.'

'I care about you.'

She turned away and spread out her fingers on the stone balustrade. 'I can't tell you about my family.'

'Why?'

'I can't tell you what happened.'

'Try.'

'I will talk myself out of loving you, out of staying with you.'

'How do you know?'

'The shame.'

'All families have shame.' He gave a small shrug. 'That's what families have.' He stood closer to her. 'Please, talk to me. Let me get closer to you. I feel the distance between us too.'

'You're never here.'

'I know,' he sighed. 'Tomorrow I leave. We don't know what will happen tomorrow.'

And so, hesitantly at first, and then with more confidence, she began. 'I am Mayambikai. Daughter of Lakshmi, niece of Sita. Granddaughter of Javanthri...'

They stayed up for hours. Piece by piece he stitched together the whole story, the life for which she was groomed, her house on West Main Road, dancing along the temple corridors, Palani and the palace of dreams. When she came to talk about her aunt's outcasting, her voice shrank. When she told him about her aunt's murder, he watched her disappear inside herself. He wanted to bring her back, and gently pulled her towards him. For a long time she resisted, her body unyielding in his arms. He let himself soften. He allowed the weight of her words to sink through his own skin. The fact that she'd told him, that she'd cracked her heart open, made him want her more. Minutes passed and then he heard a long, slow exhale. For the first time since they'd been together, and for the first time in Maya's life, she allowed herself to be truly held.

The tenderness of his embrace lasted long after that night. She kept recalling it. Through her legs, down her arms, to her fingertips. In the way his hands – smooth and soft now – had held her. The way he'd listened, as if every fibre of his body was listening. When she pressed herself against him, she felt the presence of her aunt. It was as if Sita were standing there, nodding, giving her niece the blessing she'd never had herself.

With it came euphoria unspooling through her body, a desire to dance again, a brightness inside. It was as if, all these years, she'd been carrying her aunt's own unfulfilled wishes and desires, and now she could let them go. After that evening, and in the following weeks, Maya's spirit swelled through the whole house. She ventured into the garden for the first time. She told the gardener to fix up the bungalow, which had fallen into disrepair, and she made it her own. She took Suranita out on the lawn, spread a blanket and played with her for hours in the shade of the frangipani tree. It was like falling in love all over again.

When the annual celebration of the ancestors arrived, Maya went to the temple to make offerings. After the last *puja*, she decided to take a walk along the beach. She rarely went out alone these days. Then she took a shortcut through the backstreets of Mylapore, clogged with cows, people, stalls and beggars. From behind, she heard her name being called. She turned to see a man standing on a doorstep, tall and stooped, snapping his fingers to get her attention. He was holding a violin.

'Rao *ayya*? Is that you?'

Bushy eyebrows peeked from beneath a faded blue turban. Nodding vigorously, he beckoned her over.

'Still playing?' Maya said.

'More than ever.' His words slid together as he talked.

He indicated that they should sit on the small porch to the left of the door.

'How long have you been here?'

'A few months only. I had to leave Tanjore again. Oh Maya, the city. The whole district.' He squeezed his eyes and sucked in his lips. 'You haven't been back? It's better that way. Better you remember it as it was.'

'Is the palace still there?'

'Yes, but the temple now houses the English garrison and arsenal.'

'The temple?' She was shocked.

'Troops everywhere. The prince is never seen, afflicted in body and mind. First the nawab and now Hyder Ali have plundered the town. Thousands are dead. Thousands more abducted in the villages. Hyder Ali's troops seize the children, sending the horses into the barns to sniff out the young girls. I was lucky to escape when I did.'

She shuddered, thinking of Suranita. All afternoon the child had been alone with the maid. She should get back.

'Rao *ayya*, how long will you be staying here? I have to go.'

'So soon? There is much to tell.'

'I'll come back.'

'You may like to know this much before you go. The English soldier, the one who murdered your aunt. He was captured by Hyder Ali.

He's being held with hundreds of other English in the dungeons of Seringapatam.' He was watching her closely.

'You're sure?'

'Yes.'

'What will happen to him?'

'The fair-haired ones, and he was fair wasn't he—'

'I never knew.'

'—are castrated and join the royal troupe of eunuchs. The rest are chained and left waist-deep in icy water. Many are tortured to death.'

She swallowed, her palms damp. She hadn't wanted revenge. Revenge hadn't been part of it. But perhaps this was some sort of justice.

Rao picked up his violin and started to play a slow, wistful lament. All of a sudden, he stopped. 'Do you remember that Englishman in Tanjore? I used to teach him Tamil?'

'The *sahib* who gave me the notebook?'

'Yes. Have you ever written in it?'

'No. I don't know what to say.'

'The English love to write about themselves. They write letters about their lives here and send them back to their families. They write books and books about us, Maya. Even when they don't know very much, still they write.' Absentmindedly he began to pluck the strings of the violin. 'It is not our custom to do this. This means our side of the story will never be known. Have you ever thought of that?'

She shook her head, rising to her feet.

'Five minutes more. Then you can go. There is something I need to tell you about that Englishman. There is something you should know.'

37

Walter was almost out the door, when he heard the jangle of the runner's tambourine. He stood at the top of the stairs as the man raced up, letter in hand. Immediately Walter recognised Schwarz's writing.

'Give him some water,' he called to his housekeeper Phoebe, 'and tell the runner to wait.' Then he went back inside.

Dear Reverend Sutcliffe
Events are moving apace. Prince Tuljajee has been forced into
an allegiance with Hyder Ali and already the Mysore forces have
reached Tanjore district. I fear for the future of this kingdom.

My duty lies here as counsel to the prince. However I've learned
of disturbing reports that English battalions are running riot and
require moral guidance in the Vellore region. I hope that you can
leave your school in the hands of the warden and travel there. This
is of the utmost urgency. I'm sending a reliable guide to accompany
you and have received assurance from Colonel Macleod that you
can travel with his troops.

I know this is unfamiliar territory for you, but I trust in your
abilities. Please send a full and complete report as soon as time permits.

Your humble servant.
C. F. Schwarz.
November 24th, 1780.

Walter read the letter again. It had been written in haste and the ink
was smudged. Nobody with such authority as Schwarz had ever said
they trusted in him. As he sat down to compose his response, a light
film of sweat broke out on his upper lip. He wrote his reply with a
flourish and ensured it was perfectly blotted.

Walter's hopes of travelling with Macleod's guard were abandoned
when news came through that Hyder Ali's army was forty miles
south of Madras. All English troops were rapidly recalled to protect the city. But he was determined to continue, and a fortnight
later, Walter reached the outskirts of a *kudi* by the river. Scorched
houses lined the road of the settlement. He saw a woman standing
outside the ruins of a temple. She was shouting out and walking,
her head thrust forward, as if she had lost something. Stopping,
looking, walking, with a stick in one hand. The cloth around her
waist was threadbare, her breasts shrivelled. She turned towards
the palanquin. Her eyes were red, her face bloodied with scratch
marks. He saw the same scars on her breasts. Some of the ridges
were old, raised pinky-brown lines. Others were new: weeping cuts,
suppurating yellow.

Walter alighted. The bearers told him to stay back, that the woman
was mad. He ignored them. He wanted to know what could have
happened for someone to do that to herself. Other villagers gathered
when they saw the entourage. He started to walk towards the temple.
A man behind shouted at him to stop. The woman ran towards him,
shaking her fist.

The bearers were whistling and clapping in alarm.

'Come back,' his guide called.

'*Sahib*,' a village man pulled his arm. 'Many *peys* here. Dangerous
place. Too many ghosts.'

Walter shook the man off. 'Who did it?' He stared at the ruins of
the temple, at the piles of bricks blackened by fire. The faces of the
sandstone statues were mutilated. The ornate carved door ripped off

its hinges. It was a scene of desolation. Out loud, he said, 'Damn that evil tiger of Mysore.'

'No, Sir. It was the English who did it.'

Walter spun round. Facing him was a tall man, his hair and beard wild and unkempt.

'I'm the headman of this district,' he said. 'Three months ago, we were attacked. Four hundred women and children taken from our village. All butchered and raped.'

Walter looked at the row of people standing next to the headman. They were shrunken and gaunt, grubby cloths around their waists. For the first time, he saw the depth of their hate. Without thinking, he took off his hat, placing it flat against his chest. A light murmur ran through the crowd. Then he looked across to his guide, who was nodding.

'Yes, *sahib*, it's true what the man says. The English did it. This woman was there. She is one of the few survivors.'

Walter looked slowly from his guide to the headman, and back to the woman, still prodding the ground with her stick.

'The battalion was led by Colonel Matthews,' the headman continued.

Wordlessly, he turned and walked through the people to his palanquin. He reached inside and pulled out his sketchbook, quill and ink. He told his bearers to take rest and called for water and a chair to be brought.

'What happened?' Walter said, sitting down, as the villagers gathered round. 'I want to know everything.'

His guide translated for the woman, pausing occasionally when she used a word he didn't understand. All around gnats buzzed.

'I was at home when word came that the English were coming. My husband was already in the fields. I told my girls to come quick. The four of us ran, shouting out to the neighbours to follow.'

She stopped, her voice thick. 'We could already hear the sound of gunfire and the pounding of horses' hooves on the ground. It made the earth shake. The priests told us to go inside the temple. That we'd be safe there. There were hundreds of us, pressed against each other. The gunfire grew louder. We heard the cries of men and screams of horses. My girls were clinging to me. The smell of sweat and fear was making some of the women sick. Children were pissing and shitting themselves. Flies, hundreds, thousands of them, crawling all over us.'

She squatted and rocked back and forth.

'Then came the splintering of wood. They were battering down the temple doors. The priests didn't stand a chance. The doors were flung open and redcoated soldiers poured in. The killing started straight away. The priests went down first. Then they started pulling out the women, ripping off their blouses, pushing them on the ground, against the wall, against the statues. Some they took outside and stripped naked before they set upon them.'

She stopped and let the stick fall. She covered her face with her shaking hands.

Walter waited, the sketchbook idle on his lap. The headman was tapping his foot; the crowd was restless. He wasn't sure how much he could stand to hear, how much he needed to know. The woman hadn't finished. She began to shuffle from side to side. He could imagine the scenes passing in front of her eyes. The stench of gunpowder, the baying of drunken soldiers. Legs of women, bloodied and bruised. He reached for his cross hanging around his neck and started to pray.

'For a few minutes, my girls were with me. I told them to stand behind me, that I'd protect them. Then this huge soldier approached. He pushed me aside and grabbed my eldest. She was screaming and holding on. I lunged towards him, scratching him. He punched me in the head. More soldiers came. I couldn't hold them back. They snatched each of my daughters. Then one came for me.' She picked up the stick again, and sliced the air.

Walter jerked back, his eyes smarting.

After a long silence, she continued, 'I don't know how I survived. I must have passed out. I awoke at night, my hand in something cool and sticky. I couldn't move my legs but I could lift my head. I opened my eyes. Everywhere, bodies. My legs were pinned down and for hours I lay there. Morning came, and so did the flies. The vultures and the crows. I felt the rapid beat of their wings. It was their hunger for life, their readiness to take my own, that forced me to move. They'd have had my eyes first, then my tongue. Somehow I pushed myself up through the bodies. To get out I had to walk over them. I'll never forget the crush of people under my feet. The softness. Bodies slit wide open, still soft.'

Silence shrouded the group. He looked up to see his guide brushing away tears. The villagers were staring at the ground, as if it might offer up answers; the woman stabbed the dirt with her stick. In the distance rose the mournful cry of jackals. He couldn't begin to take it in. Like a chill, numbness spread through him. This wasn't war. This was an abomination.

'Did you find your daughters?' he asked.

She nodded. 'Eventually. All three had been raped. Even the youngest. A child not yet bleeding. And they left me.' Her hands fell sideways. 'Better I was dead.'

She stood up abruptly and in the curl of the woman's blackened nails, he saw the claws of the vultures, still scouring her flesh. She turned away and began to walk towards the gaping hole in the temple walls. All around a profound and horrible silence reigned, only broken by the sound of crows.

3 8

Thomas was at the Sea Gate watching the merchants and *dubashes* vie for the best position. After so many years, he'd learned to read which native had something worth selling, which writer had money to spend, and who was bluffing. It all came down to the movement of the eyes and hands. Those with money had a relaxed stance, but their eyes were restless, constantly searching for the perfect deal. The hands of those with nothing were never still. *Like me*, he thought. *Always worried I'll lose it all.* He held his palms out. They were nearly healed. Every day Maya bathed them and rubbed herbal unguents into the skin.

He pictured Maya now. She would be nursing Suranita, sitting in her favourite spot on the verandah, looking up at the trees, watching the intimate habits of the birds. He'd not known any woman who gave them so much attention.

'Haven't you ever wished to fly?' she'd asked him the other day. 'I was watching a young Brahminy kite gathering twigs for its nest. It was perched among the coconuts, uttering high-pitched cries. Suddenly, another kite dropped down from above, falling fast. It knocked the first bird off the branch and together they twisted, spiralling around each other, falling. Then, at the last minute they straightened their wings and soared back up together. Imagine!'

That night as he lay next to her, hearing her rhythmic breathing, he felt disquiet. The image of her falling, nay, not even – of flying, of leaving him – left him hollow inside. He wanted to pin her down, to rouse her from sleep and take her. He lay very still, his cock very hard.

Her face was turned towards him, her mouth agape. Her breath had a sour-metal smell mixed with aniseed. He felt again the impossibility of his love for her.

She had told him about a famous painting of Krishna and Radha. Between them was a heart with wings. It lifted both of them up, bridging the divide between. Yet the heart was always separate: uncontrollable, unknowable. He nudged her awake.

'What is it?' Her words sinking with sleep. 'Suranita?'

'It doesn't always have to be Suranita who needs you.'

She opened her eyes.

He started to kiss her.

She pushed him away. 'Not now.'

'Think of it like a dream.'

Again she pushed him. 'Have you learnt nothing being with me?' She sat up. 'I'm not simply for you to take. I am not your wife.'

Outside the singsong chorus of frogs was mocking. He wouldn't be spoken to like that.

'No, but I keep you. I have certain rights.'

'Am I denying you those rights?'

He was confused.

'Or am I asking you to approach them differently?' She traced her fingers along his arm, to the crook of his elbow. 'What is happening to you, Thomas? What is the fight going on inside?'

He kept his arm still and stared straight ahead.

'It is the letters from your family.'

'They are there,' he agreed.

'But that's not it?'

He thought again of the two Brahminy kites, one waiting on the branch, calling out for the other as it built a nest. He guessed that was the female. Then the male came along and pushed her off and they fell together. But they could stop. When they chose they could lift their wings and fly. All he could see was the ground coming closer and closer and no way to stop himself. He turned away. She wanted answers that he could not give her. No, that was not right, that he would not give her. He wanted more than she could ever give him. There was always more to know – his longing never fully met.

Early in March 1781, Thomas sat down at his desk to write to Elsie. He'd put it off long enough. He would send it as soon as the *Charlotte* was ready to sail.

> *Dear Sister*
>
> *I pray by the time you receive my letter, the worst would have passed. This past year has been a hungry one. Even us Servants feel the pinch. Cash is in short supply making it impossible to buy merchandise. Friends have become rivals and no one trusts their neighbour. The only profession to profit is the lawyers, who are quick to lay suits against the indebted.*
>
> *The situation worsened when the Nawab of Arcot defaulted on his debts. Most of the Company are reliant on him, myself included, as he is the only one with a regular flow of money. Each time the dastardly ruler fails to honour his promises, another Servant faces bankruptcy. It is rumoured that the nawab owes the Company more than three million pounds. He has no possibility of repaying it.*
>
> *I had the sorry task of travelling to the outlying districts last month. Already famine stalks the land. Once the crops fail, the farmers have no choice but to eat their seed grain. When there is nothing else to eat, there are fears they will flock to the capital.*
>
> *We have suffered heavy losses in the war with Hyder Ali; a surprise attack on General Baillie's troops cost close to four thousand lives. Thankfully he did not advance to the gates of Madras, so for now, disaster has been averted.*

I know that you are anxious to receive an adequate income
but I cannot promise that it will arrive in the near future. Until
the situation improves, I have no surplus to send home.
Your affectionate brother, Thomas.

An odour of mildew and dust greeted Thomas when he opened the
heavy door of St Mary's. After dipping his finger in the holy water
and making the sign of the cross, he was relieved to kneel on the cool
flagstones. Outside, the heat was oppressive. His visits to the church
had begun with a Sunday service once a month. Now each time he
left to tour the districts, and arrived safely home, he made a point of
giving thanks and a modest donation.

The door swung open and Walter walked in, carrying a stack of
prayer books. 'Mr Pearce. Just back, are you?'

Thomas pushed himself up, nodding. 'You've been away too, I hear.'

'Yes.' He put the books down. His mouth quivered slightly. 'These
are most uncertain times.'

Thomas waited, but the reverend walked away, his shoulders
hunching around his ears. 'Do you think Madras is safe enough for
now?' he asked.

'I don't know.' Walter turned, his face pale. 'I don't know anything
any more.'

He'd never seen the reverend so rattled. 'At least more troops are
arriving.'

'But can we rely on these soldiers to protect us, any more than we
can rely on the council to face up to Hyder Ali?' Walter's hand cradled
the heavy wooden cross around his neck.

Thomas frowned, wondering if he'd offended the man in some
way. He wanted to get him on side for the child's baptism.

'I'm sorry, I'm making you uncomfortable. I'm much—' Walter
thought about it, '—preoccupied these days.' As if steeling himself,
he looked at Thomas. 'It is God's will what is happening. We can only
trust in that. I've noted your regular attendance at church. I see that it
helps you.'

'I never know if each trip will be my last.' Thomas shrugged. 'Reverend, I have a request. It is a delicate matter.' He hesitated, fearing the other man's judgement. He looked down at his hands and Walter followed his gaze and saw how they were chapped and weeping.

Thomas pushed his hands into his pockets. 'Can I trust you, Reverend?'

'Unburden yourself, Sir.'

'I have a daughter. She needs to be baptised.'

'How old?'

'Eighteen months.'

'You are not wed, Mr Pearce.'

'No.'

'I cannot condone such behaviour.'

'While I appreciate your view,' Thomas took a step towards him, 'my last commission that you owe me for the piece goods on the *Charlotte* is still outstanding. I have let that slip. I'm not sure Reverend Schwarz would condone that, either.'

The flicker in the man's blue-grey eyes told Thomas he'd said enough.

'If you let me know a suitable day – a quiet day, I don't want half the Fort in church – I will bring her,' Thomas said, adding for good measure, 'I'll not let any child of mine be damned to hell.'

The following Monday Walter was tidying up after morning prayers when Thomas pushed open the church door holding a young infant. She lolled awkwardly, her long white dress tangled in the man's arms. She was drowsy, her hair thick and curling, her ears already pierced with gold. She wasn't as dark as some he'd seen, but still too dark to escape detection.

He waved them towards the marble font in the nave. When he poured the water on her head, her arms shot upwards. 'I baptise you in the name of the Father, the Son and the Holy Ghost,' Walter began.

At first she didn't scream as much as give a half-hearted mew.

Then, fully awake, her eyes wide with shock, she bellowed. Thomas struggled to hold her still, her mouth gasping, fishlike and indignant.

When Walter had finished, he put his finger to his lips. 'Sssh, child.'

Her eyes slid to one side.

'Pretty little thing,' he said, leaning towards her.

Suranita reached out to grab the blue ribbon tied around his collar. Walter straightened but she was too quick. She tugged at it, her forehead crinkling.

'She's got you now, Reverend,' Thomas said, cradling the back of her head and wiping off the excess water. 'That was a drowning, not an anointment.'

Walter ignored him, extracted the ribbon from the child's fingers and wiped his hands with a towel. 'You'll have to make plans for her. She can't stay, you're aware of that, Mr Pearce?'

'It crossed my mind that she could attend your school. You have children of officers there, too?'

'A few orphans, yes. But would you want her mixing with the offspring of soldiers, below her class?'

Thomas shook his head.

'Back home, she'll have a chance. She'll have prospects.' He walked over to a cabinet, slipped his hand into his pocket and pulled out a bunch of keys, jangling them as he did so. 'Here she'd be outcaste by her own with no hope of entering gentle society.'

'Do many get sent back?'

'All the time. It's often me who arranges their passage. She can go to your family.'

'They don't know.'

'You could tell them.' He motioned Thomas to sit behind a narrow table to the side of the nave. Opening the cupboard, he reached inside.

With a thump Walter laid a thick, black, leather-bound book in the centre of the table embossed with gold writing. *Baptisms, Marriages and Burials from 1698. Property of St Mary's Church, Fort St George.* He opened the tome to the correct page, laying the quill and ink next to it. Then he pointed to the left-hand column.

'Today's date here. Then your name and the child's name.'

She was wriggling and making small bleating sounds. Walter wished she would stop. A heaviness was settling around his heart.

'Leave a blank for the mother's name. That's only to be filled if she's a Christian.' He scrutinised Thomas. 'I presume she's not.'

Thomas shook his head and transferred the child to his left arm. She started to cry again. He looked up, his lower lip twitching. 'Bit tricky to write. Would you mind holding her, Reverend?'

Walter sighed. At first he held her at arm's length. The crying grew louder. He was worried she'd foul him. That had happened before, ruining a perfectly clean shirt. He heard the quill scratch across the paper. Thomas was taking his time, pausing in between each word. It was no use, she'd never shut up. Walter rested her against his shoulder, patting her back. For a moment she quietened, before hollering again. He switched her to his other arm and dangled the keys in front of her face, and she grabbed one, pulling it towards her blossom-pink button-shaped mouth. Just like Emily used to. In spite of himself, he smiled.

'Thank you, Reverend.' Thomas was standing, his arms outstretched. 'Do you have children, Sir?'

He hesitated. 'One. Also a daughter. Sadly, she—'

Thomas reached out to pat his arm and took the child. 'I'm sorry. You understand then, the pain of separation.' He looked down at his daughter, quiet now. 'It's a wonder any survive here.'

'Many don't,' Walter said, steering him towards the open door.

'I suppose you're right. She'll be better off back home. Right now, though, I couldn't imagine sending her away.'

'You have to do it before the mother gets too attached – when the child is six or seven. The natives don't take it well. I've seen that. It's better you make all the arrangements and then at the last minute, inform the mother. In time, she'll come round. The mother must see it from the perspective of the child. If she stays here, there is no place for her.'

Walter stood watching them go. It was beginning to rain. The gate squeaked shut. Back inside, he scanned the open page of the register.

'Thomas Jack Pearce, Company Servant. Daughter, Madeline Pearce, born 18th October, 1779.'

He leaned forward, dipped the quill in the black ink and in the column for the mother's name, wrote simply, 'Native woman.'

Back home, Walter turned to face his armchair towards the open window, and stared out at the rain. It was steady now and looked as if it had set in. He curled his hand around the cup of spiced tea. Phoebe always made a good brew. He was happy with her and would be sorry when her brother returned from the village. Perhaps he could keep both on. Thomas's words came back to him. *'You understand then, the pain of separation.'*

But where was the separation in that? Walter thought. The child will go to England and a few years later, Thomas will join her. He wondered if he knew anything more about Emily. Probably not. He sat back. For a moment, he wondered who the mother of the child was. There had been no mention of her. But then, there rarely was.

A crow flew down and shuffled along the window ledge to escape the rain. Walter watched it scrape its beak either side of the ledge, as if sharpening it. Another joined and they turned to face him. *Bloody crows.* He stood up and flung his arm towards them. *Get away.*

The rain was getting heavier and Thomas knew he had to get Suranita back to the house before Maya returned. Every day, it seemed, she was attending another religious festival. This time with Mamia. He walked briskly towards the side gate inside the Fort walls, anxious not to be seen. He'd already been ribbed once about his 'piebald' daughter.

The reverend confirmed what he knew already. Suranita's best opportunity lay in going back to England. Here she would forever be betwixt and between. He thought of persuading his Scottish uncle to take her on. For a few years, at least. *Then, when I'm ready, I can join her.* His mind became hazy.

In truth, he could never see himself back there. The long, dark winters. The cold, empty streets. That's what Cheyney had said when he'd gone back on furlough. He'd left again to escape the damp and perpetual grey skies that weighed him down. Thinking of Cheyney, it dawned on him that Walter had used the same turn of phrase, *'In time she'll come round.'* But Cheyney's *bibi* never had. A light shiver ran through him. The rain was constant now and he could feel the starch on his collar begin to sag.

Opening the scalloped curtains of the palanquin, Thomas laid his daughter down on the cushions. She was quiet, her face subdued. He should go home and freshen up. He'd find a way to break it to Maya. He would explain it all. She would understand it was for the best.

Maya awoke suddenly in the night. Next to her Thomas was breathing deeply, his body curled in on itself. The air was hot and heavy. She closed her eyes. Again there came an image of a man in black. He was looking at her as if he were under water, and peering through bevelled glass. She sat up, unsure if there was a presence in the room, or if it was only a dream. Quietly, she went out on to the balcony. Outside, the moon was halfway to fullness and the garden was brushed ghostly white.

She listened. Suranita was with the maid and both were asleep. She missed the warmth of her child's body pressed against her own. She kicked and wriggled, sometimes crying out and talking in her sleep, yet there was comfort knowing she was there.

A dog howled, then another took up the cry. Soon, all the dogs of the neighbourhood were barking. She strained, listening. The *looties* had started in the west. Thomas assured her that they wouldn't come this far south. Nonetheless, two new watchmen were posted at the gates. Perhaps Thomas was right and they should move to Black Town. It was safer there, the defences were stronger closer to the Fort.

Tiredness tugged at her. She would try and sleep again.

Back in bed, the image of the man's face and his blue-grey eyes filled her mind. Rao's words came back to her. *'The Englishman had a daughter the same age as you. She was called Emily. She and her mother died in a fire at their house. He never forgave himself.'*

As she lay there, she realised that the man in the dream was *sahib* Sutt-sutt. She remembered all those years ago: the first time, when he'd tried to stop *Amma* hitting her in the temple. The way he'd reached out to touch her. And then she remembered that that wasn't the first time. She'd seen him on the day of her initiation. Perhaps *Amma* was right and seeing him on that day had been a bad omen. Next to her, Thomas stirred. She rolled towards him, fitting herself to the shape of his body. As she listened to his breathing settle, she thought of the notebook the *sahib* had given her. And Rao's words, encouraging her to write in it. She wondered if it was still fit to be used or if the mice had chewed the pages to dust.

The next day, when Suranita took her afternoon nap, Maya went to the bungalow in the garden and in the corner, found her box. Inside, was the notebook. It was the size of her outstretched palm, the cover swirling brown, like the Kaveri after heavy rains. She sat on a stool and opened the front cover with care, so as not to damage the spine. Some of the pages, thick and yellowing, were stuck together.

Maya opened it fully. The sketches still leapt off the page like the first time she'd seen them. In one corner was a parrot in mid-flight with an orange snub beak. In the centre of the page, there she was, in her lime-green blouse and skirt in between the temple pillars. She'd never realised that her clothes matched the colour of the parrot's wings. With her arms outstretched, she looked like she, too, was flying.

On the next pages were several profiles of her face and head. On some the *sahib* had used heavy strokes for the darkness of her skin. In the last sketches, however, they were softly done, featherlight, and the mole on her right cheek was sharply defined. Then, on the next page, was a larger profile of her face, except it no longer looked like her. The eyes were light hazel and the skin was milky. And yet, Maya saw glimpses of herself in this other girl's expression, in the tilt of her head and the intensity of her gaze, in the curve of her cheek and the way the lips were parted.

Maya leaned back against the wall. *This must be Emily*, she thought. *He had seen glimpses of her in me.* The *sahib's* strange fascination with her had never made sense. As a child, she'd only felt sorry for him. She thought of Suranita. If she were to die, would she see her likeness in other girls too? Would the torment of loss play tricks with her mind? She dispelled the thoughts. It was only inviting sorrow. Maya continued to turn the pages. There, in upright letters, the *sahib* had written.

It is hard to believe I have been in Tanjore for four years and not written a word. I am hoping that Maya will make better use of it than I.

It was as if he knew her. As if he were talking to a friend.

When Thomas departed on another sortie to the districts, Maya went into the bedroom and sat at the desk with an inkpot and quill in front of her. She had made her own quill from a swan feather she'd found by the river. Thomas had given her a glass pot of black grainy ink. The quill was awkward to hold, the words scratchy on the page. She should practise first. She went in search of paper, but she could not get comfortable. The chair was hard and the desk at the wrong height. Then she took a tray and carried everything out to the verandah.

She did not know the date but knew from Thomas that the month was October. Instead, she wrote, *moon waning, Aippaci*.

A week later, the notebook still lay untouched. But Maya had filled several sheets of parchment with words – English words – beginning with her name, then Suranita, Thomas. Slowly she started to transfer these to the notebook's pages.

Short phrases.

The crimson blossoms of the frangipani fall. At night I smell fear.
People are starting to go hungry.
No word from Thomas. Suranita cries out.
My wings are clipped.

Interspersed were lines of poetry in Tamil script.

The Lord is white as jasmine, Akkamahadevi.

When your husband holds you,
Push him gently with your breasts, Palani.

In December she received word from Thomas. He had been delayed and would be gone for a few more weeks. *The famine is taking hold,* he wrote in broad, sloping handwriting. *I urge you to stock food and buy what you can. I will return as soon as my work here is done.*

The next day Maya slipped his message into the front of the book.

39

Thomas had never wanted to return to Madras as much as he did now. He had gone all across the northern districts of Arcot. The English now managed all the land once belonging to the nawab, and to the west too. The Company was taking over. He passed hundreds of weavers and farmers and priests who had left their villages in search of food. Everywhere, starving mothers and starving children, too tired to mob him, too weary to cry.

The drought had lasted for two years now. Yet Thomas couldn't believe the country he was seeing. In the early years, when he was still trying to prove himself to Mudaliar, he'd visited this region, famous for its weaving industry, and found some of the best cloth – a weave so tight that it shimmered like a Gainsborough. He'd never found anything like it, before or since.

As he lay back on the straw cushions in the palanquin, he reflected that his *dubash* had taught him well. Undoubtedly the man was cunning. *But then, who among us doesn't have double standards? Each has his own secrets.* His back ached from the constant jolting and the hard ground he slept on at night. His skin itched, his guts were rotten. He wished to be on the back verandah with Maya and Suranita. He didn't want them to see what he was seeing. He prayed that the situation in Madras would be better. He knew it wouldn't.

All around was cracked earth and dry corn stubble. The fields lay untilled and the villages deserted. The people had stripped the leaves off the trees and dug up the grasses. The cattle had sunk to their knees. Their carcasses were dirty white, buckled and leathery, bleaching in the unforgiving sun.

At night the servants never let the fire go out and he slept with a pistol at hand. Tigers roared, coming within feet of the campfire. Further north herds of wild elephants were marauding, mad with hunger. He couldn't sleep. The jungle encroached, jackals yowled. Worse, though, when it came, was the silence. Then Thomas would wake and call for the flames to be stoked higher.

Things were only going to get worse. Much worse.

The next morning they set off again. Three days' march, Flam reckoned, before they would reach the outskirts of the city. Already, it was January. He'd been gone three months. Thomas slid his left hand under the cushions, checking once again that the leather bags filled with *pagodas* were there. He used them at night as a pillow; during the day he lay on them as he travelled from village to village. Not till they were safely deposited could he breathe easy.

The governor would be pleased with his efforts. The final amount had exceeded expectations. He'd made sure that every village paid their dues. He wouldn't have been gone for so long but for the tip-off to go to the far north of the district. A town had hidden the measly profits from last year's sale of grain. They'd already avoided paying their taxes once. He wasn't going to let them get away with it again. This time he saw to it that the headman was punished. One hundred lashes in the public square.

He made himself watch. Afterwards he puked in the bushes.

Lying down again in the palanquin, Thomas fell asleep. Some minutes later loud buzzing woke him. Thick black flies were swarming inside. The air was putrid. He ripped the curtain back as the palanquin swayed and shook. Suddenly, the bearers dropped the bamboo litter.

'What the hell is it?' he shouted, the coins jangling and rattling beneath him.

'*Sahib,*' Flam cried, pointing ahead.

As Thomas climbed out, the full force of the smell hit him and he staggered back, his palm pressed against his face. The smell of liquid death. As far as he could see, corpses filled the ditches. Dead from hunger and thirst, men, women and children were piled up and among them, packs of scabies-ridden dogs ripping off chunks and tearing at limbs. There were too many dead for the dogs to fight over. No barking; no need. Thomas bent double, vomit spraying out of him.

There was no choice but to go down the road. Sometimes the bearers had to step over the dead bodies half-stripped of rotting flesh. In the hot sun, the corpses putrefied almost at once. Thomas lay back, covering his face. But the flies kept on crawling on him. Each time he brushed one off, another came.

That night, they set up camp a dozen miles outside of the city. The bearers refused to go any further. They feared the restless ghosts stalking the land, looking for warm bodies to suckle on. They found a *choultry* that still had a roof and a dribble of water in the pump. The bearers went inside and cleared a space for him.

It mattered not whether Thomas was in or out. The stink pervaded everything. He couldn't sleep, couldn't eat. He didn't want to breathe. He was witnessing scenes his mind couldn't comprehend. He'd heard stories about how bad Hindustan was in a drought. He remembered the story the Dutchman had told him about the great Bengal famine the previous decade, when wild dogs took over the villages. How they never attacked their victim while he was still standing. As soon as he fell, they would set upon him. *'The poor fellow might still be alive when they went for the soft parts of the body, ripping out the bowels before the victim's eyes.'*

⌒

When Thomas entered Madras, he entered a city of the walking dead.

All along the streets, crammed into every available space, were the poor and homeless. At first he couldn't tear his eyes away. Protruding hipbones and unnaturally scrawny shoulders – they weren't people any more. Reduced to their skeletal frames, men and women looked the same, bony necks resting on each other's knees. Babies with thighs no wider than his thumb, their eyes blank.

The bearers could barely forge a path through the crowds. As they inched forward, he saw a child die, its distended belly pumping up and down in vain as the arms lifted in a sudden paroxysm, before falling in the mother's hands. She was too exhausted to cradle it one last time to her withered breast. Her eyes followed him, defeated. He thought of Maya and shouted at the bearers to move faster.

Beneath him were the uneven ridges and angles of the leather bags and safe-boxes, the coins clinking as the palanquin swayed from side to side. A wave of disgust engulfed him – that he was even worrying about such things. But he told himself to be practical. A man had to carry on. Before he could go to meet Maya in the house in Black Town, he must deposit this at the Fort. Thirty bags to the Company and five to him. A tidy sum, and no one would ever be any the wiser.

At Cheyney's earlier that day, Suranita had been playing when Maya received Thomas's message to go straight to Black Town.

Take what you can, lock up the rest. Cover the child's face on the journey. I will arrive as soon as I can.

He'd sent reinforcements. Three extra litters for their belongings; another for herself, Suranita and the maid; a cohort of armed guards. It had been weeks since she'd been outside Cheyney's gates. She had no idea how bad it had become. The emaciated and destitute lined the roads. Feeble hands hit the side of the palanquin and cried out for rice. The peons shouted, beating them down. Maya wrapped a shawl around Suranita and swallowed back her tears.

Thomas was not at the house when they arrived. The rooms were dark and stuffy. She went up to the roof and sat under the palm-leaf awning, rocking Suranita until she fell asleep. When she heard the watchman's cry, she leaned over and saw the gates open and Thomas arriving. She went downstairs. His face was ashen. He crossed the room towards her.

'You both arrived safely,' he said, looking towards the sleeping child in Maya's arms.

'Where have you been?'

'I had to go to the Fort.'

'I thought you'd be here when we arrived.'

'I came as quickly as I could.'

'Why didn't you warn me? We were mobbed in the palanquin.' Her breath was shallow. She didn't trust him and she didn't know why. Her legs were shaking and she needed to sit.

He looked at her, worried, and called the servant.

She sat on the chair. Suranita stirred, whimpering, and she pressed her lips against the child's forehead. 'Thomas, what are you hiding from me?'

He was facing away from her, so she couldn't see his expression. She saw his shoulders flinch. It was momentary and if she hadn't been watching, she would have missed it.

'Nothing,' he said, turning to face her.

They stood without speaking.

'I've never seen you look so guilty,' she said.

Throughout 1782, the days became longer and longer as the heat built. By lunchtime the flowers were wilting; the animals stopped moving; the birds started to drop from the sky. And the people went on dying. Twice in three months Maya, Thomas and Suranita returned to Cheyney's, only to flee when the warning flares were lit and Hyder Ali's warhorses were bearing down on the city. After that they stayed in Black Town. Most of the English took their families inside the Fort but Thomas insisted they stay put. Maya knew he didn't want to be seen publicly with her.

Suranita grew sick and fell into a fever. She could not keep down her food. All around people were dying for lack of it but Thomas always ensured they had a constant supply. Maya didn't ask where it came from. She didn't want to know. Her world shrank to the back rooms of the house. She never set foot outside, her heart too heavy from all she'd witnessed, her mind blunted from so much pain.

In early September, Thomas was walking slowly towards the refectory, waiting for the bell to be rung for lunch. Although the meals were smaller than a year ago, they never stopped serving.

As he crossed Fort Square he saw the reverend, who vaguely nodded at Thomas and continued past. 'It's too much. Too much,' he was saying, his eyes pinned wide. 'I've given away everything. I've moved back to my old rooms. But it's not enough. Nothing is enough. We're losing five hundred natives a day.'

'You've moved out of your lodgings?'

Walter nodded. 'Anything extra I have goes to the school.'

They fell into step together.

'It's the screams at night that haunt me. All those still outside the city gates, but there's no room for them here.'

'Are you going to lunch?' he asked.

Walter shook his head. 'I've lost my appetite.'

He looked down at the reverend's hands. They were shaking. He couldn't meet the man's gaze; the despair ran too deep.

'I know some of the English godowns are still full of grain. I've seen them with my own eyes. The council is holding their stock back while they force the Indian merchants to sell theirs. Yet it's only the blacks caught profiteering who get twenty-five lashes. Have you seen any of the Servants getting flogged? Have you?' His tone was accusatory. 'I haven't.'

Thomas lowered his head.

'You're not contributing to the suffering, are you, Mr Pearce?'

'No, of course not. I try to be fair,' he lied, thinking of the surplus grain he was still hanging on to, waiting for the best price. 'I'm just a

chink in a long chain.' Thomas gave a curt nod and walked towards
to the refectory. All down the street he could hear the reverend talking
aloud to himself.

'Nothing can prepare you. So much suffering...'

When Walter opened the door to his small rooms behind the church,
he sighed. His old rooms were pokey, but the walls were thicker than
the grand apartment on James Street. Since moving back, he had
started to sleep a few hours at night. He pulled the chair out and
slumped down. His legs were weak and his mouth was dry. He should
try to eat one meal a day. He needed to maintain his health. There was
no one else at the Fort who'd take over the orphanage if he dropped
dead. The children would be turned out on to the street.

With effort, he rose to his feet and uncorked a bottle of Madeira,
pouring himself a glass. He'd been sorry to let his housekeeper go.
Phoebe had pleaded with him to keep her, but there was no room.
He'd done the best he could, and she still worked three days a week
cleaning the church. That provided her with enough for food and
lodging. He swirled the sweet wine in the glass and tossed it back in
one gulp. Heat rushed through him and he poured himself another.

Since the famine had taken hold, he was up each day at dawn,
ready to shepherd the new arrivals to the shelter. The previous day
had started out like any other, and then a young girl of eight or nine
approached him, a puny baby in her arms. There was no more room
inside, so he ordered a makeshift palm shelter to be made at the back
and asked one of the women to feed the pair some rice gruel. Then,
both slept.

By lunchtime, when he went to check on them, the girl was up
again. Some of them made a remarkable recovery once they had
eaten. She asked if she could bring some more orphans to the shelter.

'We've been sleeping in a fishing boat and eating scraps left by the
fishermen.'

'How many are you?'

She counted on her fingers. 'Eight.'

'Are they well enough to walk?'

She shrugged.

'How far is it?'

'Not far.'

He looked around. All the workers were occupied and he wasn't needed until evensong. 'I'll come with you.'

The girl led him away from the Fort, south towards the fishing village. Once they left the main thoroughfare, the stench of human shit and rotting flesh cloaked him. He pulled out his handkerchief and covered his nose and mouth. He hadn't realised how living in the Fort still kept him from the worst. He stopped, and thought to turn back. The girl reached out for his hand. Her hands were tiny and unnaturally cold.

Ahead, the laneway narrowed and he saw the figure of a woman sitting upright. Next to her was a corpse. As they approached, the girl made a coarse chattering sound. Her grip tightened and she tried to yank him back. At that moment the woman lifted her head, too large for her bony neck, and opened her mouth. Her teeth were thickly coated with blood, and in her hand was the remains of a limb.

Walter lurched sideways. An icy gush rushed through him. He found himself running behind the girl, away from the woman, his mind exploding.

'We must get back to the Fort,' he said.

'The other children will die if I don't get them.' Her tiny frame was shaking with effort.

'You need to rest. If not, you will die too. Tell me where they are and we will fetch them later.'

That afternoon, they found the boat where the other orphans were sleeping. Two were dead, the others made a full recovery.

Walter was grateful for the charity offered by the wealthier Indians. The *dubashes* and merchants had all increased their subscriptions to close to two hundred and fifty *pagodas* a month. It was the Company servants who appalled him. The whole damn system was corrupt.

Many turned a blind eye. The balls and luncheons and dinners continued. Then, after six months of famine, when no one thought it could get any worse, came the hurricane. Only then did he weep useless tears into his pillow at night.

Thomas resorted to wearing the silk gloves again. In bed he lay listening to the monotonous drone of the surf. Unable to sleep, he went upstairs on to the roof of the Black Town property. Since they'd cleared the worst of the corpses from the streets, Maya had filled the terrace with pots of plants, plump aloe vera and pungent *tulasi*. Somewhere he caught the scent of night jasmine. He let himself breathe it in, and then started to pace.

The calls were coming from all over. The nawab. The Company. The merchants. He owed money to them all, or they to him. And no money to be had anywhere. The letters from his family were building to an unruly stack. He hadn't opened the last one from Mama. He knew it would be the same. Elsie and Charlotte still didn't have enough to enter the marriage market.

The events of Monday unravelled before his eyes. Two lawsuits had been laid before breakfast. The secretary wrote again dunning him for money – from his own account, as well as the Company's. The nawab's agents threatened to beat down the door if he didn't pay up. He had one more chance to get rid of his surplus grain before the council came after him. Already it had come down hard on two Servants who'd profiteered during the famine. Now Sutcliffe was on his back, suspecting the worst.

Thomas told himself, as he had before, that he hadn't deprived ordinary people of grain. He'd just increased his profits at the expense of the Company. Once the shipments of rice arrived from Bengal, his problems would be solved. He'd find a way to get rid of the extra grain and through the money he would make on the rice, he'd clear his debts. But as the first fingers of sunlight broke through the cloud, he gripped the balcony, enraged. Before his eyes, he saw all the years here coming to nought. He was trapped in a web of his own making.

One morning, Maya went into the front room overlooking the street. For months she'd kept the shutters closed but now she pushed one open and peered out. The streets were clear now. There was a cow eating rubbish and two skinny men pulling carts. Further up, she saw a new encampment starting on a vacant plot. The destitute still crowded the city.

Maya widened the shutters and light streamed into the room. She ran her finger along the ledge. The dust was black and thick. From the back room, she heard Suranita cry out. She went to check on her, pressing the back of her hand against the child's neck. The fever was almost gone. She wiped away the crustiness under the child's eyes, then called for the maid.

'Take her up to the roof and sing to her. It is fresher there.'

Maya went back to the front room and sat on the window seat. She saw a lizard basking on the ledge in the sun-brittled light, its back the colour of saffron. It was a relief to see something alive. Its round charcoal eyes darted from side to side, its body softening in the warmth. On the opposite side of the road there was a mother and a child dressed in rags. The mother was around the same age as she was. When she saw Maya, she lifted up her daughter with outstretched arms. She couldn't bear to see any more die, and ordered that they be taken in and fed.

40

In early October, believing the worst to be over, Thomas decided they would return to Cheyney's. 'I want to celebrate Suranita's third birthday surrounded by trees. We must get out of this stinking place.'

Since growing thin with fever, Suranita had fattened up again. Her cheeks were becoming round, and every day Maya saw more of Leela in her daughter's face. She hoped that if they moved back, Thomas would be at home more. But he was always working late, fretting over when the city's desperately needed supply of rice would arrive from Bengal. She wanted to stem the gulf widening between them. He was unreachable these days. *After witnessing so much death*, she thought, *our hearts have closed to life itself.*

On 18th October 1782, as they sat on the back verandah, with the placid Adyar flowing by, he presented Suranita with a painted wooden doll, fashioned with a bonnet and wearing a cream dress. All day she played with it on the swing seat. That night, when Maya lay next to her, stroking her daughter's forehead, the child's hands would not be prised away from the toy.

Two days later, when Thomas woke, there was no hint of a breeze. No birdsong. No hawkers. The sky was tinged mustard and copper red. As he sat in his study he sniffed, wondering if fires were to blame. Yet no wood smoke sullied the air, rather he could smell a dry, brackish odour. A large drop of sweat fell on the letter he was composing to the governor and the ink ran across the page. He pushed the letter away – it could wait. Maybe tomorrow he'd have better news. His head pounded. Neither water nor wine relieved his thirst.

By late morning the quiet enveloping the house was disturbed by sudden gusts of wind. The red clouds darkened and in the distance thunder rolled. At one o'clock he heard the whistles and ahoys from the watchman, the rattling of the tambourine and crunch of gravel on the driveway. A runner arrived with warning of a violent storm approaching and advising all Company men to take shelter in or near the Fort. Straight away, Thomas ordered the windows to be shuttered and the furniture brought inside. The boats were pulled up the bank and the horses tied in their stables.

Grabbing his telescope as he hurried out of the study, he called to Maya sitting on the verandah. 'Come. We should go up to the roof.'

As they stood at the edge of the stone balustrade, looking down-stream to the bay, Maya moved closer to him. She let the back of her arm touch his wrist. The wind was stronger now, blowing strands of hair across her face.

He reached out to hold her hand. As he did so, the memory of the night they had waltzed together came back to him, and afterwards, when they had come up on the roof and he was down on his knees staring up at her. When she was everything – she was his world. He pulled her to face him, stroking the side of her cheek. He looked at her for the first time in months. Fine lines were beginning to show around her mouth, and her eyes were tired.

When had he stopped looking? he wondered. When had the barbed comments from other Company men turned his love to shame? He wished for life to be simple again. He wanted to be honest with her, and a better man for it.

A high whinnying rose from the stables. Dogs started yelping. Down below they heard urgent shouts and window frames rattling. A pot smashed.

'We have to go,' she said, turning towards the ocean. 'Look what is coming.'

On the horizon, a spiralling column of blackness was advancing towards them. They watched as the cloud came closer. All around was a cacophony of high-pitched whistles and birds calling in distress.

Thomas put the telescope to his eye. 'Swallows! My God, hundreds of swallows, and other birds, seagulls, cormorants, all coming in from the sea.'

She snatched it out of his hand and put the telescope to her eye. He was right. The birds were coming. This time not falling from the sky but fleeing some immense unimaginable terror. The wind was gathering force. Branches were snapping.

'We have to go, Thomas.'

They looked at each other and, seizing her hand, he pulled her close, pressing her against him, inhaling the coconut oil in her hair.

'I've missed you. I'm sorry. I know this isn't the time.'

'I've wanted to leave you. If I could have done, I would have left already. I'm scared you're going to leave us. Go back to your country. Find yourself a wife.'

Suranita was screaming down below. Doors were slamming.

He pulled her closer.

'No. I'm not. My place is here.'

She looked at him, her mouth dry. He held her gaze.

'My home is here,' he said. 'With you.'

There was the sound of wood splitting. The horses were trying to break free.

'We must tie up the horses before they escape, and then go.'

By mid-afternoon their party had reached Mylapore and the charcoal-grey clouds were changing the day to night. Maya stared out of the palanquin. All along the beach, crowds gathered looking out to sea, now a churning mass of white froth. The wind was whistling, the rain falling. Cries came from the river. Boats were being ripped from their posts. In the bay the ships and men-o'-war tossed violently, tearing at their anchors. The Bengal fleet had arrived but until the storm passed, there was no chance of unloading the precious cargo of rice.

Then, with huge of claps of thunder, the hurricane struck. Cane and bushes mixed with columns of sand, palm fronds flying in every direction. Masts snapped like cribbage sticks, throwing terrified men into the sea. As the storm deepened, the wind tore in from the north-west, and sea monsters – giant squids and urchins, large glassy-eyed fish – were spewed up from the deep.

When Maya and Thomas reached Black Town, the bearers could barely hold the palanquins against the wind. Grit and sand blew around them and tore the curtains off. Trees were almost at right angles and tiles were being ripped off roofs. People were dispersing, running for shelter. Everywhere wood and debris were flying and falling. An army regiment passed them at a run and flares were blazing from the Fort. As Maya stepped out of the palanquin, a vast jaundiced yellow moon rose – beautiful, dark and tragic. The maid passed her Suranita and she felt the rapid beat of her daughter's heart and, clutching her, she began to run, heavy raindrops soaking them both.

'Move quickly, we need to get inside,' Thomas said, waving his hat. His eyes blazed forest green. As he seized Maya's hand and pulled her towards the door, love flooded through her. She couldn't deny it; she still loved this man. She didn't know how it would end, but she knew that right now she was bound to him.

'The child, keep her close to you, keep her safe,' Thomas was saying. Once inside, he ordered Flam to barricade the upstairs windows and everyone else to hurry downstairs to the godowns. They huddled together: Thomas, Maya, the maid, cook, watchman and bearers. Flam, at the entrance, stood holding a burning torch. All around were hessian bags empty of grain and outside, the howling wind.

Not two miles away in the Fort, Walter was sealing the storerooms where the grain was stored. At last, they were full. In an improbable gesture of charity, Pearce had offered to fill one for the orphanage school out of his own supply. He thought of Pearce, of when he'd first met him, back on the *Gloria*. *I mistrusted him then, and I do now.* He didn't know what the man was hiding but as Walter struggled with the bolts, buffeted by the storm, he could only be grateful. It would feed the school three times over.

In the early hours of the morning, the north-west wind suddenly dropped. An uneasy calm settled. People came out from their houses. Thomas and Flam went upstairs on to the roof to survey the damage. The north-westerly that had scoured the coast, lifting dry earth from barren fields, was transforming into something else. Thomas stared upwards. Lightening streaked across the indigo sky. After hours of deafening noise, this silence was eerie and foreboding.

'What's happening?' He turned to Flam.

'Very bad, *sahib*. Very bad.' He pressed his palms together and started to pray.

'Maybe it's over.'

'Not over. Only beginning.'

'There's more to come?'

'The signs of this storm have been there for days. This is when the gods pause before making more mischief.' Flam's voice was shaking.

Thomas looked up at the few birds still left, tossed by the wind, black shapeless forms in the squid-ink sky.

In the forest the elephants were stampeding to higher ground, trumpeting in terror. Packs of sandy-haired monkeys were swinging from tree to tree, fleeing the coast. Goats butted against each other and horses kicked down stable doors, everywhere freakish cries of man and beast.

High above, beyond the clouds, beyond where Thomas could see, the wind was making the last revolution of its 180-degree turn from the north-west to the north-east. Then, at exactly four o'clock, wrote one eyewitness, 'After waiting in awful suspense, the wind suddenly burst into a hurricane, the like of which was never before seen in Madras.'

Downstairs, in the godown, Maya heard distant droning. She held Suranita tighter, calling out to the Mother Goddess for mercy.

'Thomas,' she shouted. 'Come down. The wind is coming back.'

On the roof, Flam grabbed Thomas around the waist and pushed him down the stairs. Together they stumbled into the godown and a sea of hands pulled them in. Thomas reached out for Maya and encircled her and Suranita with his arms. He didn't let go of either of them all night.

As the wind tightened into a knot, Maya smelt the fear in the room and heard the muttering of prayers. Then it struck, and she was unable to hear anything.

The next morning, an English merchant went out to sketch what he saw. He could not. 'From the Sea Gate as far as Chepauk the whole beach was covered with wrecks.'

Maya rolled over. Her arm was stiff; she must have fallen asleep. She bent down to look at Suranita. The child was unscathed. Thomas stirred. His fingers sought out her own and then travelled up her arm to her face. He opened his eyes. She reached out to squeeze his hand and drew it towards her lips. They were alive. Somehow, they'd survived.

'She is well?' he said, looking towards Suranita.

Maya nodded. Outside, she could not imagine how the city would look.

He rose to his feet and stretched, offering his hand to her. Then he scooped up Suranita and together they went up to the roof.

The sky was ribboned red. Boats were discarded on roads; buildings were gone. Hundreds of palm-leaf shacks, as flimsy as silk, were destroyed. The homes to fishermen and their families, the camps sheltering the homeless, the schools for the children – all were flattened. Thousands were killed.

Everywhere was covered with filth. Dead dogs and cattle and corpses littered the streets. Carts and trees were turned upside down. The sun was breaking through the clouds and by evening the bodies were starting to rot. The Cooum forced its banks, flooding all the godowns and spilling all the remaining grain stores into the sea. The rice from Bengal sank without a trace. Boats littered the cemetery, and for days afterwards, brightly coloured sea snakes were found writhing on the governor's lawn.

PART 4
Madras, 1786

4 1

Suranita was in the back courtyard when Maya came out on to the balcony. She stood watching as her daughter thrust out her arms, flapping them up and down like a bird, and speeding around the statue of the dancer. *Just like I used to do,* Maya thought.

After one round, she stopped and looked up. 'I'm the eagle you showed me yesterday.'

'Come. It's time for lessons.'

Suranita jutted out her bottom lip.

'Enough of that. Upstairs now.'

Suranita took off again. 'Catch me and I'll come.'

It was the same routine each morning. By the time they sat together on the swing seat, both were breathless.

'First we learn the vowels,' said Maya, resting the slate on Suranita's lap. 'In Tamil there are twelve. I'll write; you copy.'

The child bent forward, the tip of her tongue sticking out. *Like Amma,* Maya thought. Suranita was learning fast – too fast, sometimes. Maya wondered how her daughter knew as much as she did and if she'd been the same when she was six years old.

'Is this how you were taught?' Suranita said, as if reading her thoughts.

'Yes. By my mother and aunt.'

'Tell me about the temple again, about where you used to play.'

'Afterwards, when you've finished your letters.'

'They're not as good as yours,' Suranita pointed.

'But you're just starting. In time they'll get better.' Maya looked down. Each letter was etched with deliberation and care.

On the chair opposite was a carved wooden boat from Canton. Thomas was always bringing Suranita gifts, clothes, too – stiff dresses with frills and bows. Maya didn't like Suranita trussed up like a doll. But Thomas insisted, especially when he took her out, which he did more and more.

At home, he demanded she speak English to him. 'The child needs to be taught some manners,' he'd said the day before when he caught her eating with her fingers. 'I want her at the table using a knife and fork.' When Suranita refused, she was sent to the bedroom alone. Worse than the punishment was the bewilderment on her face. The child had no idea what she'd done wrong.

'*Amma*, you're not listening to me.'

Maya felt a light tap on her knee. 'Show me the elephant dance again, *Amma*.'

'Only when you've finished.'

'Now.'

Maya gave a mock sigh and put the slate to one side. She stood tall and stretched her left arm out at shoulder height, bending it upwards at the elbow and tipping her hand down like a trunk. Swaying from side to side, she mimicked the heavy rolling gait of the elephant.

Suranita jumped up. 'Like this?'

'Opposite arm. That's it. Now trunk up. Trunk down.'

'Trunk in.'

'Trunk out.'

Suranita erupted into peals of laughter.

'In.'

'Out. And now flap the ears.'

'Stop, I need to catch my breath. My elephant can't keep up with yours. It's a baby elephant.'

Maya smiled, relaxing her arms at her sides, watching Suranita as she bent over, her shoulders convulsing with helpless giggles.

'Another. Do the peacock.'

'All right. Just one more,' Maya said as she sank her knees low and stood on tiptoes, her torso and head undulating like the peacock as it stretches its long neck, her arms and shoulders splayed out to show the fanning of the tail.

Suranita stood transfixed. 'How do you make it look so real?'

'Practice. Just like you with your letters,' Maya said, sweeping the child up in her arms, and sitting her on her lap for the rest of the lesson.

'When can I learn to dance?'

'Soon.'

'This afternoon.'

Before Maya could answer, she heard the servants' whistles announcing the arrival of a messenger. This time it was a letter for her, stamped with the Company seal of the Dutch East Indies.

'Take a break now, little one. Then we'll finish off.'

Suranita stood up and ran along the corridor towards the kitchen, where the maid was waiting with a plate of plump *laddus*, sweetened with raisins.

Maya crossed to the balustrade, the letter in her hand. She remembered the last time she'd seen Jacob, only a few weeks before in Black Town. His face was thinner, his eyes sad. He'd told her, then, that Mamia was unwell. 'She insisted on travelling with me to Pondicherry, but our boat capsized while still in the harbour,' he'd said. 'Mamia was the better swimmer and helped both of us reach shore, but now she complains of pain in her lungs.'

Maya ripped the seal open.

Mamia is gravely ill. I beg you, go to her. She is only a few days' journey from Madras and I can arrange a palanquin for you. I will arrive as soon as I can.

Maya stared down at the river. The water was calm and glassy. She'd already told Jacob she couldn't go, that she was reluctant to leave her daughter. She thought of Mamia, of the times they'd spent together, of the story her friend had told her once. 'I will die young, it is written. I will enjoy myself while I can.'

This second request, Maya could not ignore. She slipped the letter inside her blouse, wondering how she could persuade Thomas to let her go, and walked along the verandah to where Suranita was sitting on the maid's lap. From the kitchen she smelt cardamom and rose.

'Still hungry?'

Suranita nodded.

'I think cook has a treat for you.'

Two minutes later he appeared, a metal bowl in each hand.

'*Payasam, payasam.*' Suranita jumped up, clapping her hands.

Maya nodded to the cook, whose fleshy jowls quivered beneath his black curling moustache.

They ate the milk rice desert sitting on the back steps, sucking it noisily from the lip of the bowl. It was tepid, perfumed with rosewater, and green pistachios were scattered on top. Maya was glad Thomas wasn't there to insist they eat at the table and use a spoon.

Thomas and Sam were standing on the balcony of the Company offices waiting to see the new secretary. Opposite, a workman was putting the final touches to the roof of the governor's house in readiness for the visit of Lord Cornwallis, recently appointed as governor-general of India. They watched as the man's toes gripped the wood of the flimsy scaffolding, his saffron turban a shade brighter than the terracotta tiles.

'That orange,' said Thomas. 'You don't see it back home.'

'I do. Every night I take my wig off.'

'That's auburn. Here the orange is so bright and brassy it makes my eyes hurt.' He reached up his right hand to tip his hat down against the glare.

'Your hands, they're bad again,' Sam said.

Thomas stared at his inflamed fingers. 'It's the weather.'

'Is that all? You look awful tired these days.'

He slipped his hands into his pockets, wishing Sam would stop looking at him. 'Do you think we'll make it, Sam?'

'Make it back home? We have to move soon if we're to keep the profits,' Sam said.

'But how are we expected to keep any profits with the India Act forcing us to declare all our income?'

'I told you this was coming.' Sam indicated towards the governor's house. 'And when Cornwallis arrives, the rumours are that he'll clamp down even more.'

'Do you think so?'

'Thomas, we've got Edmund Burke calling Hastings a despot in a turban. The tide has turned. When you arrive back in quaint old Westbury-on-Trym, in a shining hackney, dressed in oriental garb,' he flicked a hand towards the cream silk shirt Thomas was wearing, 'you'll be known as Pearce the *nabob* and you'll be shunned.'

'By whom? None of our middling friends. They'll be pawing all over us.'

'Over you.'

Thomas frowned.

'We're staying for now, Lily's decided. Anyway she's in the family way again. We can't risk it.'

Thomas looked into Sam's lightly freckled face. All these years and he'd never changed his attire, nor let the sun brown his skin. *A proper Englishman, more decent than I'll ever be.* 'I'll miss you when I leave, Sammy. We've seen a lot together, you and I.'

'Don't get pathetic on me. You've not gone yet.'

'If my health were more robust and I didn't have the responsibility of the family back home, I would stay forever. I'll sorely grieve when I go.'

They stared at the view. The sea was quilted and scintillating blue in the bright sun. The calmness outside made him realise how jittery he was. He swallowed, trying to stop the panic rising in the back of his throat.

'What about the child?' Sam said.

He couldn't answer straight away.

Sam waited.

Inside his pockets, Thomas clenched his hands together into a fist, feeling the skin break a little more. The pain felt good.

'You're not having second thoughts, are you? Not thinking of staying because of her?'

'No, of course not.'

'Then?'

The workman was fixing the final tile. He lifted one foot to balance it on the side of the building, awkwardly reaching over to push the tile into place. A sudden gust of wind made the scaffolding teeter. His other foot slipped. For a few seconds they watched, horrified, as he hung in mid-air, his outstretched limbs at impossible angles, before he grabbed the wooden pole to save himself. The tile slid off and smashed below. His lips moving fast, the man cautiously lowered himself to the ground.

Thomas and Sam looked at each other.

'I'm making arrangements,' Thomas said, chewing the inside of his bottom lip so his chin wouldn't give him away.

'It's the right thing, Thomas. You know that. For her, for you.'

He nodded. *But what about the mother*, he wanted to say. *What about Maya?* But he couldn't do that. He'd never be able to see it through if he thought about her.

'I just wish . . .'

'No point in that.' Sam reached out, patting him on the arm. 'You just have to act now.'

The following Friday evening, Thomas was in the study at Cheyney's, a letter on the desk. A faint odour of his mother's spirit of lavender rose from the crisp watermarked page.

> *Send the girl on the first ship available. We have found a place for her. She will go to your cousin in Dundee. I have not, of course, made mention of it to your future bride.*

We would rather you travelled back with your offspring. If you
must finish your affairs, we expect you back early next year. The wed-
ding will take place in March. We cannot postpone this any longer.
I trust that your business continues to do well.
Yours faithfully etc.,
Mother.

Elizabeth Finch. He'd met her once, many years before, at a Christmas
gathering. A fair-haired creature, rather wan with unsteady eyes. They
had little in common.

He walked out on to the verandah. There was no relief from the
heat. He went back into his study. The candle was guttering, black
smoke curling from the flame. He looked down at his accounts. This
year he'd made the biggest profit since arriving in Madras – all thanks
to the recent law slashing the tax on tea from 119 to 12.5 per cent.
Overnight, Thomas had turned his entire trade over to the stuff. He
and Sam had chartered two ships and sent them to Canton. He'd tried
to talk the reverend into stumping up an advance, but he said he was
done with trade. He was a man of the cloth and nothing more.

'You'll make more doing this than you ever will elsewhere,'
Thomas had told him.

'I'm not playing the game any more, Pearce.' The disgust in the
reverend's eyes was unmistakeable.

Thomas stared down at the figure. Twenty-five thousand *pagodas*.
Equal to ten thousand pounds. More than his father would have made
in all his years of business. Yet it gave him no pleasure, only a creeping
sense of failure. His guts griped, wheezing like ancient bellows. His
hands throbbed. He emptied the glass of arrack, then poured another.

Thomas rolled up the scroll and melted a hard lump of wax in the
flame. Then he pressed his seal on to the parchment and tied it up with a
ribbon. If Sam was right, he had to get his money out before things really
tightened up. And, before, he lost it again. Nothing was certain here.
He sat down once more. Above he could hear the squeal of monkeys
and a faint thud as one fell on the roof. In the hallway, the servants were

bickering. Out in the garden, a lone night bird called. All these sounds that he couldn't imagine living without. He put the candle out of its misery and, picking up his sheaf of papers, walked back along the corridor.

Suranita cried out. She'd been having bad nights lately, calling for her mother. She wasn't used to sleeping without the maid or Maya close by. One night he'd found her standing in the centre of the corridor, her eyes vitreous. When he'd picked her up to carry her back to bed, her hands had clung to him. When he laid her down, she'd buried herself in the pillow, her hands restless, mewing in her sleep. That night, he'd given in, and laid her next to him.

But now, as he stood at the bedroom door watching her, his body was rigid. He was unable to go to her. He pushed down the doubts, the fear of what could happen on the long voyage ahead. *She's a tough girl, she'll survive the crossing.* Others had done it before her. More would follow. He should have listened to Sam and done it sooner. That was the problem. He'd left it too late.

Thirty miles to the south of the city, Maya was sleeping on the floor of a *choultry*. She sat up, panting. She felt the rising in her chest. She'd had the dream again. Suranita was stretched out in a white box and someone was sealing the lid. There was nothing Maya could do to stop it. She heard the tolling of church bells, ringing from across the sea. She saw Suranita's face, her eyes skating under the thin butterfly-wing lids, her lips half-open. She had to get home. She should never have come.

The bearers wouldn't be moved. Maya shouted and protested, picking up the pots and banging them together.

'Get up. Get up now, you lazy good-for-nothings. Move.'

An hour later they were on their way. The bearers punished her by shaking the palanquin and stumbling as they walked.

Maya drifted between waking and sleep. She could still feel the presence of her friend Mamia with her. She could feel the gratitude of her spirit that she'd been there at the end. That she hadn't been alone. *No one wants to die alone,* Maya thought.

After nursing Mamia in her final days, Maya had stayed for the funeral. Contrary to tradition, Mamia had requested Jacob light the pyre. Initially, the priests had refused, but so impressed were they by his fluency in the language and respect for their customs, finally they had agreed. His head was shaven and he wore white. From a short distance, Maya watched as the priest handed Jacob the torch. He swayed, his hand unsteady at first. Then, more firmly, he began to encircle the body laid out on the wood, before plunging the flame into the dry hay.

Within moments the fire caught. Tears welled in the back of Maya's throat but she swallowed them down. Mechanically the priests began their prayers. She watched Jacob closely. His face crumpled for a moment before regaining composure. Only his eyes betrayed the devastating loss she knew he was feeling. Together they stood as the flames crackled, devouring the flowers and silk, smoke rising, acrid with burning flesh, which even the best sandalwood could never mask.

A sharp movement jogged her awake. She heard the gruff voices of the bearers grunting and swearing and spitting.

'*Poa, poa*. Go, go,' she cried.

But her journey back to Madras was maddeningly slow. Bridges had been destroyed. Roads had disappeared, reclaimed by the jungle. All the way she kept hearing a child's laughter, loud and bright. Uneven footsteps running across a wooden floor.

As Maya drew closer to Madras, the crowds thickened, a never-ending column of people, bullock carts, cows and goats, eddies of dust and women with babies strapped to their backs, heading to the capital. Their pace slowed until they were barely moving. Maya stared out at them, at the children grabbing their mother's skirts, crying out to be held, to be loved. Mothers too tired and empty to respond. In every child's eyes she saw the eyes of Suranita.

The following evening, Thomas was sitting on his armchair, on the verandah, staring up at the blackness. The tide was high, the wind fretting around him. He listened to the water lapping against the bank and took another swig of arrack. It burned the inside of his mouth and throat. He could feel Maya reaching out to him. She wasn't far away now. He knew if she arrived, she'd do everything in her power to stop him.

He remembered the week before she had left to go to her friend Mamia. They were all together, Maya and Suranita sitting on the swing seat reciting poetry. He looked across at the identical tilt of their heads, the swanlike shape of their necks, the same delicate hands. Maya had stopped and looked over. Suranita followed her gaze. They both stared at him, eyes mirroring each other. Abruptly he had turned away.

Later that day, he and Maya were watching the maid chase Suranita around the statue of the Indian dancer. He'd said quietly to her, 'She's got to go, you know.'

'Who? The maid?' Maya said.

Thomas understood, then, that she had no idea what he was talking about. He'd let the matter drop.

Now, as he finished his drink, he looked at the empty glass, the way the candlelight shone through it, and then, with as much force as he could, threw it against the wall. For a brief moment, as the shards skittered across the tiled floor, he felt release. Almost as quickly, regret. The sound brought Flam running. He stood at the door, scratching his head.

'Leave it until the morning,' Thomas said.

The valet looked at the pieces of glass and back at Thomas.

'Sir?' He loosened and re-tied his *lungi*, his fingers fiddling with the knot.

Thomas dismissed him with one hand. 'Go to bed, Flam.'

'Sir.'

Thomas walked to the opposite end of the verandah. He had to do something, go somewhere. He couldn't just wait for the hours to pass. From inside he heard crying. Flam appeared again at the doorway.

'Suranita is awake, *sahib*.'

'Fetch the maid. Tell her to lie with her.'

'Sir.'

He walked through the house, past the rows of oil paintings, the statue of Ganesha and the sleeping watchman. Opening the front door as quietly as he could, he walked down the steps into the garden. The wet dewy grass was cool underfoot. He never came here after dark, rarely on his own during the day.

Thomas found himself walking to the bungalow where Maya liked to spend her afternoons. He tried the door. The wood had expanded in the dampness. He pressed his shoulder up against it. A musty, tired smell filled his nostrils. He kept the door open, allowing in the trickle of moonlight and walked across to the corner. There was a stool, and beneath it a box. He sat down and picking up the box, shook it gently. Nothing rattled. It was locked.

He put it on his lap, his fingers feeling the rough texture of the wood. Maya's box. He thought of that first time he'd come to Cheyney's. When he and Cheyney were standing on the roof and he'd heard Prema singing.

Maya will hate me for it. She'll never forgive me. He'd known that all along. That's how it was.

Thomas picked up the box again and shook it harder, willing it to give him an answer. He put it back down. What was he thinking? All he wanted was to be close to her. To be near her.

And yet, it riled him that she should have a box here and he'd never known about it, and that it was locked. She should have no secrets from him. He stood up and, cradling the box, he went back outside. *This is why people turn to God*, he thought, *to make them feel better when nothing else will.*

As he walked back to the house, he thought of Suranita. He had packed her sea chest with care – with some of her Indian clothes and her new cotton dresses for the journey. Her three dolls. The blanket Maya had sewn her. He wanted his daughter to have fond memories of her time here. The following morning before they left, he would sit her down and tell her she was going on a journey, and he'd be joining her soon.

Thomas woke early. All he wanted was to go back to sleep. Outside in the corridor he heard voices, laughter. Suranita was already up. When he turned over, his hand touched something hard. With eyes closed, he let his fingers feel the corners of the box.

Once dressed, he found a piece of wire, inserted it into the lock and jiggled lightly. A faint click. He opened the lid. Inside was a dark-brown notebook. Beneath that, a score of palm leaves covered in Tamil script and a *pandaan* shaped like a parrot. Thomas frowned and carried the book over to the window. It fell open to a page covered with sketches of a young girl, around Suranita's age or a bit older, dressed in green. Further on was a sketch of another girl, fair-skinned, with light-brown eyes. Underneath, in childlike writing, one word: *Emily*. He kept turning the pages. In the same handwriting, he read.

> *I have never known what to write in sahib's book but I have held it for so long, it must have a purpose. As I cannot think what to write for myself, I can write for my daughter. So she can know who she is and where her mother is from.*

Each letter was scratched into the page with care, with courage. Maya must have practised every word separately before she wrote it in the notebook. He continued to leaf through. No mistakes. Every sentence neatly blotted.

Why had she done it in English? He never knew she could write so well.

> *A beautiful baby girl born just before full moon in early Aippaci. Amma and Auntie would be proud. She reminds me of little Leela…*

An ear-splitting wail rang out from the verandah. Thomas dropped the book on to the top of the chest and ran into the corridor. Suranita was bellowing, her eyes squeezed together, her mouth wide enough for him to see her tonsils. She was pointing downwards. A trickle of blood was spreading out from her small brown foot.

'Take her inside,' he shouted. 'Flam, clear up this bloody mess. I told you to do it last night. Someone get water and a cloth.'

Drops of blood followed her.

It took an hour for the cook to extract the three glass splinters from Suranita's foot. By the time the wounds were dressed and bandaged, and Thomas had finished packing, it was past nine o'clock. She was wearing a blue-and-white chequered skirt and a white blouse with a mauve collar, clinging to the maid, snivelling and burying her head in the woman's red sari.

When Thomas tried to pick her up, she started yelling for her mother. He slapped her hand. 'Suranita, stop this. We have to go.'

The child snatched her hand away, and wrapped her arms tighter around the maid's legs.

'Get here now.' He looked across to Flam. 'The maid can come with us as far as the Fort, then we'll send her back.'

'*Sahib.*'

Inside the chaise and pair, Suranita was curled up on the maid's lap. When Thomas climbed in beside her, she turned her face away.

On the seat opposite was her sea chest. He'd packed the notebook and a few extra things in her black satchel. He checked his pocket for the pouch of money.

42

Walter was finishing lessons when he heard a rap on the door. It was one of Thomas's servants. He read the note, smoothing out the creases.

I will meet you at ten with the child in front of the Sea Gate. The ship is due to leave early afternoon.

He scribbled a response and gave it to the lad, then he walked back to the front of the class. 'Slates out, everyone. You, boy, begin the day's reading.'

When class had finished, Walter walked towards the Sea Gate. The wind was coming from the north-west and clouds scudded across the sky. A large flock of crows were massing in the palm trees. He looked towards the metallic grey ocean flecked with white. There were only two ships in the bay. Two had been diverted to Fort St David a hundred miles south. More crows were gathering; a swarm of tattered wings rose out of the trees. A sudden squall and they flew upwards.

The memory came back of Tanjore. The day when the crows fell on the town, burnt wings everywhere. He couldn't remember whether the crows were alive or dead when they fell. The whole thing seemed preposterous now. Maybe he'd dreamed it, maybe he'd dreamed it all. The glare of the Indian sun burnt away some memories and distorted others.

Walter started to say the Lord's Prayer under his breath. 'Our Father, who art in heaven...' The words kept coming. His tongue licked the back of his teeth, finding the remnants of the stringy mango he'd eaten for breakfast. He'd eaten two, just sliced the flesh off and stood there in his nightshirt, watched by his housekeeper, letting the juice drip down his chin. No matter how many he ate, it was never enough.

He should get going. Thomas would arrive before long. He wanted to get there early, choose the best fishing boat. A splash of rain fell. The wind was picking up, but the tide was going out. His chest was tight and he didn't know why. He hoped they'd arrive soon. The *masula* boats wouldn't go out if conditions worsened.

Two hours later, Walter was still waiting. For the second time the fisherman strode up the beach towards him, raising his eyes to the sky and shaking his head.

'Storm coming.' The man gesticulated towards the ship. 'They are making ready to leave.'

'I know, I know. They'll be here soon.'

Maybe Pearce has changed his mind, thought Walter. He'd seen that before.

Then, he saw Thomas's servant running towards him. Behind him was Thomas, carrying the girl, struggling in his arms. One of her feet was roughly bandaged, the bottom of the white rag stained red. When he saw Walter, he tried to raise a hand.

'Had a mishap before we came out. Just a cut. Left the child unsettled.' Pearce put her down. 'Now stand up, Suranita. Meet Reverend Sutcliffe.' He nudged her forward. She shook her head and started to sob.

Walter touched his elbow.

'Pearce, the child knows what is happening?'

'As best she can. She's too young to understand.'

He raised an eyebrow. 'But you have told her?'

Thomas turned to look at Suranita, quiet now as the maid rocked her.

'I told her she'd be going on a journey. I didn't think she needed to know more than that.'

'What about the mother?'

He hesitated. 'She's away.'

'The maid, is she going?'

'No.' Sweat was gathering on his upper lip and brow. Thomas pulled out a handkerchief and pressed it against his face. 'You've organised someone to take her on the ship?'

'Yes. She will be the charge of Miss Welch.'

They both looked at the girl, smiling now as the maid clucked softly under her breath. Walter hadn't seen the child since the day of the baptism. She'd grown to be quite lovely. She turned towards them, her eyes wide and trusting.

'She answers to Madeline?' Walter said.

'For now, just use Suranita.'

'As you wish.'

'Until she's in England. Then she can start anew...' His words petered out.

'*Sahib*, ready?' The fisherman was waiting.

'Pearce?'

But he was crouching down in front of the child, straightening her blouse. He pulled her towards him, kissing the top of her head. 'Now you'll be a good girl, won't you?' He squeezed her hand. The child looked up. 'You'll be with Miss Welch. She'll look after you. Elsie will be there at the other end.'

The child wasn't listening. She was twisting round, back towards the maid.

'Reverend, perhaps I should accompany her after all. You know, make sure she's all set up.'

'There isn't time for that. The ship is ready to weigh anchor. Once she's on the ship, there's so much to distract her.' He nodded towards the fisherman. 'Take the child's belongings down to the boat.'

As Walter followed the fisherman, he looked again at the child, now in the arms of Thomas's valet. A vague memory surfaced, only to disappear again. His feet sank into the wet sand and he had to run to keep up. He wasn't looking forward to this at all.

When Maya arrived at the gates of Cheyney's, they were padlocked. She called out for the watchman. No one came. Fumbling, she tried the latch on the side door. That was locked, too. She started hammering on the wood. 'Open up. Open up.' She tried the latch again but the door didn't budge.

She went back to the wrought-iron gates and stared through. The garden was empty. A single brown leaf fell. Her legs were shaking and she gripped the chain holding the gate shut. She had to stay in control: her daughter depended on it. She saw the child's face, smelt her milky breath.

'My petal, my sweetness. I'm coming for you.' The sound of her own voice frightened her.

The side door creaked open. The watchman was standing looking at her, as if he'd been there all along.

'*Akka?*'

Shouldering past him, she sprinted towards the house, the gravel sharp underfoot. She bounded up the main steps, through the drawing room, past the gloomy portraits. Her voice echoed back to her in the silence.

'Suranita, Suranita.'

She ran down the passageway, into the bedroom she shared with Thomas. Running, calling. '*Amma* is here. *Amma's* back!'

Inside the room, Maya stopped when she saw her wooden box open on the table. She hesitated a moment before looking inside. The notebook was gone. She turned around. Suranita's clothes, her dolls. All gone.

The cook appeared, standing at the doorway. '*Sahib* took her to the Fort.'

'Did he say why?'

'He packed her things in a chest. The sort they use for the sea. He said she was going away for a while.'

'A sea chest?' she repeated, the weight of the words sinking through her. She tried to push the fear down. She had to get there first. She felt the cook's eyes on her. She looked back into the box. How could she not have seen it? The words of Thomas came back to her. *She's got to go, you know.*

Her insides loosened. A clear image came of the day Suranita was running around the statue of the dancer, as the maid gave chase.

She's got to go, you know.

She'd looked into Thomas's eyes and they were blank. He said nothing more. But other signs were there. The weekend outings, his insistence that she wear frilly dresses, teaching her English words. 'Papa. Sister. Auntie.' Never mother. Not once did she hear Suranita say the word 'mother' in English.

All this time he'd been planning it, waiting for the moment. No wonder he'd been so quick to encourage her to go to Mamia. He'd seized the opportunity. Her hands were trembling, not with fear now, but fury.

She turned round and picked up the floor mat, and shook out the bed cover. A single doll rolled out. She grabbed it and her own wooden box with the few things left inside. Then, taking one last look around the room she retraced her steps, knowing she would never return.

'Get the bearers. We leave straight away.'

Walter had to hold the girl the whole way across. She clenched his lapels, her body shaking. The swell grew steadily worse and she vomited. The mustard-yellow spew flew back into his face and through his hair.

The oarsmen were crying, *'Yalee! Yalee!'* They battled to hold the boat upright. The catamarans were close at hand. *Too close,* Walter thought. *They expect a drowning on a day like this.*

'Give us this day, our daily bread. And forgive us our trespasses...'

He held her tighter and she went limp in his arms. Her eyes softened. It was a long time since he'd held a child so close. He pressed her face against his chest and let her warmth comfort him.

Just south of Chepauk, Maya heard beating drums and shouting. Her head jerked up and she glanced at the cook opposite, flicking her wrist towards the closed curtain of the palanquin.

He leaned forward to look out. 'It's a procession.'

'Let me see.' Ahead were knots of people and standard bearers holding billowing flags.

'The castes are warring again,' said the cook. 'Each day another protest.'

'Tell the bearers to take a different route,' she said.

But that way, too, was blocked.

She started to pray. First to Ganesha; then to the Mother Goddess. She never abandoned her children.

'We can't get through,' the bearers said. 'We have to go back.'

'No. Find another way.'

The bearers were cursing.

'It's no good, every road is jammed.'

Maya looked out again. It was starting to rain. Up ahead, the crowds were being pelted from behind by stones and shoes.

'Turn around. Turn around,' she shouted again to the bearers. But the bearers were slow, their eyes dark pits of fear, and ahead she saw the mob start to run towards them.

Back on the beach, Thomas was pacing, anxiously looking through the telescope. Every time the *masula* boat sank down he held his breath, wondering if it would crest the next wave. He thought of the waterlogged plants that covered the base of the boat. The slimy feel as they curled around his ankles. He remembered that hot summer's day all those years ago and felt his skin crawl.

The moist close heat sucked the air out of him, but his teeth were chattering. He saw Suranita, the incomprehension in her eyes as she was being carried away. *I'm a coward not to go with her myself. To send her away without telling Maya.* Maya. The thought of her made him wretched. He had no idea how he would explain himself.

He lifted up the telescope once again. If he went now, he could get there in time. He would just have to take his chances.

'Flam, find me another boat. I'm going after them.'

His valet looked at him.

'Get on with it.'

By the time Walter reached the *Neptune,* both he and the child were drenched. As the boat pulled up alongside, the navigator struggled to hold it steady. A rope ladder came tumbling down and another of the fishermen grabbed it, towing them alongside the vast wooden hull that towered above. On deck, sailors were scurrying as huge white sails unfurled and a young lad scrambled up the rigging.

'Pass me the child,' the fisherman said, hanging to the rope ladder with one arm, the other outstretched. His palm was pink and calloused.

For a few seconds, Walter held on. Limpet-like, she wouldn't let go.

'Now. You want us all to drown?'

Walter thrust her away, handing her to the fisherman. She fought against it, her arms reaching back towards him, eyes dark with terror. Holding her under his muscular arm, her legs kicking behind, the fisherman held her firm.

'You're late,' the ship's mate shouted as he reached down and took the child from the fisherman. 'We were about to leave when we saw you coming.'

Walter watched as the girl was lifted on to the ship. He tried to stand, his feet sinking into the spongy wet vegetation that covered the inside of the boat. 'I should come aboard. Hand her over myself to Miss Welch.'

'No time for that. Just pass me the girl's trunk. I'll take care of the rest.'

'I must come aboard. Check everything is in order.'

'If you're worried about the money going astray, I'll bring the lady here. You can watch as I hand it over.'

'It's not the money, Sir. It's the welfare of the child.' His voice was hoarse, the words snatched in the bristling wind. As he fumbled with the handles of the seachest, the boat swung left, knocking him back down and causing the chest to roll over and the lid to fly open. Bloody Pearce hadn't even shut it properly. He grabbed what he could, shoving the girl's wet belongings inside and slammed the lid shut. The hull was straining, the wood creaking, and the frantic yells of sailors sounded. Above it all, piercing his heart, were Suranita's frightened wails.

'Not your day, Reverend.' The ship's mate was laughing as the fisherman handed him the chest and the pouch of money. 'I'll be sure this gets to Miss Welch.'

'I'm right here, Reverend. The girl will be safe with me.'

'You're there, Miss Welch?' Walter strained to see her as the fishermen readied the boat for the crossing back. 'Take care of the child. She's a fragile—'

But his words were lost as the boat leapt forward and he was flung backwards. As they flew across the top of the waves he heard the booming cannon carry across the water. The *Neptune* was ready to sail. Minutes later, they landed on shore.

Walter started to wade through the shallows. He had only covered a few yards when he heard a shout behind. The navigator was holding a black leather satchel. Walter waited as the man sprinted towards him.

'Also, this was left,' he said, handing him a wooden doll.

Walter walked up to where the sand was firm and then paused to open the satchel. Inside was a notebook. The brown mottled cover looked familiar. The outside edges were damp, stuck together with seawater. It was hard to turn the pages, but it was even harder to stop his hands shaking. He turned to the first page, fearing what he would find. Some of the green paint had run, but the sketches – his sketches – were instantly recognisable. The tower of the Big Temple in Tanjore puncturing a chalky blue sky. A girl running and dancing, her lime-green dress flowing behind. The girl's face close up – Maya's face. Her enquiring eyes. He looked closer, then lifted his gaze.

There must be some mistake. He shut the book and turned to face the ocean, shading his eyes. The ship's sails were full. It was already moving fast, a shrinking object on a vast, endless horizon. Around him the fishermen were gathering. They wanted payment. He beckoned the navigator.

'This bag, it was in our boat?'

'Sir.'

'From the girl's trunk,' said another.

He was finding it difficult to breathe. He gave them the money, twice as much as they'd asked, and carried on up the beach. Again, another cry made him turn around.

It was Thomas's valet, Flam, running towards him.

'Sir, did you see *sahib*?'

Walter didn't understand.

'He changed his mind. He went after her.'

'Pearce took another boat? Is that what you're saying?'

Flam nodded. 'I tried to stop him. Told him, the weather no good. The boat. It hasn't come back. No sign of it.'

Walter scanned the ocean. The waves were choppy. Lightning streaked across the sky, followed by a crack of thunder. Flam jumped. 'Sir, please help.'

'What do you want me to do? He's an idiot. Nobody would be mad enough to go with this storm brewing. Go and ask the fishermen who took me.'

'Sir.'

It was all most unsatisfactory. He had to get back inside. Into the church, where it was cooler. Where he could think. As he turned to go, he called out, 'Flam, what is the name of the girl's mother?'

He looked at him, his eyes narrowing a fraction. 'Maya.'

A quiet, desperate sigh escaped Walter's lips. 'Dear God,' he said. 'What have I done?'

He looked back down at the notebook and opened it halfway through. The ink had run, but he could still make out a single word: *Emily*. And then, *He always thought I was like her.*

Below was a sketch of his daughter, as fresh as if it had been drawn yesterday.

By the time Maya and the cook arrived at the Sea Gate, there were no ships in the bay. They'd abandoned the palanquin and reached the Fort on foot. She looked around, trying to get her bearings. Her head was pounding, sweat dripped into her eyes. Around her were clusters of white men in triangular hats and tight breeches, and between them, coolies shouldering heavy loads. A line of wiry fishermen was pulling in the nets, singing as they swayed. She could hear the frenzy of exchange at the Sea Gate. She tried to make her mind slow down.

A few paces away, the cook was talking to a fisherman. He waved her over.

'The man says that a young girl was taken to a ship about an hour ago. A foreigner in black took her. He came back. The girl was left on board.'

'Which ship? There is no ship,' she said.

The fisherman spat on the ground. Slowly he turned, pointing. 'That ship.'

On the far horizon she could see one. The white sails just visible.

Down on the beach a crowd was gathering. Maya started to run. Maybe they'd brought her back. She recognised Flam, a head taller than everyone around him. He was directing people. Two fishermen were carrying a foreigner and they laid him out on the sand. His mousy hair was plastered down, blood streaming from his forehead, his skin pale, his clothes waterlogged. She didn't need to get any nearer to know who it was. Before she could see more, a man in black with looping strides pushed through the crowd, then it closed around him.

Maya stopped running. She didn't want to go further down the beach. She stood still. She wasn't sure if she was on the shore or floating out over the sea. She saw the ship fading fast and was helpless to stop it. Somewhere a trumpet was blowing. Down below, the fishermen were singing as a beggar pulled himself along on his hands and feet like a broken dog.

She could only stare at the ship shrinking on the horizon. She was soaring now. Soaring above it all. She could do it. All these years she'd waited to lift her wings, and now she could. Her hair streamed behind her. She was weightless. Below, Maya saw herself still standing there. A single Indian woman on the beach, among hundreds of men. As her mind's eye travelled across the waves, she saw the ship disappearing.

Suranita was too far. She could not bring her back.

A frantic cry burst from her lips. She shouted out the words that she wanted the whole beach to hear. 'Suranita, I'll come and find you! I'll bring you home!'

She started to walk in the opposite direction to the crowds. Then, she turned for one final look. They had covered the body of the man and were carrying him on a stretcher towards the Sea Gate. Flam was in front. Directing them was a man in black wearing a hat. The crow man. *Sahib* Sutt-sutt. So many years later, and there he was again. Her mind couldn't take it in. The four o'clock gun sounded. She needed to get to Black Town. Jacob would know the name of the next ship she could board. He'd be able to arrange her passage. He'd know how she could find her daughter again.

But Jacob wasn't there and so Maya continued to walk north, to the Shiva temple built on a rocky outcrop on the seashore. The waves showered her with salt spray. The priest had tight curls and a long beard. His skin was light and his body clothed in fine dark hair.

'Why are you here?' he said.

'To pray for my daughter.'

'Why?'

'She has been taken. I need answers on how to get her back.'

Maya placed some coins on the tray. She watched him go inside the shrine room and saw him light a dozen *aarthi* lamps. He lit the incense and she heard him invoking Shiva. The *muttirai* on her arm burned. She saw herself rising up and up, her feet leaving the floor, her body following. There could still be time if the ship stopped at Fort St David. It was worth trying. Anything was worth trying. With a jolt, she came back into herself.

She should leave now. The priest was coming back and suddenly she felt his desire. She looked around but the other worshippers had moved away. Behind the priest, Maya saw the eyes of Shiva, the colour of smoky topaz.

'Have you anything else to offer?' he said. 'The Lord is hungry.'

'He has taken enough from me.'

'Shiva is never satisfied.'

He took a step closer. She could see the individual black hairs curling around the sacred white thread across his chest. She could smell the camphor on his fingers. She touched her eyes, mouth and heart, muttered thanks and backed away. He reached out to grab her hand, but she was too quick.

'Wait,' he said. 'Wait.'

People were turning their heads, looking.

'Your daughter.'

She stopped.

'There is still time.'

She would find her. Of that, Maya was sure.

43

Walter was standing in front of his easel by the open window looking across the escarpment towards Tanjore. The air was fresher than in town and he could clearly see the low, broad building of the British Residency on the hilltop. From where he stood, the flat reddish roof reminded him of an Italian villa. The new Resident was much more amenable than that awful fellow Baldock, and every few weeks Walter rode over for a sundowner on the terrace. Behind him, strains of the morning's hymn rose and fell as Phoebe pottered around their bedroom. It was a comfort knowing she was near.

He'd asked his housekeeper to move upcountry with him not long after burying Thomas. Phoebe hadn't hesitated for a moment, but it was taking longer to persuade Schwarz to agree to their banns of marriage. He looked back down at the canvas. The watercolours from England could never match the intensity of the colours here. Phoebe had started making paints for him out of natural dyes and earth ochres. 'They'll give you what you are looking for,' she'd said that morning on seeing his dissatisfaction.

He took a step back and surveyed his work. The face of the child was still too long, the eyes too close. He rolled his shoulders back and down, as if to take charge of himself. *If only I'd thought to ask Pearce the mother's name. Damn it. Damn it all.*

The day before he and Phoebe had left Fort St George, he'd gone to the corner of St Mary's graveyard. It felt foolish speaking out loud, but he'd squatted down by the newly turned earth, to say some words to Thomas. A ray of sun cast dappled light on the graves, illuminating the dust motes suspended in the air.

He thought he might feel – what? Remorse? Guilt? He'd had no part in Pearce's death. That was the man's own volition. Yet he couldn't help feel his own determination to do right by these half-castes was misguided. Or at the very least, interfering.

He stretched his back, pressing his lips together. He had thought Maya might send a message to him. He'd wanted to give her back her notebook. If her daughter couldn't have it, then at least she could. Rao tried his best, too, but it was as if she had vanished.

He tried to console himself that he'd done that one small gesture. After saying goodbye to Thomas, he'd gone into St Mary's, unlocked the cupboard and heaved out *Baptisms, Marriages and Burials from 1698*. Laying the tome carefully on the table, he flicked back to April 1781, turning the pages to the date of Suranita's baptism. Under the column entitled 'Mother's Name', he crossed out 'Native woman' and wrote 'Maya'.

Outside he heard a tambourine jangling. Laying aside his brush he walked down the corridor to the front door.

'A letter for you, *sahib*.'

The envelope was greasy from handling, the writing unfamiliar. He turned it over, stifling a gasp when he saw the Pearce family seal. A response, at last.

Walter dismissed the messenger, went inside to fetch a knife, then walked back outside to the shaded portico and sat on the bench. He took a moment before he began to read.

Dear Reverend Sutcliffe
Thank you for your thoughtful letter regarding my dear brother, Thomas. While his untimely death brought our family great anguish, I was glad to read that you conducted a proper Christian burial. I take heart in the knowledge that his body lies at St Mary's,

as I am sure he would have wished himself.

Mother and I are grateful that you arranged the safe passage for Thomas's daughter. The Neptune arrived without mishap eight months after setting sail from the Fort. It most pleases me when I see glimpses of her father in the child's features.

Despite all our best efforts, polite society still shun the girl's company due to her being a mixed Breed. We have plans to send her to Scotland where she will be reared by a relative.

As she is still settling into her new home, we think that any reminder of her life in Madras is best forgotten. So I ask you not to send the notebook. You are free to do with it as you please.

I have only the best interests of the child at heart.

Yours faithfully etc.,

Elsie Pearce.

Walter read the letter several times, reading for what lay between the lines. It was clear that it was Pearce's mother who shunned the child. Elsie's affection seemed genuine. He checked the date again, May 18th, 1787. Sixteen months it had taken to reach him. It was a wonder it had arrived at all.

But she'd arrived. Unexpected relief seeped through him.

He wondered what they called her. Madeline? Or had they kept Suranita? *Too hard, too foreign.* By now she could be a servant in the house of this relative. Or perhaps it was code for saying she was being sent to an orphanage. He'd probably never know.

He folded the letter and placed it back in the envelope. He would tell Rao of the news another day. His heart was suddenly weary, his shoulders slumped. As he walked back into the house, he stooped down and snapped the head off a marigold, smelling its bitter scent. He placed the flower at the feet of the statue of the Virgin Mary on the shrine by the door, telling himself that in time, the child would forget her mother and her memories of India. That it was only the privileged few who were sent back to England. The fate of Maya's aunt and her children were testament to that.

In his study he opened the brown notebook and placed Elsie's letter at the back, then he reached up and put it behind the other books on the top shelf, nudging it so it fell behind. He'd done the best he could. The rest was up to God.

44

Maya did not know how her limbs could ever thaw out, or when the darkness would lift and daylight reappear. Three months she'd been here and each morning a thick soupy mist clothed the hills of Bristol. The spindly trees were bare; pools of water covered the sodden ground. Jacob had warned her about the cold, insisting she take several Kashmiri woollen shawls and had given her his own black overcoat for the crossing. She was glad of it. He'd written to her since she'd arrived and said if she had no luck, she should travel to Holland. But she'd only just started the search. It would take time. She had to be prepared.

Her lodgings were close to the docks, down a steep cobbled street. She wasn't alone. There were others from foreign parts who'd made the journey – for love, money, adventure. Some sympathised with her plight, others thought her foolish.

She shared a room with Kumari, an older woman from Karnataka, who was waiting for the monies for her return passage. The Company had promised they would pay, and a pension too, since she was the widow of an English surgeon who'd saved lives in the battles against Hyder Ali. She was small and dark with a flattish nose and a turned-up mouth that made it seem she was always smiling. Practical, with sturdy hands, she'd assisted her husband as a nurse and, since his death, earned her keep as a midwife.

'No point sitting waiting for the family to respond to your letter,' Kumari said one morning as she and Maya breathed on the embers in the grate. 'You need to get out there. Get seen.'

'By who?'

'By those who would have known Thomas. He was a local here before he left?'

Maya nodded.

'Then there would still be those that know of him.'

'He once mentioned this old man – George, I think he was called. Blind in one eye. He lived down by the docks in a hut. It was he who showed Thomas a *pagoda*, who planted the seed to travel to Madras.'

'What are you doing here, then? You should find him.'

'I've tried,' Maya said, the tips of her fingers itchy as the flames started to catch in the grate.

'Not hard enough, you haven't.'

After Kumari had gone, Maya retreated back to bed. Perhaps she was foolish to think that if she came here, she'd find Suranita. She thought it would be like home where, if you asked enough people, someone always knew the person you were looking for. Here, there were too many to ask. She didn't know where to start. Outside she heard the sound of hooves clipping on stone and muffled cries. She rolled on her side, towards the window, grimy from soot. It was impossible to stay clean here. Even harder to bathe. She and Kumari managed it just once a fortnight.

She wondered how it had come to this. If, somehow, her childhood longing to see the sea, her yearning to know what lay beyond, had conspired to bring her here. It was Palani who had told her that she had choice. But now, that choice was overwhelming. And the only direction she could see for herself was downwards. She twisted her mother's gold chain and pressed on Auntie's ring. They were her last pieces of jewellery. She had nothing else to sell. *I'm not going to become a whore. I'm more than that. Much more.* There had to be another way, another means of survival.

⁓

In late December the mouth of the River Avon was frozen grey. Chunks
of ice knocked against each other and among them, a young swan, its
off-white feathers tinged with brown, struggled to navigate through
the freezing waters. A mix of tar, dampness and rotting vegetables
coalesced into a smell Maya would always associate with England.

As she came to the quayside, a finger of wintry sunlight broke
through the cloud. A ship had just arrived and passengers were on deck
waiting for their turn to step ashore. Feet unsteady, faces pinched. A
young girl among them with a woolly hat pulled over her ears. She was
older than Suranita, her skin darker. Behind her a white woman, her
face kindly enough. The girl walked forward on the gangway, her stride
certain. So quick and then the moment was gone. Maya's heart leapt.

The air was thick with sailors' cries, jackhammers banging and a
thundering of metal as the giant anchor of the Indiaman was released
on its chain. Maya listened for the rhythm in the sounds around her,
drawing in the beat of the docks and matching it with the rapid jittering
of her heart. Underneath her black overcoat she had layers of clothes,
and under one arm a rolled-up carpet. Ahead was a musician she'd
found who was from north of Madras.

The piece she chose had to be fast, fast enough so she could forget
the cold and chilblains on her toes; a beat as staccato as life here, with
its frenzy of arrivals and departures, embraces and farewells. Fast
enough to null the fear that this act, in a world so foreign to her own,
would not ruin things forever. That instead this might be her way out.
The end of one tradition and the beginning of another.

She blew on her fingers poking through the woollen fingerless gloves
Kumari insisted she wear. She nodded to the musician to lay down the
hessian sacks on the only dry patch under an awning, on a busy corner
where she'd seen passers-by loiter. She unfurled the thin Persian carpet
and slipped off her boots. Her socks, for now, she kept on.

She gave the signal to begin, but the man's hands were clumsy, the
cymbal dull and tuneless. He tried again.

'*Tai-ya-tai, tai-ya-tai,*' she said, encouraging him.

As his hands warmed up, the cymbal responded.

She heard a catcall and a jeer. Still, she composed herself, and first made a bow to the earth beneath her feet. She wasn't on Indian soil, but the earth was the earth and she could rely on it to hold her upright, and bear upon itself the beat of her feet. She slipped off the overcoat.

Beneath, Maya shimmered: a firetail of colour, a fountain of greens, marigolds and rubies, around her neck a golden shawl. The tempo was still too slow. Her breath hung like smoke. Her lungs contracted from the freezing air. In her mind's eye she saw her daughter running among the burning oil lamps in the Big Temple and felt the ripe heat of an Indian summer.

Her hands were on her waist, her feet pointing outwards. With a benign smile on her lips, she sank to the half-sitting position, her right palm turned upwards and her left palm down. She thrust her body forward. A glance at the musician quickened the tempo. Her socks, they had to go. Her mind became sharp, her eyes focused. She turned out her right leg and her foot struck the ground with a distinct *tatt-tatt*. The sounds of the quayside became distant. And as a crowd gathered, they watched in awe as Maya began to dance.

ACKNOWLEDGEMENTS

In writing this book, I received advice and help from many people in small and large ways. The following assisted in the research process: Joep Bor, Jean Deloche, Nirmala Lakshman, S. Muthiah, P. Perumal, Miles Taylor, V.A.K. Ranga Rao, Dr P. Sambhu, V. Sriram and B.M. Sundaram. I am grateful to all at the Writing and Society Research Centre, especially Gail Jones, for her support and feedback during the early stages of the manuscript. I was fortunate to receive funding from the University of Western Sydney for research, allowing several stints in India. Thanks to V.R. Devika for patiently answering my queries and for her assistance with language and cultural references. Any mistakes are, of course, my own.

Thanks to all my family; to my friends, in particular, Verena Clemencic-Jones, Bubula Lardi, Ruth Malik and Jane Walker; to Amanda Perry-Bolt for being there on the pilgrimage in the north, and Tattwa Bodha (Dominique Bechet) for our journey together in the south; and special thanks to Suzanne Leal for all her encouragement and careful reading during the development of the manuscript.

I'd like to thank my agent, Jessica Woollard. At Unbound, a particular note of thanks to John Mitchinson for his boundless enthusiasm for the novel and to all the team there for creating this beautiful edition. Thank you to all my Unbound supporters whose generosity allowed my novel to reach new audiences. You have all taught me the value of community. I've been humbled by the support from friends, family and strangers.

Most of all, I'd like to thank Aden for being there in so many ways, for a willingness to traverse physical and emotional landscapes together, and for believing in me and in this book.

NOTES AND SOURCES

This is a work of fiction, but some of the dramatic events recounted did take place. I became fascinated by the figure of the *devadasi* after going to Tanjore (now called Thanjavur). On the eleventh-century shrine walls of the Big Temple, the names and addresses of four hundred dancing girls are still visible. I liked the idea of a continuum between past and present, and the fact that these women were once celebrated artists of their day. I was also fascinated by this particular period of Indian history. Despite the growing presence of European powers, there was still the possibility of exchange between cultures – a possibility that would not be there in the later Victorian era. It seemed to be a time of incredible beauty, discovery and brutality.

Much later I read the phrase 'shaking the *pagoda* tree'. The double meaning of the word *pagoda* – both a coin and a temple – intrigued me. It appears that coins initially became known as *pagoda*s because an image of a Hindu deity, often a goddess, was imprinted on them. I then came across the work of Jawaharlal Nehru (1889–1964), committed nationalist and the first prime minister of independent India. In his writings he made reference to the '*pagoda* tree', also noting that the English word 'loot' originates from the Hindi word 'to steal'.

In exploring this uneasy meeting between East and West, it became apparent that while British India is exhaustively documented, the stories of Indian women – temple dancers even more so – are harder to find. So where I could, I have tried to be historically accurate. Where sources do not exist, I have imagined.

The main characters in *The Pagoda Tree* are all fictional, however some of the minor characters are inspired by real historical figures. Palani is based on Muddupalani, a courtesan who lived at Tanjore court in the eighteenth century during the reign of King Pratap Singh. Her epic, *Appeasing Radha (Radhika Santawanam)*, consists of over five hundred poems and almost certainly is the first erotic poetry written by a courtesan in southern India. Its focus on a woman's pleasure and sensuality would later attract controversy, and the British judged it obscene, banning it. The ban was only lifted in 1947, after Indian independence.

Reverend Schwarz (1726–1798) was a German Lutheran missionary who lived in and around Tanjore for over thirty years. I mined his rather laborious diaries and letters for life at the time (*Memoirs of the Life and Correspondence of the Reverend Christian Frederick Schwarz*, 1835). Schwarz succeeded in realising his dream and his church still stands as a monument to his efforts.

The Dutchman, Jacob Haafner, existed, and his travel accounts are still available, although only one is in English (*Travels on Foot Through the Island of Ceylon*, 1810). In his *Journeys in a Palanquin* (*Reize in eenen Palanquin*, 1808), he tells the story of his love affair with a dancing girl called Mamia.

For the sake of the reader knowing who's who, I have not adhered strictly to Tamil kinship relations or used the many different honorary terms for family members. I am also aware that in Tamil culture there is no general word for 'cousin', and there is a custom that a wife does not call her husband by name out of respect and because it is believed to be inauspicious. For the sake of simplicity, Maya refers to her lovers by name.

There are some unacknowledged quotes in the book. Fragments from Palani's poetry in chapters 10, 14, 15 and 38 are taken from *Appeasing Radha* written by the real Muddupalani. In chapter 14, I have adapted the sixth-century poem 'So free am I', written by Mutta, an Indian nun who lived contemporaneous to the Buddha. The fragment, 'The Lord white as jasmine', is from the poetry of the twelfth-century mystic, Akkamahadevi, first mentioned in chapter 15, and repeated several times. I am grateful to the encyclopaedic *Women Writing in India* (Vol. I) edited by Susie Tharu and Ke Lalita (1991) for these quotes.

In chapter 44, the line 'but the earth was the earth and she could rely on it to hold her upright, and bear upon itself the beat of her feet', is derived from Krishna Sahai's, *The Story of a Dance: Bharata Natyam* (2003). Sahai's original quote describes how a dancer often begins a performance with a prayer to Mother Earth to 'bear upon Thyself the beat of [her] feet.' Sahai's book was essential in understanding the complexities of Indian dance.

I have compressed some historical events and occasionally shifted dates to fit the narrative. It was in 1773 that General Smith invaded Tanjore and the English switched sides, allying with the wealthy Nawab of Arcot in Madras against the impoverished Prince Tuljajee of Tanjore.

The Nabobs: A Study of the Social Life of the English in Eighteenth Century India by Percival Spear (1998) and *Nabobs of Madras* by Henry Dodwell (1926) were useful in furnishing details of the English traders and Company writers. Dodwell's text provided the following quotes. Thomas repeats two phrases from the letters of Francis Jourdan, another Company servant down on his luck, 'you are a man of fortune' (chapter 28) and 'dunning him for money' (chapter 39). The real merchant David Young inspired the line, 'The only profession to profit is the lawyers...' (chapter 38) and I quoted Young again in chapter 40, 'From the Sea Gate as far as Chepauk the whole beach was covered with wrecks.'

Descriptions of the 1782–3 Madras famine and hurricane are drawn from eyewitness accounts, among them those by Schwarz and Haafner. Mudaliar and the world of the *dubashes* were informed by the little known eighteenth-century Sanskrit work, the *Sarva-Deva-Vilasa*, translated by D. V. Raghavan (1957). Durba Ghosh, *Sex and the Family in Colonial India: The Making of Empire* (2006), was indispensable in understanding the complexities of mixed-race relations.

Margot Finn's family biography of Thomas Munro provided a valuable counter-narrative to some of the 'old school' historiography in 'Anglo-Indian Lives in the Later Eighteenth and Early Nineteenth Century', *Journal for Eighteenth-Century Studies 33* (2010): pp 49–65.

Her fascinating study of the family of Thomas Munro (1761–1827) informed the fate of Suranita. It was in fact Thomas's brother, Sandy Munro, who sent his illegitimate 'little Dark girl' to be raised by his family back in Scotland. From the Munro letters, I adapted the phrase, in chapter 43, 'polite society shunned the girl's company due to her being a mixed Breed.'

Walter's trip to the Vellore district was influenced by Jacob Haafner's description of visiting a town called Onour in *Journeys in a Palanquin*. As Haafner tended to embellish, I'm unsure whether he did go there, but the massacre that took place is historically accurate – I merely changed the location. In the Second Anglo–Mysore War (1779–1784) against Hyder Ali, Colonel Matthews besieged Onour and the English soldiers raped and murdered four hundred Indian women who had taken refuge in a nearby temple. Matthews was among several thousand British soldiers later captured and died in chains in the dungeons in Seringapatam. I thank Haafner for providing the last line to chapter 37, 'All around a profound and horrible silence reigned, only broken by the sound of crows.'

To continue the conversation about *The Pagoda Tree* and for further details on sources, go to clairescobie.com

SUPPORTERS

Unbound is a new kind of publishing house. Our books are funded directly by readers. This was a very popular idea during the late eighteenth and nineteenth centuries. Now we have revived it for the internet age. It allows authors to write the books they really want to write and readers to support the writing they would most like to see published.

The names listed below are of readers who have pledged their support and made this book happen. If you'd like to join them, visit: www.unbound.com.

Abercrombie
& Kent Australia
Jimmy Anderson
Joy Anderson
Sophia Andreadis
Barbara Mary Andrews
Caroline Apps
Martin Archer
Sarah Armstrong
Ann Kenton Barker
Kelly Benson
Moyra Blakstad

Robert Bluck
Steve Blundell
Joep Bor
Jane Bradish-Ellames
Nicky Brown
Helen Brunton
David Burlinson
Leslie Burrows
Virginie Busette
Anna Cairo
Eleni Calligas
Katie Campbell-Johnston

Barbara Carmichael
Rebecca Caroe
Helen Carroll
Wendy Cazzolato
Verena Clemencic-Jones
Chris Collins
Jan Cornall
Andrea Cowling
Ken Cox
Helen Craven
Lucy Crawford
Diana Hardwicke Davies
Giles Derry
Sil Devilly
Fiona Dewar
Kyinzom Dhongdue
Chris Doucas
Jenny Doughty
Georgina Dove
Robert Eardley
Grant Everett Eaton
Katrina Edwards
William Ellsworth-Jones
Richard Evans
Peter Ey
Michael Fountoulakis
Christine Gabriel
Gil Gillenwater
Salena Godden
Noel Grieve
Nicki Grihault

Paul Ham
Michelle Hamadache
Lenna Harris
Tamayra Hayman
Sarah Hender
Kathryn Heyman
Mary Hickson
Marilyn Hoey
Wayne Holden
Mary Horlock
Cristina Huesch
John Hutchin
Kate Impey
Johari Ismail
Susan Johnston
Glyn Jones
Peter Joy
Veena Kanda
Nicole Kelly
Nicki Kempston
Ruth Caroe Kennedy
B Khano
Dan Kieran
Shona Kinsella
Cara Kirkwood
Sophie Knock
David F Kruger
Suzanne LaPrade
Anne Lawrence
Suzanne Leal
Jennifer Lovering

Jeremy Lovering

Peter Lovering

Anna Maguire

James Marshall

Phillippa Jane Martindale

Flora Masens

Joanna Maxwell

Catherine Mcgarvey

Pamela Mclean

Shafik Meghji

Edmund Mervyn

Jane Messer

John Mitchinson

Joanna Morris

Seb Mullins

Shelly Muncaster

Judy Munday

Sara Murphy

Kali Napier

Carlo Navato

Patti Niehoff

Kirsty O'Callaghan

Mary Park

Suzy Parker

Tanmaya Parsons

Justin Pollard

Timothy Powell

Suellen Priest

Sam Pritchard

Sujata Raman

Julia Rees

Stuart Reid

Carmel Reilly

Aden Ridgeway

David Roach

Richard Robinson

Cheryl Robson

Annah Ross

Ashar Salia

Yogachakra Saraswati

Patricia Scobie

Sarah Scobie

Fiona Scolding

Stephanie Scott

Gill Shaddick

Laurence Shapiro

Shalini Sharma

Toni Smerdon

Richard Soundy

Andrew Stalbow

Mary Stewart-Hunter

Claire Storey

Virginia Stungo

Beverley Tarquini

Claire Taylor

Miles Taylor

Julia Thomas

Robert Thorogood

Gabrielle Trainor

Lavinia Tulli

Ronald van Domburg

Joel Victoria

Jane Walker
Sue-Anne Wallace
Persephone Ward
Eric Webb
Anne Whaite
Abbie Widin
Belinda Wiggs
Peter Wilson
Alexandra Wingate
Alecia Wood
Jenna Wright
Xinran Xue
Annaxue Yang
Diana Yeldham
Caterina Zavaglia
Acielle Zelenina